Relentless

PURSUIT

Selected Historical Fiction Published by McBooks Press

Alexander Kent

Relentless Pursuit

the Bolitho novels: 25

McBooks Press, Inc.
www.mcbooks.com

ITHACA, NY

Published by McBooks Press 2002
Copyright © 2001 by Bolitho Maritime Productions
First published in the United Kingdom by William Heinemann Ltd. 2001

Cover painting by Geoffrey Huband.

Library of Congress Cataloging-in-Publication Data

Kent, Alexander.
    Relentless pursuit / by Alexander Kent.
        p. cm. — (Richard Bolitho novels ; 25)
    ISBN 1-59013-026-X   (alk. paper)
        1. Bolitho, Adam (Fictitious character)—Fiction. 2. Great Britain,
History, Naval—19th century—Fiction. I. Title
PR6061.E63 R4 2001
    823'.914—dc21   2001045033

Additional copies of this book may be ordered from any bookstore or directly
from McBooks Press, Inc., ID Booth Building, 520 North Meadow St.,
Ithaca, NY 14850. Please include $5.00 postage and handling with mail
orders. New York State residents must add sales tax to
total remittance (books & shipping).
All McBooks Press publications can also be ordered by calling
toll-free 1-888-BOOKS11 (1-888-266-5711).
Please call to request a free catalog.

Visit the McBooks Press website at www.mcbooks.com.

Printed in the United States of America

9 8 7 6 5 4

For you, Kim,
With all my love,
and a yellow rose . . .

The sheets were frozen hard, and they cut the naked hand;
The decks were like a slide, where a seaman
    scarce could stand . . .

But all I could think of in the darkness and the cold
Was just that I was leaving home and my folks
    were growing old.

ROBERT LOUIS STEVENSON

from *Christmas at Sea*

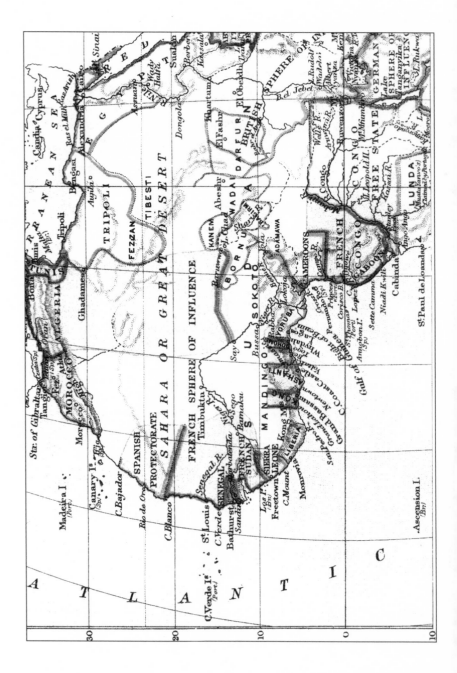

I No Turning Back

PLYMOUTH, always one of England's most important and strategically situated seaports, seemed strangely quiet, subdued. Even Plymouth Sound, notorious for its fast tides and unexpectedly fierce squalls, was almost still but for some cruising catspaws from a light offshore breeze.

But it was cold, the air bitter like a knife edge, and only a few small local craft seemed willing to contest it.

It was mid-December, six months to the day since the news had broken of the victory at Waterloo, and the final surrender of the Corsican tyrant who had held power for so long. Boys had grown to manhood in the course of that same conflict, plough hands and stable lads alike had been transformed into sailors and soldiers.

Now it was over, and seaports like Plymouth which had given so much and so many were still numbed by the reality of peace and its aftermath.

Even when the noon gun shattered the silence and rolled its echoes from the Hoe to the old battery at Penlee Point, only a few gulls rose screaming from the water, *the spirits of dead Jacks,* the sailors called them. Maybe they felt it too.

From here great fleets and powerful squadrons had weighed anchor, and had headed out to every part of the world where England's enemies were at large, and famous names, the Nile, Copenhagen, Trafalgar, had filled the hearts and minds, particularly of those who did not have to fight, and had no loved ones

facing the merciless broadsides which took the lives of volunteers
and pressed men without discrimination.

At the end of the war the fleet had been at its strongest, with
240 ships of the line, some 317 frigates and countless other smaller
vessels, ready and able to perform whatever task their lordships
of Admiralty might dictate.

There were ships here now, plenty of them. It was a Sunday,
but in those other times it would have made no difference when
the noon gun was fired. There had been signals to be exchanged,
chronometers to be checked: the daily routine continued.

But today many of those same ships were like ghosts, some
with upper yards sent down and boats removed for storage ashore,
and in some cases the scars of a last, desperate sea fight still unrepaired, as if their companies had been spirited away. Ships already
laid up in ordinary, some waiting to be hulked or used for stor-
ing unwanted equipment; a few would become floating prisons.
And some, perhaps, would live on to fight again.

Only one small craft moved with any apparent purpose and
direction. It was a gig, oars rising and falling precisely and unhurriedly, the crew smartly turned out in tarred hats and matching
blue jackets, a coxswain with one hand on the tiller bar, a midshipman beside him, eyes on the passage among the silent ships,
the phantom fleet.

And in the sternsheets, boatcloak thrown back over his shoulders to reveal his gleaming epaulettes, was the captain, who
needed no reminding of the significance of this day.

Captain Adam Bolitho did not glance at the passing ships, but
it was a moment he would never forget. He would know the
names of some, even of many of them. Silent and deserted now,
their gun ports empty like staring eyes, but he would hear the
cries and the wild cheering, still audible amidst the darker memories of war at sea.

The seaports were full of reminders, men crippled and blinded and others left to beg on the streets. And there would be many more now, thrown on the beach while the fleet was cut to the bone, their courage and sacrifice forgotten. Adam gripped the old sword beneath his cloak until his fingers throbbed. Emotion, pride, anger, it was all there on this bitter, cleansing day.

He turned and looked up as the gig passed through the shadow of an anchored seventy-four, an old two-decker like *Hyperion*. Against the bleak, cloudless sky he saw a solitary figure standing on a gangway to watch the gig as they pulled past.

Then very slowly he raised his hat, and held it above his head in salute until the jutting stern hid him from view. A watchman? Someone still finding refuge in the world which had rejected him? Or just another ghost?

He heard the midshipman clear his throat. He was new; they had met for the first time when the gig had picked him up at the Queen's Stairs. Another young hopeful, nervous with his captain in his care.

Adam had seen the wary glance from Luke Jago, his coxswain. He would allow nothing to go wrong. No matter what he thought or said, he would know what this day meant to his captain. Just as Jago would have known where and when to collect him without a signal having been made, or any instructions given.

He felt the tiller move slightly and looked along the boat, over the heads of the oarsmen, their breath hanging in the cold air like steam. Like that first day, just over a year ago, in this same place. He stared at his ship.

When I took command.

He had been away from the ship for two weeks and had barely had time to think over and remember that past year. The sea fights, the triumphs and the pain, official visits and others no less important, to him at least. And all the while he had looked forward to this moment. *Coming back.* Like being made whole again.

It was something like a shock, nevertheless. The ship had been moved during his absence and now lay at her cable, well clear of all the other vessels, and even her appearance came as a surprise. The familiar buff paint around her hull had been replaced by white, so that her strakes and black gun ports along either side made an even sharper, chequered pattern, clean and fresh against the stained and deserted hulks nearby.

His Britannic Majesty's frigate *Unrivalled* of 46 guns was one of the first to wear the new peacetime colours. She was also the first ship of her name on the Navy List.

He stood up in the boat as the hull rose above the tossed oars. And he was her first captain.

It was enough. There was nothing else.

The bowman had hooked on, and the side party would be waiting, faces, new or old, ready to receive him.

What had I expected? That they would take her from me?

He glanced at the midshipman, but the youth's name would not come.

"That was well done."

The boy blushed, and Jago remarked, "Mr Martyns is learning fast, sir."

Adam nodded. It was Jago's way. He would remember next time.

The calls squealed and he heard the slap of muskets as the Royal Marine guard presented arms in salute.

It was all as he had expected. The ensign curling against the cold sky, the seamen, faces still tanned from *Unrivalled*'s service in the Mediterranean. The smell of fresh paint, like that other December day a year ago.

He saw none of it.

Being back was enough.

Lieutenant Leigh Galbraith strode in from beneath *Unrivalled*'s poop and ran his eyes over the main deck. Everything was in order. He had made certain that nothing had been left to chance. Today the captain was returning; his own period of temporary command would soon be over.

He frowned as the hard light reflected from the water. He had been pulled around the ship as soon as the hands had been piped to work, and had still been surprised by her appearance. The white paint took some getting used to, almost frivolous compared with the moored hulks nearby, and only the experienced eye could discern the new timbers which had repaired damage suffered in their savage exchange with the frigate *Triton* only months ago. Some of the repairs had been carried out at Gibraltar and the rest here at Plymouth, where *Unrivalled*'s life had begun. Where Galbraith himself had been given another chance. He was lucky and he knew it. And with the whole fleet being cut down, halved, some said, he should count his blessings and leave the bitterness to others less fortunate.

Galbraith was 31, and he had spent nineteen years of his life in the navy. He knew and had wanted nothing else, except a command of his own. And that he had been granted. His previous captain had given him the highest recommendation, and his reward had been the little brig *Vixen*. Not a fifth-rate like *Unrivalled*, but his own, and the first step to the coveted post rank.

He saw Partridge the boatswain, big fists on his hips as he explained forcefully what work he needed done in the foretop. Thank God for men like Partridge, he thought. The backbone of any man-of-war, they were the true professionals, Partridge, Stranace the gunner, probably the oldest man aboard, and Joshua Cristie the sailing master, the best Galbraith had known. A man who never wasted words, but when he spoke it was with authority and a complete understanding of the tides, stars and winds which were his world.

As the frigate's first lieutenant, Galbraith was most aware of and concerned with the shortages. They were more than fifty men under strength, despite their presence in this naval harbour. He smiled grimly. Or perhaps because of it.

Apart from those they had lost, killed or badly wounded in the last battle, some had been paid off or had gone to other ships. But a few of the old hands had remained, even some of the hard men like Campbell, who had paid for his insolence and contempt for authority with several floggings in this commission alone. He seemed to find some brutal satisfaction in displaying his scarred back, which looked as if it had been clawed by some savage beast. A dangerous man, and yet he had been one of the first to volunteer for the attack on the corsair's chebecks when they had pulled alongside with enough explosives to kill every one of them. Campbell had been a tower of strength, but he would sneer openly at anyone who suggested he had acted out of a sense of duty or discipline.

There were others like Campbell. Men who claimed to hate everything the navy represented, and more especially the officers who upheld it.

So why did they stay, when they now had the chance to quit?

Galbraith saw Luxmore, the captain of the Royal Marine detachment, speaking with one of his sergeants. Whatever went on around them, no matter how cramped the ship, they somehow remained a separate entity. Even their quarters were called "the barracks." Luxmore had seen plenty of fighting, and he had a good rapport with his marines. Maybe that was enough. Galbraith looked away. Or was he congratulating himself on his advanced promotion? The debonair Captain Bosanquet had been killed that day. *Like me, then.* Thankful to have survived, and to have a ship, because of fear of the unknown.

He saw the boy Napier, the cabin servant, pausing to stare at the land. He probably knew the captain's thoughts better than anyone. Fourteen years old, serious and hard-working, and obviously devoted to Captain Adam Bolitho. An unusual relationship, he thought. Bolitho was not always the easiest man to understand, and had sometimes apologised for his own intolerance. As if something or somebody was driving him, forcing him on.

And yet with Napier he always seemed to have time to explain, to describe, to elaborate. *The only way he'll learn,* he once said. As if he saw something of his own youth in him. That must have been stormy enough, from what Galbraith had heard, and had seen for himself. Like that last engagement, when Bolitho had given chase to the enemy frigate captained by the renegade Spaniard, Martinez. He had deliberately misinterpreted their admiral's signal to remain on station and leave the pursuit to a smaller frigate which had been outgunned and outsailed from the start, and they had saved the merchantman *Aranmore,* which had been carrying important passengers. He glanced at the companion ladder and remembered Bolitho holding the woman's hand, kissing it. They could have been quite alone.

Galbraith began to pace the deck, his hands clasped behind him. Was it that as well? Had she reminded him yet again of the girl he had hoped to marry, and had lost when he had put his brief command first?

He thought too of Bolitho's reluctance to become close to anyone in his new command. He had lost a frigate, *Anemone,* fighting a more powerful American ship, had been taken prisoner and had escaped. It was as if he had found it impossible since then to reach out, to accept, and to trust.

And there was yet another side to the man, a stark contrast. Cristie had told Galbraith about the day when he had openly disagreed with his captain. For Cristie it was a thing almost unheard of. Galbraith's raiding party had been amongst little-known islands, and the master had advised that it was unsafe to take *Unrivalled* through a channel which was virtually uncharted, and which might rip out the ship's keel. *A captain's total responsibility . . .*

Cristie had confided after the successful recovery of the raiding party, "Fair mad he was. *I'll roast in hell before I leave Galbraith to die in their hands*, he said. I don't go much for praying, but I tell you, I nearly did that time!"

And when they had stood together in the church at Falmouth, the first time *Unrivalled* had dropped anchor there. The church full of people, the streets also, and total silence for the man who had died at sea, the captain's famous uncle, Sir Richard Bolitho.

Lady Catherine Somervell had been there with them. So beautiful, so alone despite the crowds. Where was she now? What would become of her? The woman who had defied society and had been Sir Richard's lover and inspiration, and had won the heart of the country.

The deck moved slightly, and he saw the ship in his thoughts as clearly as he had this morning. A thoroughbred. Like the carved inscription beneath her figurehead. *Second to None.*

Unrivalled was eager to move. The first and perhaps the last of her kind: in the yard where she had been laid down, built and launched, Galbraith had seen her only sister ship. The same fine lines, the pride of any craftsman. But abandoned. Unfinished. Dead.

He stared along the deck, at the two lines of eighteen-pounders, their tackles and breechings taut and neat, and recalled Massie, who had been the next senior in the wardroom. A flag officer's son and a gunnery man to his fingertips, not one you would ever know. Quiet and self-contained even on the day he had been killed, shot down as he had rallied his people.

He had been replaced here in Plymouth by Lieutenant George Varlo, a complete contrast. Lively, talkative, and in his mid-twenties, he must have had some influence; every appointment now was like pure gold. Galbraith had decided that he would bide his time with Varlo. He almost smiled. Maybe he had got that from the captain.

He turned in his pacing as the noon gun echoed mournfully across the water and the watching veterans. Even without the large, old-fashioned watch he had always carried, Captain Bolitho would be right on time.

He heard Midshipman Sandell's sharp, petulant voice, berating one of the new men. They were over fifty hands short of approved complement. Petty tyrants like Sandell would be no loss at all.

"Gig's in sight!" That was Bellairs, the third lieutenant, who had been the senior midshipman when *Unrivalled* had commissioned. It would be a challenge to him, Galbraith thought. Some of the old Jacks would recall him as just another "young gentleman," neither fish nor fowl, and still look for some weakness to exploit. But he was a popular choice and had settled into the wardroom well, and seemed grateful for his change of circumstance.

He smiled again and walked to the entry port. The marines were fallen in and dressed in two impeccable ranks, swaying very gently to the ship's quiet motion.

He saw O'Beirne, the portly surgeon, hurrying to the companion, down to his own world on the orlop, where some had died and others had survived.

He watched the gig returning, pulling around one of the abandoned ships. Bolitho's coxswain was another rebel, or so it had first appeared.

The boat was turning toward the main chains, the bowman already standing with his hook raised.

"Royal Marines, *ready!*"

The boatswain's mates moistened their silver calls on their tongues and gazed at the entry port.

Galbraith gripped his sword and pressed it to his side.

For two weeks he had been in charge of this ship and every hour of her routine. Completing repairs, taking on stores and fresh water, powder and shot. Men to be sworn in and issued with clothing. It was a far cry from some ships he had known, when some of the poor wretches dragged aboard by the press gangs had worn their own clothes to shreds before a grasping purser could be persuaded to dole out garments from his slop chest.

And now that responsibility was over. The captain had returned.

Galbraith stepped forward, his hand to his hat as the calls shrilled in salute and the marines went through their drill.

He watched the captain as he climbed through the entry port, eyes moving quickly over and above his ship. At moments like this, a stranger again.

Adam took his hand and shook it.

"A long two weeks." He glanced at the other officers and then forward, the length of the ship.

Galbraith waited, feeling it all again. They had done so much in a year of action and triumph, disappointment and grief.

He was surprised, ashamed even. This man, who could be so youthful one moment, so grimly determined when he had made a decision which might affect each one of them, was still so distant, so unknown.

Galbraith recognised it, the old enemy which he had thought laid to rest. Envy.

"Welcome aboard, sir!"

It was done.

Adam Bolitho walked to the sloping windows of the stern cabin and stared out at the anchorage. The other ships looked even more desolate through the wet, misty glass. And it was cold, only to be expected in December, but a far cry from the Mediterranean, Malta or Algiers. *Unrivalled* was a big frigate, but the only heat came from her galley stove.

He should be used to it, able to accept or ignore it. He knew

Galbraith was watching him, his tall frame slightly angled between the deck beams. The boy Napier was just inside the sleeping compartment; he could see his shadow moving up and down as he unpacked one of his captain's chests, doubtless with a ready ear cocked in case he was needed.

"You've done well, Leigh." He turned away from the damp glass in time to catch the expression on the strong features. Galbraith still found it hard to accept a captain's use of his first name. In his absence the barrier had returned. Perhaps it had never truly gone away. "Are the new people settled in?"

Galbraith seemed to consider it, as if taken aback by the question when all he and most of the others had been concerned about were their orders, their place in things, their world.

"I've warned the officers to be ready in the wardroom."

"Yes, I shall want to speak with them." He shivered and moved restlessly to the opposite quarter. Strain, excitement, or the fact that he had not had more than a few hours' sleep for days. He thought of Galbraith's words. *In the wardroom.* He had noticed the plume of smoke from the galley funnel, had caught the heavy smell of rum even as he had been piped aboard. Small, real things. They also reminded him that he had not eaten since yesterday.

He said abruptly, "Men. We must get more hands. We can train them." Almost bitterly it came out. "We shall have all the time we need!"

"I've done what I can with the watch bills, sir. A mixture of old and new hands in each part of ship."

Adam said, "I am told that we may attract some experienced hands in Penzance." He looked at the stern windows again, trying to accept it. "One of the big packet companies has been forced to give way to competition. With so many trained seamen tossed on the beach they can pick and choose, it would seem!" He made another attempt. "I have obtained some posters. Usher can deal with it."

He stared at the small empty table by the screen door, where Usher his clerk had always sat, quiet and attentive, making notes and copying letters and orders, a handkerchief always balled in one fist, trying valiantly to stifle the coughs. A nervous man who had once been a purser's assistant, he had seemed totally out of place in the crowded confines of a fighting ship.

His lungs had been diseased, all too common in a man-of-war. As the surgeon had put it, Usher had been dying a day at a time.

"Forgive me." It was as if he had spoken to the little clerk, who had finally died on their passage back from Gibraltar, within a day's sighting of the Cornish coast.

They had buried him at sea. There were no details of home or relatives. He stared at the curved beams and the reflection of the black and white checkered deck covering. This ship had been Usher's home, too.

He thought suddenly, painfully, of the big grey house in Falmouth, people crowding around, kindness, warmth, and curiosity.

He touched the sword at his hip and then unclipped it. The constant reminder, if he had needed one, like all the old portraits in the house, the watching faces, some with ships in the background, some not. But always the sword.

How empty the house had seemed. Bryan Ferguson had been overjoyed to see him, and had tried not to disturb him with the signing of papers relating to the estate and the farms, the people who had always known there was a Bolitho to care for them, or his lady when he was at sea. Now there were only memories.

He had intended to make the journey to Fallowfield to visit the little inn, The Old Hyperion, but Ferguson had persuaded him against it. The roads were deeply rutted, unsafe; he had seen ice for himself in the place where roses would bloom again in the new year. Catherine's roses.

Or had Ferguson been afraid of the effect on Allday if they had met so unexpectedly? *Or on me?*

Galbraith saw the play of emotions on his captain's face. Like a young colt, someone had once described him. Hair so dark that it was almost black, a mouth which could be determined, even hard. Equally, it could show a rare sensitivity. As it had now, at the mention of Usher's name. That was the true difference. He cared for these people he led and commanded; in some ships Galbraith had known, it was not always the same thing. Abrupt, impatient, stubborn, Adam Bolitho had revealed each mood throughout the months they had served together. But Galbraith felt privileged to have sometimes seen the other side to this youthful copy of the famous Richard Bolitho, and to have shared it.

Adam said, "I shall leave you to take charge of recruiting parties. Remember, we are looking for men, not *begging* for them." He smiled quickly. "That was unnecessary, Leigh. I am bad company today."

Galbraith was about to reply when he sensed something like an unspoken warning. Adam Bolitho had originally come from Penzance, or very close to it. Was that the reason for his dismissal of the task?

He said, "I can deal with it, sir. Our marines will put on a good display."

Adam scarcely heard him. "I saw the Flag Officer, Plymouth. Twice, in fact."

"Vice-Admiral Keen, sir. You have known him a long time, I believe."

"Yes." He saw the boy watching from the screen and said, "Fetch me something hot, will you?" He laid the sword on the bench seat. "Some cognac too, I think."

The door closed. Only the marine sentry stood between them and the whole ship.

"In confidence." He raised his hand, as if to dispel something. "But it must be between ourselves." He glanced toward the table again, as if expecting the cough, or one of Usher's usual meticulous explanations of what he was doing. "We shall leave Plymouth tomorrow." He gazed at Galbraith directly. "Does that present a problem?"

Galbraith said, "No, sir," and saw the dark, restless eyes return to the old sword.

"After Penzance, where additional orders will be waiting for us, we shall proceed to Gibraltar." He attempted to smile. "Better weather, with good fortune!" But it eluded him.

Galbraith was suddenly tense. No routine orders; they were not rejoining the fleet or one of the local squadrons. He considered all the laid-up ships. *What was left of them.*

Adam said quietly, "Sierra Leone. I shall receive full instructions when their lordships believe me fit and ready to proceed."

Galbraith waited. Like a burning fuse: that day among the islands, the charges exploding in what might have been a suicide attack, a reckless and ambitious operation. He recalled once more what Cristie had told him. *I'll roast in hell before I leave Galbraith to die in their hands!*

Sierra Leone. To Galbraith and most other sea officers it meant the slave trade. He could dismiss that idea; *Unrivalled* was too big and powerful to be wasted on hit-and-miss anti-slavery patrols. Schooners and brigs were the usual choice.

He was surprised to find that he did not care. The ship, *their ship*, was to go into service again. They were fully repaired and supplied. And if they could get a few volunteers, they would be ready. A fighting ship once more.

"I would sail her single-handed, sir, just to get away from this graveyard!"

Adam smiled. It was far better to be like Galbraith. He was reminded suddenly of Keen, in that spacious house commanding the sea and the countryside in one unending panorama. Where he himself had walked with Keen's wife Zenoria, for so short a time before her tragic death.

Keen's second wife Gilia had been there this time, and had made him more than welcome, and her pleasure had matched only Keen's pride in the revelation that a child was expected in the spring.

It was obvious that Gilia had never told Valentine Keen what she knew of Adam's love for her predecessor, who had thrown herself from a clifftop after her son by Keen had died.

If Keen suspected, he hid it well. He had confined their conversations to *Unrivalled*'s return to duty, and her performance against the renegade frigate *Triton*.

Only once, Adam had sensed something, as Keen had remarked on the "fine piece of work" when they had caught and destroyed the big ex-Dutchman. By rescuing *Aranmore*, the government had been saved the embarrassment of having to parley with the Dey of Algiers for the release of hostages. One glowing report of the chase and action had been sent by Sir Lewis Bazeley, one of the passengers and, it was said, a friend of the prime minister.

Keen's wife had commented, "Bazeley? He has a very pretty young wife, I believe," and Keen had said, "You carried them earlier to Malta, Adam."

An admiral's discretion, or was he still a friend? Once Sir Richard Bolitho's flag captain, and one of his midshipmen. *Like me.*

Galbraith probably knew or had guessed some of it.

He made up his mind. "I recommended you for a command again, Leigh."

"I did not know, sir."

Adam shrugged. "Someone might take notice." He glanced at the door as Napier opened it with one foot. He had even discarded the squeaky shoes for this special day. "I'll come to the wardroom in an hour."

Galbraith strode from the cabin, and gasped as his head banged against a deckhead beam as if someone had shouted at him.

The captain needed every trained man that he could get. The second lieutenant was as yet an unknown force; Bellairs had scarcely settled into his rank. The most important officer in the ship to any captain under these circumstances was the first lieutenant, especially one so experienced.

Galbraith rubbed his head and grinned ruefully.

"But he'd have let me go if a ship was offered!"

The marine sentry's eyes moved briefly beneath the brim of his leather hat.

Officers talking aloud to themselves. And they had not even up-anchored yet!

He relaxed again. It was something to tell the others.

Galbraith thrust his way into the wardroom and tossed his hat to a messman. They were all looking at him, while pretending to be disinterested.

I will never be offered a command. He repeated it in his mind. But the envy was gone.

Vice-Admiral Valentine Keen pulled the heavy curtain aside and stared out at the restless waters of the Sound. The sea would be livelier beyond in this steady north-easterly, and it would still be light when *Unrivalled* cleared the anchorage and found her way into open water. He thought of the growing ranks of paid-off ships and men. She would be better off at sea. Any sea.

Somewhere in this big house he had heard voices, laughter, people to be entertained, encouraged or held at bay, as circumstances dictated. There were still times when it was almost impossible to accept. He was the youngest vice-admiral since

Nelson, with two captains, six lieutenants and a veritable army of clerks and servants to do his bidding, probably more if he raised the matter with the Admiralty.

But like the captain who was uppermost in his thoughts on this cold December afternoon, the final responsibility was his and his alone.

It was to be hoped that *Unrivalled*'s visit to Penzance would bring a few more men forward to be signed on. Men who had possibly imagined that the only life worth living was outside the harsh and demanding world of a King's ship.

He thought of Sir Graham Bethune, who held the same rank as himself. They had both served as midshipmen under Sir Richard Bolitho. Keen had been promoted lieutenant aboard Bolitho's frigate *Undine* when they had set sail for India and a world unknown to him. Without question or hesitation, like the newly commissioned officer he had seen aboard *Unrivalled*. His mind fastened on the face and name. Bellairs. He should do well, if Adam Bolitho could put the pain behind him. He had much to live up to. He thought of Penzance, what it might mean to Adam. *And much to live down.*

The navy would have to change, adapt to this new, uneasy peace and brittle relationship with allies who had been enemies for so long. He felt the wind buffet the windows, but it was warm even in these huge rooms. Warm and safe . . .

He thought of the countless reports and accounts he had studied since he had become a flag officer. It was still impossible for him to remain uninvolved. Always he had felt himself to be a part of it, fleet action or ship-to-ship like Adam's fight with the renegade *Triton*. He had defied Rhodes' orders, but success protected the brave. Sometimes. Admiral Rhodes' attempt to destroy the Dey's batteries had been a costly failure. The capture of hostages would have made future dealings with the Dey impossible.

A fresh attack was already being planned, by a fleet this time, and a born fighter, Lord Exmouth, had already been selected to command it, if rumour was to be believed. But Rhodes would not forget. Like an evil web. Rhodes' cousin had died in an asylum, driven mad by the syphilis which had destroyed his chance to be Sir Richard's flag captain in *Frobisher.* Keen frowned. It had all been buried. Rhodes had seen to that. But he would never forget.

And the admiral whose son had been a midshipman under Adam's first lieutenant during his first and only command . . . The youth had caused the death of a seaman, and Galbraith had put him ashore to await an enquiry. That too had been buried, and the midshipman appointed to another ship, forgotten. Except by his father. But Galbraith would never get another ship of his own now, unless some miracle happened. He recalled the intensity of Adam's eyes, his plea for Galbraith. *As a captain, in these circumstances, would I have done it?*

He heard a door open, the rustle of her gown against the furniture, and felt her hand on his arm. So much a part of it. And now there was the child to consider.

She asked, "Have you seen her yet, Val?"

Few called him that. Only Richard and his Catherine, and Zenoria.

He covered her hand with his own and smiled. "Is it so obvious, Gilia?"

She looked toward the sea. That, too, she could share. She had sailed many miles with her father, a renowned ship designer. It was good that he was not here to see all those fine vessels, like veterans begging on the streets.

"He will be all right, Val. I feel it."

"I know. One of our best frigate captains, and a fighter." He tried to dismiss it. Adam would have to learn. *We all did.* "I am no longer sure myself any more."

He felt her fingers tighten on his arm. "Look, Val, there she is!"

They waited in silence, watching the cruising patterns of whitecaps, hearing that same wind probe beneath the eaves of Boscawen House.

And there she stood, her topsails and courses almost pink in the fading light.

Adam was taking advantage of the wind to carry him clear of the headland before he set more canvas. Even from here the occasional feathers of spray were visible, bursting up and over her beakhead and jib sails. But Keen saw it all with great clarity, as if he were there. The lovely figurehead, the naked girl with her hands locked behind her head and mane of hair, her breasts thrusting toward the horizon.

He would have liked to have seen the anchor break from the ground and rise swiftly to her cathead. There would probably have been a fiddler, keeping time for the stamping feet, some inexperienced, on that slippery planking.

As we did together so many times, so many seas. The greatest moment, until the landfall.

Some out there would be feeling the first pangs of regret. It would be Christmas before they knew it . . .

He could feel her hand gripping his arm, and knew what she was thinking. That they were together, and with God's grace she would never have to watch his ship leaving like this. Never knowing when or if he would return. Like so many others. Like Richard and Catherine.

And now Adam, who was alone.

There were more voices. Intruders.

"I'll go down, Val. You stay a while longer."

He hugged her. She always knew. Just as she had taken over this great house as if she had been bred to it.

He looked again. "No, *Unrivalled*'s cleared the Point. Adam will be eager to make more sail now."

They walked arm in arm to the door, past the great dark paintings of ships at war, smoke, flames and proud flags. But no pain, no blood. The vice-admiral, the youngest since Nelson, and his lovely wife, ready and prepared for another kind of duty.

But once, as the wind rattled a shutter, Keen did look back, although he knew that *Unrivalled* was now out of sight.

And he was with her.

2 THE *F*INEST IN THE FLEET

CAPTAIN Adam Bolitho loosened the collar of his heavy boatcloak and tugged his hat down more firmly on his dark hair as he paused at the street corner. To recover his bearings or to prepare himself, he was not certain which.

The wind off Mounts Bay was still like ice, but had dropped considerably since *Unrivalled* had made her final approach two days earlier, buffeted this way and that, her reefed canvas cracking and banging in protest. It had been a relief to hear the anchor splash down, and see the town of Penzance, bright and sharp in the wintry glare.

A relief, or a warning? He shook himself angrily. He would go through with it. He could hear his coxswain breathing heavily, as if unused to the exercise and the steep ascent from the harbour. Curious or secretly amused, it was hard to tell with Luke Jago, the man who had always hated the navy in general, and officers in particular. And yet he was still here; after the fighting and the madness of battle, he had stayed. And he was a friend, a good one.

Adam turned as two young boys ran past, one carrying a crudely fashioned model boat, the other a pirate's flag, laughing and pushing each other, without a care in the world on this bitter forenoon with Christmas only a week away.

One paused, staring at the two blue-clad figures, hats tilted against the wind.

He called, "You want a good ship, Cap'n, zur?"

Jago shook his fist. "Little buggers!" And they both ran off.

Adam gazed after them, seeing himself. More ghosts . . .

Like this street, so strange and yet so familiar. He had almost expected to see faces, hear voices he knew. He should turn and leave right now. Galbraith was ashore with his recruiting parties, not an enviable task at the best of times. Everybody remembered the press gangs, men being snatched from the streets, even from their homes, if an officer was afraid to return to his captain empty-handed.

Like Falmouth, Penzance lived off and from the sea: you could smell the fish, and on hot days the nets hanging out to dry. Hemp, tar, and always the sea. Waiting.

He had been only a boy like those who had just passed when he had left Penzance, clutching a scrap of paper which he was to give to the people he must find in Falmouth. He had never returned, except once, when he had ridden here on one of the Bolitho estate's horses, twenty miles from Falmouth and back again. As that young boy, the twenty miles had been endless and punishing. And two days ago, with the proud silhouette of St Michael's Mount across the starboard bow, he had returned once more. Not the nervous boy, but as the captain of a frigate.

He thought of the orders he had received almost as soon as *Unrivalled*'s anchor had hurled spray over the beakhead. So why waste time? Why rouse the old doubts and painful memories?

He turned, and was about to speak when he saw the tall steeple, clear and sharp against the washed-out sky. St Mary's Chapel.

Like feeling a hand on the shoulder . . . He remembered hearing the old men talk about that steeple, so fine and slender, so delicate on this storm-lashed coast of England. They used to wager on its chances when every new season of gales arrived. The old men were long dead. St Mary's Chapel and its steeple were still standing.

There were not many people about. It was market day, so most of those who ventured out would be hunting for bargains in Jew Market Street.

"This way." He glanced at the nearby houses, small details apparent, recalling what he had heard, and what his mother had told him in childhood. Ships had come to Penzance to load cargoes of copper, tin and granite. They had frequently come from Holland, and unloaded their ballast of Dutch sandstone before their return voyages. Nothing was wasted, and even now he saw the facings of houses built with Dutch sandstone and not the usual granite.

On his way from the harbour he had seen few of the notices Galbraith had posted. Some had been torn down, others removed perhaps as souvenirs. He had caught the glances too: this was a seaport, and every one would know of the powerful frigate lying at her cable. *Looking for men.* Had it ever been different? And they would know he was her captain.

He should have remembered that it was market day, a most unlikely time for a man to sign his life away in a King's ship. And an army recruiting party had been here also; he had seen a sergeant outside one of the local inns, persuading men who had already drunk too much ale for their own safety to make their marks, *to be gone for a soldier.*

Galbraith had found twenty new hands so far, almost half of them from the local magistrate's court. Better than prison or deportation, seemed to be their reasoning. Reality might come as something of a shock. He had heard Cristie the sailing master say scornfully, "Gallows bait, the whole lot of 'em!"

He stopped outside the church and looked up at the weather vane. South-easterly wind. Perfect for sailing. *Leaving here.*

Jago hesitated and then removed his hat as Adam stepped through the tall, weather-worn doors. "Shall I come, sir?"

Adam hardly heard him. "If you wish."

The church was empty but for two old women sharing a pew; they both wore the traditional cowls he remembered from his childhood. Young or old, women carried huge baskets of fish, supported by strengthened bands around their heads, to settlements around the town, or sold it fresh from the sea from little donkeys in the streets. Neither of the women looked up as their shoes rang on the tiled floor.

Jago paused by a bust of what he supposed was some local dignitary, and watched and waited.

Adam halted beneath one of the windows and stared at the memorial plaque. He knew now that she had been beautiful. But for years he had remembered only that final day when she had pushed him away, pleading with him to leave her and find his way to Falmouth. Sick, dying, but as always she had put him first. Just as she had sold herself for him. He shivered, aware of the silence, of the streets he had just walked. Like the houses, they seemed so much smaller than he had remembered.

He reached out impetuously, as Jago had seen him do many times, to a friend, to a subordinate. *To me.*

The plaque was plain and simple. Even that had been something of a struggle with the stonemason and the church.

But it was done.

In loving memory of Kerenza Pascoe, who died in 1793.
Waiting for his ship.

That was all. The most they would condone for a woman of her reputation.

Adam touched it and smiled. Surprised that it was not difficult.

"I came, Mother. God bless you."

Then he turned and walked toward the doors again.

Jago glanced at the tablet. No title, no details. Just a woman's name and something about a ship. He was sometimes glad that his father had forced him to learn to read and write when he had been a boy, working in the schooner running out of Dover. With clips around his ears if he did not apply himself. Looking back now, it was all he could find to thank his father for, a bully who had died after falling drunk into a dock. So they said.

But reading gave you an edge. As the captain's coxswain he was privileged to walk the decks as much as he chose, to the annoyance, he knew, of some of the senior rates and little squirts like Midshipman Sandell. A glance at the chart or one of the log books kept him informed. *When, where, how.* Some of the hands aboard ship were just ignorant hawbucks, bumpkins; the ship could be on the moon for all they knew.

He thought of the two old women at prayer, fishwives as they were called round here, and wondered what comfort it gave them. He had heard prayers at sea, when some poor Jack was stitched up in his hammock and tipped over the side like so much rubbish. Where was the sense in that?

He felt the breeze across his face as they stepped on to the street once more and saw the captain square his shoulders, but not, he guessed, against the wind.

The woman who was remembered in the church had been Captain Bolitho's mother. Jago knew much of the story, and guessed the rest. Bolitho was a lucky man. A good family, and an uncle who would live in sailors' legends as long as Nelson, some said. But lucky above all else. He had risked his ship, his reputation, maybe his career by flying in the face of an admiral's orders, and all because of that woman they had carried in *Unrivalled.*

He had seen her crossing swords, and glances, with the captain.

And lucky to have a ship, with the navy being cut down in numbers daily, their companies thrown ashore to fend as best they could. Until the next bloody war, he thought. Then it would be soft words and the like, to get poor Jack back to sea again.

He looked up at the houses as they walked. Most captains would try to forget their pasts if it left a gap in their defences. Like Sir Richard and his lady, and his brother who had deserted the navy to fight for the Americans, Hugh Bolitho, who had fathered *Unrivalled*'s captain. The last of the family, they said.

But not this one. He shied away from any sort of unfounded trust; it was something he could never accept.

Adam Bolitho had taken him to the church with him. And for some reason, it mattered.

They had reached a place where the sea opened up to greet them again, like polished pewter, hard on the eyes, Adam thought, even for men like *Unrivalled*'s most experienced lookout, Joseph Sullivan, whose uncanny skill had found him the *Triton*. Sullivan was one of the older hands, respected by everyone, not least because he had been at Trafalgar, although he rarely spoke of it, and Adam was grateful that he had stayed with the ship.

Sullivan had regarded him with those clear eyes, like the eyes of a much younger man looking out of his weathered face.

"Where else would I go, Cap'n?"

And there was the ship, like glass from this vantage point. Strange to think that Bellairs, the youngest lieutenant, was the only officer aboard until the recruiting venture was over and the anchor was hove short again. Doing what he had always dreamed of. *Like most of us.* Luck, dead men's shoes, who could say? Massie, the second lieutenant, had been killed. The third lieutenant, Daniel Wynter, had left the ship to follow his late father into politics. The member of Parliament had always hated his son's career in the navy and had made no secret of it.

In death he had apparently succeeded in getting his own way.

The new lieutenant, Varlo, seemed experienced and came from a naval background. He had also been flag lieutenant for a few months to a rear-admiral at the Nore.

Galbraith had had little to say about him, other than mentioning his duties. He was keeping his distance until matters had settled down. As his captain had once tried to do.

It was impossible.

Adam turned and stared at the ship until his eyes watered. He should have remained on board. There was more than enough for him to do before sailing. So why . . . ?

He heard Jago say casually, "Now who's this, then?"

Something in the tone, even the suggestion of a hand loosening the short, wide-bladed dirk he always wore. A hint of danger, like those other times. But he was mistaken. There was no threat in the two figures who were waiting by a pair of opened gates.

The man was tall, and well built, but for the way he twisted his shoulders. About his own age, but wearing an eye patch which did not conceal the terrible scar that clawed down his face and neck. One eye must have been torn out, and the flesh opened to the bone. He had only one arm.

His companion was a young woman, who wore a cap and apron. She was holding the man's arm, and her face was hostile.

Jago said, "What is it, matey?" He stood as if very relaxed, one hand resting on his belt.

The man took half a pace forward and tried to say something. His voice was confused, almost strangled, but he would not stop.

The girl cut in, "I *said* you should stay away! They don't care! I told you!" But she was sobbing, the anger a mask for something else.

Adam said, "It's all right. My fault—I was many miles away just then."

He moved nearer, but felt as if he were frozen to this place. A man of his own age, crippled, half-blind, barely able to speak. Not just a survivor, but a victim.

He said quietly, "John Powers, foretopman." He held out his right hand, but changed it to suit the one-armed man.

The head twisted round still further, so that the eye seemed to fill his face. Then he spoke, slowly, with painful gaps between each word, and all the while the girl held his arm, watching his face, sharing the anguish, as she must do every day.

"Not . . . killed . . . sir." He nodded slowly, remembering it, seeing it. "I . . . was . . . told you . . . was . . . 'ere." There were more deep scars on his throat. " . . . 'Ad . . . to . . . come . . . an' . . . be sure . . ."

Adam said to Jago, "John Powers served in my *Anemone*, when we lost to the Yankee. A day I'll never forget."

The girl reached up to brush her companion's hair from his face.

She pleaded, "Let's get back, Johnny. They will be lookin' fer us, eh?"

Adam said, "Where do you work?"

She gestured over her shoulder. "At the inn. We got a place to sleep. Don't need nobody else!"

The crippled man, who had been one of the best topmen in *Anemone*'s company, said, "Wash . . . pots . . . an' . . . things . . . sir."

Adam put his hand to his pocket but she snapped, "I brung 'em, cause he wanted it! We don't need yer money, *sir!*"

She dragged him round and pushed him towards the opened gates. From a small window Adam could see faces watching, tankards poised with interest.

The man named Powers tried again. "*Anemone* was the finest in the fleet!" He did not stammer once.

Jago stared after them and then at his captain and shrugged, his hand slipping away from the dirk. "It happens, sir. We'll always see it. It's the way of things." He felt he wanted to reach out, to touch his arm as he had seen him do so often, and reassure him in some way.

Adam looked at him, his dark hair blowing in the wind although he did not recall having removed his hat.

"Sometimes we need to be reminded." He stared up at the old steeple. *"Pride."*

One word. It was all that was needed.

Lieutenant Galbraith held his hands out to a crackling log fire. It was about noon but he felt as if he had been on his feet for days, and he was tired, frustrated and disappointed. He nodded to the inn's landlord and took the proferred glass, felt it run like fire across his tongue, and wondered where it had come from. Smugglers would be busier than ever now that the war with France was over. For the moment.

He heard the small squad of Royal Marines which had accompanied the recruiting party, voices loud and untroubled in the other "long room." Corporal Bloxham would make certain that none of his men got drunk or misbehaved; he had an eye for such things. He was the detachment's crack shot. Galbraith recalled that last hour aboard the *Triton's* scarred and bloodied deck, the captain trying to assist his servant, who had been hit by a wood splinter, and unable to reach the enemy commander who was aiming to kill him.

Like a little tableau, the injured boy cradled in Bolitho's arms, the old sword pointing impotently across the deck, and then Bloxham, quite calm, as if he had been on the range somewhere with his faithful musket.

Yes, Corporal Bloxham would keep an eye on things. He would be thinking of a sergeant's stripes before too long.

He stared around the low-beamed room, with its smoke-stained pictures and pieces of polished brass. He sighed. One more stop and it was over. He glared at the empty glass. A bloody waste of time. Three men; one man and two boys was closer to the truth. *Waste of time.*

The door banged open and he tried to relax his mind and body.

There was something about Lieutenant George Varlo which seemed to unsettle him. He scarcely knew him, and accepted that that was mostly his own fault, and yet . . . Varlo was alert, keen-eyed, efficient. Very light on his feet, like a dancer or one used to matching swords for pleasure, or in earnest. Fair hair, short and fastidiously kept, like his clothing: the perfect officer. Galbraith was not normally an intolerant man, but Varlo made him feel clumsy and awkward in almost everything.

Maybe it was because he had served as flag lieutenant to some senior officer. Or maybe you were chosen because of those qualities? But he considered George Avery, who had died when they had boarded the enemy, and his own words to Captain Bolitho. *I think he knew he was going to die. He had given up the will to live.* No, not like Avery at all . . .

Varlo glanced around, a small smile on his lips. "I've told Mr Rist to watch the others until we're ready to move."

Galbraith said, "Rist knows what to do!" He was being stupid. Unfair. How could Varlo know what Rist, the best master's mate in the ship, was like? How, on that day when they had launched a boat attack amongst the islands, Rist had been a tower of strength, even when they had landed on the wrong beach.

The landlord had reappeared. "A glass, zur?"

Varlo shook his head. "Later."

Galbraith said, "*I* will." He sensed the man's resentment and added sharply, "Just what I needed."

He made another attempt. "The next place is in Market Jew

Street." He opened his notebook. "Must have had a Jewish community at some time."

Varlo studied him, amused. "Actually, no. It's the old Cornish tongue, *marhas you*, which means Thursday Market." The smile widened. "Or close enough!"

Galbraith said curtly, "I didn't know."

Varlo shrugged elegantly. "Why should you? Not really our concern, is it?"

There were shouts and cheers from the street. The army recruiting sergeant was returning to his barracks with his haul. Probably too drunk to know what they had done.

He said, "We might have better luck tomorrow."

Varlo said directly, "You've been with *Unrivalled* since she was first commissioned? With her captain, too?" The little smile again. "A Cornishman, no less."

"Yes."

"What is he like? One hears so many things, as you well know, but if we are to be away from England and the fleet, it is sensible to be prepared."

He was goading him, drawing him out into the open, and enjoying it.

Galbraith said, "The best captain I've yet served. He has high standards, and expects them acted upon." He tried to smile, to put it in perspective. "Even from Cornishmen."

Varlo nodded thoughtfully. "Thank you for the warning. If it was so intended."

Rist, the master's mate, peered in at them. "Ready, sir!"

Galbraith picked up his hat and straightened his sword against his hip. Varlo probably had some influence behind him. A flag lieutenant, and now appointed to a fine frigate when so many were being laid up. *Influence.* With a view to getting a command of his own? He nodded his thanks to the innkeeper. *Like me.*

He felt the salt air on his lips. Back to sea. He was eager to leave.

Adam Bolitho ran his hand along the smooth, cold stone of the sea wall, worn away by every sort of weather. Peace or war, it made no difference here.

He felt for his watch and remembered, and thought of the boy who had asked his permission to keep the pieces after the musket ball had smashed it to fragments. It had saved his life. *The little mermaid.*

Tomorrow they would be leaving here. It was not the voyage to West Africa which disturbed him, or the countless demands and challenges of a ship still undermanned.

It was not that. He had held a command since he was twenty-three. He was prepared for most difficulties.

Tomorrow was the problem. Leaving here, where he had been born and brought up by the woman whose name he had touched in the church. A place where he had learned to take care of himself, even as a child, and yet he had never considered it his home. Falmouth, and the great house which was now his by right, no matter what legal arrangements still had to be made, was home, Falmouth and the ocean, wherever it beckoned him.

But not today. With *Unrivalled* at sea again he would find time to laugh at himself and his sentimentality. *It happens, sir.* He thought of Jago's words at the church. *It's the way of things.* He was down there mustering the gig's crew now, and probably questioning his own decision to stay on as coxswain. If he had ever stopped doing so.

He sighed. Galbraith would be returning very soon. They would share a glass once they were aboard. He thought of the cases of wine from the address in St James's Street, Catherine's gift when *Unrivalled* had been commissioned. A lifetime ago.

He heard Jago's footsteps on the stone stairs. It was time.

But Jago shook his head. "Thought I'd better come and tell you, sir. There's a gentleman who wants to see you." He added bluntly, "Insists, more like."

Adam bit his lip. Another one, like the crippled ex-topman and the spectre on the moored hulk. Too many reminders.

Jago watched him grimly. "He's in the coastguard post yonder, sir. I can tell him to shove off, if you like."

"No. I'll come."

The room was almost dark, a fire dying in the grate.

Adam stepped into a patch of light from the solitary window and said, "I understand, sir . . ."

The figure sitting by the window was round-shouldered, portly; there were small gold spectacles propped on his forehead.

Adam held out both hands. "Daniel Yovell! Of all people!"

Yovell got to his feet and came to him, dropping his spectacles into place with the gesture Adam remembered. A man of learning, who lived with and by his Bible, once his uncle's clerk and then his secretary and friend. Catherine's, too.

Yovell said, "When you visited Falmouth I was away on business in Bodmin. I only heard when I returned there. Bryan Ferguson was very upset that your stay was curtailed. There was so much, you see . . ." He did not continue.

"It is *good* to see you, old friend." Even that reminded him again of Allday.

"I heard that your ship was calling here. You know how news travels, sir, especially amongst sailors."

Anybody less seamanlike was hard to imagine. Stooped, devout and gentle, Yovell had been one of Sir Richard's *little crew*, as he had called them. He had been given a cottage adjoining the big house and had become a great help to Ferguson, the estate's one-armed steward. Another veteran.

"How can I help you?"

Yovell smiled, and it was like a cloud clearing from the sun.

He said, "I have a letter for you. I fear it has taken its time finding its way to Falmouth."

Adam took it, seeing the marks and the official signatures. *From Catherine.*

"I thought to send it across by the boat, but I judged it best to see you first."

Adam turned the letter over in his hands. She hadn't forgotten.

Jago was still standing by the door, arms folded, face expressionless. Yovell regarded him sternly. "This fellow said I should take cover in here, *better for one of my age,* indeed!"

Jago grinned. "No disrespect, sir!"

Adam turned, angered by the interruption. Galbraith was shouting to his men, and there were other voices, loud and excited.

Jago said patiently, "I was about to *say,* Cap'n. We seem to have gathered some recruits. Volunteers!"

Yovell was watching him, his eyes both warm and sad. "I meant no harm. But these men came across in the packet from Falmouth. With me."

"Do I know any of them?"

"Perhaps not. All of them served under Sir Richard."

"My God." Adam looked past him, knowing, understanding what it must have cost Yovell, a man closer to his uncle than almost any one.

And now there was a letter from the woman who had loved him.

He said, "I shall go out to them," and walked blindly across the familiar cobbles. Like part of a dream. *The lifeline.*

Yovell polished his spectacles with a handkerchief and remarked, "It seemed the thing to do, you see. The letter gave me the idea." He didn't add that Allday had known nothing about it.

Adam came back, inexplicably disturbed and moved. Hard hands reaching out as he had passed among them, tattoos and weathered faces, every one a prime seaman.

It was as if he had known all of them, but in his heart he knew that they had seen and heard another Bolitho when he had spoken to them.

He said quietly, "That was a fine thing you did." And to Jago, "Gig ready?"

Jago nodded. "Say the word, sir."

Adam looked at the round-shouldered man who, in his own quiet way, had changed everything.

"Will you stay in Penzance a while?"

Yovell shrugged, and seemed almost apologetic.

"I have some things with me, sir. I had heard that you lost your clerk recently, so I thought I would offer my services until something better presents itself." He was smiling, but there was no doubt of his sincerity. His need.

"Are you sure, man? She's no ship of the line, you know!"

Yovell said severely, "I was Sir Richard's clerk before becoming his secretary. I can adapt, *even for one of my age.*"

Jago picked up the newcomer's chest and followed them out into the keen air. He had seen his captain's face when those men had crowded around him, as if it was the start of some big and glorious venture, just as he had seen it in that church nearby.

He was reminded of the handshake which, for him, had decided things. And he was glad of it.

Adam rested his hand on the breech of one of the eighteen-pounders which shared his quarters and sensed the movement under his palm. Something he had never grown used to, never truly accepted, that a ship was alive and responding in her own way.

He shook his head, dismissing the notion, and glanced around the cabin. Young Napier had been busy; there was nothing lying about, everything was in its place.

How many in *Unrivalled*'s company were feeling regret and anxiety, he wondered. It was easy to laugh it off, for the old hands to brag about it after a few tots of rum on their messdecks. But that was then. *Unrivalled* was ready to leave. Alive.

The wind had backed a little, which might allow some of the new men time to become accustomed to the complications of getting under way. You never forgot the first time. Everyone else seemed to know exactly what was expected of him.

He heard the shrill of a call; the ship was restless, straining at her cable, her fully laden hull matched against the men labouring at the capstan bars. Yes, there would be a few faint hearts on this cold December forenoon.

He stood away from the gun as if he had heard someone speak, and patted his worn, seagoing coat to make certain he had everything he needed, and glanced at the small desk where he kept his personal log book. He had placed Catherine's letter carefully between its pages to press out the wear and tear of its journey.

My dear Adam. He could hear her voice, had tried to picture her writing it. How she felt, what she was doing. How she looked.

She had mentioned George Avery, and had thanked him for writing to her of his death. She had touched only briefly on its effect on Sillitoe, Avery's uncle.

But it was clear enough; she was with Sillitoe. She had spoken of his strength, his protection, and that she was accompanying him on some business venture.

Adam was still surprised by his own foolishness, his naïveté. After what she had endured, the grief and the enmity, it was a wonder she had written at all.

He half-listened to the sudden thud of feet overhead, the

shouts as a petty officer chased some confused newcomer to his right station. They would learn. They had to.

He recalled the dry wording of his final orders.

You are to repair in the first instance to Freetown, Sierra Leone, and avail yourself of the latest intelligence concerning the forts and settlements on that coast. You will reasonably assist the senior officer of the patrolling squadron in whatever way you consider conforms with these said orders.

But on passage *Unrivalled* would call into Funchal, Madeira, to replenish stores, and perhaps make more sense out of such vague instructions.

The slave trade was a fact, although banned officially by Britain. A felony, to the delight of the anti-slavery movement in Parliament and elsewhere.

A show of strength, then. He wondered how Galbraith and the others regarded it. They were safe, lucky to be employed; they had seen that for themselves in Plymouth and Penzance.

For the practical ones, like Cristie, the master, it was all a matter of sea-miles logged, favourable winds and faith in the stars. To Tregillis the purser, it was food, drink, and a minimum of waste for every one of those miles, with enough left over for emergencies.

He plucked at his shirt and felt the locket against his skin. The bare throat and shoulders, the high cheekbones . . . it was over because it had never begun. Nor would it. They might never meet again. Perhaps she only truly existed in this locket.

Napier came in from the sleeping quarters, careful, he noticed, to walk lightly on the restless deck.

He could see it now. The boy on *Triton*'s deck, falling with a jagged splinter deep in his thigh like some obscene dart. *Triton* was like many Dutch vessels; her builders had used a lot of teak, something hated by English sailors. The splinters were known to poison and cause gangrene to spread at an alarming rate. Even O'Beirne had been troubled about it, and had wanted to put the boy ashore at Gibraltar where he might have received better attention.

Napier had insisted that he wanted to stay with the ship. He had suffered for it, and would carry the scars of O'Beirne's surgery until his dying day.

O'Beirne had said severely, "You'll always have a limp, my boy!"

Napier had been equally stubborn. And he seemed to be overcoming his limp.

Adam had written to the boy's widowed mother. She should be proud of the child she had allowed to be signed on without, it seemed, much hesitation.

He touched the locket again and carefully released it. Catherine had sent no address. It was as if she simply needed him to know that she was there. Like the day at the memorial service at Falmouth, when Galbraith had asked to join him.

He looked at Napier. "It's time." He had heard the muffled chimes of eight bells, and beyond it the slow, regular clank of the capstan pawls.

He thought of the men who had come with Yovell to sign on. How were they now?

And Yovell himself. He had settled down as if he had never left the sea. He was sharing a tiny cabin space which also served as a store for the purser's records with Ritzen, the purser's assistant, a Dutchman who had played an unlikely but vital part in discovering the role and purpose of *Triton* in that last battle. Adam sensed that Yovell had needed to get away from his hard-won security, if only to hold on to something far more precious.

Napier said, "Can I come up with you, sir?"

Adam smiled. "Regrets?"

The youth thought about it, his face serious. "My *place*, sir."

They walked through the screen door, where the marine sentry was already stiffly at attention, and probably wishing he was on deck with his mates.

Adam touched his hat to the figures by the quarterdeck rail and looked at the slowly revolving capstan; its twin would be keeping time below decks. The fiddle was going, the shantyman beating time with his foot, his voice all but lost in the creak and rattle of blocks and rigging.

They were all here, Cristie with his master's mates, Galbraith by the rail, and young Bellairs at the foot of the towering mainmast. Here the marines, their coats very bright in the hazy light, waited with the afterguard to control the mizzen sheets and braces. The simplest mast in the ship, *all they were any use for*, as the old Jacks proclaimed. And right forward, one arm outstretched and dwarfed by the beautiful figurehead, was the new lieutenant, Varlo, watching the jerk of the incoming cable.

And young Midshipman Cousens with the big signals telescope turned toward the land. He was Bellairs' successor, and the next obvious candidate for promotion when the opportunity offered itself. If he was lucky.

Adam nodded to Galbraith. "The wind's steady. Stand by." He even recalled his own words that day before the fight. *Trust me.* So many times.

Another midshipman's voice. That was Martyns, the one who had been with Jago in the gig.

"Anchor's hove short, sir!" Repeating Varlo's call from the beakhead, his voice broke in a shrill squeak.

Adam saw one of the helmsmen glance away from the flapping masthead pendant just long enough to grin at his companion.

"Stand by, the capstan!"

More calls and running feet. "Loose th' heads'ls!"

Adam tensed. This was the moment.

"Hands aloft and loose tops'ls!"

The cable was coming home, much faster now. Or was it his heart? He looked toward the shore, hardly another sail moving. But many eyes would be watching today. Some relieved, others already feeling the ache of separation.

He thought of the crippled seaman who had served with him in *Anemone*, the ship which had begun so much, and had opened the way for him. A shattered man, who lived from day to day with his woman, two lost souls, each needing the other.

They would be there today.

Men scurried past him, one pausing to stare at him. The captain. *What's he like?*

The yell from forward. *"Anchor's aweigh, sir!"*

He felt the deck stagger, and dashed spray from his face as the ship appeared to ride her bowsprit up and over the timeless barrier of St Michael's Mount.

Small details stood out. Cristie's hand gesturing at an extra man to throw his weight on the wheel as the helm went down. Hoarse cries from overhead as the sails broke free, then filled and bellied out to the wind. Blocks squeaking, men hauling on the braces to drag the great yards round still further, to capture the wind, so that the rudder-head sounded like a drumbeat.

"Steady she goes!"

Adam looked again. That would be Newlyn village over there as *Unrivalled* continued to pivot round, but it was lost in haze and drifting spray.

"Sou'-west by south, sir!"

Galbraith, his hands cupped to make his voice carry. "More men on the weather forebrace, Mr Partridge! *Lively there!*"

Adam gripped the quarterdeck ladder rail, reminded of the night Napier had come to tell him of the girl who was lying just there.

And what had happened later, in Malta . . . A dangerous madness, potentially no less lethal than a teak splinter, or the shots which had cut down so many over the months . . . the years.

He pushed away from the rail and walked stiffly up to the weather side. He knew Jago was watching him, standing near the signals party in case he was needed, but careful not to show it. Perhaps that was his strength . . .

He said, "Steer sou'-west until we weather the headland, Mr Cristie!" and saw his approval.

To Galbraith he shouted, "We'll get the fore and main courses on her directly!"

The ship heeled still further, some bare feet sliding, a few men sprawling, too concerned with watching the land which was already fading away.

There were kicks and curses too. Leadership and knowledge would follow.

"Steady she goes, sir! *Full an' bye!*"

He considered the calculations he had made and compared with the taciturn sailing master.

With a pause at Funchal, *Unrivalled* could complete her passage to the Windward Coast in about a month. Less.

He looked up as more shouts came from the maintop.

Galbraith was peering aloft also, but seemed satisfied. Drill, drill and more drill; there were no passengers in a King's ship.

Time to train and to prepare. Adam shaded his eyes and stared across the quarter, but the land was just a blurred, misshapen barrier.

He touched the locket beneath his sodden shirt.

And time to forget.

He was free.

3 "TO SERVE THIS SHIP"

LIEUTENANT Leigh Galbraith paused at the foot of the companion ladder and clung momentarily to the handrails, gauging the mood and energy of the ship and the deck which awaited him. It was four in the morning, or very soon would be, but time seemed to have lost all meaning. Even during the middle watch he had been summoned from his cabin in response to the call for *all hands*. To shorten sail yet again, the sea a wilderness of leaping spectres, and waves surging along the hull like a tide race.

His whole body ached, and he could not remember being dry and warm. Five days of it, not long when you considered what they had already achieved in this ship. He smiled bitterly, hearing his captain's words. *That was then.*

Even the handrail was clammy, and his stomach contracted as he heard somebody retching uncontrollably.

He climbed the rest of the ladder and waited for the wind to greet him. A few moments more while his eyes grew accustomed to it: the wet, huddled shapes of the watchkeepers, the three helmsmen joined like statuary as they clung to the big double wheel, eyes seen occasionally in the compass light as they peered aloft at the iron-hard canvas, tightly reefed though it was, fighting their own war with sea and rudder.

Varlo was waiting for him, slim figure angled to the deck as if nothing could shift him.

Galbraith listened to his report, although the chart had been engraved on his mind even in the discomfort of his swaying cot, the boom of the sea alongside.

Nine hundred miles since they had tacked clear of Mounts Bay. It felt ten times that.

Beating clear of Brest and then down into Biscay, the weather following them with barely a let-up. It was surprising that they had got this far without losing a man or sustaining any serious damage. There were injuries a-plenty, especially amongst the landmen, who had never set foot in a ship of any kind before. Brave lunatics, the surgeon O'Beirne had called them. Men thrown from their feet by water surging over the gangways, or flung against stanchions, or worse, one of the guns. Others caught by the unexpected rush of a line snaking through a block to catch the unwary in a noose like a trap. A man could lose fingers in a block, or have the skin scored from his bones by the deadly cordage.

Varlo said, "South by east, sir!" Clipped and formal, perhaps to remind Galbraith that his watch was waiting to be relieved. "Wind's steady as before."

Galbraith winced as spray dashed against his face. On the chart it was clear, certain. *Unrivalled* was eighty or ninety miles to the north-west of Lisbon, across the fortieth parallel. But even Cristie seemed doubtful, and had muttered, "I'll feel better when we can see something!" It was quite an admission for him.

Galbraith said, "It's easing." Water was still splashing down from the shrouds, but not cutting across the deck like the last time. He groaned. *Was that only three hours ago?* He waited for the moment and seized the quarterdeck rail. His eyes could make out details now; the deck and rigging was stark against the seething water as it surged abeam.

He pointed suddenly. "Those men. What are they doing?"

Varlo replied offhandedly, "Bailing the boats. Idle bastards, they'll know in future not to drag their feet on *my* watch!"

Rist, the master's mate of the morning watch, called, "The watch is aft, sir!" A good man. Astute too, and wise enough to have marked the friction between his officers.

Galbraith said, "Most of them are raw, untrained! You can't expect them to learn it all in five days, man!"

"I see no sense in being soft with them, *sir!*"

"I'll be the judge of that, Mr Varlo! Now carry on, and dismiss those hands." They faced one another like enemies, all else forgotten. "Or bring them aft and charge them. Make it official!"

Varlo turned and walked to the companion-way without another word.

Galbraith peered at the swaying compass card, giving himself time. Angry, because he knew he had overreacted, or because Varlo had seemed unmoved by it.

Rist said, "We can get some 'ands aloft at first light, sir. There'll be a bit o' fancy splicing to be done after this little lot."

Doing his best. Bridging the gap.

Galbraith nodded. "Aye, we'll do that. And thank you." He walked to the opposite side, alone again.

Rist sighed. A warrant officer was always in the middle, had to be.

Galbraith was a good first lieutenant, brave too. But Varlo . . . he was just plain dangerous.

But still, a couple more days and they should sight Madeira, or Mr Cristie would be wanting to know why not.

That would take the edge off things, for a while anyway. Some of that heavy red wine, and bold stares from the women.

Someone called to him urgently and he turned away.

The sailor's dream.

Adam Bolitho put his signature to yet another letter and stared at the pile beside it on the desk, all in Yovell's effortless, round hand.

He was sitting opposite, gold spectacles perched once more on his forehead.

"I thought you were over hasty in offering your services in Penzance. I thought you might well live to regret it." He smiled, the strain already gone. "Now I am only thankful!" His mind returned to Falmouth, the big grey house. "Bryan Ferguson will be cursing me for taking you."

Yovell regarded him thoughtfully. "It was time, sir. I knew that within a few days of my return. I did manage to complete a few details with the lawyers," and glanced away. "It is their world, not mine, I fear."

Adam leaned back in the chair and felt the sun across his cheek from the stern windows. The glass was thick and the warmth an illusion, but it was enough, after days of wind and angry sea.

He heard muffled shouts from the deck, and the sound of fresh cordage being hauled over the planking, ready to be spliced and then hoisted to the upper yards to repair some of the storm damage.

And tomorrow they would sight Madeira. A first landfall for many of *Unrivalled*'s people. It might make up for the hardship, the knocks and the bruises along the way. At least they had not lost a single man. A real risk on any first passage.

He thought of the letters which would be landed in Funchal to await the next courier to England. Yovell had advised him on some of them. Was there nothing he could not do or understand? *Their world, not mine.* The estate had to be run, the farms overseen and encouraged. In his mind he had often seen that room overlooking the sea, with its portraits of Cheney and Catherine. A place full of memories and hopes, but an empty house for all that.

Yovell watched him, seeing the changing emotions, recognising some of them as he had known, and perhaps feared he would.

It had not been easy, and on more than one occasion he had found himself questioning his own common sense for putting himself in this position. As Adam had warned him, *Unrivalled* was no liner, and in the long nights as the ship had reeled and plunged in that invisible sea, he had been close to despair.

He had been surprised how easily he had been accepted in the ship. Perhaps because he was a stranger.

He saw Adam glance at the skylight and tense again, his ear catching some false note in the constant chorus of wind and rigging. Others saw him as the captain, the final authority as far as sailors were concerned, the one man who could promote, reward, flog or destroy any of them, if he chose. It was only at moments like this that one glimpsed the real man. The uncertainties and doubts, that rare wistfulness in his dark eyes when his mind had slipped away from the role he was expected to play at all times.

Yovell was a patient man, and had always been prepared to wait before forming his true opinions.

He turned his head as the door opened and the young servant, Napier, padded into the cabin.

Of Napier Adam had said, almost casually, "He has no father, and I've never been able to discover his mother's thoughts about his future, if she has any. He can read and write, and he has courage, true courage." Yovell had seen that look just now when Adam had been thinking about Falmouth. He had added, "See what you can do for him, will you?"

Just like that. Few would ever see that side of their lord and master.

Napier said, "I've got out your best coat, sir."

Adam looked at him, his mind clearing. "I had all but forgot. I am to sup in the wardroom tonight. Mr Cristie assures me it will remain calm enough for that!"

He glanced at the two of them. "You may make use of these quarters while I am being entertained."

He walked to the stern bench and leaned both hands on it, watching the sea fling spray up from the rudder. A flock of gulls rose and dipped soundlessly, their shapes distorted by the salt-stained glass, waiting for scraps from the galley. They probably nested in Madeira.

The youth placed two goblets on the desk beside a bottle, and then quietly departed to the adjoining cabin.

Yovell waited. Somehow he knew this was the real cause of the tension, the quick changes of mood, the eagerness to find some kind of solution in routine ship's affairs. Like all the letters and reports they had gone through together; he had felt it even then.

Something which was holding them apart, like a barrier. And it was the one thing which had first drawn them together.

Adam said quietly, "This is a good ship. I am a lucky man to command her, for so many reasons, but most because I need her." He smiled, but only briefly, so that Yovell saw the youth again, the image of his uncle. "There were so many who were there, *that day*. I was not one of them."

Yovell sat very still in the chair, feeling it, seeing it.

Adam continued, "Sometimes I feel he is still very close to me." He nodded. "I have known it several times. Always the hand, reaching out. I have spoken of this to no one else, except . . ." He turned away from the glass. *"Tell me."*

"I was not there, either." Yovell was polishing his spectacles again, probably without realising he had removed them. "I was assisting the wounded. I prayed with some of them. But something made me go on deck, although he always ordered me to stay clear of the guns." He looked at Adam but his eyes were very distant. "They were all cheering, and some were firing their muskets to signal a victory. But on that deck there was utter silence; all the din was outside, somewhere else."

Adam nodded, but did not interrupt.

"It was over. I knelt down on that bloodied deck, and I prayed. Not for him, but for us. I shall never forget."

In the adjoining sleeping cabin, Napier crouched with his ear against the slats of the screen partition, one hand resting on the fine dress coat which had been brought aboard in Plymouth. To replace the one the captain had been wearing when they had boarded the enemy ship, and the splinter had pierced Napier's leg.

The captain could have been killed that day, like the uncle they had just been talking about. *But he came to help me. He put me first.*

He glanced at the swaying cot where the rebel captain Lovatt had died, *thinking I was his son.* Captain Bolitho had even cared about that. Just as he had been concerned about his mother's failure to reply to his letters. She had other things on her mind now that he was here in *Unrivalled.* A man. It had not taken her long to forget.

But how could Captain Bolitho be expected to understand anything so cheap, so heartless?

It could not last forever. Nothing did. His mother had said that often enough. Other ships, and perhaps one day . . . He almost ran from the screen.

"You called, sir?"

They did not move, and Napier realised they had neither heard, nor called out for him.

He stood quite still, feeling the regular rise and fall of the cabin around him. *And he was a part of it.*

Lieutenant James Bellairs turned his shoulders into the wind and peered at his list. It had been handed round from watch to watch and was barely readable. Fortunately there were only a few more names left on it. Midshipman Deighton stood close by, frowning with concentration. Learning, listening or merely pretending to be interested, it was hard to tell. Bellairs had been a midshipman himself so recently that he often found himself thinking like one, especially when he was left to explain something.

He knew the old arguments. *We had to learn the hard way, so why not them?* He might even become like that himself. One day. He tried again.

"The first lieutenant wants to reduce the number of idlers

before we reach our destination. And more hands are needed for gun drill."

Deighton asked, "What is Sierra Leone like, sir?"

Bellairs tapped one foot impatiently. Deighton was new to the ship but experienced, and had served in another frigate which had since been paid off for refit. At fifteen, his previous service put him ahead of most of the others. Reserved, almost withdrawn, he had proved what he could do under fire. But he rarely smiled, and Bellairs knew it was because of the rumours which surrounded the death of his father, an acting-commodore. Killed in action; he had heard the others talking about it. But it was now said that he had in fact been shot down by one of his own men. Another ship, but Captain Adam Bolitho had been in command of her also.

He recalled Deighton's question. "Oh, one of those rough-and-ready places, you know." He had never been there.

Deighton saw some figures below the poop. "There they are, sir."

Bellairs waited for the gunner's mate, Williams, to hustle them over. Two men and a youth. The last was not merely pale, his skin was white.

Williams reported, "Cooper, Dixon and Ede, sir."

Bellairs surveyed them. Just three new hands, nothing out of the ordinary. Except . . . He glanced at Williams, but his face gave nothing away.

"You will report to Mr Varlo in the first division tomorrow. Gun drill is essential to a man-of-war, and . . ." He looked at the white-faced youth. "Are you unwell, Cooper?"

The man at the other end of the group called, "I'm Cooper, sir!"

The third one grinned broadly.

It was a bad start. Bellairs said sharply, "I asked you a question, Ede is—*that* right?"

Landmen, untrained, and somehow out of place.

Bellairs tried to put it to the back of his mind. He was a lieutenant now. He must look at everything firmly, but fairly.

Even in his own service he had seen most of them. The hard
men and the cowards, volunteers and pressed hands, the godly
and the liars. But these men stood apart. They had been released
from prison only on the understanding that they would redeem
themselves by serving in a King's ship. There had been about
twenty of them all told, but these last three were still without a
proper station in the ship.

Ede said, "I was sick, sir."

Williams said, "Speak up, boy!"

Bellairs peered at his list. "The surgeon has passed you as fit
for work."

"Yes, sir."

"Well, then." Bellairs looked past him. "Do your work with a
will and attend your duties, and you'll have nothing to fear!"

He strode aft and added, "He'll soon learn, Mr Deighton." He
caught himself in time. He had almost said, *we all had to.*

Deighton glanced back at the three figures with Williams. It
was strange that the third lieutenant had not noticed it, he
thought. The youth called Ede was not merely sick or feeling out
of place. He was terrified.

He put it from his mind. They were heading for Sierra Leone,
and there was talk of the slave trade. And today he, Midshipman
Richard Deighton, was being invited to the wardroom. Perhaps
the first step . . .

He thought of Ede again. Even when these same guns had
roared out and men had been cut down in front of him, he had
not been afraid. Not as he might have expected. A need to prove
something, maybe? No, it went even deeper than that.

But not like the youth named Ede. Deighton had been afraid
of only one man. His own father.

He thought suddenly of the way the captain had treated him

when he had joined the ship at Malta. It had been like sharing something, as if . . .

"I trust I am not *tiring* you too much, Mr Deighton?" Bellairs had turned to watch him.

Deighton touched his hat.

"Ready, sir!"

Bellairs strode on. He felt more like a lieutenant again.

The meal in *Unrivalled*'s wardroom was a surprisingly good one. The centrepiece was a saddle of mutton which had been brought aboard at the last moment before sailing, with a remarkably strong sauce which was one of the cook's own inventions. The fresh bread from Devon and Cornwall had already been consumed, but ship's biscuits, cheese and a variety of wines made it a lively occasion.

As a young lieutenant, Adam had often wondered how a captain felt when he was invited to the wardroom. *A guest in his own ship.* Even now he was not sure, nor was he used to it. A small brig like his very first command, or an ugly bomb like those he had seen off Algiers was a much closer community. A frigate, despite the lack of space, preserved the same barriers and distinctions as a lordly ship of the line.

Only at times like these, with the wine flowing at will, did you see the other side of the coin, the men behind the allotted ranks and roles. As varied as Cristie the sailing master, the true professional whose family had been raised in the same humble street as Lord Collingwood. O'Beirne the surgeon, stabbing the air through the drifting pipe smoke to emphasise the point in some Irish story he had been telling. He was a good surgeon, who had proved his worth several times over, after and during action at sea, or when dealing with the hundred and one accidents that befell even the most experienced seaman going about his work.

Adam eased his back against the chair and knew he had eaten

too much. It was nothing compared with his companions, more out of habit. As captain he could choose what and when he ate. Consuming too little was as dangerous as drinking too much, when there was nobody to enchourage or restrain you.

He glanced down at his new coat, made by the same Plymouth tailor as the one he'd worn when *Unrivalled* had been commissioned. The one he had worn for that last fight with *Triton*. Part of the Bolitho legend, or a reckless indifference which might one day kill him?

Either way, it was loose around his body, even though the soft-tongued tailor had insisted it had been cut to the original measurements. He had made it sound almost inconvenient.

He heard shrill laughter from one of the three midshipmen, who had been invited for this special evening while their captain was present. It was the youngest, Hawkins, who was twelve years old. *Unrivalled* was his first ship. The son of a post-captain, grandson of a vice-admiral. He thought of Napier. At least Hawkins would have no doubts about *his* future.

He stared at his goblet, but could not recall when it had last been filled. It would soon be time to make his excuses and leave. Galbraith would go on deck and check the watchkeepers, wind and weather, and that would give the others a chance to speak out, to discuss what they chose without fear of crossing that forbidden bridge, the chain of command.

"May I ask you something, sir?"

It was Varlo, who had been silent, almost detached, for most of the evening.

He kept a good watch, and had never failed to request permission to reef or shorten sail if he considered it necessary. Some lieutenants would rather tear the sticks out of a ship than disturb their captain, for fear of showing a lack of ability or confidence. And yet . . .

He said, "Fire away, Mr Varlo."

Varlo leaned forward, his neat hair glossy in the lantern light.

"Slavery is illegal, sir. Most of the world powers are agreed on it. I read in the *Gazette* that even the Portuguese have accepted that the Equator shall be the boundary line of the trade." He glanced along the table, one hand in the air. "But how can we *enforce* such a ruling? We shall have fewer ships, and less senior officers with the authority and experience to carry out anything so widespread."

Adam said, "That is what we must discover—the purpose of this mission, as I see it."

Varlo smiled, quickly. "Many people in England do not agree with the ruling, sir. They were and still are against the Bill as it went through Parliament . . ."

Captain Luxmore leaned forward and slopped some wine down his sleeve. Fortunately, it matched the scarlet well.

"No more speeches, George! Leave that to the damned politicians!"

Adam said, "I take your point, Mr Varlo. Some people do not understand. Others perhaps see slavery as the only way to work and produce from those lands for which we are responsible. It is an old argument, but loses its strength when set against the act of enslavement itself."

Galbraith said, "I have heard it said that Negroes are far better off working in a Christian country than being left in their native barbarism." His face was troubled. "But it will be hard to contain, no matter what the true rights and wrongs of it."

Varlo nodded, satisfied. "An enormous task, as I have said. And a proportionate responsibility for any captain."

He stopped, his hand still in mid-air as Adam brought his knife down on the table.

"We have a proud ship, Mr Varlo." He looked along the table. This was not as he had intended it to be. "And now, thanks to all your efforts, we have men to serve her. It can be said that conditions in the navy have at times been little better than slavery." He glanced at his goblet. It was empty. But he could not stop now. "Things will be different, eventually. A man becomes a sailor for all sorts of reasons. Because he is hungry and unemployed, or unemployable. He may be on the wrong side of the law." He saw Cristie nod. "He may even be driven by dreams of glory. Our company is probably no better and no worse than any you have known, but it will be up to us to mould them into something of true value. *To serve this ship.*"

Varlo smiled. "Thank you, sir."

Adam held his hand over the goblet as a messman hovered beside him. It was time. Varlo, by design or accident, had made his point. Few people today cared about the rights and wrongs of slavery. It was a fact of life. *So long as they were not ill treated.* He had heard James Tyacke on the subject. He was back on anti-slavery patrol duty, where it had all started for him. Where he had first met Richard Bolitho, and his life had been changed. He could hear him now. *He gave me back my pride. My will to live.* Another face. Another unbroken link with the past.

He was at the wardroom door; faces were beaming, some shining in the damp air. All the toasts, the stories, the small, tight world which was theirs. *And mine.*

Galbraith followed him and said, "It was good of you to come, sir." He gave a crooked smile. "Sorry about the second lieutenant. Some of it was my fault." He did not explain. "I'll be glad when we've got some real work to do!"

Adam nodded to the marine sentry and entered his cabin. Only two lanterns were still alight. He saw his boat-cloak hanging near the sleeping quarters, and remembered the girl who had left a lock of hair in the pocket. Where was she, he wondered. Laughing now at that brief but dangerous liaison in Malta. He must have been mad. It could have cost him dearly. *Cost me this ship.*

But he had kept the lock of hair.

He saw a goblet wedged in a corner of the desk, the dark cognac tilting and shivering to the thrust of wind and rudder.

He touched the locket beneath his shirt before looking around the cabin, as if he expected to see or hear someone.

Then he raised the goblet to his lips and thought of the toast they had avoided calling in the wardroom. *To absent friends.*

Don't leave me. But the voice was his own.

The afternoon sun was poised directly above the mainmast truck, the glare so hard that it seemed to sear the eyes. The forenoon watch had been relieved and were now below in their messes for a meal, and the smell of rum was still heavy in the air. During the day the wind had veered slightly and dropped, so that the ship appeared to be resting, her decks quite dry, for the first time since leaving England. To any landsman the activity on the upper decks might appear aimless and casual, after the urgency and constant demands which time and time again had dragged all hands to their stations for shortening sail, or for repairing damage aloft.

But to the professional sailors the deck was often "the marketplace," and any trained eye would soon pick out the many and varied activities which were all part of a ship's daily life.

The sailmaker and his crew sat cross-legged like tailors, needles and palms rising and falling in unison. No canvas was ever wasted. Sails had to be repaired and wind damage made good before the next gale or worse. Scraps were used for patching, for crude but effective pouches, for making new hammocks. For burying the dead.

The boatswain's various parties moved through the hull, greasing block sheaves, replacing whipping on strained or worn ropework, repairing boats, touching up paintwork wherever needed.

Occasionally men would shade their eyes and peer across the

bows to the low, undulating humps, purple and dark blue against the horizon's hard edge. Like very low clouds, except that there were no clouds. It was land.

The shift of wind, with courses and topsails hard put even to remain filled, had changed things. The old hands understood well enough. No captain would want to skulk into a foreign port under cover of darkness without showing his flag. The wiser ones realised that Madeira consisted of five islands, with all the extra hazards of a final approach for the captain to consider.

It would be tomorrow.

"Stand to your guns!"

In the meantime, work and drill would continue.

Only two guns were being used to instruct some of the new hands, the first pair right forward on *Unrivalled's* larboard side. She carried a total of thirty 18-pounders, her main armament, divided along either beam. They also made up the biggest top-weight, quick to make itself felt in any sort of heavy swell. When the ship had first been laid down, the designers in their wisdom had ordered that the eighteen-pounders be cast a foot shorter than usual, in the hope that the decreased weight would assist stability in bad weather and, more important to their lordships, in action.

At the first gun, its captain Isaac Dias wiped his mouth with the back of his wrist and glared at the next group of men. Dias was thickset and deep-chested, a gun captain of long standing both in *Unrivalled* and in other ships before that. His gun was in the first division, and as such was usually the earliest to engage the enemy. He wore his shaggy hair in an old-style pigtail, and stripped of his shirt his body was scarred in several places from splinters and from brawls ashore and afloat, and like his massive arms was thick with hair. Fiercesome and incredibly ugly, he was also the best gun captain in the ship, and he knew it.

He squinted up at the topgallant mast and noted the lie of it toward the horizon. The windward side of the ship. Not much of a blow, but still a muscle-tearing sweat to haul the gun up to the open port. He ran his eyes over the waiting hands. You were *born* a gunner. You didn't just become one because some poxy officer said it was to be.

Someone murmured, "'Ere comes trouble, Isaac."

Dias grinned. It made him look even uglier. "Goin' to tell us what to do, eh?"

The trouble in question was Midshipman Sandell, walking as he always did, with his dragging springy step, as if he was already *strutting his own quarterdeck,* Dias thought.

But Dias was an old hand. He knew about the young gentlemen and how far you could go. Not like some of them, Sandell actually enjoyed being hated, and hated he was. When he was eventually commissioned lieutenant he would make life hell for everyone. It was to be hoped he would be killed before that happened.

Sandell stood, hands on hips, his lips pursed in what might have been a smile.

"You know your places. When I give the word, go to them, *roundly so!*"

The last words came out sharply and he turned to point a finger at one who had been startled.

"Name?"

It was the youth Ede, even paler in the harsh glare.

"Ede, sir."

Sandell regarded him keenly. "I remember. Yes. The one who would not go aloft when ordered!"

Ede shook his head. "No, sir, I was excused at that time."

Sandell nodded. "Of course. Afraid of heights, someone said." He glanced round; some men had stopped work to watch or listen, and Midshipman Deighton was at the second gun with more untrained hands. Sandell was beginning to enjoy the audience.

He snapped, "Gun captain, take your station now! Facing the port!"

Dias said, "I know my station, Mr Sandell!"

Sandell flinched. "San-*dell*, damn you! I shall be watching you, Dias, old Jack or not!"

Dias looked away to hide his grin. It was so easy with this little maggot.

Sandell cleared his throat. "Now take stations!" He flicked the starter he always carried across a man's bare shoulder, and added, "In action you might find yourself *in charge*, everyone else killed, think on that, you oaf!"

The man's name was Cooper. He had been picked from Bellairs' list along with Ede. They had been in the same prison together.

Cooper ducked down and seized the handspike nearest him. Sandell was already snapping at someone else and did not see the fire in his stare. Almost to himself, he muttered, "And you'll be the first to get it!"

The drill continued, with some of the regular gun crews going through every move before handing over to the others.

Sandell had seen Dias looking at the foremast and said, "Prepare to run out!"

Dias stooped over to add his weight but stood aside as Sandell shouted, "Not you, Dias. You were just killed!"

It was heavy going, backs and muscles unused to handling a great gun, bare feet slipping on the deck as it tilted over yet again, the eighteen-pounder dragging at its tackles to make their efforts seem puny.

At the second gun Deighton shouted, "Together, lads! Heave!"

The two guns trundled up to their ports and groaned into position.

"*Point! Ready! Fire!*" Sandell was beating time with his starter as if he alone could see and hear this empty gun in action.

He lashed out again at the one named Ede. "Don't let go,

you idiot! Put your weight on it!" He struck him again and Ede slipped and fell, his legs beneath the truck.

"*Belay that!*" The voice was sharp, incisive. "*Secure the gun!*"

It was Lieutenant Varlo, his eyes everywhere as he walked along the gangway and stopped directly above the first gun.

Sandell exclaimed, "It was deliberate, sir!" He gestured towards Ede. "Nothing but trouble since we began!"

Varlo said, "Stand up, Ede." Then, "Had this gun been in action it would have recoiled inboard when fired and you would have had both legs crushed." He watched him calmly, but his voice was meant for the midshipman. "*Do you understand?*"

Ede nodded shakily. "Yes, sir."

Varlo looked at the foremast. "Afraid of heights, eh? That won't do. This is a *fighting ship*. We depend on one another." He glanced coldly at Sandell. "We have no choice."

A boatswain's mate touched his forehead. "Cap'n's compliments, Mr Varlo, sir, you can dismiss the drill now."

Varlo nodded. "Carry on." He looked at Ede again. "No choice. Remember that."

The others gathered round, the regular gun crews peering at everything as if their own smartness and efficiency was being questioned. Isaac Dias spat on his hands.

"Come on, show 'em how it's really done, eh?"

The laughter seemed to break the spell, although nobody looked at Sandell as he strode aft, barely able to contain his fury.

Only Ede remained, one hand on his arm where Sandell's rope starter had left its mark.

Deighton was about to leave when something made him say, "I was scared of going aloft." He checked himself. What was the matter with him? But he added, "For a long time. But I learned a lot from the old Jacks, watched how they did it. *One hand for the King,* they always said, *but keep one for yourself!*"

Ede was staring at him, as if he had just realised he was there.

"But . . . you're an officer, sir . . ." He stared aft, watching for Sandell.

Deighton said, "It makes no difference, up there." He thought suddenly of his father's intolerance. "Come up with me in the dog watches." The youth was still staring at the criss-cross of rigging, the aimlessly flapping foretopsail, and he recognised the fear and something more.

"Would you, sir?" Almost pleading, almost desperate. "Just the two of us?"

Deighton grinned, relieved, but for whom he did not know.

"I'll try, sir, if you think . . ." He did not go on.

Deighton touched his arm. "I'm sure." Then he walked away, into the market-place.

He did not know how gratitude would look, but now he knew how it felt.

He thought of the captain's words in the wardroom. *Things will be different. Eventually.*

For both of them it was a challenge.

After the blinding glare of the sun, the dazzling reflections thrown up from a clean blue sea, the night was like a cloak.

Galbraith moved occasionally from one side of the quarterdeck to the other, and was surprised that it could still hold him, move him, after all the watches he had worked, all the sea miles logged. A ship at her best. He looked up and through the rigging at the batlike shadows of the topsails, barely moving in a soft, steady breeze. No moon, but the stars stretched from horizon to horizon. He smiled to himself. *And he was not yet used to it.*

He glanced at the helmsmen, one at the wheel, the other standing by. Joshua Cristie, the master, took no chances; he had only just gone below himself. It was as if it was his ship. Like the gun captains he had watched at the drills. Possessive, resentful of unnecessary interference. He had spoken about the new midshipmen, one in particular, the youngest. Cristie had been instructing them, taking the noon sights, and it would be some time before they satisfied him. Of Midshipman Hawkins he had remarked, "Should be at home playing with his toy soldiers! Did you see the sextant his parents gave him? A beauty. Not something for a twelve-year-old child to cut his teeth on!"

Galbraith had said, "You were about that age yourself when you were packed off to sea, or have you forgotten?"

Cristie had been unmoved. "That was different. Very different. For us."

He felt the deck tremble and saw the wheel move slightly. The helmsman was watching the little dogvane, a tiny pointer made of cork and feathers perched on the weather side of the quarterdeck rail. On a dark night and with such light airs, the dogvane was a trained helmsman's only guide to the wind's direction.

Trained: that summed it up, he thought. Like the drills, sails and rigging, guns and boatwork. It took time for raw recruits. It was different for the old hands, like that brute Campbell, and the gun captain he had seen glaring at Sandell behind his back; they might not see the point of it any more, now that there was no real enemy to face and fight, no cause to recognise, no matter how uncertain.

It could change tomorrow. They had already seen it for themselves, when Napoleon had broken out of his cage on Elba. He glanced at the dimly lit skylight; the captain was still awake. Probably thinking about it too. His uncle had been killed then. A cross on a chart, nothing more. No better and no worse, he had said of *Unrivalled*'s company. Galbraith thought of Varlo's comment about a captain's responsibility. *Why should that have touched me as it did?* Varlo never seemed to make casual remarks. Everything had to matter, to reflect.

He lifted a telescope from its rack and levelled it across the empty nettings.

Over his shoulder he said quietly, "We'll warn the middle watch, Mr Deighton. Those lights are fishermen, if I'm not mistaken." He heard the midshipman murmur something. Tiny lights on the water, miles away, like fireflies, almost lost among the stars. It would be a safe bet to say that every one of them would already know about *Unrivalled*'s steady approach. He added, "Remind me to make a note in the log."

"Aye, sir."

He liked Deighton, what he knew of him. He had more than proved his worth in battle, and the captain had remarked on it.

Galbraith put it from his thoughts. *As my captain wrote of me when I was recommended for command.*

He heard the midshipman speaking to the boatswain's mate of the watch, and he thought of what he had seen during the dog watches when Deighton had gone aloft with the young landman who had been terrified.

Nobody else took much notice, but Galbraith had watched and remembered his own first time, going aloft in a Channel gale. He smiled. A million years ago.

And he had seen them return to the deck. They had climbed only to the foretop, and had avoided the puttock shrouds which left a man hanging out over the sea or the deck below, with only fingers and toes to keep him from falling.

A voice murmured, "Cap'n's coming up, sir."

Some would never tell an officer, warn him. When it came down to it, it was all you had to prove your worth.

He was surprised to see the captain coatless, his shirt blowing open in the soft wind.

The helmsman reported, "Sou'-sou'-east, sir!"

Galbraith waited, sensing the energy, the restlessness of the man, as if it was beyond his control. Driving him. Driving him.

Adam said, "A fine night. The wind holds steady enough." He turned to look abeam and Galbraith saw the locket glint in the compass light. He could see it in his mind. The bare shoulders, the dark, challenging eyes. Why did he wear it, when Sir Richard's flag lieutenant, Avery, had brought it to him? Before he himself had been killed, on this deck.

The captain would be about his own age, and the lovely woman was older, beyond his reach, if that was the force which was tearing him apart.

Adam said, "Call all hands at first light. I expect this ship to look her best. If and when we are given the time I want more boat drill. The waters we are intended for are not suitable for a man-of-war."

Galbraith waited. He was thinking ahead. Going over his orders again, sifting all the reasons, and the things unsaid. *For the Captain's discretion.*

Adam said suddenly, "I was pleased about young Deighton's work today. A good example. God knows, some of these poor devils have little enough to sustain them." He turned and Galbraith could almost feel his eyes in the darkness. "I'll not stand for petty tyranny, Leigh. Attend to it as you see fit."

Galbraith heard his shoes crossing to the companion-way. He missed nothing. But what was driving him, when most captains would have been asleep at this hour?

He was pacing the deck when the middle watch came aft.

He noticed that the cabin skylight was still glowing, and his question remained unanswered.

4 OBSESSION

FRANK RIST, *Unrivalled*'s senior master's mate, pressed one hand on the sill of an open port and stared at the colour and reflected movement of Funchal harbour. He had visited Madeira several times, a place always ready with a bargain to tempt the sailor-man, even if the price doubled at the first sign of a King's ship.

He felt the heat of the timber through his palm, something he never tired of, and smiled as a boat loaded with brightly painted pottery hovered abeam, apparently deaf to the bellowed warnings to *stand clear* from one of Captain Luxmore's "bullocks."

He withdrew his head into the chartroom and waited for his eyes to accept the gloom of the low deckhead after the glare off the water. He rubbed them with his knuckles and tried to shrug it off. It was when he looked at a chart in uncertain light, or by the glow of a small lamp on the quarterdeck during the night watches that he noticed it most. Like most sailors Rist was used to staring into great distances, taking the bearing of some head-land or hill, or gauging the final approach to an anchorage like this morning.

He heard the first lieutenant's footsteps overhead and the shrill of a call as another hoist of stores was hauled inboard, the purser doubtless counting every item and checking it against a list, as if it was all coming out of his own pocket.

Unrivalled suited him, despite the gaps in her complement, and the new hands who were either old Jacks who had volun-teered for a further commission, or those totally untrained in the ways of the sea like the youth Ede, who was quietly clearing up the chart space as if the ship was still out of sight of land, or he was afraid of making contact with those people and boats out there in the harbour.

Ede was so young, and it troubled Rist when he considered it.

He was a good master's mate and the senior of the ship's three. He tried to push it aside. He was also one of the oldest men in the company. Rist was forty-two years old, twenty-eight of which had been spent at sea in one sort of ship or another. He had done well, better than most, but he had to face it, unless old Cristie was offered another appointment or dropped dead, any hope of promotion was remote. And now his sight. It was common enough in sailors. He clenched his fist. *But not now.*

He glanced at the youth, still so pale despite the sun which had greeted their course south of Biscay. Neat, almost delicate hands, more like a girl's than a youngster going to sea for the first time. He could read and write, and had been an apprentice at some instrument maker's shop in Plymouth or nearby.

In the navy it was usually better not to know too much of a man's past. It was what he did now, how he stood for or against the things which really mattered in a man-of-war. When it came down to it, the loyalty and courage of your mates counted more than anything. Rist looked around the chartroom. *Old Cristie's second home.* You could still smell the paint and pitch from the repairs after that last savage battle.

He stared through the port again. There was a Spanish frigate at anchor nearby. She had dipped her ensign when *Unrivalled* had glided past her. Hard to accept, to get used to. He shook his head. Such a short while ago and their young firebrand of a captain would have beaten to quarters and had the guns run out before the poor Spaniards had finished their siesta!

It was strange. But it was what he did best. He thought about the rumours and the endless gossip in the mess. To most of them slavery was just a word. Others saw it as a possibility for prize-money, even slave bounty, or so the lower deck lawyers insisted.

Rist had already considered something else. If *Unrivalled* was to be involved, which seemed unlikely at close quarters, there might be prizes. Any such capture would require a prize-master.

It was hard *not* to consider it. Captain Bolitho could not spare a lieutenant for the task, and the midshipmen were either too young or incompetent. It would be the one chance he needed. He could see no other.

He turned and exclaimed, "If the master sees you handling that, he'll hang your guts out to dry, my lad!"

Ede looked at him across the sextant, which he had been about to place in its well-worn case.

He said, almost shyly, "I used to work with these, sir. A Parsons model, one of the earliest I ever saw."

In the sudden silence Rist saw the pain in his eyes, and wondered how it had all gone wrong. Attempted murder, they said. Youth and something else had saved him from the gibbet. Rist pushed it aside. *It happened.* Ede was paying the price for whatever it was. After all, you didn't ask forgiveness when you were trying to hack out an enemy's guts with dirk or cutlass!

He asked, "What about magnifying glasses? For chart work and that sort of thing." He turned away. *Far enough, you idiot.*

But Ede said, "I can repair them, sir. I made some once for my . . ." *His employer,* he had nearly said. The man he had stabbed almost to death.

Rist nodded. "I'll speak to the first lieutenant. Can't promise anything, but we could find work for you here." He added scathingly, "Anything to keep some snotty blowhard out from under my feet!"

He did not mention Sandell. He did not need to.

Rist was thinking of Galbraith, how they had been together in that raid off the African coast, the exploding charges, the chebecks like fireballs while they had floundered to safety. He liked the first lieutenant; they got on well. Galbraith would be thinking much the same about his own dwindling chances of promotion. Others seemed to get it as if it were their right. Or because they knew somebody . . .

He heard the bell chime from the forecastle, and thought of the rum which would soon be served in the warrant officers' mess. After that, he had been ordered to take a boat ashore and stay in company with the captain's new clerk, a strange old bird if ever there was one. But afterwards, if he could find the house, if it was still there, he might seek a little pleasure with one of the girls.

He was forty-two, but told himself that he did not look it.

Adam glanced through the open port again, at another vessel which was swinging to her anchor, to make a perfect twin with her reflection.

A Portuguese flag; it was a joke when you thought about it. All the big powers beating the drum about banning slavery, Portugal most of all.

He gave a wry smile. And yet they shipped more black ivory than any one.

He looked at his hands in the dusty sunlight.

Slavers, then. He turned away. *And I was one of them.*

Captain Adam Bolitho climbed through *Unrivalled*'s entry port and paused to raise his hat to the quarterdeck, and the flag which hung so limply that it was scarcely moving. As he walked past the side-party he felt the sweat run down his spine and gather above his belt, and yet despite the busy afternoon ashore, the rituals of meeting the Governor and clearing the ship to take on supplies and fresh water, he felt strangely alert. Perhaps it was just being back on board, something he knew and trusted.

Like the faces around him, some so familiar they could have

been aboard since the ship had first run up her colours, when the world had been so very different. *For all of us.* Yet he knew that several of them had only joined at Penzance, mere days ago. Were they regretting it? An impulse, seeking something they had believed lost?

Galbraith greeted him and said, "Fresh water will be brought out by lighters in the forenoon tomorrow, sir." His strong features were full of questions, but he added only, "Two hands for punishment, sir." It sounded like an apology. "Working on the jetty, drunk. There was a fight."

Adam glanced past him, feeling the heat striking down through the taut rigging, the neatly furled sails. "Who was in charge?"

"Mr Midshipman Fielding, sir. He is usually very good in such matters. He is young . . ."

"All the more reason why he should be respected, not abused because of it."

Fielding, the midshipman who had once awakened him from a dream. That same dream. Another memory.

He said, "Deal with it when we are at sea." He shaded his eyes to study the other anchored ships nearby. Mostly small local craft, they would have no difficulty clearing the harbour even with a light breeze. He thought of the people he had seen on the waterfront. The watching faces, interested, indifferent, it was impossible to tell. Like some Spanish officers from the visiting frigate; there had been a group of them waiting for their boat by the stairs. They had doffed their hats; a couple of them had smiled politely. Was it really so simple, so easy to forget, to wipe out the madness, the ferocity of battle which they had all suffered? *Could I?*

He saw Partridge, the barrel-chested boatswain, giving instructions to one of his mates. A flogging, then. Partridge would never even question it. When it came down to it, the Articles of War and a thin line of marines was the final extent of a captain's authority.

He turned his head, missing something Galbraith was saying.

It was Partridge, big fists on his hips, an amused grin on his sun-reddened face.

"She may 'ave a fancy Portuguese name, my son, but I knows 'er of old!" He seemed to realise that Adam was listening and explained, "The brigantine over yonder, sir. The old *Rebecca* as she was in them days. First tasted salt water in Brixham."

Adam stared over his massive shoulder. Like the flaw in the pattern, the face in the crowd which is so easily missed.

"You're certain?"

Parker, one of the boatswain's mates, grinned. "Never forgets, sir!"

Partridge seemed to realise it was not merely idle comment. He said, "My father worked at the yard in Brixham, sir. There was money trouble, and someone else paid for *Rebecca* to be completed." His eyes sharpened. "The rig I remembers most. The extra trys'l. Rare, unless you've got spare 'ands to manage 'em. She were in all kinds o' trouble, even had a run-in with the Revenue boys. Then she vanished out o' Brixham. Disappeared." He looked around at their faces. "Till now."

Galbraith said, "She's taken on no stores since we anchored, sir. And she's unloaded none, either. Time in harbour costs money. Unless . . ."

Adam touched his sleeve. "Come aft with me." He looked across the water again. Perhaps it was meant to be. Or maybe he needed to delude himself. There was no mail or message for *Unrivalled*. Nothing. So why had he noticed the black-hulled brigantine? Even the name *Albatroz* across her counter, when the gig had pulled him back to the ship.

"You've a good memory, Mr Partridge. It may be a great help."

Partridge rubbed his chin and said, "Well, she's not in ballast, sir. My guess is she'll be up an' away before dawn. I could take a party o' picked men an' go over . . ."

He looked down, surprised as his captain gripped his arm.

"A Portuguese ship, in a Portuguese harbour, Mr Partridge? It goes beyond our powers. Some might even say it is what certain people are expecting, *hoping* we might do." He smiled suddenly. "But we shall see, eh?"

Galbraith followed him aft beneath the poop, saw him glance at the nearest ladder as if he had remembered something.

Adam said, "Call all hands early, Leigh. Mr Partridge may be right. I want to work clear of the anchorage as soon as possible. We shall use boats to warp her out if need be." He gave that rare smile again. "My orders state quite clearly, *with all despatch.* So be it, then."

He entered his cabin and hesitated. "There was no mail for the ship, Leigh, new or old. It will doubtless catch up with us one day!" The smile would not return. "Now, if you'll excuse me, I have a letter to write."

He walked to the stern windows and stared at the nearest ships and the waterfront beyond them. On his way to pay his respects to the Governor he had seen a little stall; it could hardly be called a shop. But it had reminded him of the one in Malta, where on a reckless impulse he had purchased the small silver sword with the single word *Destiny* engraved on the reverse. Like some mindless, lovesick midshipman. But she had taken it, and had worn it. With him and for him.

And she had been here, in this ship. In this cabin.

He sat down and pulled open his shirt to cool his body.

Destiny. Perhaps that, too, was another dream.

Daniel Yovell laid down his pen by its little well and tugged out a handkerchief to mop his brow. It looked soiled and crumpled, but he was an old enough hand to appreciate the value of fresh water, no matter what size the ship.

He had heard the familiar slap of feet overhead, the bark of orders, the response of squealing blocks and sun-taut cordage. He had always allowed it to remain a mystery, something outside his own daily life. Even here in the great cabin it was stiflingly hot, the deck barely moving, the shadows angled across the beams and frames, unchanged.

He looked over his spectacles and saw the captain leaning against his table, his hands pressed on a chart, some brass dividers where he had just dropped them.

It was over a week since they had quit Funchal, with a better wind than anyone who was interested had expected.

Yovell picked up the pen once more and was thankful for his freedom to come and go in this part of the ship. And more so for the privilege of sharing it without being compromised.

He watched Adam Bolitho now, one hand moving on the chart, as if it was feeling the way. Testing something. Preparing for some unknown obstacle.

Only here, in his own quarters, did he ever seem to show uncertainty, doubt. Like the day they had left Funchal, after discovering that the Portuguese brigantine which had caught his attention had weighed and slipped out of harbour without anyone seeing her leave.

The water lighters had come out to the ship, and once again Yovell had sensed the captain's mood. Why waste time taking on water when they might be at sea, chasing and running down the mysterious *Albatroz?*

But it had been the right decision. Water was like gold dust, and along this invisible coastline it might be weeks before they could obtain fresh supplies.

And the brigantine? Like most of *Unrivalled*'s company, he was beginning to think that she was a need rather than a threat.

It was like being totally abandoned, he thought. Every day the horizon was empty, with not even a cry from the masthead. He watched Adam's hand move again, the dividers marking off some new calculation. Yovell had seen the other side to the captain, despite whatever doubts he might have about the purpose of his mission. He had told the first lieutenant to reduce the time spent aloft by all lookouts. *They are my eyes. I want them always to be fresh and alert.* And he recalled when Galbraith had come aft to ask about the new hand, Ede, and the possibility of his working with the master's mates, for which he seemed more suited than general seamanship.

Some captains might have told their senior lieutenant to deal with it, and not to distract them from more important duties. Instead, Captain Bolitho had said, "I read his report. I think it is a sensible idea. Keep me informed."

As watch followed watch, the daily routine took precedence over everything. Sail and gun drill, boat-handling when *Unrivalled* had been becalmed under a cloudless sky, before a light north-westerly had taken pity on them. Out of necessity or discipline they were becoming used to one another. Making the best of it.

Despite his inner caution, Yovell often found himself making comparisons. He had seen Sir Richard Bolitho trying to distance himself from the hard reality of punishment. As an admiral he had been spared the tradition and spectacle of a flogging, something which he had seemed unable to accept even after his years of service from midshipman to flag officer. *My Admiral of England,* as he had heard Lady Somervell call him several times. A secret between them, and something very dear to her.

Adam Bolitho could not do that. As captain he had to order the relevant punishment, according to the Articles of War, which held the power of life and death over every man aboard.

The old Jacks made light of it. *Getting a checkered shirt at the gangway* was their casual dismissal of a flogging, no matter what they thought of the rights and wrongs of the punishment. The hard men like Campbell bared their own scars from the cat with something like pride. Or Jago, the captain's coxswain who had once been unjustly flogged, in defiance, even against the author-ity he served and upheld.

Adam Bolitho would have been at the quarterdeck rail with his officers while the punishment had been carried out. The beat of a drum, the master-at-arms counting each stroke aloud, the boatswain's mate wielding the lash, probably with little thought for the victim but very aware of his own performance, *without fear or favour* as Partridge would put it.

Neither of the two men under punishment were new to the navy. After two dozen lashes each they were cut down and hauled below to the sickbay, without uttering a sound.

Curiously, Yovell thought, the midshipman who had been involved in the drunken affray had almost fainted.

A shadow dipped over the desk; the captain was looking down at him.

"A few more days, my friend." Adam glanced at the skylight. "No wonder the West African station is so unpopular. For us it is bad enough. Imagine how it must be for the anti-slavery patrols, small vessels for the most part, brigs, schooners, even cutters." He thought suddenly of James Tyacke, who had served on such patrols. *The devil with half a face,* the slavers had called him. Tyacke, who had become his uncle's flag captain in *Frobisher. Who had been with him.* He swung away from the desk, angry for allow-ing it to pierce his defences.

And Tyacke was back there again. In a frigate, but not as a frigate. Adam had heard one long-serving lieutenant describe the work as fit only for "the haunted and the damned."

He heard Napier padding about beyond the screen, shoeless, because he was feeling the heat. *Or because he does not want to offend me.*

He looked at Yovell's round shoulders. *Have I been so intolerant, so obsessed?* He strode to the stern windows, feeling the deck tilt more steeply. *The wind.* But when he thrust open one of the windows he felt the air on his face and chest, like the door of an open furnace.

He stared at the blue water, the small ridge of crests breaking towards the ship. Little slivers of silver too, flying fish, so there would be sharks as well. Something else for the new men to get used to. Not many could swim if they fell overboard.

It was like sailing into nowhere. His orders were vague, to be interpreted by the senior officer at Freetown, or by the Crown Agent, as the new appointment was grandly called. Probably a civilian, and conferred as a reward or an escape.

He walked away from the glare and then paused abruptly by the desk again.

"What was that?"

Yovell peered up at him. "I heard nothing, sir."

Adam listened to the sounds of rigging and the occasional thud of the great rudder.

He clenched his fists. Sailing into nowhere.

Feet outside, then the marine sentry's call. "First Lieutenant, *sir!*"

Galbraith entered, his forehead reddened where his hat had been jammed down to shade his eyes.

"What is it?"

Galbraith glanced at Yovell, as if to share it.

"Masthead, sir. Sail on the larboard bow. Standing away."

Adam wanted to swallow, to moisten his mouth. He could do neither.

He said, "Call the hands, Leigh. Get the t'gallants on her. My compliments to Mr Cristie. I'd like him in the chartroom without delay." He looked at him calmly. "It could be any vessel." It was infectious; even Yovell was nodding and beaming.

Galbraith grinned. "I think not, sir!"

Adam snatched up his notes and strode to the screen door, but stopped and looked aft again, where Yovell remained hunched at the desk in silhouette against the dazzling blue backdrop.

He said simply, "When next you have the will to pray, my friend, I'd be grateful if you'd speak for me."

Then he was gone, and for the first time since he could remember, Daniel Yovell was guilty of pride.

Lieutenant George Varlo jumped down from the mizzen shrouds, his shirt blackened with tar. Everyone on watch was busy about his duties, like badly rehearsed players, he thought angrily. Careful to avoid his eyes, and no doubt amused by his stained and dishevelled appearance.

He looked up at the topgallant sails, free and bulging now to the steady north-westerly, such as it was, the seamen already sliding down backstays to the deck while the landmen and novices took a slower but safer route by the ratlines, urged on by threats and yells as one mast vied with the other.

The masthead pendant was licking out towards the southern horizon, and Varlo could feel the ship coming to life again, dipping her lee bulwark towards the water.

The masthead lookout had reported a sail, somewhere out there beyond the larboard bow. Miles away; even by climbing up into the weather shrouds Varlo had been unable to see it. A desert of glaring water. And even if the lookout was not mistaken . . .

He turned and saw Galbraith climbing through the companion hatchway. Strong, dependable, and as popular as any first lieutenant could safely be, he thought. And yet they were rivals, and would remain strangers through this or any other commission.

Galbraith strode to the compass and consulted it after checking the new display of canvas, *Unrivalled*'s *skyscrapers,* as the old hands termed them. The first thing you ever saw of a friend or an enemy, cutting above the horizon's edge.

Varlo was twenty-six years old. He glanced at Midshipman Hawkins, the newest and youngest member of the gunroom, a *baby*, the one with the beautiful sextant which the master had admired. Impossible to believe he had ever been so shallow, so ignorant even of the basic terms of seamanship and naval discipline. He moved to the side again and felt his shoes sticking to the deck seams, his stained shirt clinging like another skin.

He thought suddenly of his father. It was common enough over all the years of war for families to be separated, held together only by memory and the occasional letter. His father had been a post-captain, and one of considerable merit. Varlo accepted that he had learned more about him from others who had known or served with him; when he considered it, he realised that he had probably only seen his father half a dozen times in his life, if that. Grave, overwhelming in some ways, warmly human at other times. Each like a separate portrait. Different.

His father had died in a ship-to-ship action in the West Indies nearly ten years ago. It was still hard to believe. He had not lived long enough to be proud of his only son when he had eventually been commissioned.

He heard someone say, "Captain's coming up, sir."

He felt it again. Like an unquenchable anger. *Would they have warned me?*

He waited while Captain Bolitho checked the wind direction and studied the set of every sail.

Old Cristie had come up with the captain, his expression giving nothing away. He was the same in the wardroom. Like an oracle: while some of the others chatted emptily about the possibilities of prize-money, or moving to a better station, he remained aloof. Unless he was with his charts, or like now, gauging the captain's mood, like those of the wind and tide.

Varlo had found nobody he could talk to, or meet at what he considered a like level. Not O'Beirne, the surgeon, the listener, who hoarded information and indiscreet revelations perhaps for some future yarn, or one of his endless Irish jokes. Nor Lieutenant Bellairs, who was keen and very conscious of his new rank. Still a midshipman at heart. Like Cristie, the other senior warrant officers who shared the wardroom and its privileges, because of their circumstances were kept apart. And there was Galbraith. Brave and obviously respected, but yearning for a command of his own. A rival, then.

He heard the captain say suddenly, "Masthead lookout?"

And Galbraith's immediate reply. Expecting it. "Sullivan, sir."

Bolitho said, "I wonder . . ." He looked at Cristie. "Bring her up two points. If the wind holds . . ." Again he left it unsaid.

"Man the braces! Stir yourselves!"

Bolitho took a telescope from the rack and glanced briefly at Varlo.

"If he runs, we can head him off."

Varlo watched him as he trained the glass to windward, sidestepping as some seamen bustled past him, gasping with exertion as they hauled at the mizzen braces, the marines clumping along with them.

Varlo had heard most of the stories surrounding the captain. About his famous uncle, killed aboard his flagship at the moment of Napoleon's escape from Elba, and of his father, Captain Hugh Bolitho, a traitor to his country who had fought with the Revolutionary Navy of America.

Not married, but it was said that he was popular with women. Gossip, but where was the *man?* As calm and unruffled as he now appeared, turning to smile as a young seaman cannoned into a corporal of marines and paused to apologise. The marine, who was built like a cliff and had probably felt nothing, answered with equal formality, "One 'and for the King, matey!"

Spray spattered over the quarterdeck nine-pounders, to dry instantly in the unwavering sun.

"Deck there! She's makin' more sail!"

"Then so shall we. Set the forecourse, Mr Galbraith. More hands on the main brace." He looked round briefly as the helmsman called, "East by south, sir! Full an' bye!"

Unrivalled was taking it well, her weather rail rising to the horizon and remaining there, the great shadow of the forecourse spreading and darkening the scurrying figures at sheets and braces.

A good wind, across the larboard quarter. More spray, and Varlo saw some seamen twist their half-naked bodies, grinning as it soaked them like rain. He noticed that one of them had been flogged. But he was sharing the moment with his mates. Men he knew and trusted. Perhaps the only ones.

Varlo swung away, angry with himself. There was no comparison.

"Mr Varlo?" Adam Bolitho did not move nearer nor did he appear to lower his glass. "I suggest you go below and seek out a clean shirt."

Varlo saw Galbraith turn, suddenly stiff-backed. Surprised? Shocked? Then Bolitho did look at him, frowning. "It may be nothing, but we have to know what this vessel is about. Whatever we do, we shall be unpopular, both with those who are making money out of slavery and those who are losing it because of us." He smiled. "You are the King's man today, Mr Varlo. Dress accordingly." He levelled the glass again. "My cabin servant will give you one of mine if you are in need. Believe me, I have not forgotten the failings of the wardroom messmen!"

Varlo swallowed hard. He did not know what to say. Even Galbraith seemed taken aback.

Varlo tried again. "I'm to board her, sir?"

Bolitho's jaw tightened, then he said, almost lightly, "Take the jolly-boat. I suggest you have Mr Rist with you. He is an old dog when it comes to a search!"

He handed, almost tossed, the telescope to Midshipman Hawkins and said, "I *saw* her." He glanced around the quarter-deck, embracing them. "*Albatroz,* as I thought it might be!"

Varlo had one foot on the companion ladder when the voice stopped him.

"Take care. Be on your guard when you board her."

Varlo ducked his head below the coaming and did not hear Galbraith say, "I could go over to her, sir."

Nor did he hear the quiet but incisive answer.

"Perhaps you are *too* experienced, eh, Leigh? My responsibility, remember?"

He saw Jago at the weather ladder, one foot on the top step, his head turning as if searching for danger.

Adam said, "A different war, my friends, but just as deadly to those who must fight it."

Afterwards Galbraith thought he had been speaking to himself. And the ship.

5 THE *H*AUNTED AND THE DAMNED

ADAM BOLITHO could not recall how many times he had climbed into the weather shrouds to obtain a better view of the brigantine, or how long it had been since the other vessel had been sighted. He had played with the idea of going aloft where Sullivan, the eagle-eyed lookout, was watching the performance of both vessels in comparative comfort.

But there was no time. It had to be soon. The wind had freshened still more, and he could feel the ease with which *Unrivalled*'s hull was ploughing over and through the new array of shallow rollers.

The wind was an ally; it was also a possible threat. Even without his small telescope, his spyglass as he had heard young Napier describe it, he had seen the brigantine standing away on the larboard bow, not running but standing close to the wind, reaching into it, it seemed with every stitch of canvas spread, thrusting over as steeply as any vessel could lie under such pressure.

He glanced now along the full length of his command. Men not employed at braces and halliards were watching, probably betting on the outcome of this unlikely contest. The new hands were openly excited; it was their first experience of ship-handling. The reasons were unimportant.

He had to admit that *Albatroz* was being handled superbly. Her master knew exactly what he was doing. By clawing closer and closer to the wind he held on to a chance of coming about and cutting across *Unrivalled*'s stern. If he succeeded, he could wait for darkness and with luck make a full escape. He had the whole ocean. On the other hand, if he ran south-east with a soldier's wind he could not outpace the frigate, but if the wind grew any stronger it would be impossible to put down a boat with any hope of boarding her. *He cannot fight us, so why must he run? Unless he has something to hide.* A Portuguese vessel, sailing from a Portuguese harbour, should have nothing to fear. By the latest agreement, it had been reluctantly accepted that Portugal could even continue loading and shipping slaves from her own territories, provided they were south of the Equator.

Adam strode to the rail where Cristie and two of his master's mates were in close discussion, but they had to raise their voices to be heard above the boom of canvas and the noisy sluice of water which surged almost to the lee gun ports.

One, Woodthorpe, was saying, "Bastard's got everything but the cook's bloody apron spread! He'll give us the slip yet, damn his eyes!"

Cristie saw the captain and said harshly, "Two miles, sir. Another hour and he'll see some sense. But if he luffs, an' comes hard about." He shook his head. "You know what it's like."

Some of the others were listening, and his own words came back to him like a fist. *My responsibility.*

He shaded his eyes to look up at the yards, the quivering thrust of the topgallant sails, holding the sun now to mark the change of direction. Cristie had made his point.

He said, "Ask the gunner to come aft."

Rist, the other master's mate, showed his strong teeth in a grin.

"Mr Stranace is here now, sir!"

"Old Stranace," as he was called behind his back, shuffled out of the driver's great shadow and touched his forehead.

His face was a mass of wrinkles, and his years at sea, much of the time bent and groping in one magazine or another, surrounded by enough powder to blast him and the ship to fragments, had given him a permanent stoop. But his eye was as sharp as Sullivan's and his judgment relating to his precious artillery had not been faulted.

He asked, "Two mile, did 'e say, sir?" He bared his uneven teeth, a grin or disdain it was hard to tell. "Less 'n that in *my* view." He nodded. "You want 'im dismasted?"

Adam stared across the water, to give himself time. What would people say in England, he wondered. With their fixed ideas of the Heart of Oak, or the *sure shield* as William Pitt had once called the navy, if they could witness this? The frigate captain with his grubby shirt, a rent in one shoulder, hatless, with no sword or gold lace to mark him out from those around him. And Old Stranace, bent, with shaggy grey hair, and the shapeless felt slippers he wore to guard against striking sparks in or around the magazines.

He said, "If I alter course a few degrees to the south'rd, the wind will lay us over still further." He saw the gunner's eyes move quickly to the larboard battery of eighteen-pounders, the sea barely visible as the hull tilted across her own shadow.

Then he grunted, "I'll lay it meself, sir. Number One, larboard."

Adam added, "I want her stopped, that's all." He was never sure if Old Stranace could hear him. So many broadsides, and countless other occasions from saluting to putting down a careering chebeck, had left him partially deaf. It was common enough among deepwater sailormen.

But there was nothing wrong with his ears today.

"I'll part 'is bloody 'air, sir!"

"Stand by on the quarterdeck! Braces, there!"

"Helm a-lee! Steady! Hold her, steer sou'-east!"

Cristie rubbed his chin and watched the gunner clawing his way down the lee ladder, calling out names as he went, his cracked voice carrying effortlessly over the chorus of wind and rigging.

Cristie said dourly, "*Albatroz*'s master will think we're giving up."

He sounded mistrustful of the new arrangements.

By the time *Unrivalled* had settled on her new course the first gun on the windward side was almost ready, its crew kneeling and bowing around their charge like worshippers at some pagan ritual.

Old Stranace had been a gun captain himself. It must have been a long, long time ago, but he had forgotten nothing. He selected one ball from the garland, fondling it in both hands, then changing it for another with the same performance until he was satisfied. He even supervised the loading of the charge and the tamping down of the wad, and then the ball itself, but allowing one of the gun crew to tap it home.

Cristie said dryly, "He'll not use a flintlock either. The crafty old bugger!"

Adam found time to recognise the affection as well as the amusement. Unlike the hammer of a musket which was brought violently into play by a strong spring, the deck gun was worked by jerking a lanyard. If it failed to strike a spark instantly, the gun misfired. So great and regular was the risk in close action that slow-matches were always kept ready burning in protected tubs of sand.

Adam raised his spyglass again and waited for the brigantine to lift above the blue water like some great, avenging bird.

"Ready, sir!" That was Galbraith, his voice unusually hushed.

Adam looked forward at the small pattern of figures around the eighteen-pounder closest to the forecastle. The port was open, the gun had already been run out, extra hands were throwing their weight on the tackles to haul the weapon up to and through it. He saw Old Stranace put his hand over the forearm of one of the crew, guiding the handspike while the muzzle was raised to its full elevation. And to his satisfaction.

If the shot scored a direct hit, the repercussions would be severe. If it went widely astray it would be no less harmful. He wondered only briefly if the men on the brigantine's deck had noticed that 46-gun frigate of the world's greatest navy was standing away. Giving up the chase. *And would it really matter?*

He closed his mind to it. *"Fire as you bear!"*

He saw Stranace glance aft for just a few seconds. The responsibility was not his to carry.

Adam saw his arm move with the speed of light, the puff of smoke like steam from a heated pipe. He felt the grip of ice around his stomach. *Misfire.*

There was a sharp bang and the eighteen-pounder seemed to come to life, hurling itself inboard, down the sloping planking until the tackles slowed and then brought the truck to a jolting halt.

Nobody made a move to sponge out the gun, as if the single shot had somehow paralysed them.

There was something like a great sigh, changing and rising to a wild cheer as a tall waterspout, white and solid against the dark water, burst skywards off the brigantine's quarter. At this range it was impossible to determine the exact fall of shot.

But Everett, the sergeant of marines, exclaimed, "Much closer an' them buggers'd be swimmin' with th' sharks!"

Adam said, "Bring her back on course, if you please."

Rist called, "They're shortenin' sail, sir!"

"Call away the boat's crew and inform the bosun." Adam plucked at his shirt. It did not sound like his own voice. What had he expected, and what would he have done?

He looked again. The brigantine was broaching to, her canvas in disorder while they prepared to await instructions.

Varlo was close by. "Ready, sir!"

Adam barely heard him. "So let's be about it, eh?"

Lieutenant Varlo made another attempt to get to his feet in the swaying jolly-boat, but had to find support in the coxswain's shoulder.

It was a hard pull, the small boat veering and dipping in a succession of troughs and broken crests, spray bursting over the oarsmen like rain.

He shouted, "Don't *feather*, man! Lay back on it!"

Rist sat wedged in the sternsheets with two armed seamen, his eyes slitted against the spray, gauging the flapping sails of the drifting brigantine, waiting for the unexpected.

A part of him was still able to sense the bitterness and resentment in the boat. It was a hand-picked crew; he had chosen each man himself. Good, experienced seamen, every one of them. Not one would crack and run if shooting started, or worse, a burst of grape was fired. It could only take one shot to finish the jolly-boat at this range. No matter what *Unrivalled* did after that, it would not help any of them.

He caught the stroke oarsman's eye, then saw him look away, astern, while he lay back on his loom, probably watching their ship. It was better not to look back once you had started, Rist thought. The ship always seemed so far away. He peered hard at the brigantine again. Pierced for several guns, six maybe, but none run out or manned. Yet.

Varlo called, "We'll go under her lee!"

Rist swallowed hard. He did not *know* Varlo. Never would, in all likelihood. One thing was clear, he was out of his depth in this sort of trick. He had been some admiral's flag lieutenant, the gossip said. More used to picking out the right people for his lord and master to meet and entertain than doing his stuff as a sea officer.

He said, "She's still swingin' sir. But the chains are the best chance!"

Varlo turned and stared at him, as if searching for criticism or defiance.

"So I can see!" He gripped the coxswain's shoulder again as the hull bounced over.

Then he said, "Suppose they don't speak English?"

Rist almost grinned. "No matter, sir." He touched the hilt of the short fighting sword under his coat. "This'll do the talkin'!"

The brigantine was right over them now, or so it appeared; they could even hear the clamour of loose rigging and flapping canvas above the din of oars and sea.

Rist watched closely, trying to stay unruffled. *Like all those other times.* Just one stupid mistake. A man loosing off a pistol by mischance. It was all it took.

But seamanship came first.

"*Bows!*" He held his breath as the bowman boated his oar and changed it for a boat-hook. Just in time: with this sea running they could have driven straight into the other vessel, splintering oars. Disaster.

He saw the helmsman glance at him, hardly a blink. It was enough. The tiller bar swung over and the boat reeled around toward the brigantine's rounded hull.

"*Oars!*" Varlo had recovered himself. "Boat your oars!"

They were alongside, the trapped water leaping between the vessels while men groped for their weapons, some staring up at the nearest gun port.

Varlo snapped, "With *me*, Mr Rist!"

Rist stumbled after him, gripping a shoulder here, a steadying hand there. It was all wrong. For both of them to board together was madness. They could be killed as they climbed aboard. *Now.*

It was then that it hit him. Varlo would never admit it in two centuries, but he needed him.

The next moment they were pulling themselves up and over the bulwark. Figures and peering faces seemed to loom on every side, and Rist felt the menace like something physical.

Through it all a voice boomed, "By what right do you board my ship?"

Varlo had drawn his sword, and set against the brigantine's seamen looked completely out of place in his spray-dappled blue coat. He had somehow managed to retain his hat through the crossing.

His voice was quite unemotional and steady. As if on parade. Or, Rist thought, facing a firing squad. He would be the same in either situation.

"*In the King's name!*"

The remainder of the boarding party had climbed aboard,

peering around, weapons ready. Something they knew and understood from hard experience. A false move now and there would
be blood. Rist strode forward. *But not our blood.* He stared through
the shrouds and saw *Unrivalled* for the first time since they had
shoved off.

He had never thought of a ship as being beautiful before. As
a trained seaman you saw her in so many different guises. And
she was there. *Waiting.*

He turned as Varlo finished his little speech about the right
to stop and search, and the fact that *Albatroz's* master should be
well aware of the said agreement.

Rist examined the master. Broad and heavy without being over-
weight, all muscle: a man who could and would know how to use
it. About his own age, he thought, but it was hard to tell, the face
was so weathered and tanned by sun and sea that he could have
been anything. But Rist was certain of one thing: this man was as
English as he was. He had a hard but vaguely familiar accent, like
Loveday, *Unrivalled's* cooper. Loveday was a Londoner, and had
been a Thames waterman in the Limehouse district for several
years before he had volunteered or been pressed by some over-
eager lieutenant. As a waterman, he would have had the precious
protection.

Varlo said sharply, "Post guards!" He pointed to one of several swivel guns. "Put a man there!"

The master said, "This is a Portuguese vessel, Lieutenant. We
have no part in smuggling or unlawful trading." He shrugged.
"You can see my papers."

Rist watched carefully. Very sure of himself. But he must have
known *Unrivalled* was the ship which had been in Funchal, and
been ready for this. So why had he tried to run? In the end they
would have caught him, blown this vessel out of the water had
he fired a single shot. With slaves you had a chance, given time.

But to fire on a King's ship was another matter. Piracy. A hanging matter, and briskly done.

His own thought came back at him. *Given time.*

Varlo was calling to a boatswain's mate, gesturing at him as if he were a new recruit. The vessel would be searched.

Rist glanced at the brigantine's powerful master. He was speaking with another man, probably his mate. Like one of those prizefighters you saw in more doubtful harbours around the Mediterranean, squat, bald and neckless, with bare arms as thick as a youngster's legs. Turkish, maybe. The man looked over at him now; you could almost feel his eyes. Like metal. Merciless.

Varlo strode over to him. "Now we shall see, eh?" He snatched out his handkerchief and dabbed his mouth. He sounded out of breath.

Rist jerked his head towards the two figures by the wheel. "What about the master, sir?"

Varlo had to drag his mind back. "Him? Name's Cousens. English. This is all he can do, I suppose. It will be up to the captain . . ." He broke off as two seamen emerged from a hatchway and one called, "Nothin' down there, sir!"

Varlo dabbed his mouth again. "Must be something. He was running away." He stared around at the silent, staring figures. "I can't simply take his word for it!"

Rist waited. That same uncertainty. *But never an admission.*

He was suddenly angry. Of course this vessel was a slaver. The fresh paint and tarred-down rigging meant nothing. She was empty, probably on passage to one of the countless islets which stretched along the Atlantic shoreline where larger ships waited to bargain and to complete their business for the most valuable cargo in the world.

He had seen it and been a part of it. Shut his eyes and ears to the inhuman treatment, as men, women and sometimes children had been dragged aboard and packed into darkened holds where the conditions had been too foul to believe. *And I did it.*

He tried to contain his anger. *Leave it to Lieutenant Varlo. You'll get no praise or recognition for doing his work for him. Nor would he recognise it if you did.*

Someone else reported, "Empty, sir."

Lawson, the jolly-boat's coxswain, touched his arm. "Reckon the Cap'n'll be spittin' fire by now!" He was enjoying it.

Then he murmured, "Watch out for squalls!"

It was *Albatroz's* master, very confident, even pushing a levelled musket aside as he walked over to join the small group by the main hatch.

"I have work to do, money to earn so that my men can be paid!" He did not attempt to conceal his contempt. "We stopped for you because you fired on my ship. But my employers will take this to a higher authority than your quarterdeck!"

Varlo snapped, "How *dare* you speak to me in this fashion . . ." He looked down as Rist plucked his sleeve. As if he had been struck.

Rist said calmly, "You had a lively passage, Cap'n. We were hard put to catch you!" He was still gripping Varlo's coat, and was more conscious of that than his own self-control.

"So you can speak too, eh?" Beyond, the bald, neckless mate gave a grimace, probably intended as a grin.

Rist smiled. "I've been at sea all my life." He felt Varlo staring at him, doubtless unable to accept that his subordinate was daring to interfere. "One thing I was taught, on pain o' death. Never light fires in a bad seaway. There's nothin' that can't wait 'til you're snug at anchor, *right?*"

He turned aside and added evenly, "Pitch, sir. I could smell it when we came on board. My mind didn't grapple it, that's all."

Varlo said, *"Tell me."*

Rist beckoned to the boatswain's mate. "Selby, take two hands down the main hold." He raised one hand. "An' yes, I know you've already searched it."

Selby glared at his companion and said, "Saw the pitch boiler, sir. Coolin', so I thought best to leave it be."

Rist touched the hilt of his hanger and allowed the coat to fall open so that it shone dully in the late sunlight.

"Tip it out. The rest of you, stand fast where you are!" To Lawson he added, "Be ready with the signal." At any second he expected Varlo to shout him down, even put him under arrest for insubordination, although he doubted if the others would obey any such order.

It was no longer mere routine. *The sailor's lot with nothing at the end of it.*

Rist looked at the brigantine's master and said almost softly, "If you try any tricks, *Captain Cousens,* I promise you'll get it first!"

It took another ten minutes. It felt like an hour or more. Across the glittering strip of water *Unrivalled* had changed tack again, almost bows-on to the smaller vessel, as if poised to draw even closer in case of a delay, or some trick which might still give *Albatroz* time to prolong what Adam Bolitho probably now believed was a calculated error on his part.

Rist saw Varlo take a pace away as Selby came on deck, with what appeared to be a wad of tarred rags grasped in a pair of tongs. Varlo said nothing and nobody moved, so that the sea and shipboard noises intruded like some wild fanfare.

Rist said, *"On the deck!"*

The metal was so clogged with partly set pitch that it could have been anything. Rist's hanger was quite steady in his hand, although he barely recalled drawing it.

"Easy, *Mister* Cousens. I'd not want to spit you here an' now, but in God's sight I will if needs be!"

Selby shook out some more pieces of metal, iron manacles. Rist stared at them. *For that first horrific voyage.*

It was Varlo who broke the silence.

"Very well, Lawson. Make the signal to *Unrivalled.*"

Rist took a long, hard breath. A close run thing.

Freetown, the largest natural harbour on the African continent, was always teeming with vessels of every kind, and a nightmare even for any experienced master making his first approach. Some of the larger merchantmen, loading or discharging cargo, were surrounded by lighters and local traders, while stately Arab dhows and smaller coastal craft wended amongst the busy moorings with apparent disregard or any respect for the right of way.

Slightly apart from the merchant shipping, the frigate lay at her cable, her black and buff reflection almost perfect on the barely moving water. Awnings were in position, white and bar-taut in the relentless glare, windsails too, to bring even slight relief to the close confines of the lower decks. She mounted a fine figurehead, a fierce-looking kestrel with widely spread wings, head slightly turned as if about to take to the air.

She was in fact His Britannic Majesty's frigate *Kestrel* of 38 guns, although any trained eye would quickly notice several of her ports were empty, without even the customary wooden "quakers" to give the impression that she was fully armed. There were some men working aloft on the braced yards and neatly furled sails, their bodies deeply tanned, while others did what they could to find patches of shade beneath awnings or the tight pattern of rigging. A White Ensign at the taffrail was barely moving, a masthead pendant occasionally lifted and licked out like a whip to make a lie of the oppressive heat. All her boats were in the water alongside, to ensure that the seams remained tightly sealed, and a Royal Marine sentry paced along each gangway, undaunted it seemed by his full scarlet uniform, his sole occupation to watch out for thieves. It was not unknown for swimmers to pick upon a moored longboat, cut its painter and remove it without anyone seeing or raising the alarm. A replacement was hard to get, and the marine would not hesitate to use his musket if it was attempted during his tour of duty.

Apart from Lion Mountain, there was little to distinguish the shore from any of the other anchorages on the Windward Coast. Huddled white dwellings and some native huts by the water, with the unending backdrop of green scrub and forest which seemed to be waiting to reclaim its territory from the intruders. And the whole panorama appeared to be moving in a heat haze, dust too; you could feel it between your teeth, everywhere, even out here, in a King's ship.

To some of the newer hands it was still something of an adventure. Strange tongues, and the noise and bustle of harbour life, something completely alien to men from villages and farms in England.

For others, the endless patrols were hated above all else. The monotony of handling salt-hardened canvas in blazing heat, again and again throughout each watch to contain the light tropical airs, and the periods of windless calm when men would turn on each other at the slightest provocation, with the inevitable aftermath of punishment. And always the fear of fever, something never far from a sailor's thoughts along this unending coastline.

A few could see beyond the discomfort and monotony. One was *Kestrel*'s captain.

Standing now in his stern cabin, his body partially in shadow, he watched the haphazard pattern of harbour traffic with professional interest. Captain James Tyacke was used to it, even though his return to the anti-slavery patrols had been a fresh beginning. He touched the hot timbers. And in a new ship.

Although classed as a fifth-rate, *Kestrel* had been prepared for her new role. A third of her heavier armament had been removed, to allow for more stores space and the extended sea passages she would be required to take. She carried a full complement, however, enough for excursions ashore when needed, and for prize-crews should they run down a slaver when the chance offered itself.

Tyacke was an old hand at it. He had gained his first command, a little brig, when he had been pitting his wits against the slavers. He touched the mutilated side of his face, burned away like wax, with only the eye undamaged. A miracle, they had said at Haslar. That had been after the great battle at Aboukir Bay, Nelson's resounding victory over the French fleet, which had destroyed Napoleon's planned conquest of Egypt and beyond. The Battle of the Nile, it was called now, although most people had probably forgotten it, he thought. He could even do that without bitterness now, something he had once believed impossible. He touched his skin again. The legacy. It had earned him the nickname, *"the devil with half a face,"* among the slavers.

It had been very different then. England had been at war, and the anti-slavery patrols had taken second place to everything else. Slavers had been active then, war or not, and justice had been swift, when you could catch them.

Now, with the coming of peace, there were pious demands from the old enemies for stricter controls not only of slavery but also the administering of justice. *Irrefutable proof of every crime.* The word of a captain and his officers was no longer enough. So it took longer and it cost more money. They never learned.

He stiffened as he saw a vessel moving, seemingly at a snail's pace, towards the roadstead. A pyramid of pale canvas, each sail expertly braced to catch the air in this windless harbour.

Going to England. He could think about that without regret, without questioning his motives.

More to the point, she was carrying the recently appointed government agent who had been sent to Freetown to investigate and assess the navy's anti-slavery activities. The climate had got to him almost immediately, and drink had done the rest; he would not live very long after the ship landed him in England.

He glanced around his cabin. Spartan, some would call it, with little to hint at the character and the courage of *Kestrel*'s captain.

The government agent had come aboard soon after his arrival. Tyacke could see him now. Concerned, sincere, probably genuinely interested in what he had been sent to discover. To pass back to some desk in London. At least their lordships of Admiralty, no matter what you thought of them, were usually content to leave it to the flag officer or captain in charge of the station in question. Not so with the civilian authority, the Foreign Office.

Even trying to describe the area which was required to be under constant surveillance had been like talking to a block of wood. Just a handful of men-of-war like *Kestrel,* but relying for the most part on smaller vessels, brigs and schooners. The area extended from twelve degrees north of the Equator to some fifteen degrees south. Even using a chart, he had been unable to make the agent understand, so he had described the navy's patrol as being akin to sailing from the northern tip of Scotland down and through the Dover Strait and back up and around to the Clyde. He had made some impression, but he doubted if it would make much sense when it reached that desk in London.

A needle in a haystack. Perhaps that was what appealed to him.

He heard footsteps, firm and assured: John Raven, his second-in-command. Old for his rank, he had come up the hard way, from the lower deck. If they were good, there were none better. And John Raven was good.

They had grown to respect one another more as individuals, men, rather than through the necessary division of ranks. If it was personal, it went no further than this cabin. Unlike some ships, where a captain's habits and weaknesses would become common gossip in the wardroom and throughout the command. Raven had been married, but was no longer. He had served in brigs also, and was at ease in the cramped familiarity of smaller craft.

And doubtless he knew his captain, how his face had been burned away at the Nile, how he had lost his girl because of it. And had found her again.

He turned towards the door as the sentry called, "First lieutenant, *sir!*"

Then I left her, for this.

He smiled. "News, John?"

Raven was strongly built, with a still young face, at odds with hair which was completely grey.

"The guard-boat has just come alongside, sir. *Seven Sisters* is returning from patrol. They report the frigate *Unrivalled* making her final approach." He hesitated, watching his captain's blue eyes. It had been impossible at first not to stare at the terrible disfigurement, but he had noticed almost from the beginning of the commission that Tyacke seemed able to accept it. Carry it.

The eyes were considering now. *Seven Sisters* was one of their brigs, but it was not that.

"*Unrivalled,* sir. Forty-six guns." He paused, but saw Tyacke's expression soften.

"Yes, I know her. She's commanded by Captain Adam Bolitho."

He turned away to watch the guard-boat pulling strongly around the larboard quarter. They all said the navy was a family. Love it, hate it, damn it or die for it, it was still a family.

Like that last time in England, when *Kestrel* had called at Falmouth. He had intended to call upon Catherine Somervell. He did not notice that he was touching his face again, nor that Raven was observing him, perhaps discovering something; he was thinking of the day when she had boarded his ship, and had kissed him, *on this burned skin,* in front of the whole company. And they had loved her for it. *As I did.*

He was still not sure if he had been relieved that she had been away, in London, they had said. That neither of them would have been able to surmount it. The one thing which drew them together now forced them apart. *The Happy Few.*

Now, another memory.

But John Allday, Sir Richard's coxswain, his oak, had come aboard in Falmouth. Had sat in that very chair where John Raven was standing. Bolitho had died in his arms on that day Tyacke could never forget.

He spoke again, calmer now. "Sir Richard's nephew. A fine officer."

They both looked up at the open skylight as a call trilled, and hands were piped to some new task on the forecastle.

"I knew another frigate would be joining us." He smiled. "Perhaps it's time to stop running, eh?"

Half an hour before sunset, *Unrivalled* dropped anchor.

6 THE WITNESS

DESPITE the heat, *Unrivalled*'s chartroom seemed almost cool, compared with the quarterdeck above.

Adam Bolitho waited by the table while the sailing master wrote a few more notes in his log.

They had been on deck for the noon sights, but with the sun blazing down from almost directly above the mainmast truck it had been hard to concentrate. The same undulating green coastline, on and on, without any apparent change. Even the midshipmen with their sextants had been unusually subdued. Like sailing into nowhere.

He watched Cristie's strong brown hands, clumsy, most people would think. And yet his notes, like his carefully pencilled bearings and calculations, were fine, almost delicate. Adam sighed. It was as he had expected. They had logged some eight hundred miles since leaving Freetown, south-east, and then east again into the Gulf of Guinea. And it had taken them nearly nine days. *Unrivalled* had been designed to sail and fight in another sea, against the Americans with their powerful frigates, larger and better armed than most British ships. *Unrivalled* was fast under the right circumstances, and had more than proved her agility in close combat. *But this . . .* He clenched both fists and felt his shirt tug against his back like a wet rag. This snail's pace was a test of endurance.

He thought of his meeting with James Tyacke before receiving his orders to put to sea again. He stared at the chart, and wiped the sweat from his eyes to calm himself.

He had expected to meet Tyacke, but he knew *Unrivalled*'s arrival had come as a surprise to the other captain, and he had recalled their reunion many times since they had quit Freetown. Warm but wary, some sentiment present which was stronger than perhaps he had realised.

Tyacke had done his best to explain the immediate problems of the anti-slavery patrols, and had even provided some notes on the subject and about some of the other vessels and commanders Adam might encounter along the way. Tyacke made no secret of his displeasure at being kept in harbour. The station's commodore, Arthur Turnbull, was at sea in one of the patrol schooners. It was his way, Tyacke said. He could not, apparently, accept the need to remain in Freetown, tied to a shore administration for which he was probably unsuited in any case.

Adam had known several captains like that. Promoted suddenly to commodore or flag rank, something totally unexpected in most cases, they had still yearned for the separate and personal authority of command. A ship.

So until Turnbull returned to Freetown, Tyacke was in charge.

He obviously hated the prospect.

There had been reports of several suspicious vessels in the area. A big ocean, but, as Tyacke had remarked, the landing points where slaves could be bargained for and then shipped out were known, even though some were almost inaccessible for anything bigger than a cutter.

It had been brewing for months. Slaving captains were becoming more daring, and prepared to bargain against their own kind for one more rich cargo. Their ships were built for the purpose, designed for service in the light airs of these latitudes. Against them, the British fleet had older ships which had been constructed for the endless blockade of Ushant and all the French ports where ships of war might lie, and for riding out those heavy seas. A few ships like *Unrivalled* might tip the balance, and allow smaller craft to penetrate the rivers and lagoons and confront the slavers before they could reach open water, and run to the markets of Brazil and Cuba.

Tyacke had said, "Diplomacy has many pitfalls, Adam. Good intentions and greed go hand in hand. And with Turnbull at sea, the acting governor seems unwilling to lift a finger!"

And a new Crown Agent was expected at any time. An improvement?

Tyacke obviously doubted it.

"Let me get *Kestrel* back to sea, Adam. The diplomats can stew!"

Adam realised that Cristie had said something.

Cristie gave his twisted grin. "A few more days, sir. Five maybe, an' we shall sight the island of St Thomas." He tapped the chart and waited for Adam to lean over it. "The furthest leg of the patrol area. After that . . ."

Adam nodded. "We shall return to Freetown." He felt a drop of sweat splash on his hand. Even then, they might fail to make contact with the commodore. And then what? More orders?

He tried to recall what Tyacke had written in his notes about St Thomas. A small Portuguese island right on the Equator. Barely twenty miles long. Insignificant. He straightened his back and frowned. But it had shipped many thousands of slaves, protected by the clause in the agreement which allowed Portugal to use her own ports to trade in human lives south of the Equator without interference. It was madness, and it was cruelly unfair. He shrugged, and said, "I wonder what will happen to our prize, the *Albatroz?*"

Cristie did not blink. He was becoming used to the captain's occasional disclosures, and his doubts. Strangely, it seemed to add to the man rather than the reverse.

He had heard Lieutenant Varlo bragging about the brigantine they had taken into Freetown. The impression it would make.

His mate Rist had said hotly, "A few manacles? It'll take more than that to pin a charge on that bugger Cousens!"

Cristie had hoarded that, too. Rist knew more than he realised. But he was probably right. With bounty being offered for every slave freed and recovered, a captain and his ship's company could be expected to share among them a purse which ranged from sixty pounds for a male slave to ten pounds for a child. But the prize court would require more than a few irons or manacles as proof.

It was all most of the sailors could think about.

It was strange about Rist, he thought. He wanted to be a prize-master, the only way up the ladder for a man of his service and rank, but had returned from the *Albatroz* angry, troubled about something. It was unlike him. He was a good master's mate, and a good friend when you needed one.

In a man-of-war, that was most of the time.

Adam did not notice the master's amusement. He was looking at the open log, the notes and the observations, ship's position and course, a man for punishment, an issue of grog. *Unrivalled*'s life story.

But it was the date. Almost a year since his uncle had fallen. Tyacke must have been thinking of it too, but had said nothing. He felt the locket sticking to his skin. *And Catherine.*

He crossed to an open port and stared at the unchanging pattern of land abeam. Misty in some places, hard and sharp in others. Were there eyes over there watching this ship, he wondered. Like the playful dolphins he had seen around *Unrivalled's* slow-moving stem this morning, or the gulls which seemed too tired to leave the water as the ship had passed them by. The hot, unmoving air quivered very slightly. More a sensation than a sound. He straightened.

"A storm, d' you think?"

Cristie turned. Bare feet thudded overhead as the watch on deck came alive. He studied the captain's profile, and thought unexpectedly of his home on the Tyne. It was probably snowing there. Bitter too.

But all he said was, "Gunfire, sir."

Lieutenant Galbraith strode to the larboard nettings and levelled the telescope he had just snatched from its rack by the compass box. He winced as the sun burned across his shoulders when he stepped out of the driver's shadow. He had sent Midshipman Deighton clattering down the companion ladder, but knew in his heart that the captain would have heard the distant echoes.

He ignored the buzz of voices nearby, speculation, a welcome break from the airless torpor of watchkeeping.

He swore under his breath. The lens had misted over. The masthead lookout might see something. *But it had been gunfire.* Not heavy, but rapid. Now there was utter silence.

He heard the captain's voice now. He smiled to himself. *No longer a stranger.*

"Bring her up a point, if she'll take it. Mr Deighton, aloft with you and speak with the masthead." He turned away and must have glanced at the serious-faced midshipman. "An extra pair of eyes won't do any harm!"

Galbraith cupped his hands. "Pipe the hands to the braces, Mr Partridge!"

Cristie was here, too. "T'gallants, sir?" A question, or a gentle reminder; you could never be sure with the master.

Adam nodded. "Yes. Hands aloft. East-nor'-east."

Galbraith waited for the confusion to settle into a pattern. Topmen swarming up the shrouds like monkeys, marines at the mizzen braces. A master's mate using his hat to deflect the glare from the compass so that the helmsmen could see it.

"Helm a-lee!"

The big double wheel creaked over, like everything else bone dry. Galbraith licked his lips and tried not to think of a tankard of ale in some impossible situation.

He started, as another sound sighed against the hull. Just one. An explosion. A ship in trouble? On fire?

Adam joined him by the nettings. "Too much haze coming offshore. And in any case . . ." He did not finish, as Deighton called down, "Deck there! Sail on the larboard bow, sir!" He paused; perhaps the lookout had told him something. Then, "Very *fine* on the bow, sir! Moving inshore!"

Cristie said, "Not too smartly charted hereabouts. We'll be close enough presently!"

Someone else murmured, "I'll bet the bastard knows it, too!"

Galbraith accepted it. A few sounds, a vague sighting of a sail, probably quite small to be standing so close inshore. Not much to go on, and yet these men around him had already given it a form and personality. Somebody to hate.

Adam took a glass and climbed into the shrouds again. The coastline was unchanged, moving slightly in the haze. No wonder men went mad in the desert. He forced himself to ignore the tarred cordage which was burning through his breeches like a furnace bar.

It was a sail. Maybe two masts, but not very large. He was already losing it in the clinging heat haze. He bit his lip. They were getting a better share of the wind than *Unrivalled*, that was certain.

A waste of time. But there had to be a reason.

"Get the t'gallants on her *now*." He stared up, surprised as the maintopsail writhed and then banged away from its yard. Wind. Like an omen. He heard the creak of steering gear and saw one of the helmsmen turn to grin at his companion.

"That's woke 'er up, Ted!"

Adam walked to the opposite side, his mind busy with the frugal intelligence at his disposal. An explosion. Only the one. And yet a vessel was standing away from whatever had caused it. Fear or guilt? There was nothing to choose.

He knew that Cristie was watching him. Thinking of that last time when his captain had taken this ship through a channel which was scarcely known. Adam often thought about it. Holding his breath while *Unrivalled*'s great shadow had risen inexorably from the sea bed for a final embrace.

A terrible risk, and Galbraith would remember it better than anyone. It had saved his life that day.

He glanced at the ensign as it curled away from the peak. It would not last. But while it did . . .

Deighton yelled down again. "Deck there!" He seemed to falter. "Something in the water, sir! Same bearing!"

"What the hell does he think he's doing?" Varlo had arrived.

Adam cupped his hands and waited as the sudden flurry of wind through canvas and shrouds eased into a sigh.

"Tell *me*. Take your time." Somehow he knew it was Sullivan up there. It was his watch, but he would have been there anyway.

Would have known. The seaman who had fought at Trafalgar under Our Nel, and who was still working on a fine model of his old ship, the *Spartiate*. Strange how one thought linked to the other. *Spartiate* was a French prize taken by Nelson at the Nile, seven years before Trafalgar. His uncle's last flagship, *Frobisher*, had been a prize too. Did ships feel it . . . ?

"Deck there!"

Adam stared up at the mainmast, seeing the midshipman's struggle, his efforts to remain calm.

"Some wreckage, sir. Very small, and . . ."

Adam said quietly, "Tell *me*. Between us!" He did not realise he had spoken aloud, nor did he see Galbraith's look of compassion.

"Blood, sir."

Cristie said, "How could it be? Even with a glass he could never see . . ." He broke off as his senior mate Rist retorted harshly, "He would, you know, if there's enough of it!"

Adam folded his arms. "Mr Cousens, go aloft and bring him down." He held the signals midshipman's eyes. "With care, do you understand?"

He did not turn. "Take in the t'gallants, Mr Galbraith, and have the jolly-boat made ready for lowering." He counted the seconds and said, "Go yourself, Leigh."

Then he crossed to the quarterdeck rail and stood beside the sailing master.

"I shall take every care, Mr Cristie." He tried to smile. "But put a good leadsman in the chains if it will help to ease your mind."

All the unemployed hands turned to watch as Midshipman Deighton jumped down from the shrouds and walked across to his captain.

Adam said, "You did well, Deighton. Now tell me the rest. In your own time."

He saw Jago by the hatch. He would know what to do.

The midshipman said, "I—I thought it was the sea, sir, changing colour. But it was spreading, and spreading." He looked at the water, unable to believe it. "It was all *alive*, sir." He dropped his head and said in a small voice, "Sullivan said they were sharks, sir. Hundreds . . ."

Jago was here, guiding the youth to a fire bucket, roughly and without sympathy.

"Here, spew into this!"

Deighton would have cracked if he had offered gentleness.

It seemed to take an eternity, the ship gliding through the offshore current with scarcely a ripple beneath her stem. And all the while the sea seemed to open up across the bows, stained in drifting patterns of pink with tendrils of darker red reaching up like weed to wander amongst the surface litter of flotsam. Broken spars, an upturned boat, planks and scraps of canvas, most of which were charred.

And in the centre, as if there by accident, was a drifting hatch cover, and on it a human figure, stretched out, staring at the sun, as if crucified.

Varlo said thickly, "Must be dead too!"

And then Partridge, the boatswain, abrupt, angry. "Don't say that, sir! Th' poor devil wears *your* coat!"

Adam said, "Heave-to, if you please. Mr Varlo, take over the watch. Stand by to lower the jolly-boat. Lawson, pick your crew, don't waste time asking for volunteers! It's running out!" He glanced over the nettings and saw the sea come alive again as two sharks or more broke surface, somehow lithe and graceful. Obscene in their frenzy.

He knew Midshipman Deighton was watching, nodding as if to reassure Jago, or himself.

Their eyes met and Adam smiled. He was sickened by it, but it was important, perhaps vital for this youth who would one day be a King's officer. And would remember.

Unrivalled came unsteadily into the wind, her sails scarcely flapping in protest, as if she was glad to be standing away from the invisible murders. Adam barely heard the boat pulling away from the quarter but saw Galbraith standing in the sternsheets, one arm out-thrust, leaning over to speak with Lawson the coxswain.

Then he took a glass and levelled it with care. The jolly-boat, Galbraith's head and shoulders leaping into focus, one of the oarsmen squinting in the glare as he lay back on his loom. Then past and beyond, the small pieces of flotsam, and the hatch cover. Even as he watched he saw a shark thrusting against it, lifting it slightly in an effort to pitch the inert figure into the water. Partridge was right. The man was wearing a lieutenant's coat, *like seeing yourself.* Someone gave a gasp as the figure let his arm slip to the edge of the hatch cover. Another exclaimed, "'E's alive!"

The shark surged against the cover again, the cruel crescent-shaped mouth starkly visible in the telescope lens.

A last hope or some lingering instinct, who could tell after what he must have seen and endured? But he moved his arm again, so that the shark scraped past, lashing at the misty water, turning instantly for another attack.

Adam lowered the glass and wiped his forehead. It was as if he had just climbed from the sea himself. The jolly-boat was there, the sole survivor already manhandled across the stroke oarsman to the sternsheets.

Adam heard the surgeon's deep tones as he gave instructions to his assistants.

He moved to the compass box, his feet dragging on the melting pitch.

Perhaps they would discover what had happened, and why.

He shook himself impatiently. "When we recover the boat, you may bring her back to her original course." He glanced at the curling masthead pendant and saw Sullivan framed against the empty sky, looking down at him.

Adam raised his hand in a slow salute. Then turned towards Cristie again.

The rest would have to wait. The ship came first.

Cristie watched and was satisfied. For a short while he had been troubled; now it was past.

The captain was himself again.

And the ship came first.

Denis O'Beirne, *Unrivalled*'s surgeon, had already rolled up his sleeves, and was gesturing unhurriedly as if to impress the need for care rather than haste.

Adam stood in one corner of the sickbay as the loblolly boys carried the survivor to the table, their faces intent but devoid of expression. They were hardened to it. They would not survive otherwise.

He hated the sounds and smells of this place; it was something he had never grown used to, in any ship. He had known men pray and plead to be left on deck to die after being wounded in battle, anything, rather than face the saw and knife on the orlop.

He half-listened to the sounds from overhead, muffled and somehow remote. Galbraith was in charge now, bringing the ship round to catch the feeble offshore airs. He had said quickly, "Name's Finlay, sir. Lieutenant in the *Paradox*. He was in charge of a prize crew aboard a slaver. He kept losing track of it, delirious. I don't think he knew what was happening when we pulled him on board."

Adam watched O'Beirne's hands, deft, busy, like extensions to his mind. A big man, awkward in many ways, but his hands were small, and very strong.

The figure on the table could already be dead, one arm hanging over the side as on the hatch cover which had saved him. Skin badly burned, a livid bruise on his forehead where he had been struck down.

Adam forced his brain to examine the few, bare facts at his command. *Paradox* was one of the anti-slavery schooners. For a few seconds he wondered why the name seemed familiar, then it came to him. She had been mentioned in Tyacke's notes, as the vessel Commodore Turnbull had been using to visit the limits of the patrol area. She was small, so this lieutenant was likely her senior officer. A rich prize, then. But where was *Paradox* now? And why had the captured slaver been left unescorted?

He heard a gasp and saw the man named Finlay trying to prevent O'Beirne's assistants from removing his coat. Perhaps in his tortured thoughts it represented a last link, his only identity.

O'Beirne was saying, half to himself, "A bad wound, left hip, knife. Deep, and infected." He laid one hand on Finlay's shoulder and said quietly, "Easy now, you're among friends." He nodded sharply to his men, and the uniform coat was removed.

Then Finlay spoke, his voice quite strong.

"Must tell the captain . . ."

O'Beirne was watching his senior assistant, the instruments gleaming in the swaying lantern light like something evil.

He said, "The captain is here now, as you speak!" He looked at Adam. "A few words, sir?"

Adam approached the table and saw the man trying to focus his eyes, fighting to retain his senses.

"My name is Bolitho. I command here." He put one hand on the arm. The skin was cold, clammy.

He was naked now, and Adam did not have to look around to know that the others had taken up their positions, ready to pin him down, to hold him still, no matter what. Only their shadows moved, leaping across the white-painted timbers like ghouls.

The other man murmured vaguely, "New out here." He tried again, pausing while a hand came out to dab his mouth with a wet cloth. "We ran down a slaver." He groaned and moved his head from side to side. "Three days back, I—I can't remember. The commodore was with us. We had struck it lucky!"

"What happened after that?"

"I took command. Boarding party, ten good hands, and young Mr Coles. His first attempt." He closed his eyes tightly. "*Paradox* had to leave us. Can't remember why. We were to make for Freetown as ordered."

O'Beirne remarked, "Not much longer, sir."

Adam glanced at him. "A minute."

Finlay said suddenly, "Then we saw this other vessel closing with us. A brig. Spanish colours. Nothing unusual about that." He was remembering, seeing it. "Then she ran up a black flag and ran out her guns. I had the slaver's crew locked up and under guard, but poor Coles must have got careless. They broke out and attacked my people. It was over in minutes."

Adam felt the men tense around him and saw O'Beirne reaching into his bag. He persisted, "The slaves, what happened to them?"

Finlay let his head fall back on the table, his eyes suddenly dull. Defeated.

"There were over two hundred of them. Most were in manacles, we couldn't spare the time to free them. But they knew they were *saved*. Some of them used to sing about it."

Adam realised that the eyes were now looking directly into his.

"They must have sighted your tops'ls, Captain Bolitho. I was helpless." He attempted to touch his side, and perhaps knew for the first time that he was being held motionless. "They slaughtered my lads there and then. Young Coles took longer. Even out there on that raft, I thought I could hear him screaming. Like a girl being tortured, I thought. They must have thought me dead.

Then there was an explosion. They'd planted charges before abandoning her. Then I was in the water. I think somebody pulled me on to the raft. I—I can't remember. And there were sharks. As the slaver went down I heard them screaming. It's shallow there. The sharks would get them before they drowned, poor bastards!"

He did not speak again, or resist as a leather strap was forced between his teeth, and the knife showed itself for the first time.

Adam walked from the sickbay and thought of the unknown midshipman who had been tortured to death, and the seamen who had been killed like pigs in a slaughterhouse. And he thought of Midshipman Deighton, who had seen it. The great, spreading stain, to mark where over two hundred helpless captives had been torn apart.

They would never know who Finlay's unseen rescuer had been. He had probably been taken by the sharks too.

He heard Finlay's strangled cry, and wanted to go back to him. To tell him that he and his men would be avenged.

Instead he went on deck, his mouth raw, as if he had vomited like Deighton.

Everything was as before. A glance aloft told him that the yards were braced to hold the breeze, but the ensign was scarcely lifting.

Galbraith stood by the larboard ladder, but made ready to move when his captain appeared. Nobody looked at him, but Adam knew they saw his every emotion.

Napier, the cabin servant, was waiting with Jago. The boy hesitated and then moved towards him, a tray held carefully in one hand, a clean cloth covering it.

"That was thoughtful, David." He did not notice Napier start at the use of his first name.

It was a glass of white wine, kept almost cool somewhere in the bilges. Until now.

He looked at Galbraith and shrugged. "They were all killed."

Then he tilted the glass, his eyes blinded by the sun, or something stronger which he could no longer control.

He saw O'Beirne's heavy figure climbing the quarterdeck ladder, peering around as he always did when he visited this place of command. Different from the man in the sickbay, with the strong and steady hand. His world apart.

O'Beirne said, almost casually, "Lost him, I'm afraid, sir. I don't know how he stayed alive as long as he did." He spat out the word. "Poisoned. Deliberately, if I'm any judge." He turned only briefly as the sailmaker and one of his loblolly boys crossed the main-deck together. A burial then. The corpse well weighted for a swift passage down into eternal darkness.

He added softly, "Just before the end he looked up at me." He smiled, and it made him appear intensely sad. "Right at me, and he asked, *where were you?*" He shook his head. "Then he died."

Who had he meant? His own captain? This ship? Adam turned abruptly and stared astern. The sea was smooth again. The stain was gone.

Perhaps he was speaking for them.

At dusk the masthead sighted a sail to the east. It was *Paradox*. At daylight tomorrow they would speak.

But before that, with the purple shadows of sunset suddenly upon them, they buried Lieutenant Finlay in the same ocean which had decided that he should remain the only witness.

As he closed the prayer book Adam heard instead those other words, and knew he would never forget them.

Where were you?

Commodore Arthur Turnbull walked easily across the black and white checkered deck covering, pausing only to touch one of the beams above his head.

"I relish the *space*, Bolitho, room to stand upright instead of ducking to save your skull! They become used to it in small vessels, I'm told." It seemed to amuse him. "The drawbacks out-weigh the advantages, I'd say." He turned with his back towards the stern windows, the movement light and without effort, like his walk. "You did well, Bolitho. We'd have been totally ignorant but for your prompt action."

Framed against the dancing reflection and the glare from astern it was impossible to see his face, gauge his attitude.

Turnbull was younger than Adam had expected, or so he seemed. But he was a senior post-captain, and Tyacke had told him that prior to being appointed to Freetown he had been in command of a big three-decker. He had done well. But even in the short time since he had arrived on board Adam had sensed a restlessness, an impatience which was at odds with his air of self-assurance.

Finlay, who had been buried the evening before, had been *Paradox*'s first lieutenant, the same age and rank as the com-manding officer. Turnbull had listened carefully to the account of his rescue and subsequent death but had said only, "*Paradox*'s cap-tain will miss the fellow. They were quite close, I believe. But there it is."

Adam had thought it strange that he had not been summoned to go aboard the topsail schooner, which was even now tacking slowly across *Unrivalled*'s quarter. A smart, well-handled vessel, and he could well imagine how two officers could become close and dependent on one another. Perhaps Turnbull preferred that this interview should be here, away from the eyes and ears of the men among whom he had lived on this last patrol. Certainly the last for Finlay and his boarding party.

"The other ship, sir. A known slaver, perhaps?"

Turnbull shrugged. "Could be one of three which *I* have in mind." He did not elaborate. "Recaptured the prize and intended to take her inshore, where the cargo would be transferred to a larger vessel. As it is, nobody has gained anything, and we have lost a prize." He sat down in a chair and crossed his legs, his eyes moving around the cabin again as if seeking something. "Your arrival on the station will carry some weight, Bolitho. Endless patrols are not enough. We must hit the slavers on their home ground. Destroy them before they make our efforts look like a useless campaign to save face in London." He glanced at Napier as he walked carefully into the cabin with a tray and some glasses. The boy waited beside the desk, his eyes averted from the visitor.

Turnbull said suddenly, "Of course, you have known Captain Tyacke for some time. In fact, he was your uncle's flag captain?" He hurried on. "But he learned his skills out here too. I'd see him commodore when I leave, if their lordships would agree." Again, something appeared to amuse him. "Tyacke is the only one I've met on this godforsaken station who seems at ease here!"

Adam relaxed, muscle by muscle. Turnbull was letting him know how well informed he was about all those under his command. And from his last remark, it was obvious that he was already thinking of his own next appointment.

He poured two glasses of wine, while Napier dared to look at the commodore for the first time.

Turnbull said, "This is a fine ship, Bolitho. Your record matches it, I believe. A frigate will bring you fame, but beyond that, I'm not so sure." He sipped the wine and smiled gently. "You put into Funchal, I see. Fair, I'd say, but a mite too sweet for my taste." He changed tack again. "When we return to Freetown we shall be busy. The new Crown Agent should have arrived, and I intend to impress on him the need to carry out some sharp attacks on the various collecting areas. The trade is thriving, the prices are going higher by the day, and some of the traders are making it worse by bribing local chiefs to get the slaves for them." He looked up, his eyes sharp. "Bribing them with muskets. And you know where that will lead."

There was a tap at the door and the sentry shouted, "Midshipman of the watch, *sir!*"

Napier hurried to the screen, bare feet soundless on the painted canvas. Turnbull took out his timepiece. It seemed to glow in the cabin, and Adam guessed it was set with diamonds. He would be amused to know that the cabin servant always carried a broken watch, engraved with a little mermaid.

Quite useless, and yet it seemed to mean everything to the boy. The realisation angered him suddenly. He was being unfair, and as intolerant as his visitor.

In the same breath he knew how different it was. Not once had Turnbull shown the slightest pity for the murdered slaves and *Paradox*'s boarding party. The loss of the prize and its potential bounty seemed to matter more to him.

Midshipman Deighton entered the cabin, his hat under his arm.

"Mr Galbraith's respects, sir, and the wind is freshening." He glanced up as feet thudded overhead. Perhaps remembering what he had seen from the lofty masthead. Was that only yesterday?

Turnbull said, "I shall require my boat, Bolitho. We don't want to lose the wind!" He became serious again. "As soon as we clear the land and gain sea room we can pick up the south-east trades. That will knock a few days off the passage."

Adam said, "Carry on, Mr Deighton. I shall come up directly. Have the commodore's boat called alongside."

He wondered why Turnbull had not chosen to shift his broadpendant to *Unrivalled* for the return passage. It was all a cloak of mystery, some image of dash and daring which he seemed to consider appropriate for his present role.

The door closed and Turnbull asked casually, "Deighton? His father was killed, wasn't he? A commodore, too!" He chuckled again. "I shall have to watch myself!"

At the door he said abruptly, "I would appreciate it if your clerk could complete two copies of your report before we sight Freetown. It will be useful to me, and I expect the new Crown Agent will be concerned to read it when he hears about the boarding party. An act of piracy, no less, which no turtleback at the Foreign Office will dare to ignore, not this time!"

Adam led the way to the companion ladder, glad he was leaving. Turnbull glanced back towards the deserted wardroom, and once more his eyes missed nothing. Perhaps he was recalling a face or some moment in his past.

He said, "The Crown Agent is or was a sea officer himself—that's something in our favour, I *hope*."

He turned again, one perfectly polished shoe poised on the ladder.

"Name's Herrick. Rear-Admiral Thomas Herrick—mean anything to you?"

Adam gripped the handrail to steady himself. Turnbull had not waited for or expected an answer. He already knew.

On deck again it was still with him, and those who waited by the entry ports or stood smartly aside as he passed wore the faces of others he had known. *We Happy Few*. Very few now. And Thomas Herrick had been one of the first.

So many questions, unanswered and unexplained. Like some of Cristie's calculations, the neat lines on a chart which somehow seemed to convene and join again and again.

The vessel which had perished, and screaming, trapped men and women left to drown or be savaged by sharks. Tyacke, who had been unable to speak of the memory which still ruled his life, and George Avery who had died because of it. And now Thomas Herrick. Down over the years. *My uncle's best friend.*

He raised his hat to the commodore, and the calls shrilled in salute as the marines presented arms.

On the face of it, Turnbull should be more than satisfied. An unblemished record, and the seniority to prepare him for the next step to flag rank. When so many others had been cast aside with the running down of the fleet, he had a bright future within his grasp.

He watched the boat pulling clear. The commodore did not once look astern at *Unrivalled.*

Adam replaced his hat, and recalled the two barely touched glasses of Madeira in his cabin.

Looking back, it was hard to discern the real man beyond the authority.

All he could recognise was envy.

7 SECRETS

UNRIVALLED'S gig came smartly alongside a sagging, sun-blistered pier and hooked on. Luke Jago tilted his hat and stared at the buildings on the waterfront, one of which displayed the Union Flag, with two scarlet-coated marines finding what shade they could inside the arched entrance. Then he glanced at Midshipman Deighton, who was in charge of the gig. He had said nothing more about the bloodstained water, the pathetic fragments, all that remained to mark the scene of the slaughter. He was doing well, and even Jago had to admit to something like admiration. It was as far as he would go.

He waited while Captain Bolitho climbed on to the pier. In his best frock coat, cocked hat and fresh breeches, he could have been someone else entirely, he thought. The open shirt and scuffed hessian boots belonged elsewhere. Jago hid a grin. *Like me.*

Adam said, "Not too far to walk." He turned to look back at the ship, clean and sharp against the sprawl of merchantmen and busy coastal craft. Awnings and windsails already rigged, some boats lurking nearby to offer their wares, always hopeful.

Jago watched him, remembering his expression, his change of mood after they had dropped anchor this morning. It had happened after Captain Tyacke's first lieutenant had come aboard to see him, as if he had judged their arrival to the minute. Then Jago had seen it for himself. Their prize, the Portuguese-owned *Albatroz*, had gone from Freetown. Released, they said, on some small legal detail, point of law as he had heard Cristie call it. He knew most of *Unrivalled*'s company had been so certain of their share of the prize-money that they had spent it already in their dreams.

But it was not that. It was something deeper, more personal. Perhaps he knew the captain better than he realised, and could sense his moods in a way he would never have believed likely. Nor wanted to. Like young Deighton, and his father the commodore who had been killed by one of their own men. They shared it, but it remained private all the same.

He looked at the people milling along the waterfront. Black, brown, as many colours as the flags in the harbour.

"I'll lead the way, sir." He glanced into the boat as Deighton asked uncertainly, "What shall I do?"

Jago frowned. "Keep the boat in the shadow, if you can. An' if any bugger tries to steal somethin' . . ." He could not keep it up with Deighton. He grinned. "You've got a pretty dirk on yer belt, Mr Deighton. Use it!"

Adam climbed the last of the steps and looked at the town, the dust and the haze rising beyond it like woodsmoke.

As he had brought *Unrivalled* up to her anchorage he had seen another vessel already at her moorings; she had probably entered Freetown an hour or so earlier. A brig, sturdy and typical of those which served as maids of all work in the fleet. Tyacke would have seen her too, and been reminded of his first command. *As I was of mine*. But it was something else. She was a courier brig, most likely from England, her scarred hull and weathered appearance speaking more than words of the seas he knew so well. Grey, stormy: the enemy. And there were men working aloft on the yards, spreading new canvas, or sending down the remnants from their recent passage to be repaired.

Courier brig. So there would be mail, for somebody. Men unable to read or write would have the letters recited to them on the messdeck, while others who perhaps never received news from home would sit and listen. Share it.

He stopped by a tall, dangerous-looking cargo hoist and tried again to come to terms with the thought uppermost in his mind. Tyacke had considered it important enough to send his lieutenant, Raven, across to prepare him. *Or to warn me?*

Rear-Admiral Thomas Herrick. To everybody else the name would signify just another flag officer, perhaps not even that.

But Adam had known Herrick for as long as he could remember. The navy's way, on and off, like a family. They all said that . . .

He could not accept that Valentine Keen, now Flag Officer Plymouth, had not known, had not forewarned him. He had served both with Richard Bolitho and Thomas Herrick more times than he could count. And yet, just weeks ago, when he had visited Keen and his wife while *Unrivalled* was completing repairs at Plymouth, Keen had said nothing. He must have heard about Herrick's appointment as Crown Agent, so why not mention it? Adam had sensed for a long time that there had been a coolness between the two; Herrick had once put Keen in front of a court of enquiry, which he had bitterly resented. And now their roles were reversed. Keen outranked Herrick, and still had several avenues of advancement before him; there was surely no need for continued animosity.

He had been, and still was, hurt by the realisation that Valentine

Keen had kept it from him. Did rank really reach so far above friendship?

He was reminded suddenly of his brief visit to Falmouth, when Ferguson had dissuaded him from going over to Fallowfield to see John Allday at the Old Hyperion. In a quiet moment, Ferguson had told him something Allday had said about that day when Richard Bolitho had been marked down by a sharpshooter.

He had spoken of Allday's pain when he had been trying to explain his own feelings, how, despite the aftermath of battle, and the people all around them, he and his admiral . . . his friend . . . had been "quite alone."

He was going fast, Bryan. Then suddenly he looks up at me an' asks, where was Herrick? Somehow he expected him to be there, y' see?

His oldest friend.

Adam shook himself free of the memory, and said, "Let's get it over with, shall we?"

Jago shrugged. Another mood. He had seen Captain Bolitho like a young lion in the heat of a fight, yet still able to take the hand of a dying man. He had heard him exclaim in a moment of despair, "Can't they be allowed to die with dignity? Is that so wrong?" And another time, he had heard the catch in his voice when reading over the sea burial of a man he hardly knew.

He heard the sentries stamp their boots together. Plymouth, Gibraltar, or on the deck of a flagship, the bullocks never changed.

He smiled. Even in the heat. *No sense, no feeling.*

"Captain Bolitho, sir?" A lieutenant had come to greet them, his face set in a practised smile.

Adam said, "I'll not be long, Luke."

That was the other thing. He would use your name, natural, like a friend, not like an officer at all, let alone a post-captain. As if he really knew you, and that you would never take advantage of it. Not like some. Like most.

Jago watched him vanish into the shadows of the entrance and glanced around for a suitable place to wait. People would look at the captain and see only the trimmings, he thought. The frigate captain who had everything, who would turn any woman's head. He thought of the one they called Lady Bazeley, so proud and beautiful. Knew it, too. And when he had seen them together, her half-naked, her robe plastered to her body, he had known there would be more to it. He looked around as two native women walked past, each with a huge basket balanced easily on her head, saw the way they rolled their eyes at the two sweating sentries. Just what the captain needed. He grinned and patted his jacket. He was not the only one.

Adam followed the lieutenant along a passageway, their heels strangely loud on a tiled floor. An old building, he thought, one accustomed to temporary occupation and function. It was not hard to imagine this place when there had been only the sea and jungle for company. Who had come first? Traders, and merchants, missionaries perhaps? Eventually the military would arrive to protect them. It had happened many times. The traders and missionaries might leave; the military and the flag always remained.

"Here, sir." The lieutenant opened a door and announced, "Captain Bolitho, sir." In a quieter, almost confidential tone he added, "About ten minutes, sir."

As the door closed behind him Adam found himself in semi-darkness, or so it seemed after the walk from the landing stage.

A long, narrow room, with a window filling most of one wall. It was heavily shuttered, the slats tilted to allow a minimum of sunlight, so that he had to stand motionless for several seconds to find his bearings. Then he saw Rear-Admiral Thomas Herrick by the far end of the window, his head half-turned as if he were listening for any sounds from the harbour.

"Do sit down." He gestured to a table. "I can offer some

ginger beer, and I owe that small luxury to the army hereabouts!"

The same voice. But as his eyes grew accustomed to the shadows Adam could scarcely believe it was the same man. He had been prepared for some of it. He knew how Herrick had suffered after his arm had been amputated, how the death of his beloved wife Dulcie had broken his heart. But in his mind he had always held on to the man he had known for most of his service, and what he had heard from others, mainly his uncle. Brave, loyal, and stubborn to a point of maddening obstinacy, but always a man you could trust with your life. Herrick must be approaching sixty, this man who had never expected to be posted because of his humble beginnings, let alone reach the rank of flag officer.

Adam said, "Are you well, sir?"

Herrick dragged at a cord beside him and opened the blinds a little further. Adam could see the effort, the way he bent his shoulder, as if the stump of his right arm still troubled him greatly. His hair was completely grey, but as he turned away from the glare he glimpsed the same bright blue eyes he had always remembered.

Herrick said, "*Unrivalled* will make a fine addition to the force here. A "temporary arrangement," more like a show of force than anything which might suggest a breach in the agreement. I understand Commodore Turnbull has a plan of action. I shall see him again presently."

Adam tensed. So Turnbull had already been here to see Herrick. Before anyone could dispute his appraisal of the brutal murders of slaves and British seamen alike.

Herrick continued in the same unemotional tone, "They will need a lot of smaller, faster vessels to compete with the trade. I am informed that at least one new barque is operating along this coastline. Fast, well armed, and able to carry three hundred or more slaves for a quick and profitable voyage. And there are others, one of which you apprehended with *Unrivalled*."

Adam waited. It was not a question. Herrick had been busy since his arrival in Freetown.

Herrick walked to the table and poured a glass of ginger beer. "*Albatroz* is a slaver, make no mistake on it. But she is owned by Portugal, and she is not hampered by the equipment clause which our government is trying to make universal. Manacles are an indication, but no longer, it would appear, a proof." This time he did not attempt to contain his contempt. "Piracy is a very different matter, but I don't have to tell you that. People in England do not begin to understand the misery and depravity of this foul traffic. Like the highwayman, who may appear a hero to some, but not to those who suffer at his hands! I used to warn . . ." He stopped abruptly and walked back to the window, leaving the ginger beer untouched.

Adam felt pity for the first time. He had almost said her name.

Herrick said, "I'd never shed a tear when they dance the Tyburn jig!"

Adam recalled the bitterness his uncle had shown on one occasion, when Herrick had displayed his disapproval of his "liaison" as he had called it, with Catherine.

And yet when Herrick's wife Dulcie had lain dying of typhus, which she had caught when trying to help Spanish prisoners of war from some nearby hulks, she would have been alone but for Catherine. Yovell, who was even now out there in the harbour, had been with her when she'd called at the house to see Herrick's wife; she had refused to allow him to stay and risk his own life, but had sent him to fetch help and medical assistance. And Catherine had remained to the end. Caring for her every need, washing and changing her soiled clothing, knowing as she did so that every hour was putting her in greater peril.

His uncle had spoken of it with both anxiety and pride. Now, in this dim, airless room, with a fan swaying back and forth overhead to the pull of some unseen hand, it seemed like yesterday.

Adam said, "We have taken on a tremendous task, sir."

Herrick looked at him directly, perhaps suspiciously. "I accepted it because I could stand the inactivity no longer!" His voice was stronger, as he relived something still too close to put aside. "Their lordships suggested my name for the position. An officer who could be trusted to perform the task without fear or favour, as I have always tried to do in my duty." He swung away, his pinned-up sleeve all the more apparent against the filtered sunshine. "And a suitable scapegoat, of course, should the need arise!"

There were voices in the passageway, and Adam could imagine the lieutenant listening outside the door.

Herrick said, "You will receive your orders from the commodore within two days. At no time will you discuss the proposed exercise except with your officers, and then only the bones of your instruction."

"They are all experienced, sir." He felt unreasonably irritated. With himself for sounding so defensive.

Herrick said, "I know your record. The Algiers affair, and your fight with the renegade frigate, did you credit. But you chose to ignore your admiral's signals, to interpret them as you thought fit. As a result you carried out the rescue of a valuable merchant ship, and more to the point some very important passengers. As hostages, at best they could have brought disaster to any future bargaining with the Dey of Algiers."

"I did what I thought was right, sir."

Herrick glanced at the door. "You were lucky. You would not find me quite so understanding."

The door opened an inch but Herrick said sharply, *"Wait!"* It closed.

Then he walked across the room, one shoulder hunched unconsciously, like so many veterans Adam had seen in the seaports of England.

He said quietly, "I did not intend our meeting to be like this."
He held up his hand. "No, hear me. Perhaps I am alone too much.
I did not mean to speak of it—not here, not now. But you will
know, more than anyone, what your uncle meant to me. He never
forgot, and neither shall I. Like all great men, and he was a great
man, although he'd be the last to admit it, he made enemies, far
more cunning and treacherous than those who use powder and
shot for one cause or another. So be warned. Hatred, like love,
never dies." Then, suddenly, he thrust out his remaining hand.

"I'd ask for no better captain." He smiled. "Adam."

It was the saddest thing Adam had seen for a long time.

He left the darkened room without even noticing the vague
figures who were waiting their turn for an audience.

Like a stranger. It would have been far better if he was. He
paused by another window and touched the old sword at his
hip. Herrick had once told him how he had returned to Falmouth with Bolitho, and had been present when Captain James
Bolitho had given this sword to his son. A captain and his first
lieutenant . . .

What had happened to that tough, stubborn young man?

Commodore Arthur Turnbull came out of another doorway
and stood gazing at him. Adam guessed he had been waiting for
this moment.

"Rough, was it?"

Adam regarded him calmly. "He was frank with me, sir."

Turnbull might have smiled. "That says a lot, Bolitho." He
glanced towards the other door, where the lieutenant was already
poised with another list.

"Then I shall be equally frank. Rear-Admiral Herrick is here
to advise us. But never forget, I command."

Adam listened to his shoes tapping unhurriedly back along the
passageway, self-assured and confident.

He picked up his hat from the table and jammed it on to his unruly hair. *And ruthless.*

He saw Jago by the entrance, and the same two sentries as before. Only the shadows had moved.

What would John Allday have said, had he heard Herrick just now?

Then he saw *Unrivalled,* swinging at her cable, a shipbuilder's dream. People changed, ships did not.

And for that, he was suddenly grateful.

Adam lay back in the deep chair and listened to that other world beyond the white-painted screen, with its ever-present sentry.

It was evening, another of the changes of colour and texture which seemed common in Freetown. An intense ochre sky, crossed with long ragged banners of dark cloud, moving even as he watched. Cristie had said there was a better chance of a favourable wind. Coming soon. Tomorrow perhaps, when *Unrivalled* weighed and left harbour.

Through the thick glass of the stern windows he could see the riding lights of other moored vessels, growing brighter in the shadows. Tomorrow, then.

Perhaps Cristie was right in his prediction. He thought of Tyacke's *Kestrel;* it had taken her hours just to work clear of the anchorage, and at one time boats had been lowered to offer a tow and give her steerage-way. Outside the approaches she had remained motionless, or so it seemed, as if becalmed. It must have been a test for every man aboard, especially James Tyacke. Commodore Turnbull had sailed earlier, without his broad-pendant flying above the graceful topsail schooner *Paradox.* Adam had wondered how her company felt about the deaths of their fellow seamen. Galbraith had told him he had heard that another officer had already been appointed to replace the dead Finlay. It would be even harder for him, on his first passage amongst strangers.

Adam glanced at the folder on his lap: facts and figures, and three possible locations where slavers might be expected to rendezvous. Much of the intelligence had been gleaned from trading vessels, as well as the hard-worked brigs and schooners of the patrol flotilla, and he knew from frustrating experience that most of it was pure speculation. He thought of Herrick again. He had often spoken of his faith in *Lady Luck*. It was hard to believe now.

He picked up the letter, and turned it over in his hands. Well travelled, it must have left Cornwall about the same time as *Unrivalled* had quit Penzance.

He had already read it twice. He had been able to picture his Aunt Nancy writing it, pouting every so often as he had seen her do when composing a letter. Nancy . . . he could never think of her as Lady Roxby, as the crest on the notepaper proclaimed.

She never allowed him to forget that she was always there, in surroundings he knew so well, thinking of him. Much in the same way as she had written to her brother Richard.

She was alone now, in that other house on the estate adjoining the Bolitho land. Her husband, known affectionately or otherwise as the King of Cornwall, had died suddenly. A man who had lived a full and boisterous life, and enjoyed it to excess, he had been a local magistrate, and more than a few had paid with their lives after appearing before him. He had helped to raise the local militia, at a time when England daily expected and feared a French invasion, and he had had an eye for women, but Adam had never forgotten that he had been the first to go to Catherine's aid when she had cradled Zenoria's broken body in her arms.

And the other Nancy, who had greeted him like her own son when he had walked all the way from Penzance after his mother had died. He knew Roxby had had doubts about his identity. Nancy had changed that, too.

She had written about the child Elizabeth, *your cousin.* He had never thought of her as that. He smiled. And hardly a child; she must be all of fourteen years old, or would be in June. The same month as his own birthday . . . Elizabeth was Nancy's ward, and there could be none better. She would give her the love and care she needed. But Nancy was sharp too, and missed nothing. The girl would be in good hands.

She had written of her last visit to the Bolitho house; it must have been shortly after his own brief stop in Falmouth. She had taken Elizabeth with her, and had shown her the family portraits. Adam wondered how she had explained the painting of Catherine.

It is a tradition in the family that each shall have a portrait. It would be right and proper for you to have yours beside the others. As if sensing his reluctance, she had added, *For my sake, if for no other reason.*

She had enclosed a small piece of notepaper, with Elizabeth's writing beneath a drawing of a beach, and a sail far out at sea. There was also the figure of a girl, back turned, obviously watching the distant ship.

The handwriting was well-formed and strangely mature.

My dear Cousin,
I would so like to meet you. This is a picture of your ship.
Coming home.

It was signed *Elizabeth.*

Adam folded it, and was oddly moved by it. She was well cared for; Nancy and her lawyers would see to that. Otherwise, she had lost everything.

He thought of the little drawing again. It was uncanny: so

many women had waited for the first sight of a homeward-bound ship, or prayed whenever one had departed.

Nancy would understand. She came of a family of sailors, and as a young girl she had been in love with a midshipman who had been Richard's best friend in his first years as a "young gentleman." She had come to love Roxby, but he knew she had never forgotten the young man who had visited Falmouth, and had been taken from her.

He looked at her letter again.

Catherine called upon me. She was visiting Vice-Admiral Keen and his wife at Boscawen House. I hope and pray she may discover some future happiness. My heart went with her.

He looked up. Napier was watching him from the pantry door.

"*Yes?*" Then he waved the letter, softening it. "You did not warrant that sharp welcome."

Napier rubbed one foot over the other.

"Are you not eating, sir?"

Adam stood up, and watched a boat pulling beneath *Unrivalled*'s counter. The guard-boat. Their own. Galbraith had not questioned the need for secrecy, nor would he.

He folded the letter. So Keen had known about Catherine's visit too. He confronted it. With Sillitoe; it had to be. She needed someone.

He stared at the closed skylight. The cabin was like an oven, but the lanterns would draw insects like bees to honey. And they stung. He sighed. A far cry from Nancy's Falmouth.

He realized that Napier was still staring at him.

"Some sliced pork, David, you know the way I . . ."

The boy nodded gravely. "Fine-sliced, fried pale brown with biscuit crumbs." He gave a rare grin. "With black treacle!"

He hurried away.

Adam opened the skylight a few inches and heard the hum

of voices, men passing the off-watch hours on deck, seeing the sights, enjoying the breeze, no matter how feeble. A violin, too. Not the shantyman this time, but well played, one of those sad melodies beloved by sailors.

Something stung his wrist and he closed the skylight abruptly. He heard Napier leaving for the galley, no doubt mystified that his captain should eat such spartan food when he could enjoy better fare ashore.

He had begun a letter to his aunt and would finish it tonight before he turned in. And tomorrow they would stand out to sea again. Like those converging lines on Cristie's charts. Meeting where, and for what?

He crossed to the inner screen to study the old sword hanging in its place, catching the lantern light. Napier took care of that also.

He had often thought about the sword, long before it had come to him. In so many of those portraits . . .

He smiled sadly. *And it would have been given to my father.*

He recalled Herrick's words, his bitterness. *Hatred, like love, never dies.*

He saw the goblet on his desk, the cognac, where Napier always placed it.

It was a warning.

Frank Rist, master's mate, closed the chartroom door and made his way to the companion ladder. He had examined the charts that Cristie would require a day or so out of Freetown. It was never necessary, but Cristie always expected it. Nothing left to chance. Rist had taken the opportunity to test the new magnifying glass the boy Ede had made for him. It was amazing, he thought. From a few oddments, he had explained. *Oddments.* It looked as if it had been made in a top-quality instrument shop, and somehow he knew that Ede had wanted to do it for him.

Need would be a better word for it. As if it was his way of hold-ing on to something, and not to beg favours as some might expect. A quiet, almost gentle youth, who certainly did not belong in these rough, brutal surroundings which only a seasoned Jack would recognise as offering comradeship.

It was hard to think of Ede as dangerous, although Rist had heard that he had been seized and charged for wounding his employer with a pair of scissors. Attempted murder, they said. Somebody had spoken up for him, and a lesser charge suggested, and it had not been opposed by the victim, which was strange. But young or not, he would have hanged otherwise.

He was good with his hands; Rist had even seen Joseph Sul-livan allow him to fix some tiny fitting on his model of *Spartiate*. And Rist knew that Sullivan, an otherwise calm and easy-going man, would have beaten anyone senseless who dared to touch his work.

He rested on a gun and stared across the harbour, all in deep shadow now. A few boats still on the move, but most of them had given up trying to get alongside *Unrivalled*. It was not unknown for women to be smuggled on board, through gun ports, even up the anchor cable itself, to remain undiscovered but well used until the morning watch. But not *Unrivalled*. Marines at entry port and beakhead, on the gangways and out in a guard-boat. Just to be sure.

They were going to sea for a purpose. Anything was better than rotting in harbour.

He had thought a lot about the boarding party which had been slaughtered. Men like those here on deck, yarning and pass-ing the time. After a meal of salt beef from the cask, hard biscuit, all washed down with some of the purser's coarse red wine, Black Strap, the sailors called it. They were in the mood for gossip, and outrage over the cold-blooded murders. And now, they did not even have the prize *Albatroz* to pass bets on.

Rist watched the lights ashore and found himself wondering again if there were people there who knew about the proposed mission, which would begin tomorrow. He tried to laugh it off. *If so, it's more than we do!* But it would not come.

He had never forgotten the risks in the trade. When they had boarded *Albatroz* with the high-and-mighty Lieutenant Varlo, he had been tensed up hard, and ready. And once aboard he had made sure that two of the swivel guns were loaded and primed, and trained inboard. At the first hint of danger, a daisy-cutter could have swept the decks as clean as a parson's plate.

Somebody must have got slack, over-confident. The appearance of the second vessel had tipped the balance. He had heard some of the hands exclaim, "There was no need to kill our lads! They could've let 'em run for it!"

Rist knew differently. There would be *every* need to kill them.

It was when they had arrived in Freetown and the boarding party had been relieved by a military guard from the barracks that it had happened. The big, hard-faced master, Cousens, had called out, "You'll never hold on to us!" Then, as Varlo was climbing into the jolly-boat, he had added sharply, "I knows you from somewhere, don't I?" And he had smiled, sneered. "Don't worry, matey, it'll come to me, then we'll see!"

It was unlikely. But it was not impossible. All those years, some he could scarcely remember, others he still tried to forget. It was just possible.

"You have the watch, I believe?"

Rist knew it was Varlo. You couldn't help knowing.

"Sir?"

"Time for Rounds. Send for a bosun's mate and ship's corporal."

Never a please, or offer of thanks. He could smell the drink on his breath too. Maybe he would fall down a ladder and break his poxy neck.

Albatroz had sailed. They would probably never lay eyes on her again.

He turned as two more figures appeared by the companion-way. One was the first lieutenant; the other was Hawkins, the ship's newest and youngest midshipman.

Varlo said, "I'm about to carry out Rounds, Mr Galbraith."

Rist relaxed, muscle by muscle, glad of the interruption. The evening ritual of Rounds, when the lieutenant on duty would inspect all aspects of cleanliness, security and safety. Mess-deck to magazines, defaulters, if any, to be inspected also or given extra work.

Galbraith said, "Hands will be called two hours early. Both watches will be fed before the boats are hoisted. Weigh anchor at eight bells."

Rist could almost feel their exchange of glances. No love lost there.

Galbraith continued in a more informal fashion, "And, Mr Hawkins—first time doing Rounds, I hear?" The boy stammered something, and Galbraith said, "Just remember, when you are on the mess-deck it is a part of ship, but it is also *their home*. So show respect, as I'm sure you would elsewhere!"

Rist kept his face straight. For Varlo's benefit, he thought. The boy was too young to know anything.

Galbraith watched the little group move away, and soon he could hear the shrill twitter of the call, and imagined men in their messes, at their scrubbed tables, loose gear stowed away, illegal bottles of hoarded rum well hidden from the officer's prying eye.

Men who would fight and if necessary kill when ordered. Die too, if the cards played a false hand. Tough and hardened men like Isaac Dias, the gun captain who could measure the fall of each shot with accuracy, although he could neither read nor write. And Sullivan, who had been at Trafalgar, and Campbell who seemed to cherish the scars on his back like battle honours. And youngsters like Napier, the captain's servant, somehow untainted by the violence and crude language around him. He wondered if Adam Bolitho realized what he had done for the boy. It went far beyond hero worship. Or the youth he had seen talking to Rist, who now had work he understood and could usefully do in the chart room. In some ways, an escape from the past which must still haunt him.

He frowned. And Rist himself. He had probably worked more closely with him than anyone. Except the captain . . .

But Rist was still a stranger despite their mutual respect.

He leaned back on his heels and peered up at the masthead, the pendant barely visible against the banks of stars and patches of cloud.

But he could *feel* it. The ship beneath his feet. The shrouds and running rigging, the blocks clicking and rattling quietly in the offshore breeze. And breeze was all it amounted to.

Tomorrow might change everything. He thought of Varlo. A man he would never know, and he realised it was mostly his own fault. He was the first lieutenant. Mess-deck or wardroom, hero or villain, he was supposed to be able to assess each man's value, as well as his weakness.

Varlo had been a flag officer's aide. He should have had his life and career at his feet. Something had gone badly wrong. It was said that another officer had died because of it. A fight, a duel, an accident? Perhaps even the captain did not know.

Varlo's admiral had obviously thought enough of him to arrange his appointment to *Unrivalled*, at a time when such chances were almost impossible to come by. Or perhaps, and he knew he was being unfair again, perhaps the admiral had done it to rid himself of any possible embarrassment?

He recalled the captain's return on board after his visit to the headquarters building, just over there across the black water. Rear-Admiral Herrick . . . Galbraith had scarcely heard of him. Except

that he had known Sir Richard Bolitho, and had once faced a
court martial for misconduct and neglect of duty.

It was little enough to go on. Perhaps Captain Bolitho had
summed it up when he had told him about the new orders.

"I'll not be sorry to see the back of Freetown, Leigh. Let's get
to sea again!"

In his way, he had spoken for the whole ship.

8 DIRECT ACTION

CAPTAIN Adam Bolitho shaded his eyes to peer up at the flapping driver and the masthead pendant. He could feel the deck
shudder as the rudder responded slowly to the thrust of wind, the
helm creaking while the bare-backed seamen put their weight on
the spokes.

"Hold her steady!" That was Cristie, his eyes flitting from
compass to flapping topsails. "Nor'-east by north!"

Adam let his arms drop to his sides, his mind blurred by the
heat, the slow response from the tall pyramid of canvas, and
always, always aware of the monotonous coastline. The Gulf of
Guinea again, and it had taken them nearly two weeks to work
into position, a cross on the chart south of the Niger delta and
some two hundred miles north of the notorious St Thomas Island,
where slaves could be loaded and shipped with impunity once
they had been brought from the mainland.

A handful of vessels, stretched across the approaches and the
escape routes like the noose of a trap. On a chart it was easier to
see Turnbull's strategy. Tyacke's *Kestrel* was in position to the east,
Unrivalled on the western side, while in between, and trying to

maintain contact with one another, were the brigs and schooners which made up the flotilla.

"Take the slack off the lee forebrace, Mr Fielding! Your people are like old women today!"

Galbraith's voice, unusually sharp. Adam walked to the nettings and stared at the empty sea. It was even affecting his first lieutenant. The endless strain of wearing ship, altering course a degree or so throughout every watch, just to gain a cupful of wind. The seamen were responding well enough, but boredom, the barely edible food, salt pork or beef from the cask, and the need to conserve water were taking their toll. The usual water casks, where a man could snatch a mug or wipe his mouth to give an illusion of refreshment, were gone, and marine sentries were posted below decks to ensure that the daily ration was strictly observed.

Adam turned slightly to allow the warm breeze to fan his body through the open shirt. He wondered how the commodore was managing aboard the topsail schooner *Paradox*, "the flagship," he had heard some of the older hands scornfully call it. No matter what shortages they had aboard *Paradox*, he imagined Turnbull always clean and smartly turned out.

He thought about *Paradox*'s captain also. Galbraith had discovered from someone or somewhere that his name was Hastilow, a lieutenant, and like many of his contemporaries on this station senior for his rank. He and Finlay, his second-in-command, had been together for two years. On this station that must be an eternity. Like brothers, Galbraith had heard. So like the navy, Adam thought; there was always someone who knew, or who had been told a piece of the whole story. Hastilow was also dedicated, as if the anti-slavery campaign had become something personal. It was not difficult to imagine how he would be feeling now.

He saw Lieutenant Varlo walking along the starboard battery of eighteen-pounders, gun by gun, with Williams, a gunner's mate, at his side. He thought he saw Williams glance up at Galbraith as they passed. Williams was good, and with Rist had been on the island raid when the chebecks had been destroyed. They were closer than some of the others because of that. Unconsciously, he clenched a fist. *When I risked this ship.*

The helmsmen were being relieved, the last topmen sliding down backstays to the deck, their work aloft done. Until the next pipe.

Adam looked at the unending panorama of glittering water again. No wonder men driven to desperation had been persuaded by the ever-lurking devil to slake their thirst from the sea. He had seen two men die, mad and unrecognisable, after doing just that.

And there was always the other temptation. At night, when the ship offered a hint of cooler air, and the sounds were muffled by the cabin timbers, there was no law to prevent a captain from drinking too much in a different way, but one no less dangerous in the end.

And night brought other forms of torment. Lying naked in his cot, his limbs bathed in sweat, and unable to sleep, listening and interpreting every sound, no matter how small and unimportant. As if the ship were driving herself, indifferent to all the souls she carried.

And in sleep there were dreams, one in particular. The girl, beckoning and arousing him, sometimes speaking his name, reaching out. Mocking him. Only the faces remained blurred, uncertain. Zenoria or Catherine, neither of whom had ever been his to love, or even the desirable Lady Bazeley, Rozanne, who had taken and responded with a fierceness of passion which had surprised, perhaps shocked them both.

He thought of the little tablet in the church at Penzance. *Or perhaps my own mother?* At such times he had been thankful that Napier had taken to locking the cabinet where the cognac was stowed.

He paced slowly aft, his feet avoiding flaked lines and ring-bolts without conscious effort. He pictured his aunt, dear Nancy, reading the letter he had put ashore in Freetown. *Trying to imagine what we are doing here,* sharing it as she had done with others in her family. *While we shall be tacking up and down, week in, week out. Going slightly mad, and wondering why we do it.*

Or we might all be dead by the time she reads it.

"Deck there! Sail on the starboard bow!"

Men about to creep into the shadow of gangway or bulwark, or those who had just been relieved from trimming the great yards and now making for the mess-deck's brief refuge, paused and stared up at the masthead.

Friend, enemy, prize or victim, it did not matter. They were no longer alone on this blistering ocean.

Adam returned to the quarterdeck rail.

"Must be looking for us, Leigh. She'd have run by now otherwise." He was thinking aloud, only partly aware of the listening, watching faces, tanned or burned raw by the sun. "We shall alter course two points to starboard. It will make it easier for our friend to converge on us. He'll be finding less wind than we have under our coat-tails at present."

He grinned, and felt his lips crack as if the effort had drawn blood. But it was infectious.

Some wag called, "Moight be 'nother prize, Cap'n! Fair shares this toime!"

Others laughed and punched their friends' arms, something which only seconds ago would have been answered with a genuine blow.

"Pipe the hands to the braces! We will steer nor'-east by east."

Lines and halliards came alive, snaking through blocks as more men ran to their stations, their fatigue momentarily gone.

"Put up your helm! Now steady, lads! Handsomely does it!"

"Be ready to make our number!" That was Midshipman

Cousens, very conscious of his position in charge of the signals party.

And just as quickly, "Belay that, Mr Cousens! Everyone will know *this* ship!" Lieutenant Bellairs, who such a short time ago had been a midshipman, doing Cousens's work.

Adam saw the swift exchange, and felt it for himself. Pride. It never left you. Like Galbraith and young Napier, or the scarred and mutilated seaman who had come to see him at Penzance. Pride for *Anemone,* the ship which had done that to him, but had left him no less a man.

"Nor'-east by east, sir! Steady as she goes!"

Adam saw Cristie making some notes in his personal log. *The lines meeting on a chart somewhere.* It would probably amount to nothing. A few words on a page, soon forgotten.

A captain's responsibility was total. He saw Cristie pause to look at him. The date, perhaps: had he remembered?

Adam resumed his pacing. All he could do was wait, then decide.

On this day, his beloved uncle had died.

He nodded to a seaman who was expertly coiling a halliard, although he did not notice his surprise.

He could still reach out. The hand was still there.

Luke Jago watched the jolly-boat being warped alongside, then turned to stare at the topsail schooner which lay hove-to downwind of the frigate. The signal *Captain repair on board* had been hauled down in time with *Unrivalled's* acknowledgment, and Jago was still fuming about it. The commodore's broad-pendant shone like silk from *Paradox's* masthead, and as Cristie remarked, "They could shout a message from there, damn them!"

Jago heard Galbraith calling to a boatswain's mate, and knew the captain was coming up. *Bloody Turnbull. Who the hell does he think he is?* He had been surprised that the captain had shown neither surprise nor resentment at the signal. Jago looked at him now and was partly satisfied; he was wearing his old sea-going coat and had tied a neckcloth loosely into place. Jago smiled to himself. The commodore could think what he liked.

He said, "I could have the gig swayed out, sir."

Adam smiled. "Take too long. Ceremonial can go too far!" He touched his hat to the side party and looked directly at Galbraith. "Maybe the waiting is over?"

The jolly-boat seemed to plunge into a deep trough as they cast off from the chains and the oars dipped for the first pull.

Adam twisted round to look at his ship. How large she appeared from the boat, the yards and flapping canvas blotting out the land completely. She never seemed so big when you shared her hull with some 250 seamen and marines.

He shifted on the thwart to study the other vessel. Smart, low-lying, rakish. A fine command for a young officer with one foot on the ladder. For one more senior, like Hastilow, it might appear very different.

"*Bows!*" Then Jago said under his breath, "I'll be ready, sir."

Their eyes met.

"Never doubted it."

Hastilow was waiting to receive him as he clambered up and across the bulwark.

"Welcome aboard, Captain Bolitho."

Hastilow's eyes said the opposite. Tall and lean, even thin, with his lank brown hair tied back in the style still followed by some older sailors. But the eyes were very different, dark, almost black in the glaring sunshine, deepset and wary, as if on guard for something.

He added, "The commodore is below." The slightest hesitation. "Sir."

Each commanding one of His Majesty's ships, and yet miles apart. The lieutenant and the post-captain. Schooner and fifth-rate. Usually it did not matter when men met like this. Here, it obviously did.

Adam followed the other officer aft, but glanced at the sailors working on deck, or waiting to trim the sails for getting under way again. All were so burned by the sun and wind that they could have been Africans. A large company for so small a vessel; for prize crews. And he could sense hostility, as if he was from another world which they had all rejected. They were probably remembering the men who had been butchered.

He could almost hear Finlay's words. *Where were you?*

Below deck it was very dark, and Adam was reminded of the meeting with Herrick. The thick shutters, the narrow strips of sunlight, the remaining hand drumming on the table beside the tray of ginger beer.

The cabin was small, the deckhead low enough to make him stoop. There was one skylight, so that Commodore Turnbull appeared to be on display in the shaft of dusty sunlight. He was, Adam saw, as immaculately dressed as if he were in a ship of the line.

"A fortunate rendezvous, Bolitho." He gestured to a bench seat; he even did that elegantly. "You came with all haste." The eyes moved only slightly, but seemed to take in Adam's threadbare coat and soiled shirt. "Captain Tyacke is in position by now." Without seeming to move he dragged a chart from another seat and laid it flat on the table. "Here, and here. As planned. *Unrivalled* will remain on station at the south-west approaches." He tapped the chart to emphasise each point. "The slavers are there, in the delta as reported. Three vessels, maybe more. It's a maze of channels and sandbars, safe for them, dangerous for a ship of any size." He smiled gently. "But then, you're aware of that?" He hurried on. "I intend to catch them before they can reach open water. They might try to withdraw upriver, of course. In which case it will take longer." He looked around the dark cabin as if seeing it for the first time. "Hastilow's fellows know their work well. They can outsail most slavers, and can use carronades to settle the majority of arguments."

Adam bent across the chart, and studied the location where *Unrivalled* would mount guard, almost precisely as Cristie had described. A perilous place on a lee shore. Worse if you ran on to one of the sandbars.

Turnbull said, "You will anchor."

Adam studied the chart again, wondering why Hastilow had not been asked to join them, in his own command.

Turnbull might have taken his silence for doubt.

He said, "Slavers know these inlets and beaches far better than we do. But once at sea, it is a different story. My latest information is that these vessels are to transport slaves to St Thomas, as I anticipated. There they will be transferred to a larger ship. But we will take them before that. None will escape, no matter which way they run."

Adam leaned back, and felt the schooner moving around him. Eager to go.

He said, "They may sail at night." Why had he stated the obvious? Giving himself time. Turnbull's plan made sense. If the worst happened and they only seized one of the slavers, it would show others that the navy could and would take action *on the doorstep*, as Jago had put it.

Turnbull reached down and opened a cupboard. "I hope they do, but I doubt it. Hastilow thinks it will be at first light." He lifted a bottle and two goblets from somewhere and looked questioningly across the table.

"Not Madeira, I promise you!"

Adam watched him pour two large measures. Cognac. So what was wrong? Confident, pleasant enough. He saw the beautiful cuffs, the glittering lace on the coat. The new navy emerging? He was younger even than Hastilow.

"Provided nothing changes before we can act, I intend to make an attack as close to dawn as possible." He sipped his cognac. "At least we'll not have to depend on this damnable wind!"

For a second or two Adam thought he had misheard.

"Landing parties, sir?"

Turnbull poured himself another drink. "You surprise me in some ways, Bolitho. A fellow with your record—I'd have thought you would be fully aware of such tactics." He shook his head. "Direct action, that's my belief!" He pushed the chart aside. "Hastilow understands. He's cut out for the work, and he wants revenge."

"A boat action, sir?" It was like hearing someone else's voice.

Turnbull regarded him curiously. "You were hoping for something different, a sea-fight or a chase. A true frigate captain to the end!" He gave the soft chuckle again. "I shall need *Unrivalled* right enough, but the first blow will be dealt in amongst them. The brig *Seven Sisters* will be there, and *Kittiwake* in reserve." He looked up, his eyes very steady. "I shall lead the attack in *Paradox*."

Adam heard voices somewhere on deck, and pictured Jago in the jolly-boat, and the others in *Unrivalled* waiting and wondering at the outcome. He thought of the shoreline, closer now, somehow threatening, or was that only his imagination? Because of a boat action which even in the most favourable circumstances could end in disaster.

He looked at the commodore again. It was already decided. You could almost feel it in the man.

Turnbull took out a large envelope. "For you, Bolitho." He smiled broadly. "In case anything unpleasant should happen to me." He was serious again. "I'll not come on deck just now. I've some last details to arrange. I am sure that our new Crown Agent will want to be fully informed."

It was a dismissal.

Hastilow was waiting to see him over the side; he could barely conceal his impatience. But he could not prevent his deepset eyes from settling on the bulky envelope under Adam's arm.

Then he said bluntly, "The commodore's told you then, sir?"

"Most of it."

Hastilow said, "We'll teach them a lesson they'll never forget!"

He seemed to contain his anger with a physical effort and stood aside to allow Adam to climb on to the bulwark.

Adam saw some of the schooner's company watching him leave. Defiant, contemptuous, glad he was going back to his own ship.

Perhaps Turnbull was right. It was their kind of action. But all he could think about was the one glaring flaw. *Revenge*. He thought of the renegade captain who had died of his wound in *Unrivalled*'s great cabin. Perhaps he had been right after all. He had called it vanity.

After the shuttered lanterns in the chartroom, the quarterdeck seemed pitch black. But not for long. Adam walked to the rail and stared along the full length of the ship, his eyes eventually picking out shapes and small groups of seamen at their stations, bodies pale against the guns and the familiar rigging. For another long day they had remained clear of the land, using the light airs to tack this way and that, but never losing their mean course for a final rendezvous.

Apart from the occasional slap of canvas, or the creak of the wheel, you could believe the ship to be motionless. There were no lights anywhere on deck, so that the tiny glow of the compass lamp seemed like a beacon.

It was always the same, he told himself. You could feel the solid landmass creeping out on either bow, like some giant trap. But he held the image of the chart firmly in his mind. Most of the anonymous figures relied on trust. They would do what they were told when the time came. That hardly ever changed. But Cristie would know, and would be measuring his own doubts against his captain's skill, or lack of it.

Adam moved aft again and saw the white crossbelts of the marines, stark against the dark water alongside and beyond. Armed and ready, with others, the best marksmen, stationed in the fighting-tops somewhere overhead.

He turned quickly as a large fish broke surface and then splashed down into a trail of phosphorescence, like submerged fireflies.

His lips felt parched. He could smell rum; it was all they had found time for after the galley fire had been doused. He tried to think clearly. Two hours ago?

He heard Cristie murmuring to one of his mates, then he called, "Ready to begin sounding, sir."

"Carry on." He imagined the leadsman up forward in the chains, swinging the great lead, beyond and behind his perch, then up and over, the lead and line snaking well ahead of the ship's slow progress.

He walked to the rail again and rested his palms on it. Cool and wet. In another couple of hours it would be like a furnace bar.

He tensed as the splash came from ahead, like another leaping fish.

The leadsman's voice was clear and unhurried. "No bottom, sir!"

He sounded almost bored. Even Galbraith had seemed surprised by the precautions. Doubtless he thought his captain was overdoing it, had lost confidence in himself.

Adam gazed up at the topsails, which, with the jib, were the only canvas spread for this final approach. Some overnight fisherman might otherwise see the frigate. He gritted his teeth. *And do what?* Turnbull was no fool, and would take no unnecessary risks. The horizon already seemed paler; in an hour *Paradox* and the others would begin their plan of attack.

He thought of Hastilow, experienced and eager to avenge his men and his friend. How much might he be influenced by a senior officer like Turnbull, whose last command at sea had been a ship of the line?

"By th' mark thirteen!"

Adam imagined the leadsman, up there in the gloom, hauling in his line and feeling for the telltale marks, bunting, pieces of leather or simple knots. Strong, tarred fingers, an expert in his work.

Thirteen fathoms. Cristie would be making calculations. *Unrivalled* drew three. A safe margin, but with so many sandbars and unmarked spits you could never be confident.

He heard something fall heavily on deck, and an instant mouthful of curses from whoever was in charge.

The anchor party was in position, poised and ready to let go. As soon as they were anchored Galbraith would supervise the running out of a stern rope, right round the ship and then fastened to the mooring cable. An anchored man-of-war, even one as powerful and well-drilled as *Unrivalled,* was almost helpless to defend herself against oared vessels which could work around a ship's stern and fire directly into it. The chebecks had reinforced that lesson, and it was not one he would forget, no matter what Galbraith thought about it.

He saw the chart in his mind again. So many channels which led from the main river and into the first open water.

"By th' mark ten!"

Galbraith had joined him. "Soon now, sir." It sounded like a question.

Adam did not reply directly. If they anchored too far out, there might be a dozen passages of escape for any slaver which slipped past Turnbull.

"Not yet." He walked to the compass box and peered up at the maintopsail. He could see the entire span of it now. The sun would appear over those hills which Cristie had noted so carefully. After that . . .

"An' deep eight!" Not so bored now.

It was not difficult to imagine the seabed rising relentlessly to greet *Unrivalled*'s keel.

He peered at the little dogvane, and knew the helmsmen were watching him intently.

Cristie said meaningly, "Wind's freshened a bit, sir."

Adam considered it. Cristie never wasted time with idle comment. And he could feel the strengthening offshore breeze, hear it in the sails. It would be hard work for Turnbull's boats, pulling directly into it. The slavers, if any were still there, would use it to advantage. Perhaps Turnbull had already decided to wait and allow their quarry to make the first move. At the same time, he knew he would not.

He recalled something he had heard his uncle say, as if he had spoken the words aloud. *The only thing a captain can take for granted is the unexpected!*

He was surprised that he could sound so calm.

"Bring her about, Mr Galbraith. We will anchor."

Orders were passed with no more than necessary noise, and men who had tripped and fumbled with every move only months, weeks ago, scampered to sheets and braces as if they had been doing it all their lives.

"Lee braces, there! Hands wear ship!"

Adam reached for the locket beneath his shirt and was surprised that it was missing. He had left it in his strongbox, where it would remain until this episode was just another entry in Cristie's log.

But it felt strange, different. The ship cleared as if for action, but none of the main armament loaded. Over cautious? *Or losing it,* as the old Jacks termed it.

He listened to the rebellious canvas as the seamen kicked and fisted it into submission.

He saw the two Royal Marine officers by the boat tier, every feature so much clearer now.

The leadsman coming aft along the starboard gangway, his line neatly coiled over one shoulder.

Midshipman Deighton standing beside Galbraith . . . thinking what?

"Let go!"

He saw the spray burst up beneath the larboard cathead, heard Varlo calling out somebody's name.

Then he saw the land, swinging slowly past the bows, the beautiful figurehead's naked shoulders suddenly etched against the hills which were still in deep, purple shadow.

"All fast, sir!"

Adam saw Napier speaking with the other youth, Ede, gesturing as if to explain something which was happening by the capstan. One with a mother who no longer wrote to inquire after her son's well-being, the other, so deft and gentle with his hands, who had tried to murder his employer.

So he was being over cautious this time. It was his decision.

He smiled briefly. And they were ready.

Daniel Yovell stood below one of the quarterdeck ladders, his hat pulled down to shade his eyes from the first fierce glare of sunlight. He disliked the heat, but made no allowance for it in his dress. His father had been much the same, as far as he could remember. *What keeps out the cold, keeps out the heat* had been a rule with him. He knew it was a source of amusement to *Unrivalled's* ship's company, but he was used to that too.

He took a deep breath as he watched the golden glow spreading across the choppy water, giving life to the shoreline with its hills and the darker green of forest further inland. It was a time of day he tried never to miss. He had no responsibilities, no duties; he could merely observe and enjoy it. He had grown used to avoiding the normal rush and urgency of a man-of-war, without being a part of it.

Like now, he thought. One of the boats had been pulling a long rope from aft and had hauled it beyond the bows to lash it to the anchor cable. He had heard that it was to swing the ship if need be, to train the guns when there was no other way.

He heard Partridge the boatswain bawling at some men on the capstan bars.

"'Ard work, did you say, Robbins? If the wind gets any livelier it'll be a bloody sight 'arder!"

Without turning or looking up, Yovell could hear Captain Bolitho speaking with one of his officers. Calm, unruffled. But in the great cabin Yovell had seen the other side of him. Not the captain, but the man, who cared, and was often hurt because of it.

Like the time he had returned on board after his visit to the headquarters at Freetown, after he'd met Rear-Admiral Herrick. Yovell knew a good deal about Herrick, and had served with him when he was Sir Richard Bolitho's secretary. Stubborn, pigheaded, with a fine edge between right and wrong. He had known of Herrick's refusal to accept Lady Somervell . . . Catherine . . . to see her true strength and value as more than merely Bolitho's lover.

He felt privileged to have shared it. He had seen Catherine's courage in the open boat after the loss of *Golden Plover*. Unable to conceal her discomfort, her borrowed sailor's garb barely hiding her body from a boat full of men, she had still managed to inspire and encourage them all. Most of them had given up any hope of survival. Yovell had taken comfort from his Bible, but even he had had moments of doubt.

He had heard Adam Bolitho refer to the navy as a family. Richard Bolitho had done so as well. It was no mere coincidence that the other frigate anchored at Freetown when they had arrived had been under James Tyacke's command. Tyacke in his brig *Larne* had found that open boat and saved them from certain death.

And now there was Thomas Herrick. To Yovell it seemed only yesterday since he had accompanied Catherine to Herrick's house in Kent, where they had found his wife in the grip of typhus. Sir Richard's wife Belinda had been there but had left immediately when she had realized the nature of the illness.

He had heard that Herrick had asked for forgiveness for his behaviour after that. Yovell was ashamed that he found it hard to believe.

Galbraith strode aft and paused to say, "Nothing to see, I'm afraid." He glanced at the partly-manned capstan. "But there's still time, I suppose."

He half-turned. "You going up, Sullivan?"

The seaman nodded. "Cap'n asked me, sir." He sounded troubled. "I hate this place. I was here before, once. Long time ago." His clear eyes were distant, reminiscent. "We was ashore on a waterin' party, and them devils took one of our lads. The cap'n sent th' marines ashore, but they was too late. They'd cut off his eyelids so that he couldn't close them against the sun, then they pegged him out on an anthill an' watched him die. It must have taken a long time, sir."

They watched him leap into the shrouds, like a young boy, before he began to climb up towards the maintop.

Yovell removed his spectacles and mopped his face with a large handkerchief.

"I often marvel that such men return to sea again and again, even after what they have seen!"

Galbraith grinned. "He's no different from the rest of us!" He touched Yovell's plump arm. "Or you, for that matter!"

"Deck there! Sail to the nor'-east!"

Galbraith almost ran up the ladder and saw Bolitho already opening a telescope. Sullivan might resent the other lookout calling a sighting before him.

Galbraith nodded to Midshipman Cousens as he offered his own glass. He heard Bolitho say, "She's *Paradox*. Makes a fine sight!"

Galbraith adjusted the telescope with care. It was strange at first: with *Unrivalled* lying at anchor the other vessel appeared to be much further out. It was an illusion; *Paradox* was standing towards the larger of the two inlets, tacking well enough, although the offshore wind had her almost aback at one point. She had all her boats in the water, towing or alongside. Galbraith bit his lip. That would do nothing to help steerage-way. The dawn haze was clearing slowly. He moved the glass again and saw another fan of sails, the hull still hidden in mist or smoke, as if she had fired a silent broadside. That would be *Seven Sisters*. He looked at *Paradox* again. Clearer and sharper now. The broad-pendant seemed far too large for so sleek a vessel, he thought. She had shortened sail, and he could see one of the boats, then another, being hauled alongside, the occasional glint of weapons as men clambered down into them.

Adam Bolitho said, "Too soon! The oarsmen will be exhausted before they can work into position!"

Galbraith handed the big signals telescope to Cousens. "Watch the commodore." He looked forward. All work had ceased, and most of the hands were either standing on the guns or clinging to the shrouds, spectators, as if they had no part in it.

"Deck there!" This time it was Sullivan. "Sail in sight, sir!"

Adam raised his glass again even as he heard Cristie exclaim, "There's another of 'em, fine across the inlet!"

Paradox was on the move again, her sails changing shape as she shifted to the opposite tack.

Cousens called huskily, "From Commodore, sir! *Enemy in sight!*"

Adam flinched as a gun banged out over the cruising wavelets. Small and dull, without menace.

Paradox would close with the other vessels and fire a few shots into them. There would be no point in their trying to resist, especially with *Seven Sisters* already making more sail.

Adam walked quickly to the rail, barely seeing the marines standing by or against the packed hammock nettings. He felt helpless, anchored and unable to offer support.

He turned abruptly and asked, "How long shall we hold this lie to the cable?"

Cristie answered instantly, "'Bout an hour, sir. Then we shall begin to swing."

Adam stared at the green mass of land. Between *Unrivalled* and the first sandbars there was a channel. It was badly charted, but doubtless well enough known to the slavers and those who hunted for them. Hastilow must know this coastline better than most. Creeks and beaches, inlets and places where even the biggest craft could lie undisturbed.

Paradox fired again. Aiming for the sails. If the vessel was packed with slaves it would be sheer murder to fire into the hull.

"Deck there! Third sail leavin' the inlet, sir!"

Adam heard Galbraith say, "They've left it too late! They can never come about in time!"

Adam turned as Cristie said, "I may be speaking out of turn, sir, but . . ."

Afterwards, Adam recalled the sailing master's surprise when he had gripped his arm as if to shake him.

"*Tell me,* man! What's wrong?"

"*Paradox* is on the wrong bearing." Then, more firmly, "No, I'm damn sure of it."

Adam said, "Mr Galbraith, beat to quarters, if you please, and have the starboard battery loaded." He held up one hand, like a rider quieting his mount. "But not run out!" He swung round and saw Jago watching him. As if he was waiting for it. "You were offering to sway out the gig, remember? Then do it now, larboard side."

He sensed his servant, Napier, by his side and reached out to grasp his shoulder. All the while he was watching the converging pattern of sails, like the fins of sharks closing for the kill.

"Fetch my coat and sword, David."

"Sir?" Napier stared at him, not understanding.

He squeezed the shoulder. A boy his mother should be proud to have.

"They might think twice before firing on one of the King's captains!"

Galbraith must have heard him; the urgent rattle of drums beating to quarters had ceased, the spectators had formed into tried and tested patterns. The ship seemed suddenly still, the occasional bark of gunfire remote and unreal. He exclaimed, "You will not do it, sir!" He was shaking with emotion.

There was a great chorus of shouts and groans, and Adam heard someone cry, "She's struck! *Paradox* has driven aground!"

He looked past Galbraith and saw it for himself. *Paradox* was slewing round, her fore-topmast falling as he watched, soundless in distance but no less terrible.

"You know, Leigh, I don't think there's any choice." Then, half to himself, "There never was."

When he looked again, *Paradox* was mastless. A wreck.

Seven Sisters would not be in time, and the other vessels in Turnbull's flotilla would be hard put to cut off the remaining slavers.

There was only *Unrivalled*, and she was anchored and impo-

tent, unable to move even into the other channel without sharing the same fate as *Paradox*.

"All guns loaded, sir!"

He held out his arms for Napier to assist him with his coat.
Then he took the old sword, and thought again of the renegade's
words. Bravado, courage, or vanity?

Cousens called, "They're firing on *Paradox*'s boats, sir!" He
sounded sickened, outraged.

The flat, dull bangs of carronades, packed with canister and
at point-blank range. Turnbull's proud gesture was in bloody rags.

He said, "Man your capstans, Leigh. Let us see what we can
do today," and looked directly at him. "Together."

9 PIKE IN THE REEDS

ADAM BOLITHO forced himself to remain motionless, his coat
brushing the quarterdeck rail while he stared along *Unrivalled*'s
deck and beyond to the main channel. The other vessels were still
making good use of the offshore breeze, sails barely slackening as
they altered course slightly, their outlines overlapping and distorted in the harsh light. He could hear more shots, small and
individual now, marksmen, he thought, shooting at anyone in the
water who had survived the carronades. *Paradox* had swung with
the wind and tide but was still fast on the sandbar. The nearest
slaver, a brig, fired two guns as she drew abeam, but there was no
response.

The third vessel changed tack again, showing herself for
the first time since she had left the inlet. A brigantine, if he had

harboured any doubts. Cristie quenched them. "It's that bloody *Albatroz!*" And his mate's quick response. "And not empty this time, by God!"

Adam said, "Keep your men down and out of sight, Mr Varlo." He wanted to move, to climb the shrouds for a better view, but he did neither. He did not need a telescope to see that the brig *Seven Sisters* had come about and was attempting to alter course on to a converging tack with the leading slaver. How they must be hugging themselves, the first shock of seeing *Paradox*, and then an anchored frigate, giving way to something like jubilation. People would yarn about it for years, and more and more slavers would be prepared to take the risk because of it.

"Ready on the capstan, Mr Galbraith. Take in the slack from aft." He did not raise his voice. "Impress on the gun captains to aim high, rigging and nothing below it."

"Heave, lads! *Heave!*"

Adam saw Lieutenant Bellairs urging more men from aft to add their weight to the capstan bars, feet and toes slipping as they matched their strength against the ship and the anchor cable.

Adam watched the land; it was moving, but so slowly. He stared at the three other vessels, spreading out now, with all the room they needed to avoid *Unrivalled*'s challenge. Except for the unmarked channels. Each of the three masters would know all about them, and be ready to choose his escape route to the sea.

If they took no chances, they could do it. Full human cargoes would increase their risk of sharing *Paradox*'s fate. And they had fired on a King's ship, had killed Turnbull's men in the water. Yes, every man aboard would know the penalty of failure now.

Unrivalled was swinging, but not fast enough. It had to be soon. Adam gripped his sword and pressed it against his thigh until the pain steadied him. It was now.

"*Open the ports! Run out!*"

He watched the leading and nearest slaver. It would surprise them if nothing else.

But they would know that *Unrivalled* could not move. If she weighed now, it would take an eternity to clear the treacherous anchorage and give chase. He had already told Varlo what to do; the gun captains would lay and fire without even the movement of the deck to disturb them.

He realized that Yovell was still on deck, instead of having gone to the orlop, his station when the ship was cleared for action.

The gun captains were peering aft, fists raised, eyes on the blue-coated figure by the rail, surrounded by many but totally alone.

"A prayer today, Mr Yovell, might not come amiss." He raised his arm, and gauged the glittering arrowhead of water which separated them. There was no sound on the quarterdeck; each man was waiting, wondering. Perhaps it was not merely prize-money this time. He thought of Hastilow. *Or revenge.*

"As you bear!" His arm sliced down. *"Fire!"*

The deck jerked violently, the sun-dried wood flinching to every shock as gun by gun along the ship's side each eighteen-pounder hurled itself inboard to be restrained by its tackles and crew.

Many of the shots went far too high. One even splashed down alongside the mastless *Paradox.* Adam found a moment to wonder if Turnbull had survived, at least long enough to see what he had caused.

He heard Rist say, "Got that bugger!" Then he seemed to realise he was beside his captain, and added, "Nice one, sir!"

A lucky shot or a skilled aim, the result was the same. The vessel's topmast had cracked like a carrot, and the rising wind did the rest. The spars and heavy canvas splashed hard down alongside like one huge sea-anchor, dragged her round broadside-on, and Adam could see tiny ant-like figures running about the brig's deck, probably expecting the next broadside to smash directly into them.

Her sails flapped in sudden confusion, as if her master was going to attempt to wear ship, and claw back into the narrows.

Cristie said flatly, "Aground. Hard an' bloody fast, rot him!"

The second vessel was already changing tack. *Unrivalled* could not fire again without raking the first one.

Adam said, "Number one gun, larboard battery!" He saw Galbraith turn and stare at him. "We might lose the other brig, but not *Albatroz,* not this time!"

Then he took a telescope from its rack and walked to the larboard side. The brigantine, even fully laden, would still draw less water than the others. That one channel, which had always been avoided by larger craft, was *Albatroz*'s obvious choice. He thought of his uncle's words again. *The unexpected . . .*

And there she was, exactly as he had remembered. Well handled, her rig, which Partridge had first described, bracing now to carry the vessel closer inshore, where she would tack again and cross *Unrivalled*'s bows unharmed.

Galbraith had gone forward and was standing with the gun crew, gesturing, and the gun captain was nodding, red neckerchief already tied firmly around his ears.

It might take a few more minutes, but one gun firing and reloading without support from the rest of the battery might avoid confusion and over eagerness. Gun crews were used to competing with each other; it was all a part of training and familiarity, not only among gun captains but every member of the teams. A pull here, a turn there, handspikes ready to edge the long barrel around perhaps a mere inch, to get that perfect shot.

Someone growled, "The bugger's run up the Portuguese flag!"

Another retorted, "'E'll need it to wipe 'is backside with!"

Adam glanced at the main channel. The first brig was still aground. She had boats in the water. To escape, to attempt to kedge her off? One was pointless; the latter would take too much time. *Seven Sisters* would be there before long. And the other vessel was making good her escape. He pressed his knuckles against his thighs and stared at the brigantine.

"Slack off aft, Mr Partridge. Handsomely, now." He lifted his hand again and saw Rist turn to watch him. "Easy, lads!"

He knew Varlo was signalling from the forecastle; *Unrivalled* was taking up to her cable again; the shoreline was as before, as if they had never moved.

But all he could see were the tan-coloured sails moving slowly from bow to bow, the masthead appearing to brush beneath *Unrivalled*'s jib-boom.

"*Run out!*" After the squeal of trucks and the rumble of heavy guns being run up to their ports, it was almost gentle. And yet nobody moved, and speech was in whispers.

Albatroz's master was standing into the narrow channel. There was no turning back. Soon, any second now, and he would see the solitary gun. And he would know. He might run ashore; he could even attempt to kill every slave aboard, but he could not escape. The Portuguese flag was the only thing between him and the rope.

He heard the gun captain's voice, saw him lean over to tap one of his men's shoulders. The seaman even looked up and nodded, his tanned face split into a grin.

Adam felt some of the tension drain away. He had spoken to that same seaman a few days ago, but at this moment he could not recall his name.

Cristie remarked, "She's got a couple of guns run out." He looked at his captain. "They might, if they're desperate enough."

No one answered him.

Adam straightened his back and felt the trapped sweat run down his spine and between his buttocks. The brigantine was on course now, all sails drawing and filling well, as if *Unrivalled* were invisible.

And if they did open fire? *Unrivalled's* guns would offer no quarter.

He thought suddenly of Avery, and Deighton's father, and his hand moved as if to touch the locket.

It only took one shot.

"Now, as you bear!" He folded his arms and stared at the brigantine's flag, a splash of colour against the hazy backdrop. *"Fire!"*

For an instant longer Adam thought it was another overshoot. Then the maintopmast began to dip very slowly, almost wearily towards the deck, and as shrouds and running rigging snapped under the strain the complete mast with driver and trysails fell with sudden urgency, the sound mingling with the echo of the last shot.

Adam wanted to wipe his face, his mouth, but could not move.

Strike, you bastard, strike! His own voice or someone's beside him, he did not know. Another few minutes and they would have to fire again. He knew from instinct as much as experience that the gun had already been reloaded and run out. After that *Albatroz*, crippled or not, would be beyond their reach.

"Ready, sir!"

It was not his concern. The seizure of any slaver was *his duty above and beyond all else.* The words of his orders seemed to mock him. But all he could see was the effect of one 18-pounder ball smashing into a hull packed with helpless, terrified humanity.

He lifted his arm, but held it there as Bellairs yelled, "They're anchoring, sir! The buggers are going to strike!"

Adam breathed out slowly. It sounded like the exhalation of an old man.

Galbraith stood at the foot of the starboard ladder, staring up. "Permission to board, sir?"

Adam looked across at the anchored brigantine. It was not over yet.

And there was always the flag.

The thought made him want to laugh. But, as in the past, he would not be able to stop.

"No, belay that, Mr Galbraith. Is my gig ready?"

He ran lightly down the ladder, for a moment shutting out all the others.

"Take charge here, Leigh. Fire if need be, for by that time it will be your decision."

Galbraith walked beside him.

"Then take Mr Rist, I pray you, sir. He knows these people. You and I do not."

There was no sane interlude. He was in the boat, the oars already hacking at the water without, it seemed, moving a limb.

Like some of the nightmares. It was not next week, or tomorrow. It was now.

"Stand by to board!"

Now.

Suddenly, the other vessel was right here. Small compared with *Unrivalled* and yet she seemed to tower above the gig, as if to overwhelm them.

"*Oars!*" Jago swung the tiller bar, glancing only briefly at the last few yards, conscious even in this moment of danger of how it must be done, be it for the last time.

Adam was on his feet, feeling the bottom boards creaking under him, intent on keeping his balance when at any second he expected a shot to smash him down. Figures lined the brigantine's bulwarks, and some of them shook their weapons, apparently ready and eager to use them.

"*Stand away! Stand off! I warn you now and but once!*"

The voice was loud and clear, and Adam guessed he was using a speaking-trumpet.

Rist murmured, "It's Cousens, sir. He's the one."

Adam did not even look at him, but recalled Galbraith's last words. *He knows these people. You and I do not.* And there was another sound, which tension had forced into the back of his mind. A strange groaning, many voices blended into one despairing protest, as if *Albatroz* herself was in pain.

As the gig moved into the vessel's shadow he was aware of the stillness, the finality. So unlike the wildness and sometimes the exhilaration of a true sea fight, the triumph and the suffering as an enemy's flag fell into the smoke. He looked up at the faces; even they were motionless now. It only needed one hothead, that brief incentive to kill, but all he could think was that his own voice seemed detached, disembodied, like someone else, an onlooker.

"In the King's name! Stand down and lower your weapons! I am going to board you!"

"And who speaks with such confidence?" Laughter, an unnatural sound, and Adam noticed that the voices from the vessel's hull had fallen silent, as if they all knew and thought they understood. They would be expecting more treachery, no different from that which had beaten them into captivity.

Rist muttered, "He's bluffing, sir."

Jago reached out to prevent it; he had heard Rist's remark, like the leadsman's chant. Deeper and deeper into madness . . .

But Adam looked at him. "If I fall, get the boat away." He smiled faintly. "Luke."

Then he seized the hand-ropes and felt the heat on his face as his head rose above the bulwark. This was the moment. He thought of the broken watch and the boy who treasured it, of Galbraith's concern, of the church in Penzance . . .

He jumped down on to the deck. A press of figures seemed to fill it. Seamen: they looked more like pirates. And each man would know that they could hack him down and dispose of the boat's crew with neither risk nor effort.

The burly man in a rough blue coat he assumed was Cousens

confronted him, his eyes flitting across the epaulettes and sheathed sword, then coming straight to his face. He said again, "And who are you, *sir?*"

"Captain Adam Bolitho. My ship you can see for yourself." He heard an undercurrent run through the listening, watching seamen. "You and your vessel are under arrest, and will be taken to face charges as laid down . . ."

Cousens did not let him finish. "I had nothing to do with that shooting. Those vessels are barely known to me." He folded his thick arms. "I am under charter to do this work. I have nothing to hide." He leaned slightly towards him. "And nothing to fear from you!"

Adam heard Rist move very slightly by his shoulder, and imagined Jago waiting in the boat alongside. *Your decision.*

He said abruptly, "Tell your men to put down their weapons. Now."

Someone shouted, in French, Spanish; to Adam it could have been anything. But Cousens turned away, eyes glazed with fury or disbelief as *Unrivalled's* larboard battery ran out into the sunlight as if controlled by a single hand. Like a line of blackened teeth.

He gasped, "I'll see you in hell first!" And then stared at his men as, singly or in groups, the cutlasses and boarding-pikes clattered to the deck.

Rist stepped forward. "I'll take the pistol!" And dragged it from his hand. It was cocked and ready.

Cousens stared at the frigate again. "They wouldn't dare!"

Rist wanted to kill him. It had been too close this time. Insanity.

He answered, "And would any captain dare to board a slaver alone?"

Jago and the gig's crew climbed aboard, and Adam knew other boats were pulling across to join them.

He was unsure if he should or could move. Dazed, sick, afraid, it was all and none of them.

Cousens was staring around, baffled, unable to believe what was happening, perhaps wondering if the frigate would have fired, when her captain would have been one of the first to die.

Adam took two paces away from the side and looked up at the Portuguese flag, but he saw only Galbraith. *And would he have fired,* had it been his choice alone?

And suddenly there were familiar uniforms and faces, taking up positions on deck and aft in the brigantine's quarters. Varlo had come across with a fully armed party of seamen and some marines, and they were in no mood for threat or argument now that the tension was broken.

Rist saw the lieutenant placing some of his men at the swivel guns. He had at least remembered that lesson.

Rist licked his lips and nodded to Williams, the gunner's mate who was one of the boarders.

"Near thing, Frank!" His Welsh accent seemed even more alien here.

Adam said, "Search the vessel, Mr Rist. Papers, evidence—you know what to do." He looked at the hatch covers. The silence now was almost unnerving. "Is it safe to open those, d'you think?"

"It can be done with care, sir. Slowly."

Cousens, a Royal Marine on either side of him with a fixed bayonet at the ready, shouted, "I am within my rights, Captain!"

Adam looked at him, and found himself thinking of his aunt. Dear Nancy, she had so wanted a portrait for the old house. She had nearly lost her chance. But once again the laughter remained trapped in his throat.

He said, "I would dispute that, but others better qualified will decide in good time. For my own part, I would happily run you up to *Unrivalled*'s main-yard." He thought he saw the man flinch, and seemed to hear Rist's voice. *He's bluffing.* "And enjoy it."

He swung round at the sound of shouted orders, and a disturbance of some kind from the companion-way by the wheel.

Williams and another seaman slowly emerged, carrying what looked like a corpse wrapped around with a filthy blanket.

Williams got down on his knees and laid the bundle carefully on the deck.

"In the cabin, sir. Tied up, she was."

She was a child, naked, wrists and ankles scarred by ropes or shackles. Her feet were badly torn, as if she had been force-marched for some time before she had been dragged aboard *Albatroz. To this.* She was alive, but unable to see or think, on the verge of hysteria or madness.

Williams was murmuring softly to her, holding the blanket to shade her face from the glare.

But Adam was looking at her thighs and legs, caked with dried blood. There were teeth marks on her skin where she had been bitten; she must have been raped repeatedly. *A child.* He thought of the letter and the sketch . . . maybe the same age as Elizabeth, a girl he did not know any more than this one.

Varlo said, "One hold is full of women, sir. All ages."

Adam looked at Cousens. "Is this your work, too? You are the master of this unspeakable vessel. What say you now?" He did not wait for an answer. "Open that hatch, Mr Varlo, but be well prepared." So calm still. The tone he might use when asking a midshipman about the weather on deck, when he already knew.

Then he walked to the hatch as two marines prised it open. The stench he had expected. He had sailed downwind of slavers before, when the world had turned its back. But you never accepted it, or became accustomed to it.

Jago was beside him; he could hear his breathing. Anger, disgust, or just glad he was out of it. Alive.

To Rist he said, "Tell them, if you can, that we are here to free them." He averted his eyes as screams and wild cries burst from the hold. What must it be like, flung aboard, chained, not knowing where they were or where bound? Days or weeks, scarcely able to breathe or move in their own filth. Until daylight found them. As slaves.

Williams called, "She wants to go down to them, sir." He sounded both anxious and protective. The same man who had helped to blow up a chebeck with his bare hands. With Galbraith, and Rist.

"Easy with her." He almost touched the girl as they carried her past, but saw her stare at him with eyes full of terror.

His fury helped in some way, or perhaps it was some lingering madness after toying with death. *Vanity* . . .

"You say you are the master?" His voice must have been low, for Cousens leaned forward to catch his words, and two bayonets rose level with his throat as if to some whispered command. But he managed to nod.

"You will know the name of the ship with which you intended to rendezvous, to relieve yourself of this cargo. This is too small a vessel to remain at sea for long with so many captives."

Rist called, "Three hundred an' fifty, men an' women, sir." He consulted a list in his hand and glanced at Williams. "An' children."

Cousens smiled. Relief, surprise; his confidence was returning. "My orders were to deliver them elsewhere. I will tell any government official, but not here or now. I know my rights, damn you!"

Adam saw one of the marines watching from the hatchway. It was Corporal Bloxham, the crack shot. A good man in every way, and with luck listed for sergeant at the next opportunity. Adam knew he would kill Cousens here and now at the drop of a hat.

He repeated, "The name of that ship. Tell me."

Cousens did not even shake his head.

Adam walked to the lip of the hatch again. Staring faces, eyes white in the shafted sunshine, skins like ebony, shining with sweat.

They had seen him. They would know, understand, or most of them would.

Without looking over his shoulder, he said, "As master you are expected to care for all persons carried in your vessel, at all times." Then he did look at Cousens. "We have much to do before we can get under way again. Repairs, a jury-rig, and a prize crew to be quartered aboard when we leave this place." He watched the smirk on Cousens's face fade. "I think it fair and proper that as master you should remain below with those women, to reassure them, if you will." He strode to the side. "See to it, Mr Rist, directly!"

Jago muttered, "They'll tear him apart, sir." He was staring at him, searching for something. Like that day in the church.

"I don't doubt it. Call the gig alongside. Mr Varlo can remain in charge. He is discovering a great deal today, I believe!"

The marines were dragging Cousens along the deck. Others ran to assist. He was a powerful man, but his voice, strong as it was, broke in a scream as they reached the open hatch.

The scream was almost drowned by the combined din from the hold. Like one great beast, baying for vengeance.

Rist stared at Jago and then at his captain.

"He wants to talk, sir. To tell you . . ." He glanced at the hatchway. "Anything but that!"

Adam looked across to *Unrivalled*, so bright, so clean in the sunlight.

He said, "It soils all of us. Not only the guilty!"

The master's mate strode away, and Jago said, "Would you have done it, sir?"

Adam swung around sharply, and felt the claws slackening, releasing him.

"I hope I never know." And punched his arm. "Luke."

Galbraith ducked beneath a deckhead beam and stood by the small desk. On the opposite side of the great cabin Yovell was seated at his table, absorbed in the notes he was copying unhurriedly in his round hand. No wonder they called them quill-pushers in the navy, he thought, Yovell was utterly engrossed, as if completely alone. As if this had been an ordinary day.

And the captain. Hard to believe he was the same man Galbraith had watched through a telescope climbing aboard the anchored *Albatroz,* unaccompanied and vulnerable. He was still scarcely able to accept what had happened.

As if to mock him, he heard eight bells ring out from the forecastle. Noon: six hours, if that, since they had seen *Paradox* strike bottom, and her masts and sails fold over her on the water like a dying seabird.

Work had not stopped since. Boats plying back and forth, slaves being released on *Albatroz's* deck, carefully guarded and separated from the vessel's crew, some of whom were in irons. Varlo was obeying orders. Take no chances. *With anyone.*

The brig *Seven Sisters* had been busy, too, securing the other slaver, *Intrepido,* and kedging her into deeper water. Other boats had been ferrying guns and stores from *Paradox,* anything which might be used against her original owners. *Paradox* could not be moved, and in these currents and this climate it was doubtful if she would last much longer.

Commodore Turnbull had survived, completely unhurt. Before he had come below Galbraith had seen one last boat lying alongside the dejected topsail schooner, by then a mastless wreck. They would set her ablaze, a suitable pyre for all those who had died for one man's folly. Hastilow had been killed, among others. The wounded were shared between *Unrivalled* and *Seven Sisters.* Some would not last until Freetown.

He looked at the captain now, shirtless, his dark hair clinging to his neck and forehead. Galbraith had heard that he had stripped naked and had ordered some seamen to use a washdeck pump to drench him from head to foot. Salt water maybe, but it seemed to help. To cleanse away something foul, and not only from his body.

Adam raised his eyes from the log book on his deck. They were clear, the aftermath of what he had done fallen into place, recognised if not accepted.

They had clasped hands when he had returned aboard. Even his voice had sounded different. Hard, as if he were expecting a confrontation.

"Fast as you can, Leigh! Tell the carpenter, and have Mr Partridge send a crew across. I want us out of here today."

Shortly afterwards another brig, *Kittiwake*, had arrived. She had not managed to catch the third slaver; she had not even been a spectator.

She had sailed past them, heading for open water, many of her company clinging to the shrouds to cheer and wave. They were going to Freetown.

It had been then that they had seen the commodore's broad-pendant streaming from the brig's masthead, and through the glass Galbraith had glimpsed Turnbull himself, aft with one of the lieutenants. He had raised his hat to *Unrivalled*, and he had been smiling.

Galbraith had turned to comment but had heard Adam Bolitho say, "I'll see you damned for this."

They had not been alone together again, until now.

Adam said, "How goes it, Leigh? I can see from here that the jury-rig is raised and working. And the surgeon tells me that the wounded are settled in. Are we ready?"

"One hour, sir. The wind is holding and steady. I've told Rist to remain with the prize. He's doing well."

Adam leaned back in the chair and tasted the coffee which

Napier had made for him. That had been almost the worst part of his return on board. He had been only just holding on. Facing them, the captain again. And then here in the cabin, his sanctuary, Napier had taken his hand in both of his and had stammered, "I thought . . . I thought . . ." It was all he had been able to say. Even Yovell, who rarely revealed emotion, as if it was something too private to share, had said, "What you did was pure courage." He had paused, perhaps to measure how much more Adam could take. "But if another had done as much, you would have been the first to call him foolhardy and reckless."

Adam said, "You all are, Leigh." He put the cup aside; the coffee had been laced with rum.

"We will remain in company with *Seven Sisters* and the two prizes. We can't be certain of anything yet. The other slaver had six hundred on board. In a brig, how can they expect them to stay alive?"

Galbraith said, "I have put Cousens in irons, sir. I would not trust him an inch."

Adam opened a drawer and took out the bundle of notes Tyacke had given him.

He said, "The ship everyone knows about but no one has seen is named *Osiris*." He shut the pitiful gibbering from his mind. Maybe he should have had Cousens thrown into that hold. He looked at the paper with the vessel's name scrawled on it. Cousens had hardly been able to grasp the pen.

Galbraith repeated it. "*Osiris*. Strange name, sir."

Yovell's pen paused in mid-air, and he murmured, "Judge of the dead."

Adam smiled. Like a severe schoolmaster with a slightly backward pupil.

He said, "Rist discovered a few pieces of the puzzle, I did not ask how. *Osiris* is, or was, an American vessel, built around 1812 for use as a privateer."

Galbraith nodded. "Against us." He saw the captain's hand move unconsciously to his side, to the ugly, livid scar he had seen only once.

"Yes. She's big and fast, and well armed. As the war against the trade becomes fiercer and more dangerous, so the prices will rise, and the rewards will be all the greater for those successful or aggressive enough to fight it." He realized that his hand had moved to the wound. The mere reminder of it. *Anemone's* last fight against the American frigate *Unity*. When he had been cut down by a metal splinter, *as big as your thumb*, someone had told him at the time. It had never left him. The colours cut down in surrender, when he had been unable to prevent it. Afterwards, as a prisoner of war, he had escaped, only to face a court martial for the loss of *Anemone*. He saw the crippled sailor again in his mind. *The finest in the fleet.*

He glanced around the cabin. *Until you, my lass.*

He looked towards the stern windows, but *Unrivalled* had swung again to her cable. There was only the land. *Albatroz* and the wrecked schooner were temporarily hidden from view.

"Feed the hands by sections, two parties to each watch. A double tot of rum too, no matter what wringing of hands you get from Mr Tregellis."

He touched the wound again, without thinking.

"We'll man the capstans this afternoon. Make it seven bells— the light will be good for hours, God and Mr Cristie permitting!"

They both laughed. Yovell did not raise his head but gave a quiet sigh of approval. Like sand running from a glass, the strain was going. This time . . .

Then he heard Adam say, "But I'll find this *Osiris*, somehow, some day. Cousens and his breed are dangerous, but without the power behind them they are little fish." He banged his hand on the scrap of paper. "The pike in the reeds, *he's* the one we want!"

His mood changed just as swiftly. "But the Crown Agent must

decide. And our commodore will see him before any of us."

The explosion was like something thudding against *Unrivalled*'s lower bilges, only a sensation. But a ship was dying.

Adam walked to the quarter window and shaded his eyes to watch the column of black smoke rising above the middle channel, torn by the hot wind like some ragged garment, or shroud.

No ship should die like that. He thought of Hastilow, and the action which had cost him so dearly.

What price revenge now?

Foolhardy and reckless.

Like a court martial, the sword could point in either direction at the end.

10 CODE OF CONDUCT

"CAPTAIN'S comin', sir!"

Denis O'Beirne straightened his back and wiped his hands on a piece of rag. A seaman lay on the sickbay table, his naked limbs like wax in the spiralling lantern light. He could have been dead, but a faint heartbeat and the flickering eyelids said otherwise.

"Move him presently." O'Beirne looked at the bandaged stump and sighed inwardly. Another one-armed survivor to end up on a waterfront somewhere. But at least he was alive. He seemed to realise what his assistant had said and turned to see Captain Bolitho in the doorway, his body at a steep angle as *Unrivalled* leaned her shoulder into the sea, the wind strong and steady across her quarter.

"You wanted me?" He glanced around the sickbay with its bottles and swabs, its smell of suffering and death. Above all, the stronger aroma of rum. The navy's cure, to kill pain, to offer hope even when there was none. He hated this place and all like it. It was stupid, but he had long since given up fighting it.

O'Beirne took it in with practised eyes. Strain, anger perhaps. "There is someone asking to speak with you, sir. One of *Paradox's* men, her boatswain." He paused briefly to examine his hands. "He has not long, I fear."

Some last spark of resistance or disbelief; a dying declaration was not unknown among sailors. *What would I say?*

"Very well." He regarded the surgeon more closely. Outwardly he showed no sign of exhaustion, although he had been working here or aboard the prize, *Intrepido,* since the brief action had ceased. *Seven Sisters* also carried a surgeon. O'Beirne's comment, *of a sort,* said it all.

Adam followed his large figure into the darker interior of the orlop, which seemed to be full of wounded or injured men. Some lay still, recovering or quietly dying, it was impossible to tell. Others were propped up against the ship's timbers, their eyes moving, following the swaying lanterns, or just staring into the shadows. Stunned by the realisation that they had survived, and as yet only half-aware of the injuries O'Beirne's small, strong fingers had explored and dealt with. And here too was the stench of rum.

Three had died, and had been buried after dark, their second night at sea after leaving the anchorage, with the wrecked and burned-out *Paradox* a lingering reminder; each corpse was double-shotted to carry it swiftly into the depths. There were always sharks following patiently, but sailors believed the dead were safer at night.

O'Beirne murmured, "His name is Polglaze. It was grapeshot. There was nothing more I could do."

Adam gripped his arm, sensing his sadness, so rare in a man-of-war, where a surgeon often had to face sights far worse than in the height of battle.

He knelt beside the dying man who, like the others, was propped against one of the frigate's massive frames; he could hear his breathing, the rattle in his throat. He was bleeding to death.

Adam felt the steeper roll of the hull. The wind had found them, too late for this man and others like him.

"You came, zur." The eyes settled on his face, reflecting the light from the nearby lantern, and fixed on the tarnished gold lace and gilt buttons. Something he understood. Not a young man, but powerfully built, or had been. When he reached out to take Adam's hand it was unable to grasp him.

Adam said, "Polglaze. A fine Cornish name, am I right?"

The man struggled to sit up and perhaps lean forward, but the pain halted him like another piece of grape.

His grip strengthened almost imperceptibly. "St Keverne, Cap'n."

"You can't get much further south than that. A wild coast when it wants to be, eh?" He wanted to leave. He was not helping. This man who had been born not so far from Penzance was beyond aid now.

But the boatswain named Polglaze might even have smiled as he muttered, "'Tes a wild shore right enough. The Manacles claimed more'n a few vessels when I were a lad there!"

O'Beirne said softly, "I think that's time enough."

Adam half-turned, wondering which one of them he meant.

He felt the man's hard hand tighten around his, as if all his remaining strength was there, and the need which was keeping him alive.

He said quietly, "I'll be here. Be certain of it."

He listened to the uneven breathing. Wanting it to stop, to end his suffering. He had done enough; this hard, rough hand said it all. The countless leagues sailed, ropes fought and handled, sea, wind, and now this.

He could hear Tyacke's words. Bitter, scathing. *And for what?*

Polglaze said suddenly, "I wanted to tell you about *Paradox,* Cap'n. How it was, what they did. A fine little craft she was."

Adam tried not to swallow or move. Did he know what had happened in the end? The rising pall of smoke.

"It was all planned, see, the boats was put down, and some of our best men sent aboard." His voice seemed stronger. Reliving it. "Our Mr Hastilow was ready, too. He'd done it often enough, see."

He broke into a fit of coughing. A hand came from the shadows with a cloth to dab his mouth. There was blood on it when it withdrew.

Polglaze groaned and then said, "We was too far off, an' the wind too hard on 'em. I thought mebbee we should have waited 'til the others came. An' then the lieutenant orders a change of tack. I dunno why, exactly."

Adam recalled Cristie's surprise. *The wrong bearing.* And the schooner's ragged sailors, their obvious hostility. But as a company they were as one. Polglaze could not even remember the lieutenant's name. He had replaced the luckless Finlay, but he was not *one of them.* Now he never would.

Polglaze gave a great sigh. "An' then we struck. Nobody's fault, we was just obeyin' orders." He sighed again, but the grip was just as strong. "We never carried a senior officer afore, see?"

Adam bowed his head to hear other, unformed words. Turnbull must have ordered the change of tack, and the new lieutenant would obey; he did not know that coast like the others.

Polglaze was looking at him intently. "The winter'll be lettin' go in Cornwall now, I reckon?" His head fell forward and he was dead.

O'Beirne stooped to prise the fingers from Adam's hand.

"Yes, it will." Adam stood, his hair brushing a deckhead beam, the cool timber quietening him, sustaining him, although his mind was still blurred with anger and with sorrow.

He said, "Thank you for fetching me. It was something he needed to tell me, to share, in his own fashion." He knew O'Beirne's men were lurking in the shadows, ready to carry the dead boatswain to the sailmaker. *For his last voyage,* as one captain had described it.

And one day perhaps, in the tiny village of St Keverne, where the land looked out over those treacherous rocks, the Manacles, if there was still anyone who cared, the man named Polglaze would be remembered, he hoped for his courage and his loyalty.

He turned to leave, to face Galbraith's unspoken questions.

But he paused and looked down again.

You were murdered.

O'Beirne watched him go. He had not caught what the captain had just murmured, but he had seen the dark eyes in the lantern's glow, and believed he knew him well enough to guess.

He recalled the sights which had confronted him upon his visit to the slaver *Intrepido.* Spanish, but she could have been under any flag. Only a brig, yet she had carried over six hundred slaves crammed into her holds, packed so tightly that they could barely breathe. In a hold filled with women, like *Albatroz,* one had already died and others were in a terrible state, corpse and dying chained together amongst the ordure.

He signalled to his men. Sailors like the dead boatswain endured much on this godforsaken coast. They obeyed orders. He thought of Adam Bolitho's face. Sometimes it was not enough.

At nightfall, that same captain read the familiar lines from his prayer book, and they buried his fellow Cornishman with full honours.

The last voyage.

Leigh Galbraith walked to the entry port, wincing as he left the shadow of one of the awnings. Freetown was unchanged, except that it seemed even hotter, as if all the air had been sucked out of that wide harbour, up as far as the majestic Lion Mountain.

Even the excitement of their return had dimmed. He shaded his eyes and looked across at the two anchored prizes, *Intrepido* and *Albatroz,* abandoned now but for a few red uniforms, under guard to await developments. Galbraith recalled the wild cheering from some of the ships when they had come to their anchorage, the slaves being ferried ashore, laughing, sobbing, and confused. They were free. But how they would manage to return to their villages or settlements was difficult to understand, and, far worse, some would doubtless be trapped and returned to one of the barracoons along that same hostile coast to await the next ship, and another buyer.

Unrivalled had been at anchor for two days, and only the purser's crew and two working parties had been allowed ashore. *To await orders.* He heard the bell chime from forward. And that was today.

The brig *Kittiwake* had taken on stores and had departed almost immediately. Commodore Turnbull was with the Crown Agent. Galbraith had sensed the disappointment and resentment amongst *Unrivalled*'s people. Two slavers as prizes. There would have been none but for their action, anchored or not.

A courier brig had arrived, but no mail had been delivered to them. Galbraith was not expecting any, but hope was always contagious.

Adam Bolitho's friend, and his uncle's last flag captain, James Tyacke, was still at sea. In case the missing slaver attempted to return to the inlet, which seemed unlikely, or to continue with another endless patrol.

I hate this place. He wiped his face and tried to dismiss it. Better here than on half-pay in some place full of others rejected by the one life they knew. Needed. Slavery was evil. Weighed against that, their presence here was necessary, if colonies were to survive against peacetime conditions. It still did not make sense . . .

He had heard some of the older hands talking about it. A few had boasted of their liaisons with women like those they had freed only days ago. Campbell, it would be him, insisted there was nothing to touch them. *Nice bit o' black velvet to get you goin'.*"

Midshipman Cousens called, "Boat shoving off from the jetty now, sir!"

Always alert, perhaps thinking of his hoped-for promotion.

"My respects to the captain. Would you tell him?" He beckoned to a boatswain's mate. "Pipe for the guard, Creagh, then man the side."

He relented; his voice had been sharper than he intended. It was affecting him more than he had believed. Maybe it was only the heat. And all for just another official visit, this time the Crown Agent.

He thought of the captain's expression, the last time they had been here. Rear-Admiral Herrick had been his uncle's oldest friend; he had heard that several times, but when Bolitho had returned on board it was as if they had met as strangers.

The Royal Marines were already falling in by the entry port, Sergeant Everett checking the dressing, watching for any flaw in the pattern. There was none. Guard of honour or shooting down an enemy, it seemed to be one and the same to this elite corps. The seamen often joked about it; it made no difference. Captain Luxmore was also present, his face almost matching his tunic. Galbraith turned to watch for the boat. An ornate affair, almost a barge, it belonged to the governor, and was manned by seamen "borrowed" for His Excellency's convenience.

He refrained from using a telescope; the rear-admiral would know. He half-smiled. They always seemed to know such things.

He heard the captain's step on the companion ladder and said, "Clear all idlers off the upper deck, Mr Cousens." He turned and touched his hat. "Right on time, sir."

Adam glanced along the main deck. Galbraith had done well. Everything was in its place. *Ready for sea.*

Herrick would miss nothing. He had once been Richard Bolitho's first lieutenant, a lifetime ago. He wondered if he still remembered.

Galbraith said, "I spoke with the purser, sir. There *is* ginger beer in the cabin." He did not think it was the time to mention Tregillis's list of complaints after he had returned with his crew from the stores.

"Drinking water, they call it? I'd not wash a horse in it! And the salt beef! Three years in the cask—that fellow Sullivan could carve a fleet of models from it. It's like iron!"

But a purser was rarely content.

Adam watched the approaching boat. *Another senior officer. Think of it like that.* He had noticed that Cousens's signals party had already bent on a flag for Herrick, and were ready to run it to the mizzen truck as he came aboard. Herrick would decline it; he was coming as an agent of the government, not in the capacity his rank implied. A matter of courtesy then.

He saw the bowman toss his oar and replace it with his boathook. The barge was still turning, and the man almost lost his balance.

Jago was looking on. It was not hard to guess what he was thinking.

He could see Herrick's cocked hat now; he was wearing his best uniform. Then he thought of *Unrivalled,* how she must appear to Herrick, not just another frigate, surely, but as a singular ship. *Perhaps I misjudged him. Thought of my own pain rather than his.*

The boatswain's mates moistened their silver calls on their tongues, and Captain Luxmore brought his sword to the carry.

"*Pipe!*" As the calls shrilled in salute and the marine guard brought their muskets to the present, Herrick's head and shoulders appeared in the entry port.

Adam removed his hat and stepped forward. He heard a gasp of alarm and saw Herrick lose his grip on the guide-rope. He knew Herrick never made any allowance for having only one hand, but this time he had misjudged it. The guard of honour, the hard glare from the harbour, an error of timing. Or was it emotion? Could it be that?

Jago was there in a second, before even the boatswain's mates could move, seizing Herrick by the wrist, yet still managing to remove his own hat, while even the disciplined marines gaped with astonishment.

Herrick stepped on to the planking and doffed his hat. Then he looked for Jago and said, "That was nearly a very short visit. I thank you for your alertness." Then he glanced up. In the sudden confusion Cousens's assistant, Midshipman Fielding, had misunderstood his instructions. Lazily, defiantly even, the rear-admiral's flag had broken from the mizzen.

Herrick nodded, as if he had heard someone speak, and looked directly at *Unrivalled*'s captain.

The full uniform gave him a stature which had been lacking at their last meeting. There were lines about his mouth but his eyes were as blue and clear as that young lieutenant of years past.

Adam said, "You are welcome here, sir."

He saw Herrick wince as he shook his hand. The empty sleeve was a constant reminder.

They walked aft beneath the poop, and Adam was aware for the first time that the same eager and anxious aide had come aboard with him. The marine sentry snapped to attention, the screen doors were open wide, and young Napier was waiting, wearing his best jacket. And shoes.

Herrick hesitated and looked closely at the Royal Marine. "I know you! Lucas, isn't it?"

The man's eyes barely blinked beneath his leather hat.

"Yessir. Th' old *Benbow*, sir!"

"You were younger then. We all were."

It would be all over the marines' mess-deck, the barracks as they called it, within the hour. No, Herrick had not forgotten.

They walked into the great cabin, Adam sensing that Herrick was moving almost uncertainly, as if unprepared for this moment. So many ships, so many situations; he must have seen it all on his way up the ladder of promotion from his humble beginnings.

Napier said anxiously, "This is the best chair, sir."

The blue, clear eyes turned to him. "And you look after the captain, do you?"

Napier considered it, frowning slightly. "We take care of each other, sir, that is . . ."

"Well said."

But he went to the wide bench seat beneath the stern windows, and gazed out at the anchored shipping and tangle of masts and rigging. His eyes were far away; he was somewhere else.

Adam said, "We have some ginger beer, sir. From the army mess."

Herrick grimaced. "It would be." He looked past him towards the sleeping cabin. "I would relish a *drink*, however."

Adam nodded to Napier, and saw him frown once more as his shoes clicked noisily across the deck.

Herrick said, "I have read your reports with great care. The seizure of the two slavers was commendable, and a useful example of what can be achieved with the will behind it. This ship performed well, although I cannot judge if her exact position at the time was the most suitable." He looked up calmly. "For I was not there." Then he smiled. "That was an observation, not necessarily a criticism," and repeated, "I was not there."

Adam heard the shoes returning and said, "I was obeying orders."

Herrick glanced at the silver tray and the two goblets. "From the very beginning we are told, orders will be carried out at all times without question. Obey. Do your duty." He took the proferred goblet of cognac and studied it gravely. "But as we move up the ladder, we discover that there is more to it than obeying orders. There is the responsibility, the conscience, if you like. You will know that better than many, I suspect." He swallowed some of the spirit and closed his eyes. "This takes me back." He changed tack again, as if he had momentarily lost control of his thoughts. "My aide will give you all the relevant details, or as much as you and I are intended to know, but I want this to remain *between us.*"

"You have my word on it, sir."

"You see, I have always done my duty, or tried to. I never allowed myself to question the minds of those who dictated the orders. You make friends and you make enemies. A friend is everything, but he can break your heart." He did not explain. He did not need to.

"I never wanted to quit the sea, the navy, even after this . . ." He looked down at the empty sleeve with more than a suggestion of hatred. "In the end I was offered an appointment with the revenue service at Plymouth. Someone blocked the way—I'll not mention his name, but his word was accepted, and I was given this role of Crown Agent. At best a dead end, at worst a scapegoat." He shrugged. "I accept that. I have no choice. Not anymore."

Adam looked quickly at his own goblet, surprised that it was empty; he remembered nothing of it. Herrick was speaking of Valentine Keen. It explained so much. A missing link.

Herrick continued, "So personal matters can intrude, even with the wary and the righteous." He waited until Napier had refilled the goblets and the pantry door was closed.

He said quietly, "Commodore Turnbull made full use of his

time after *Paradox* was disabled—er, wrecked. He is a lucky man."

Adam waited, but there was no hint of suspicion, whatever he might voice in his private report to the Admiralty and the Foreign Office.

Herrick shifted his position and reached for his drink.

"I am all but finished here. I have seen and made enough reports to carpet Portsmouth Point. Some will be acted upon, others will be 'considered.' The fleet was cut down to a dangerous level when the last French flag was lowered. As Our Nel, and—" he hesitated "—Sir Richard proclaimed many times to deaf ears, the main need will always be for frigates. There have never been enough. Nothing has changed."

Adam watched his hand smoothing the goblet as if to seek a reason for breaking his own severe code of loyalty.

Then Herrick did look at him, his eyes very direct, calm. As if he had come to a decision, any previous doubts dispelled.

"There is to be another offensive in the Mediterranean. Very shortly. Frigates are few enough, experienced captains hard to find. You will know what I am saying, where the last offensive failed." He almost smiled. "You were there."

"Lord Rhodes?"

Herrick shook his head. "You may discount that." He leaned forward on the bench, the sun across his shoulders and epaulettes. "*Unrivalled* will be leaving for England in a day or so, after Captain Tyacke returns here." He gazed at him impassively. "You were asked for *by name*. More, I cannot say."

Adam stared around the cabin, scarcely able to believe what he had heard. England, the Mediterranean again, and there could be no doubt in his mind that Algiers was the destination. It was like turning back the calendar to last year, when men in this ship had paid dearly for Rhodes' arrogance and stupidity.

Herrick said quietly, "Slavery does not begin or end here. I fear you will be ordered back to Freetown when you are available

for duty. Small, fast vessels, and their lordships will have to pro-
vide them." He smiled again. "Eventually. I shall be leaving too,
in the courier, for Spithead. We shall say our farewells today." He
doubled his hand into a fist and added, "Take heed. Lord Rhodes
is still powerful, and he makes a bad enemy." He dragged out his
watch and opened the guard with some difficulty; his wrist seemed
to be troubling him after his near accident at the entry port.

Adam waited, and imagined the aide loitering and bobbing
beyond the screen door. He was leaving Freetown, and returning
to something familiar, which he had trained himself to accept.
But he had known Thomas Herrick long enough to be sure he
had not come out to the ship merely to wish him well. Perhaps
Unrivalled was the only venue where he felt safe. At liberty to
speak.

Herrick said, "You're like him in many ways, you know. Head-
strong, reckless . . . he was often like that." He stood up and
looked for his hat.

Then he turned and stood beneath the sealed skylight, his face
suddenly determined.

"In your report you wrote of the barque *Osiris.* We lost her
this time, but in the end we shall meet up with her again. And
there'll be others like her, while the pickings get richer." He
looked slowly around the cabin, like someone who did not expect
to see it again.

"I wronged Lady Somervell. I have tried to make good my
ignorance, but I wronged her nonetheless. She was very dear to
your uncle, and now I can understand why." He added with sudden bitterness, "Now that it's too late!"

Adam faced him by the desk. "Tell me."

"*Osiris* is a slaver, and she wears Spanish colours." He glanced
at the screen door where a marine he had once known stood at
yet another post. "But she plies her trade for a company in the
City of London. Baron Sillitoe is the force behind it." He

clenched his fist again. "His father built his empire on slaves, did you know that?"

There were shouts from on deck; another boat was coming alongside.

Adam could hardly believe what he had heard. Sillitoe, feared, respected, influential, a confidante of the Prince Regent, and his Inspector-General until recently. And Catherine had nobody else to protect her when she most needed it.

He said, "Thank you for telling me, sir. I will never forget."

Herrick examined his hat, as if he was glad he had unburdened himself.

"I wanted to tell you when we first met in this damnable hole!" He smiled, and it made him look incredibly sad. "Duty, remember?"

They left the cabin together, Napier wearing an expression of surprise, Herrick's lieutenant of relief.

As they passed the wardroom Herrick stopped, and saw Yovell stepping aside to lose himself in shadows.

He did not offer his hand, but said, "So you could not leave it either, eh? I wish you well."

Yovell watched them walk forward, towards the sunshine beyond the poop. The grey-haired rear-admiral, with one shoulder stooped against the constant pain, and *Unrivalled*'s captain, *like a young colt,* Richard Bolitho had often said. So unlike one another, but the bond was there.

"God mind *you,*" he said quietly. *"But keep up your bright swords."* He shook his head. The coxswain was right, he was getting past it.

Herrick stood by the entry port as the governor's gilded barge was manoeuvred alongside. He saw Partridge with some of his seamen trying to conceal a boatswain's chair, in case he was unable to make the descent unaided.

He shook his head. "But thank you." He turned and looked

up once more at the listless flag at the mizzen, then at the waiting officers and midshipmen, the scarlet-coated marines. No detail escaped him.

He held out his hand and said, "Short and sweet, how every flag officer's visit should be. Take good care, Adam. I shall think of you. And heed what I said. There are many enemies in our work. Not least is envy!"

He doffed his hat abruptly to the quarterdeck and walked to the entry port, where Jago was standing, vigilant but apparently unconcerned.

Galbraith watched the barge pulling away from *Unrivalled*'s shadow and into the relentless glare.

Adam said, "Fall out guard and side party, Mr Galbraith." Their eyes met and he smiled. "Leigh."

Galbraith glanced again at the slow-moving barge. Herrick did not look back. Perhaps he dared not.

Adam said, "Come aft presently. We are to receive orders today." *When Commodore Turnbull has discovered their content.*

He followed Galbraith's gaze and added, "There goes a part of the old navy, Leigh." He touched his arm and walked aft again. "None better!"

Captain James Tyacke pushed his servant to one side and finished tying his neckcloth himself.

"Don't fuss, Roberts! I have to see the commodore, not the Almighty!"

He looked into his hanging mirror and then at Adam, who was sitting in one of the cabin chairs with a glass in his hand. "Good of you to come aboard at such short notice, Adam." He seemed to hesitate over the name, as if he were not yet used to such informality. "I met up with *Seven Sisters* on passage here and spoke to her captain." He looked at him in the mirror again. "About this and that."

Adam smiled. He had watched *Kestrel* enter harbour, working her way slowly and expertly under minimum sail to where the guard-boat loitered to mark her point to anchor.

He said, "I've received orders. To return to Plymouth." He heard the words drop into the silence; he had not yet accepted it, nor did he know his true feelings.

Tyacke nodded, buttoning his waistcoat. "So I heard. You know the navy—I expect the whole west coast knows about it by now!" He turned and regarded him thoughtfully. "I expect you'll be ordered to return here. One step at a time."

Adam noticed that Tyacke no longer betrayed any discomfort or self-consciousness. *The devil with half a face,* the slavers had called him when he had come to this station, and had welcomed its solitude. He had said more than once of Sir Richard Bolitho, *he gave me back my self-respect, and whatever dignity I still possess.* People still stared at the melted skin, his legacy from the Nile, young midshipmen dropped their eyes; others showed pity, the one thing Tyacke despised.

Adam had told him about *Osiris,* and what he had learned about her. Tyacke was like steel, and would never indulge in gossip, especially if it concerned, no matter how remotely, the reputation of Catherine, Lady Somervell.

While Adam sipped some wine Tyacke had shaved himself, waving his harassed servant aside with the razor. "If I can't shave my own face, I'm ready to go over the side!"

A difficult captain to serve, but he had the feeling that they thrived on it.

"All a long time ago, Adam. When it was fair and respectable to grow rich on slavery. Now, as controls grow even stronger, the price goes up, but it's still the same market." The eyes held his steadily. "I heard about Sillitoe's father—he made his fortune out of it. He's long dead, but the profits live on." He walked to the stern windows and back, his burned face in shadow, so that it was possible to glimpse the man who had been cut down that day, and had lost the girl he loved because of it. Now she wanted him back, and Tyacke had seen her, in the house she had shared with her late husband and the two children of her marriage.

All Tyacke had said was, "Never go back. Ships, places, people, they're never the same as you chose to remember."

Adam said, "What about *you*, James?"

"I'm content on this station. Probably the only one who is!" It seemed to amuse him. "But the work wants doing, and it needs men who care enough to do it without thinking all the while of prize-money and slave bounty." Then he took Adam's hand and said, "You're still finding your way, and the navy is going to be hard put to find good captains at the rate things are moving . . . I wish you luck, Adam. We both share the memory of the finest man who ever lived." His eyes hardened. "And I'll not stand by and allow others to defame his lady!"

He held out his arms and allowed the servant to help him into his coat.

"Take care, Adam, and watch your back." He shouted, *"Enter!"*

The screen door opened instantly; it was Fairbrother, the captain's coxswain.

"Unrivalled's gig is alongside, sir."

"Very well, Eli, we shall be up in a moment."

Adam grinned. The story had gone around the squadron when Tyacke had chosen his new coxswain. "Fairbrother? What sort of a name would *that* be in half a gale, man?" So it was left at Eli. Adam wondered how John Allday had got along with him, in the flagship together.

Raven, the first lieutenant, was waiting with the side party. He shook hands too, as if they were old friends. As it should be, in frigates.

Adam looked over to his own ship, and another prize which *Kestrel* had brought in with her. A small schooner or, as Tyacke had described the capture, "Just a rabbit sneaking out when it believed all the foxes had gone elsewhere." The rabbit had carried a hundred slaves nevertheless.

As the gig pulled slowly amongst the anchored shipping, Adam sat with one hand on the sun-heated thwart, and tried to assemble the events and his reactions into some sensible pattern.

The orders were precise but suitably vague. Four months since they had left Penzance, with a long commission the only likely outcome.

They would be home in the spring. Like the words of *Paradox*'s dying boatswain . . . But he recalled Tyacke's flat statement. *Never go back . . . they're never the same as you chose to remember.*

Jago saw his sun-browned hand grip the edge of the thwart and wondered what was going through his mind. *The captain, who had everything.* He watched a boat pulling across the channel, and scowled.

Back to some other squadron with another admiral who probably didn't recognise his backside from his elbow. *Officers.*

Adam was aware of the scrutiny, but was glad of it. Something honest, even if you were never quite sure what he might come out with.

What might be waiting this time? He allowed his mind to explore it. Falmouth, perhaps. The empty house. More memories.

Perhaps there would be a letter waiting for him. He touched the locket beneath his damp shirt.

He said, "What d'you think about our returning to Plymouth?" As Tyacke had remarked, the news was all over the station.

Jago kept his eyes on the water ahead of the gig's raked stem.

"So long as I've got 'baccy in my pouch, an' a wet when I needs one," he gave the smallest hint of a grin, "an' a few coins to jangle in the right direction, then I'm not too bothered, sir!"

Adam saw the stroke oarsman contain a smile. *We are all deluding ourselves.*

"Bows!"

He glanced up at the ship's curved tumblehome, the faces at the entry port.

Lieutenant Varlo met him with the side party, and he recalled that Galbraith was ashore to offer support to the purser.

He looked at the masthead. A fair breeze, but the air was like an opened oven. Would it last?

Varlo said, "Some mail came aboard, sir." His face was full of questions. "Official, for the most part."

Adam walked aft, seeing their expressions, hope, expectation, anxiety. The sailor's lot.

He strode into his cabin and tossed his hat on to the chair Napier had offered to Herrick. *The chair.* He smiled a little. Sparse, for the captain who had everything.

He heard a quiet cough and saw Yovell waiting by the pantry door.

"Well, I expect you know all about it, but . . ." He stopped, his troubled mind suddenly alert. "What is it?"

Galbraith would leave everything in order, and Varlo had said nothing. He asked again, "Something troubles you. Tell me."

It was unusual to find Yovell so hesitant, unsure of himself.

"There was a letter, sir. Some people might say it was not important, that it was not our concern . . ."

Adam sat down, slowly, to give Yovell time to compose himself.

He said, "If it concerns you, or anyone in my ship, then it matters. To me."

Yovell removed his spectacles and polished them on his coat.

"The letter was for your servant. The boy, Napier, sir. From his mother. He asked me to read it."

Adam said, "But he reads well . . ."

"He was too distressed to read anything after that, sir."

"She's getting married again."

Yovell cleared his throat. "*Is* married again, sir. They are going to America—her husband has work offered there."

It was not uncommon. Boys signed on for the fleet or some particular ship, but always with a link to sustain them. Then a new marriage, and the new husband or "friend" would consider the youth in question to be so much inconvenience, a burden.

Adam was on his feet without knowing it. It had been right here when Herrick had asked him the question, and Napier, in his own serious fashion, had replied without hesitation, "We take care of each other, sir." And the same boy, with a jagged teak splinter spearing his leg, concerned only with helping his captain.

Yovell went to the door and brought Napier right aft to the stern windows. He saw Napier's chin go up, with defiance, or a determination not to give in; he might even regard Yovell's behaviour as some sort of betrayal. It only made him appear younger. Defenceless.

Adam said, "We'll not talk on this, David. But I *know*. We weigh anchor during the morning watch, so I shall want to be up and about early."

He saw the boy nod, not understanding.

"*Unrivalled* will be in Plymouth in June, earlier with fair winds. Think of that."

Napier stared at the deck; he had even forgotten to remove the offending shoes.

"I know, sir."

Adam did not look at Yovell. He dared not, but put his hands on Napier's slight shoulders and said, "After that, my lad, you are coming home. With me." He swung away and added abruptly, "Some cognac for myself and Mr Yovell. I have some letters to dictate."

The boy paused by the pantry and looked back. It was enough.

Yovell said gently, "We have no letters, sir."

It was a day he would never forget.

11 HOME FROM THE SEA

ADAM BOLITHO winced as his elbow slipped from the window rest and he was tossed against the carriage side. He was astonished that he could have fallen asleep, when every bone in his body ached from the lurching motion. The roads were dry, the ruts left by the last rainfall iron-hard, a match for even an expert driver like Young Matthew. He looked out at the passing countryside, the contrasting greens, the rugged stone walls, which were so familiar. And so alien.

It was hard to recall *Unrivalled*'s return to Plymouth, or even set each event in its true order.

Plymouth, in contrast to their last departure, was no longer full of ships laid up in ordinary, or stripped and forlorn, awaiting the ignominy of being hulked or broken up. It was alive with men-of-war, from towering liners to seventy-fours, and support craft of every shape and size. But not many frigates, he noticed. Not a full fleet, but it soon would be, from what he had been told.

He glanced at Yovell, sitting opposite him, filling both seats and fast asleep despite the sickening motion, gold spectacles still on the top of his head.

Yovell had the gift of acceptance. He had been neither surprised nor excited by the prospect of their return. As if it was ordained.

He heard the boy Napier's voice above the clatter of wheels and harness, and the steady thud of hooves on the narrow road. He had wondered about the impulse, if that was what it had been, which had compelled him to tell Napier he was coming with him to Falmouth. Not any longer. He could hear Young Matthew, the

Bolitho coachman, answering his many questions, laughing at some of them, but enjoying his new companion.

Young Matthew: even that was part of the story which went with the old grey house. His grandfather had been Old Matthew, the head coachman for many years. The boy's father had been lost at sea in one of the famous Falmouth packet ships, so it had seemed only natural that the name should remain, even though he must be over forty by now.

Strange that they should have sighted a homeward-bound packet while they had been beating up the Channel to Plymouth. Long enough to close with the other vessel, and pass a message to her master.

Ferguson would have seen to the rest. Young Matthew had been in Plymouth waiting for him when he had left *Unrivalled*. For ten days . . . He had never been absent from his ship for any such length of time. He had wanted it more than he had realised. Needed it. But his other self had forcibly opposed it.

He thought now of Vice-Admiral Keen. When you were at sea only the ship mattered; it had to be so, for any captain. You tended to believe that everything else would remain the same in your absence, like a familiar landfall, or the face of a friend.

He had realised what was happening as soon as he had gone ashore to make his report to the Flag Officer, Plymouth, at the magnificent Boscawen House, with its sweeping views of sea and coastline.

Furniture "all anyhow," as Jago would put it, packing cases and bustling servants, Keen's flag lieutenant with what appeared an armful of lists. He seemed barely able to remember that *Unrivalled* had anchored that morning; he had had more important matters to deal with, and a new flag officer was arriving the following day.

Keen accepted it. He was appointed to the Nore, the Medway, and a whole new dockyard with facilities for the next generation of ships, and men. It was important, and he had the knowledge that his immediate future was secure. He might even rise to the rank of admiral. It did not seem possible; physically he had changed hardly at all, and only once did an inner disappointment reveal itself.

"Each command their lordships pass my way takes me further and further from the sea. In many ways I envy you, Adam. You'll never know how much."

His wife Gilia had been there too, and had added her insistence to Keen's on the subject of taking leave from duty while there was still time.

Keen had said, "You've been at sea almost continuously for years! The longest time you had ashore was when you were a prisoner of the Yankees, and even they couldn't hold you!"

And there was the child. Only a month old, squawking in the arms of a nurse and barely larger than a woollen glove, he had thought.

They had named her Geraldine, after Keen's mother.

When Keen had been called away to deal with something which one of his staff found beyond his abilities, Gilia had spoken with the same candour and sincerity as when Adam had confessed his love for Zenoria.

"He loves the child, of course, Adam." She had rested one hand on his sleeve, like that other time. "But it's the navy. He wants a boy, to carry on the tradition he began."

Adam knew Keen's father had done everything within his power to persuade his son to quit the service, and take up more important work in the City, like himself, or even in the Honourable East India Company.

Then she had said, "I shall miss this place. So many memories. But, as Val is constantly pointing out, I've travelled with my father almost as much as any sailor!"

Yovell said, "We're slowing down." He put his head on one

side. Like a wise owl, Adam thought. "Stopping, in fact."

He was suddenly alert, the dreams and uncertainties scattered. It had been a long, long drive, with halts from time to time for the horses to rest and water, all of fifty miles or so from the Tamar to this place, on a road somewhere in Cornwall. For much of it they had been out of sight of the Channel: hills, fields, pastures and men working in the sunshine, hardly glancing at the smart carriage with the Bolitho crest on each door, well coated with the dust of travel. They had stopped for a meal at an inn at St Austell, and more notice had been taken of them there. They were an oddly assorted group, he supposed, a sea officer and a large, benevolent figure who might have been almost anything. And the boy, proud, and showing it, of his new single-breasted blue jacket with its gilt buttons, which Adam had obtained from the tailor he occasionally used in Plymouth.

So many memories. He thought of Gilia again and smiled. Like Galbraith's repeated assurances that he would keep good charge of the ship while his captain was away, and the surprise which even he had been unable to conceal when Adam had responded, "It is *my* behaviour I care about, not yours, Leigh."

The carriage quivered to a halt, the leathers creaking in time with the horses stamping on the hard ground. They knew better than anyone; they would be in their stables within the hour.

He heard someone jump down and knew it was Napier. Perhaps his confidence was running out. *Like mine.*

So young, and yet so adult in many ways. At the inn at St Austell, when some old man, probably a farmer, had scoffed, "Bit young for a King's man, bain't 'ee? Lucky th' war's over, I say!"

Adam had turned from speaking with the landlord, ready to intervene, but had said nothing.

Napier had bent over and unhurriedly pulled up the leg of his new white trousers. In the filtered sunshine the jagged wound left by the splinter had been stark and horrific.

He had answered simply, "Not too young for this, sir."

The door opened and Napier resumed his seat beside Yovell, who had made room for him.

He looked at Adam and asked naïvely, "Almost there, sir?"

Adam pointed at a slate wall which was turning to follow the narrow track, downward now, all the way to the sea.

He said, "Hanger Lane, they call this, David. In the old days you were mad to walk here alone without one on your belt." He recalled the ragged corpses hanging in irons by the roadside when they had skirted the moor. It was not very different today.

Yovell readjusted his spectacles. "After six hours in this seat, I feel as if I've been round the Horn!"

It was a casual comment, to break some indefinable atmosphere. He was not certain if this youthful man, who seemed to have been born to his captain's uniform, was suffering some last-minute misgivings.

Napier said quietly, "You said we'd be back in England by June, sir." He glanced up at Yovell. "We were faster than that!"

Yovell saw Adam clench a fist against the worn leather.

It was the first of June, 1816. It would be his birthday next week; he had heard Sir Richard speak of it on several occasions.

Adam was thinking of *Unrivalled* lying at anchor. She was in good hands. He had heard Galbraith mention the risk of men deserting, and Cristie's gruff response. "We'll not lose a soul, sir, which is a pity in a few cases I can think of! But 'til their lordships see fit to pay them their share of prize- an' bounty-money, you can sleep safe on it!"

And he thought of Luke Jago. What would he do? Who did he care about, if anyone?

And his characteristic answer when Adam had suggested he spend some time at the house in Falmouth.

"Not for me, sir! A few wets ashore an' mebbee a lass when I feels like it, that'll do me fairly!" He had laughed at the idea.

And yet . . . Adam shook himself and leaned out of the window. The smell of the land, but above it the sea was there. Waiting.

"Drive on, Young Matthew! Before I change my mind!"

Young Matthew peered down at him, his face like a polished red apple beneath his hat.

"Then us'd be real sorry, zur!" He flicked the reins and clicked his tongue. The carriage rolled forward.

Adam leaned back in his seat and looked at Napier. Was that it? Was he trying to emulate his uncle's "little crew"? Jago another John Allday, and this grave-eyed youngster perhaps as he had once been himself.

The sound of the wheels changed, and he looked out as the carriage rattled past a pair of cottages.

Two women were talking by a gate, and he saw them point, then wave. Smiling as if they knew him.

He raised his hand in greeting and felt Yovell watching him.

The crest on the carriage door would tell them. A Bolitho was back.

Coming home.

Bryan Ferguson shaded his eyes and looked across the stable yard, where a few of the estate workers had gathered to watch Young Matthew giving another riding lesson to his new friend. The boy Napier sat upright on the back of the pony, Jupiter, face determined, and still unable to believe he was here. Barefooted and stripped to the waist, he already wore some bandages to mark his progress, and his falls in the stable yard. Young Matthew had remembered his grandfather's golden rule, that to ride a horse you must first know how to sit properly. No stirrups or saddle, not even reins at this stage. Young Matthew guided the pony with a halter, giving an occasional hint or instruction, letting the boy learn for himself.

Ferguson thought of his wife Grace; there was no friendlier

person alive, but as the Bolitho housekeeper she regarded all new-comers with suspicion until proved otherwise. It had taken only one day with Napier, after his first fall, when he had cut his knee on the cobbles.

She had come down to Ferguson in his estate office, unable to contain her tears.

"You should see that poor lad's leg, Bryan! He's lucky he didn't lose it! How could they let boys take such risks, war or no war!" She had relented immediately and had touched his pinned-up sleeve, his own reminder of action at sea. "Forgive me. God's been so good to us."

He turned away now from the sunlight and looked at his old-est friend, John Allday. Captain Adam had been back from sea for three days, and the time seemed to be running out like sand from an hourglass.

This was Allday's first visit, and Ferguson knew he was trou-bled by it, perhaps even relieved that Adam Bolitho had been away from home for most of the day.

The mug he always kept for his friend was grasped in his big hands like a thimble. His "wet," which they always shared on these occasions, had barely been touched. A bad sign.

Allday was saying, "Couldn't get away earlier, Bryan—lot going on at the Old Hyperion. Two new rooms being built—you know how it is."

Yes, Ferguson knew. With the new road and a carriage toll, business at the inn would be improving. He thought of Allday's pretty little wife, Unis, and was glad for him. She had done well for both of them, and for her brother, "the other John," as she called him, who had done more than anyone else to help her when Allday had been at sea. Her brother had only one leg, a legacy of his service in the Thirty-First Foot, when he had been wounded on the bloody field of battle.

"I thought Dan'l Yovell might be here too?" Allday looked around as if he expected to see him.

"Gone to see somebody, John." Keeping away, was the truer reason. Ten days, Captain Adam had said. And even that might be cut if some damned messenger came galloping up to the house with an instant recall to duty.

He heard a great chorus of laughter, then cheering, and looked at the yard again. Napier had nearly lost his seat, but was even now releasing the pony's shaggy mane, upright again, his face all smiles, something he sensed was rare, especially for one so young.

They were all busy, making each day count in its own way. Lady Roxby had apparently persuaded Captain Adam to sit for a portrait, to hang eventually with all the others in the old house. Ferguson closed it from his mind. One he might never see, something all sailors must consider.

He turned to his friend once more. Allday had none of it, the old dog who had lost his master. He did not belong. Unis, their little daughter Kate, the inn, and a life now unshadowed by the prospect of separation and danger . . . they were a part of something else. Even his trips into Falmouth to watch the ships anchoring and departing were fewer. Nor could he bear to mingle with all the loud-mouthed veterans you found in every tavern and ale house. At least the village of Fallowfield, where The Old Hyperion remained the only inn, was usually free of sailors. And with the press-gangs only an evil memory, no King's men ever reached that far.

"Grace'll fetch some food presently." He sat down opposite. The big, heavy hands were unchanged; they could wield a cutlass or create the most delicate of ship models, like the one of the old seventy-four *Hyperion* which occupied a place of honour in the inn parlour.

A strong man yet, although Ferguson knew better than

most how Allday still suffered from the terrible wound in his chest. A Spanish blade, and the story had it that Sir Richard had thrown down his own sword in surrender in order to bargain for Allday's life.

Allday said, "I ain't sure, Bryan. I'll be wanted over at Fallowfield."

Ferguson picked up his own mug and studied the contents. The wrong word or some false sentiment, and his old friend would get up and leave. He knew him that well.

He thought about it often, how unlikely it would sound in the telling. How he and this big, shambling sailorman had been seized by the press-gang here in Falmouth, or very close to it. And their captain had been Richard Bolitho, and the ship his frigate *Phalarope.*

After the Battle of the Saintes when he had lost his arm, Ferguson had been nursed back to health by Grace, and had risen to become steward of the estate. Allday had gone one better. He had become Bolitho's coxswain. And his friend, his oak.

Ferguson made up his mind.

"Stay here until the captain gets back. He wanted to see you before, but the roads were awash and he had to leave for his ship. You should know that, better than anyone."

Allday swirled the rum around in his mug. "What's he like, then? Full of himself now that he's captain of a new frigate, his deeds argued about when the ale flows? Is that it?"

"You know him better than those lamp-swingers, John. People will always compare him with his uncle, but that's stupid and unfair. He's still learning, and would be the first to say so, I'd not wonder! But he's his own man now." He broke off as there were more cheers from the yard. The lesson was over, and Young Matthew was grinning hugely, one arm around the boy's shoulders.

Allday said, "When Sir Richard was his age we'd just taken over the *Tempest.* Thirty-six guns, an' smart as paint, she was . . ."

His blue eyes were far away. "That was when he took fever. Nearly died, he did." He jerked his shaggy head towards the window. "Used to make me take him up the cliff walk, every single day. Then we'd sit on that old bench up there. Watch the ships. Yarn about the ones we knew."

Ferguson almost held his breath. *Like you do now, old friend.*

"We had some good times in *Tempest*. Bad 'uns, too. Mr Herrick was the first lieutenant, I remember. Went by the book, even in them days."

He stood up, and paused as if to get his bearings, and Ferguson knew it was to prepare himself for the pain, should it be lurking to bring him down. He had been lifting a cask of ale over at Fallowfield once, and he had heard him cry out and fall. Had it been anyone else he might have been able to accept it.

Allday said, "That boy down there—"

"Napier, the captain's servant."

"An' he brought him *here*, with him?"

"He has nowhere else, you see."

"So I heard." Allday frowned. "His mother cut the strings."

Ferguson stared at the stable roof, with its Father Tyme weather vane. How many Bolithos had that seen? And time it gave him, to think, and consider what Allday had said. He must have asked about Captain Adam's servant, and probably Yovell as well, although *he* could well take care of himself, Bible or not. Allday was feeling his way. Afraid of being outgunned, as he would put it.

He said quietly, "Captain Adam has nobody now, John."

Allday turned and walked heavily to the table. "I seed the roses when I got here. A fine show of 'em this year." He looked at his friend, searching for something. "I used to talk with Lady Catherine about them."

He nodded slowly. "I would like to stay, Bryan. Was it roast duck, you said?"

"Did I?" And smiled. "I'll tell Grace. It'll be the making of her, old friend!"

Allday put down his mug; it was empty.

"Needed that, Bryan." The grin was returning. "An' that's no error!"

Horse and rider paused, silhouetted at the top of the hill where the narrow road divided into separate lanes.

Adam released the reins and patted the horse's flank.

"Easy, Lukey, *easy* now."

The horse stamped on the hard-packed ground, shaking its head as if to show disapproval, impatience perhaps, at being held to such a slow, meandering pace.

Adam eased his body in the saddle, surprised that such a short ride along the winding track from Falmouth could make itself felt. Every muscle seemed to throb; the close confines of a frigate had taken their toll.

He stared at the sprawling house at the far end of the second lane, framed by trees, with the glint of water proving that Carrick Roads and the sea were ever close.

The Old Glebe House, they called it. Once owned and occupied by high churchmen from Truro, it had fallen into disrepair after a fire had broken out in the small chapel adjoining it. Derelict for years, a birthplace for rumours and tales of ghosts and evil spirits which found a ready audience in these parts, it was said to have been used by smugglers, the Brotherhood, when it suited them.

The church authorities had agreed to sell the place, although most local people had considered any prospective buyer either mad or eager for ruin. The eventual owner proved to be neither. Sir Gregory Montagu, one of the country's most distinguished painters, had bought it, repaired and refurbished it, but had left the gutted chapel untouched.

Montagu rarely mixed socially, and was said to spend much of his time in London where his work was always in demand. Eccentric, and reputedly a recluse, he was certainly different, Adam thought. He had heard the story of Montagu as a young, half-starved artist who had scraped a living from selling small paintings in the form of silhouette or profile which could be used as miniatures, gifts from departing sea officers to their loved ones. There were many such artists working around the various naval ports, but Montagu, who had rented a tiny attic on Portsmouth Point, had attracted the eye of an admiral, a man of taste as well as charity. For reasons buried in time, the admiral had sponsored Montagu, and allowed him to accompany his squadron to the Mediterranean where he had paid for professional tuition by a notable painter in Rome.

Nancy's influence, or the great Montagu's curiosity, had brought Adam here. An honour? To take his place with all those other proud portraits, or just to please his aunt, who had done so much for him? He hated the prospect, and had even toyed with the idea of turning back at the first crossroads to the village of Penryn. Years of inbuilt discipline had prevented it.

Adam disliked being late, just as he had little sympathy with those who kept him waiting. In the navy you soon learned that *presently* meant *immediately*.

He nudged the horse forward again.

"Come along, Lukey. They may have made other arrangements."

They had not.

Even as the horse clattered across loose cobbles, and the house's tall shadow closed around him like a cool breeze, a stable boy and a dour-faced servant who might easily have been a priest himself appeared at the main entrance.

He climbed down and patted the horse.

"Take care of him, will you? I may not be long."

The servant eyed him sadly. "Sir Gregory is expecting you. It *is* Captain Bolitho?"

The implication was that Sir Gregory alone would decide how long he would be.

Inside, it seemed very still, and the high, arched windows would not have been out of place in a church. Well-polished furniture, dark and probably very old, and plain, flagged floors added to the atmosphere of spartan tranquillity.

The servant cast his eyes over Adam's appearance. In the filtered sunlight the dust on the blue coat and gold lace must be very evident.

"I will inform Sir Gregory." The slightest hesitation. "Sir."

Alone again, he recalled Nancy's enthusiasm as she had told him about the appointment with the great man. She had taken his elbow and guided him to the wall where the portrait of Captain James Bolitho caught the reflected sunlight from one of the upper windows, and had turned him so he could catch the precise angle of the light across the painting. Captain James, her father, had lost an arm in India, and when he had returned from sea it had been Montagu who had been called in to paint the empty sleeve over the original work. He had also painted the portrait of Richard Bolitho, in the white-lapelled coat of a post-captain which Adam heard had been Cheney's favourite. It still hung with hers in the main bedroom. Catherine's self-commissioned portrait was with them. They were at peace there.

"Ah, Captain Bolitho, at last. A great pleasure!"

He did not walk in, nor did he suddenly appear. He was *there*.

Adam was not sure what he had been expecting. Montagu was not tall or imposing, yet he dominated the place with his presence. Very erect, square-shouldered like a military man, but wrapped up in a paint-smeared smock which looked as if it had not been washed for years. There was dried paint in his hard handshake, and his thick white hair was tied back with a piece of rag like any common seaman.

But his eyes revealed the real Montagu. Alert, restless one second and then fastening on to some feature with the intensity of a hawk.

He said abruptly, "I'll make a few sketches. You can sit and talk while I'm thinking on it. Or you can hold your peace and enjoy some reasonable hock, which might slake your thirst after a hard ride."

Adam brushed some dust from his sleeve to give himself time. *A hard ride.* To put him at ease? Or was it sarcasm? Montagu would know very well that it was only three miles from Pendennis.

They walked together along a high-ceilinged corridor. There were, Adam observed, no pictures of any sort on display. And all the while he could feel the other man studying him, although he was looking directly ahead.

He said, "I understand that you recently painted the Prince Regent, Sir Gregory?" Nancy had told him. It had not helped.

"Yes, that's true." He gave a quiet laugh. "But another man wearing his garments for most of the time. He was 'too busy,' they said." Then he did turn to look at him. "I know you do not wish to be here. Neither, as it happens, do I. But we are both good at our work, and for that reason if nothing else, it will qualify."

There were voices, unreal and echoing, like an empty vault. Montagu said sharply, "My protégés. We shall take another route. A barn of a place, but it suits."

The gaunt servant had reappeared, by magic, it seemed. He had a finger to his lips.

"Sir Gregory, your nephew—"

Montagu said curtly, "We'll slip past them. He must get used to interruptions if he hopes to line his purse!"

He opened another tall door and entered what appeared to be

one huge room. It was hung with sheets and there were trestles, a bench of clean brushes, beyond which another figure in a paint-daubed smock stood stockstill, one arm out-thrust as if he was painting some invisible canvas.

The room had a glass roof, with rolling shades to contain or deflect the bright sunlight.

Montagu said, "This way."

Adam did not move. He could not.

Sitting on the floor directly opposite him, with one leg bent under her, was a girl. She was so still that for a second longer he imagined it was a work of beautiful statuary. Then her eyes moved, seeing him, accepting, dismissing him. Her gaze returned to the motionless, out-thrust arm of the painter. She was naked but for some sort of robe which had fallen across her thighs while her arms were pulled above her head, fastened by a chain around her wrists.

Montagu paused. "Do not overwork her, Joseph." He lifted part of a sheet to shield the girl's shoulders, with the casual disinterest of a housekeeper covering an unwanted chair.

They walked past another screen and into an adjoining room. Over his shoulder Montagu said, "Imagination as well as skill—something you will doubtless appreciate, Captain Bolitho?"

Adam looked back at the closed door. As if it had never happened. But he could still see her, her body poised, motionless in the unwavering light.

"What were they doing?"

Montagu gestured to a solitary chair. "Doing?" He smiled. "Soon it will be the beautiful Andromeda, chained to a rock to be sacrificed to the sea monster, before she is rescued by her lover Perseus. Imagination, you see?"

Adam was seated in the hard chair, one arm resting across it although he had scarcely felt Montagu move him. He attempted to adjust his neckcloth and coat but Montagu held up his pad.

"No, Captain. As you *are*. The man others see, not necessarily the one you would have him be."

Uncanny that he could ignore the restless, sometimes piercing stare, the accompanying squeak of crayon.

Someone's wife, or mistress? Who could she be? He could laugh out loud at himself, but he wanted to keep that image fixed in his mind. She was lovely and she would know it. And yet in that single moment he had seen only indifference, or was it contempt?

Montagu walked back and forth, muttering to himself, darting occasional glances at his subject. Adam tried not to move, and wondered if the chair had been chosen especially to remind each victim of its importance.

Montagu said, "Lady Roxby tells me that you are in Falmouth for only a few days." He made stabbing adjustments to his sketch. "That is a pity. I understand that you have seen a great deal of time and action at sea of late?" He did not wait for or expect a reply. "I shall require you here again, of course."

Surprised again, Adam found himself nodding. "I will do what I can."

"A fine woman, Lady Roxby. I never truly understood how she came to enjoy her life with Sir Lewis." The quiet chuckle again. "The King of Cornwall. But they succeeded when many do not." He gazed at him for several seconds and said, "Your sword. *The* sword. I am surprised that you came without it. I need it, you see. Part of the legend. The charisma."

There was no scorn or sarcasm. He heard himself say, "I still find it difficult to wear without misgivings, Sir Gregory."

The crayon hesitated in mid-air. "That does you credit, Captain." He inclined his head graciously, as if to confirm it. "I knew your late uncle, of course. Very like you in some ways, especially when it came to sitting for a mere painter! Restless, always searching for excuses to leave." He turned his pad to the light. "It is coming." He stared at Adam again. "It's there, right enough. The same look, and yet . . ." He swung round as the servant peered around the door.

"What *is* it? You know I will not be interrupted!" Just as quickly the mood changed and he winked at Adam. "Not exactly what I told my nephew, is it?"

Adam realised for the first time that Montagu had a short, pointed beard, which had been concealed by the untidy smock. It was not hard to imagine him one of the King's cavaliers. What age was he? Seventy, or more?

He was ageless.

Montagu swung away from the door. "My nephew is about to leave. I must just speak with him. He will not like what I am about to tell him, but he will listen, and he *will learn.*" He tossed back his smock, the cavalier and his cloak.

In his absence Adam looked around the littered room. Empty canvases, a half-finished painting of sea birds circling a ruined belfry, the chapel he had seen when he had approached the house. How long ago was that? Even the filtered sunlight should have told him. He had been here for over an hour.

How had it happened? Was it Montagu's restless energy, his ability to switch moods and subjects with the ease of creating different images in his mind? He had not thought of *Unrivalled* once during this time. Not of Turnbull, nor of Herrick, nor even of the array of shipping at Plymouth. The smell of action. This was another world. He thought of the girl again, her arms pinioned above her head, her breasts full and taut. Montagu saw beyond the sheets and the untidy trestles. It was or soon would be a great rock, where the beautiful Andromeda waited, chained and helpless, a sacrifice to the monster. It was clear, without doubt or question. Imagination, he had said. It was far more than that.

Montagu was back, wiping his stained fingers on a rag.

"I think that will suffice, Captain. I shall work on it tonight.

I find it suits the subject." The keen eyes settled on him again. "You have been badly hurt, I think. That will come into it."

Adam smiled, surprised that the tension within himself had dissipated.

"In the navy, it is a risk we have to accept."

Montagu smiled politely. "The hurt I see goes deeper than any wound of battle." He shook his head. "But no matter, Captain, it will come to me." He gestured to the tall harp Adam had seen by an open fireplace; he had assumed it to be mere set-dressing for another painting. "Music of the gods, yes?"

Then he said, "Tomorrow, then?" Again, he did not wait for an answer. "I would not wish to interrupt your birthday celebrations, when you have so little freedom from the sea."

The adjoining room was deserted, the sheets folded untidily, the trestles waiting to be transformed into a rock for a lovely captive. The chains lay where she had been sitting. Only the sunlight had moved.

Adam heard the horse stamping outside the entrance. In seconds he would make a fool of himself, perhaps destroy the only moment of peace he had found in this old house and its strange, ageless owner.

But he heard himself say, "Please, the girl who was here, Sir Gregory . . ."

Montagu faced him again, almost like a duellist now, measuring the distance, the threat.

"She sits for me, and those I choose for their potential. She is very skilled. It is not merely the act of disrobing, posing before men with neither expertise nor scruples." He smiled, but it did not reach his eyes. "And she plays the harp to perfection."

The main doors were open, the sky was still clear; in a moment he would be out on the road again.

Montagu held out his hand. "Does that answer your question —the one you did not ask me?"

Adam saw the stable boy waiting expectantly and felt for a coin. They would doubtless laugh at him once the door had closed behind him.

"She is very beautiful." He expected the other man to interrupt, but Montagu said only, quietly, "She was badly hurt also. Do not harm her." He hesitated. "Do I have your word?"

It was hard to believe they had only just met. That he could respond without any hesitation.

"You have it, Sir Gregory."

He tried to smile, to reassure him, or perhaps for his own sake. He would never see her again, and she would remain as much a mystery as the poses of those myths of which he knew so little.

He climbed into the saddle and heard the boy call something and grin up at him. He could have put a guinea into his hand for all the notice he had taken.

He reined the horse round towards the gates and halted, hearing the harp from one of the tall windows, and imagining her as he had seen her.

Then he urged the horse out on to the road; he did not once look back. He dared not; he was afraid of destroying something.

He felt the horse pounding beneath him, as if his mood was infectious.

It made no sense, it defied all reason. He had always been made welcome in Falmouth. Nancy, Bryan Ferguson and his wife, and faces he knew only by sight on the estate or at the harbour. But he had always felt like a stranger, an intruder.

This was the first time he had ever felt he belonged.

12 TRUST

LUKE JAGO slitted his eyes against the reflected glare and gauged the gig's passage through the mass of anchored shipping. It must have been a long time since Plymouth had seen such an array of naval strength, he thought. Not a day had passed since *Unrivalled*'s return from West Africa without more vessels arriving, gathering around the flagship, *Queen Charlotte*. It was strange if you considered it. The flagship was only ten years old and carried a full armament of one hundred guns, a new vessel by naval standards. Some other well-known ships of the line had been over forty years old when they had been abandoned to the breakers, or had become melancholy hulks like those he had seen elsewhere. And yet *Queen Charlotte* was unlikely ever to stand ship-to-ship in any line of battle. They had seen the last of it.

He glanced at Lieutenant Galbraith, upright in the stern-sheets, his strong features composed. On his way to the flagship, and Jago could guess what he was thinking. The captain was still away, and Galbraith had the weight. He smiled inwardly. *Why I called away the gig. Make it look right.*

Midshipman Martyns was in charge, but Jago had to nudge his arm as a barge-like craft pulled slowly abeam, obviously looking for trade like the rest of the boats which were never far from this impressive fleet. There was a colourful canopy rigged aft, and he could see several women sitting beneath it, their gowns and painted faces leaving no doubt as to what they were preparing to barter.

Midshipman Martyns gulped and actually blushed. There was some hope for him after all, Jago decided.

His thoughts returned to the captain. He had never seen anyone so torn between taking leave of absence from his ship and remaining for everyone to see, *in command.* Others would never have hesitated, especially with a flag officer's blessing.

He had considered the captain's suggestion that he join him in Falmouth; he had laughed at the idea, but it had not gone away. He had even mentioned it to Old Blane, the carpenter, who had responded scornfully, "I always thought you was a fool, Luke, but never that much of one! I wish t' God someone'd make *me* the offer!"

And now they were on the move again. There had been no official orders, or speeches from the officers; you just knew it. The collection of ships had become a fleet. The flagship was like the hub of a great wheel, and when the word came, it would be sudden. The navy's way.

He glanced at the young midshipman's hand on the tiller bar, the watchful eyes of the stroke oarsman, as if the flagship's presence had touched each one of them. If not the big three-decker, then certainly the admiral whose flag curled only occasionally at the masthead: Lord Exmouth now, but better known and remembered as Sir Edward Pellew, who during the wars with France and Spain had become famed and respected as the navy's most successful frigate captain. The new title had been bestowed on him at the end of hostilities. Like most of Jago's contemporaries, Pellew had grown up in the navy, and wanted nothing else. He might have been expecting enforced retirement; it had happened to many officers of similar stature. Jago looked up at the towering masts and crossed yards. *Not for me.* He himself had served in a ship of the line, an old two-decker and by no means as grand as *Queen Charlotte.* He had been with her for over a year before being transferred to a frigate, and in all that time he had never ceased to meet people he had never laid eyes on before. A floating town, names you never remembered, officers who did not care to find out about any man outside his own immediate authority.

"*Boat ahoy?*"

Jago grinned and cupped his hands. "*Aye, aye!*" Just to let them know there was an officer coming aboard, *but, dear me, not a ship's captain who'd need all the proper ceremony and respect. Only a lieutenant, this time.*

He touched the midshipman's arm and murmured, "Take 'er in now."

He remembered the rear-admiral named Herrick; he would have fallen outboard but for his quick action. Strange, he thought; there were plenty of senior officers he would have happily aided over the side if he had believed he would get away with it.

Oars tossed, bowman hooked on to the chains, and the flagship's gleaming tumblehome rising above them like a cliff.

Galbraith said, "Stand off, Cox'n. I'll not be long delayed, on this occasion."

Jago touched his hat and watched him seize one of the hand-ropes and jump on to the lower "stair." As he had observed before, Galbraith was very light on his feet for so powerful a man. He was not soft or easy-going, nor did he try to be popular like some first lieutenants Jago had known.

Being close to the captain, he had got to know him better than most, or so Jago told himself. Enough, for instance, to catch the bitterness in Galbraith's tone. He knew the story, or most of it. Galbraith had had his own command. He watched the blue and white figure moving steadily up and around the curved hull, his sword slapping against his thigh. Not a big ship, just a little brig, *Vixen* she was named. *And his own.* A lot of junior officers started that way. Captain Bolitho's first command had also been a brig, and so, he heard, had been the cruelly disfigured Captain Tyacke's.

But Galbraith's promotion had stopped right there. The full story would be worth knowing.

He saw Galbraith reach the entry port and barked, "Cast off! Shove off forrard! Be ready to out oars!" The last order was for the midshipman's benefit. Martyns was daydreaming again. Staring at the flagship. His eyes saying *if only.*

Jago snorted. He could have it.

Lieutenant Leigh Galbraith paused to doff his hat to the quarterdeck and the flag, pleased if surprised that he was not out of breath after the steep climb. The deck seemed vast after *Unrivalled*; you could lay two hulls here and still have room enough to drill the marines.

A lieutenant took his name and sent a midshipman scurrying away with a message. He recalled his own brief command. It was like no other feeling. Lowly or not, you were received with honours paid, as if you were already posted. He thought about it a lot. Too much.

"Ah, Mr Galbrice!"

He turned to see a lanky lieutenant with the twist of gold lace on his shoulder that distinguished him from all other mortals. The admiral's flag lieutenant.

He corrected calmly, "*Galbraith,* sir."

"Quite. Your captain is not aboard, I understand?" It sounded like an accusation.

"Flag Officer, Plymouth, insisted he should take some days' leave of absence . . ."

The flag lieutenant shrugged. "Vice-Admiral Keen has hauled down his flag. Things are moving more quickly. I have a letter for you to take when you leave this ship. Arrange a fast courier, will you? Now, if you will follow me you may sign for your orders." He let the words sink in. "*Your* responsibility, you understand?"

He did not need to hear it from the lieutenant. Captain Bolitho was being recalled. Galbraith could not determine if he was relieved or resentful.

He followed the other officer beneath the poop. Everything was larger than life. And there was no sense of movement, as if the great ship were hard aground. He was reminded suddenly of Varlo: he had been somebody's flag lieutenant before he had joined *Unrivalled,* replacing the dead Lieutenant Massie.

Wounds healed quickly under such circumstances. It was only a short time ago, and yet he could scarcely recall what Massie had looked like, how he had sounded. The unwritten rule. His name was never mentioned, either.

He signed for the sealed orders, observed by a small, darting man who must be the clerk or secretary to someone higher. No one asked him to be seated.

The flag lieutenant said, "That seems in order, Mr, *er,* Galbraith." He looked up, startled, as a shadow fell across the door.

The newcomer was tall, well-built, and dressed in what appeared to be a towelling robe, of the kind Galbraith had seen worn by wealthy people at a local spa. His large feet were bare, and he had left wet impressions across the perfect deck covering.

He could only be the legendary admiral. Nobody else would dare.

He held out a big hand and said abruptly, "Exmouth. You're from *Unrivalled,* I believe." He smiled, easing out the lines and wrinkles. A sailor's face. "Glad to have you with me. I read the report your captain left with Valentine Keen. I found it inspiring. Could make all the difference when I am *allowed* to proceed with matters." He looked piercingly at his aide, who was open-mouthed at this casual display of informality. "A glass of something would not be unappreciated!"

Galbraith said, "I had better call my boat, my lord."

The admiral nodded gravely. "It takes some getting used to, believe me."

He waited for the flag lieutenant to scuttle away and added,

"Gunnery, that will prove and win the day. If anything will."
His eyes were distant. "All these ships at my command. But
Unrivalled is the only one which was *there*."

Galbraith felt the tension drain from his muscles. So it was
Algiers. He was surprised to discover that he was heartened by
the confirmation. The land had nothing to offer anymore.

The admiral regarded him steadily. "I shall be glad to have
Captain Bolitho in the van." His voice softened. "I knew his
uncle. Great days." He patted Galbraith's arm. "Best not to dwell
on old times, but great they were. And he was a fine man." His
eyes hardened as the lieutenant returned with some wine.

"You will stay and take a glass with me?" Again, the unexpected smile. "It is an order."

The admiral waited, the glass delicate in strong fingers. "*Yours*,
Mr Galbraith."

Galbraith presented his own glass and said quietly, "Absent
friends, my lord."

Their eyes met.

"Well said."

Later, when Galbraith waited for the gig to be signalled alongside, he thought of that encounter with the admiral. It would be
all over the flagship within the hour, about the lieutenant who
had joined Lord Exmouth for a glass of wine. Like old shipmates.

And tomorrow Captain Bolitho would receive his recall. Glad
or sorry, which would he be?

He considered his own feelings. The bitterness was gone.

The old glebe house was exactly as he remembered it: he had
thought of little else since his visit. And yet there seemed so much
more to see and hear; the hedgerows along the lane were alive
with movement, birds, and other furtive sounds of the countryside. Some jackdaws watched his approach, as if to time the exact
moment when they would all take to the air in noisy unison,

before returning after he had ridden a few yards. And wild roses. He reached down and plucked one, remembering that other time, the only time . . .

The same stable boy hurried to greet him and waited as Adam swung himself down from the saddle.

There were flowers here too, foxgloves, almost wild in the sprawling garden. A place of memories, he thought, where time had come to a halt.

The boy said, "Th' master's with a gentleman, zur." His eyes were fixed on the old sword at Adam's hip. Young though he was, he probably knew of the Bolitho family, the sailors commemorated in the church of King Charles the Martyr. Where he had stood beside Catherine at the memorial service, and Galbraith had asked to attend with him. It had been their first true moment of intimacy and understanding, not merely as captain and first lieutenant, but as men.

The dour-faced servant had arrived, and said unhelpfully, "You're a piece early, Captain. Sir Gregory's engaged at the moment."

The stable boy, anxious not to offend, and with the prospect of another coin or two glimmering in his mind, said, "I told 'n." He pointed to a walled garden. "You could look at th' bees, zur?"

Adam patted the horse's flank. He must have ridden harder than he had realised. Nervous? Anxious? *What is the matter with me?*

He had hardly touched his breakfast, and he had felt Ferguson's eyes on him as he had waited for Lukey to be brought from the stables. He had even tried to concern himself with *Unrivalled*, and what might lie ahead when the final orders were settled. He had gone to the room and looked at his uncle's portrait again. Could almost hear his voice. *Trust the professionals in your ship. You lead, they'll not let you down.*

He had heard him say that several times. *The professionals.* The warrant officers, and the time-serving men like Sullivan, the sharpest lookout he had ever known, and Partridge, the bluff, heavy-handed boatswain. And Cristie, with a lifetime's experience of currents and tides, shoals and stars. He *knew* them, and had been with them in calm and storm, broadside and the grim aftermath.

The servant took his silence for annoyance, and said almost grudgingly, "I can tell you the instant Sir Gregory is ready, sir." He shuffled away. Maybe he had been with the old house when Montagu had bought it . . .

Adam walked slowly along a winding path, and found himself listening for the sound of a harp. He tried again to shrug it off. Like a bumbling midshipman . . . But it would not release him.

He thought about this day, his birthday. Nancy would be coming to the house. There would be a few friends, Grace Ferguson would supervise the food and wine, and would probably cry a little. And perhaps John Allday would come across from Fallowfield on the Helford River. To celebrate, or to mourn? There was only one would have made it complete.

He looked up and saw her coming towards him. She was dressed from neck to toe in pale grey, a gown so fine that it seemed to float around her body. She carried an armful of yellow roses, and he noticed that her skin had been browned by the sun, that her throat was bare, and the gown had almost slipped from one shoulder.

She had stopped on this same path, her gown catching at other flowers Adam neither saw nor recognised.

Above all, he knew she was about to turn and retrace her steps. If need be, run, to avoid the inevitable contact.

His hat was in his hand although he had not moved. He bowed his head, clumsy and awkward, words sticking in his throat, afraid that when he raised his eyes she would be gone.

"I beg your pardon. I did not wish to disturb you." He dared to look at her. "I arrived too early, it seems."

He saw one hand detach itself from the flowers and rise to adjust the gown across her bare shoulder. And all the while she was looking at him. Into him, with neither smile nor recognition.

Her eyes were very dark, as he remembered them. In a single glance, but it was the same. He had not recalled her hair, other than that it was also dark, almost black in the dusty sunshine. But much longer, waist-length, perhaps more.

He said, "It was good of Sir Gregory to make the time for me. My aunt . . ."

She continued along the path but then stopped again, a few feet away.

She said, "He *wanted* to do it." She gave what might have been a shrug. "Otherwise you would not be here."

Her voice was soft, but strong, cultured, not a local girl. Assured, as she would be when composing herself for a painting. And yet, there was something else. He heard Montagu's voice. *She was badly hurt also.* What had he been trying to say?

She said, "I must leave you, Captain Bolitho." She lingered over his name, testing it as Montagu would assess the quality of a new canvas.

In a moment he would step aside, and she would not look back.

He said quietly, "I heard your harp when I left here before. I was very moved by it." Unconsciously, he gestured. "In this setting it seemed so right, so perfect. Now that I have met you I understand why."

She stared at him, defiant or angry, it was impossible to tell. She was taller than he had realised, and the gown did nothing to free his mind from that first time. The chained wrists, the painter's motionless arm, her eyes touching his for no more than a second.

But she said, "You have a way with words, Captain. With women too, I suspect. Now, if you will allow me to pass?" She looked down, startled, as two of her yellow roses fell to the ground.

He stooped to retrieve them, and saw her feet, barely covered by leather sandals, as brown as her throat and arms.

She stepped back, and almost lost her balance as her heel snared the hem of the gown.

He gripped the roses, one of the thorny stems drawing blood, but without any pain. He felt nothing. It had been her quick withdrawal which recalled it, a stark, ugly picture. The young black girl, violated, beyond anything but terror and revulsion. When he had reached out to reassure her of her safety she had responded in the same manner.

He said, "I—I am so sorry. I never meant to offend you." There were voices now, someone laughing, a horse stamping, ready to leave. It was over. It had not even begun.

Adam stepped from the path and felt her pass him, so close that the gown touched his hand.

He looked after her, and saw that her hair was as long as he had imagined. She was probably going now to adopt a pose for another artist. Disrobed, perhaps, her lovely body open to another man's stare. What did she think about? Was it a way of avenging herself for what had happened to her? To prove she was inviolable?

If he could find that stable boy he would leave now. Before . . .

He stared at her, unable to accept that she had turned back, her face no longer calm. She reached out and seized his sleeve. "Your hand! It's bleeding!" She prised the two roses from him and laid the entire bouquet on the scorched grass at her feet.

She had produced a handkerchief from somewhere and was wrapping it around his fingers as Montagu, followed by his servant, appeared in the walled garden.

"Now then, what have we here?"

Adam saw it clearly. Anxiety, suspicion; it was far deeper than either.

She said, "Roses. My fault." She looked directly at Adam and said, "I have seen many men of war, Captain. But only in portraits. I was unprepared." She knelt to recover the roses, or herself.

Montagu said, "You see, Captain, your reputation precedes you!" But he was smiling, unwilling or unable to hide his relief. "So let us begin. I've roughed out some ideas." He beamed. "Besides, we must not detain a man on his birthday!"

He turned and called something to his servant.

She stood, very upright and composed. "I did not know, Captain." She broke off a rose and attached it to the lapel of his coat. "To remember me by." Then, very deliberately, she broke the other stem and placed the rose in the bosom of her gown; his blood made a bright stain on the silk. "And I shall remember you."

He watched her walk unhurriedly along the path and out of the garden.

Montagu was waiting for him. "Come along, while the light is good."

Adam thrust his hand into his pocket. The handkerchief was still there. Not a dream.

"I'm delighted that you remembered to bring the sword. Memories, eh?"

The same room, the same unwelcoming chair.

Adam saw the canvas for the first time. An outline. A ghost.

Montagu placed the sword carefully on his bench and made a few swift sketches.

"I would not ask you to leave the sword, this sword, with me. I think, Captain, that you will need it again soon." Adam waited, his eyes on the tall harp. Montagu was giving himself time. Weighing the chances, like an experienced gun captain watching the first fall of shot.

He said suddenly, "I see that you are wearing the rose. Shall I keep it in the finished work?" So casually said. So important.

"I would be honoured, Sir Gregory. I mean it, more than ever now."

Montagu nodded slowly, and rolled up one sleeve.

"I shall tell Lowenna what you said."

He began to paint very briskly.

He had made up his mind.

Lowenna.

Adam Bolitho entered the church and closed the tall doors behind him. After the heat of the morning and his walk into Falmouth from the old house it seemed a cool haven, a refuge. He was still wondering why he had come. He felt his shirt clinging to his skin, as if he had been in haste or had some pressing reason for being here.

It was dark after the sunlight of the square, and the streets where people looked at him as he passed. Interest, curiosity or, like some of the old Jacks by the ale house, hoping to catch his eye for the price of a drink.

Perhaps he had come to clear his head, unused as he was to the awesome meal which Grace Ferguson had prepared in his honour. Duck and local lamb, fish as well; it would have satisfied *Unrivalled's* midshipmen for a year.

And John Allday had made an appearance. It must have cost him dearly to come, Adam thought. Older, heavier, shaggier, but otherwise the same. Unchanged. The first moments had been the hardest. Allday had taken his hand in both of his, and had stood in silence, holding it. Remembering, so that he had shared it, seeing it as it must have been. *The hardest part.*

Allday had told him about meeting Tyacke when his ship had called here. And other names had been mentioned, faces appearing as if from the shadows. *The hardest part . . .*

He walked deeper into the church, seeing the tablets and sculptures, soldiers and sailors, men who had died in battle, at sea or in some far-off land for some cause few would now remember. There were all the Bolithos, their wives too, in some cases.

He looked back through the church, at the aisle where he had given his arm to Belinda when she had married his uncle.

There were others in the church. Resting, escaping from the heat, praying, but all separate, alone with their thoughts.

He thought of the untidy studio, and Sir Gregory Montagu's sharp, assessing gaze while his brushes had moved tirelessly as if controlled by some independent force.

And the girl. He'd not seen her again, and yet, as he had ridden from the house he had felt that she was there. Watching him.

He had sensed Nancy's immediate interest when he had mentioned her, but even she knew very little. Born in Cornwall, but had moved away when still a child. As far as London, where the family had somehow become involved with Sir Gregory Montagu. Her father had been a scholar, a man of refinement, but there had been some scandal and Nancy had heard little more, except that the long-haired girl named Lowenna sometimes came to the old glebe house with Montagu, but was rarely seen anywhere else, not even in the adjoining village of Penryn.

She knew more than she was telling. Before she had left for her own house, she had taken his arm and murmured, "Don't break your heart, Adam. Not again."

A warning, but she had not been there in the walled garden. Like stripping away a curtain of secrecy, when he had seen the girl Lowenna, her defences momentarily broken down . . . Andromeda, the captive waiting to be rescued from sacrifice.

He had paused opposite a finely crafted bust of Captain David Bolitho, who had died in 1724, fighting pirates off the African coast. He had been the first Bolitho to carry the sword Montagu admired so much. And now *Unrivalled* would be going back there. He touched the scabbard at his thigh. *Will I be the last Bolitho to wear it?*

Montagu expected him to make another visit. He was afraid of hope, afraid of hoping.

"Why, Captain, you are not wearing my rose."

He swung round, his shoe scraping on an iron grill, and saw her sitting at the end of a pew, her face pale against something dark, even black.

He gripped the back of the pew, hardly trusting himself to speak.

"I would have walked right past you! I had no idea." He saw her hand gripped around the polished woodwork, like some small, wary creature. "I still have it. I will *never* lose it." He saw some faces turn towards him, disturbed, irritated. He lowered his voice. "May I ask why you are here at King Charles the Martyr?"

"I might ask the same of you, Captain. Perhaps you came to bask in the past glories of your family? Or to find peace, as I do on occasion."

He reached out to cover her hand with his own, but it had vanished. He said, "I wanted to walk, to think." He hesitated. "To remember."

She looked down, her face almost hidden. "You asked for the rose to remain in the portrait? Is that so?"

He nodded, sensing her sudden uncertainty. Like panic.

He said, "It will always be there. Even when I am not."

She shook her head and he saw her hair shine briefly in the colours from a stained glass window.

"Do not say such things." She looked at him directly again, her eyes very dark. "And do not think of me as you first saw me. It would be better for you if we never saw one another again."

He felt her hand close on his, slight but surprisingly strong. "Believe me, for my sake if not your own."

The building quivered to the slow, deliberate intrusion of the great clock chiming the hour.

She stood suddenly, the contact broken. "I must leave. I am already late. Forgive me."

She had opened the pew gate and was very close to him. Her perfume, or perhaps it was her body's scent, was almost physical.

He said, "I would wish to see you again, Lowenna." He felt her start at the use of her name, but she did not pull away.

Instead she said quietly, "He told you." Then, "He trusts you."

She stepped out of the pew and he was vaguely aware of other faces turning to stare.

She said, "It is a long walk. You may ride with me." And put a hand to her mouth, as if surprised, even shocked by her own suggestion.

Then she tossed her head, the hair spilling across her shoulder. "They can think what they choose!"

He stepped aside for her, unable to believe it was happening.

He said, "There will always be thoughts." Like a voice from the past.

There were some empty vases waiting to be filled, and he took her arm gently to guide her around them. He felt the sudden tension, so strong that he thought she would turn upon him.

But she halted and faced him, quite deliberately, and her voice was heavy, even sad.

"Don't do that again, Captain." Without anger. Without hope.

They walked in silence to the big doors and he saw a pony and a smart little trap waiting in the square. It was the same stable boy, neatly turned out and without his grubby apron. He showed neither surprise nor hesitation as he hurried to lower the other seat. Side by side, not touching. But Adam could think of one thing only. This meeting was no accident. She must have wanted it.

Don't break your heart, Adam. Not again.

He glanced at her profile as the little trap rattled out of the square. Her head and shoulders were covered with a fine black shawl. Only one hand showed itself on the safety rail. A temptation, and a risk he would never take. Like the girl on board the slaver. Afraid of what might happen.

Worse, what she might do.

It seemed to take no time at all. The old stone wall, the house beyond, and always the sea. He said, "You could step into the house. I could show you some of the portraits." It sounded meaningless. He tried again. "You would not be alone. There are people here."

She was not listening. She said only, "Someone is waiting for you, I think."

The little group stood motionless by the entrance. Ferguson and, surprisingly, Allday. Yovell was here too, a little apart from the others. A spectator.

But all Adam saw was the man in uniform, the dust still on his shoulders from his ride. The horse was with Young Matthew and the boy Napier, who was rubbing his eyes with his wrist.

She murmured, "Is it bad news?"

Adam turned on the seat and looked at her. He did not need to be told; he had experienced it many times. *Without question.* Sometimes he had welcomed it. But not now.

He answered, "I am recalled."

She did not take her eyes from his. "I think I knew. It was why I had to see you. To speak . . ." She attempted to pull her hand away as he covered it with his own, but instead stared at it, as if fighting something, unable to break free.

"I felt it too, Lowenna." He looked around, the house, the group of people he cared about; they were not here. There was only the sea. Like an old, familiar enemy. "I shall never forget . . ."

She shook her head. "You *must.* For both our sakes."

Adam felt a tear splash on to his hand, and released hers very carefully. Then he stepped down and stood beside the little trap and said simply, "I want to know you, and for you to know me, to share and confide. To trust."

She watched him, one hand to her breast as he lifted his wrist and touched the fallen tears with his lips.

"Until we meet again, this must suffice."

He didn't know if she'd heard him, or even if she had answered.

The trap was rattling away and was lost almost immediately around the bend of the road. She did not look back.

He walked towards the house and saw the courier unfastening his pouch.

The rest were dreams.

Adam Bolitho stood by the stern windows in a patch of deep shadow and stared out at the great array of ships. It never changed except when *Unrivalled* swung to her cable. He traced the outline of an anchored brigantine with his finger on the thick glass. You could almost feel the impatience of the vessels and their companies, eager to leave before the excitement lost its edge.

It was his first full day on board, and yet he still felt as if part of himself had remained with the land. He had tried to lose himself in his command, something he had always been able to do, even if only to give confidence in moments of doubt.

Galbraith had done well during his absence. No deserters, perhaps because of the unpaid bounty- and prize-money, and only a few defaulters, petty for the most part.

He turned his back on the glistening panorama and looked around the cabin. Two hours ago he had assembled all the officers here, senior warrant officers included. He smiled faintly. *Trust the professionals.* Two hours, yet he could still see them, just as Joshua Cristie's rank tobacco lingered as another reminder.

He had explained the main points of *Unrivalled*'s orders. In three days' time, unless otherwise instructed, she would proceed to sea, to carry despatches of importance to Gibraltar, then return to

Plymouth with the latest intelligence for Lord Exmouth himself.

Unrivalled's captain was commanded to act upon these orders with all despatch, *and at no time deviate from them.*

Exmouth was an admiral, but he was still a frigate captain at heart, and knew better than most of the temptations which might intervene with loosely worded orders.

Unrivalled was quiet now, during the first dogwatch, the hands in their messes, the "young gentlemen" and boys under instruction.

Adam had listened to his own voice as he had stressed the need for extra care, the final testing of standing and running rigging. Galbraith and Partridge would deal with that. Powder and shot; he had seen Old Stranace nod, his experience of many years priceless in a campaign which might well explode into a full-scale war. He had been aware of some surprise when he had emphasized the importance of provisioning the ship to her full capacity, especially with fresh fruit and vegetables.

Tregillis, the purser, had met his gaze without expression. He, more than anyone, would know how easy it was to barter with traders at a better rate if the goods were overripe before they were even stowed away. It would do no harm for him to be aware of his captain's interest.

There had been only a few questions, most referring to a particular officer's duties or part of ship.

Only Lieutenant Varlo had broken the pattern.

"If we are indeed to confront the Dey of Algiers to stamp out his capture and enslavement of innocent Christians, why do we require a fleet to carry out the necessary measures? Commodore Turnbull has only a handful of worn-out brigs to end the trade in Africa, as we have seen for ourselves!"

Cristie had intervened bluntly, "'Cause there are too many people making money out of Africa, *Mister* Varlo!"

Lieutenant Bellairs had raised a question about the prospect of promotion for some of the new hands, and Varlo's comment had remained in the air. But it had not gone away.

He walked to his desk and unlocked a drawer. His personal log book was still open, but the ink was dry. He wondered who would ever read it. Almost cautiously he turned back the pages, and lifted the yellow rose to hold it to the light. It would not last, even if carefully pressed. But in his mind he could see it exactly as she had given it to him. The one he had worn for the benefit of Sir Gregory Montagu's darting brushes.

It was past. There was only the next horizon. And the next.

He closed the drawer and locked it.

It would be better if they could leave, put to sea right now, no matter what the mission entailed.

Three more days. He thought he heard young Napier tidying things in the small pantry. How did he feel about leaving again?

It had all been so new, so different. Young Matthew allowing him to share the box on the carriage, and teaching him to ride the new pony, Jupiter. Being spoiled by Grace Ferguson, and cheered by the stable lads when he had fallen from his mount and struggled up again.

Adam had been unable to look at Yovell as he had dictated the last of his letters and instructions.

"Should I be unable to act on this request, through death or disablement, the youth, David Napier, shall be discharged at the expense of my estate, and taken into care by those listed at Falmouth."

Yovell had placed the document with the other letters for his signature, and had said nothing.

Adam thought of his return to the house, riding beside but separated from the dark-eyed girl. And the recall, unexpected, and yet, in some strange way, inevitable.

The boy Napier, wiping his eyes with his hand, so unwilling

to leave the first real home he had ever known, yet determined, proud even, to stay with his captain.

We all need somebody.

He glanced at the old sword on its rack, remembering the church in Falmouth. The first Bolitho to wear this sword. And the last?

He returned to the quarter gallery and stared at the hazy out-thrust of land. He knew nothing about her, might never see her again. *And even if I did . . .* He swung away, seeking anger to offer an escape.

But all he could see was her face, uplifted in that old church. Asking, telling, pleading?

Feet thumped overhead and he heard someone laugh. Galbraith would be here shortly. Corporal Bloxham's well-deserved promotion had been sanctioned. A sergeant in the Royal Marines was a big step up the ladder, and in a crowded hull like this it was an event. One to be celebrated.

The man who had saved his life that day when Martinez had paid with his own.

He reached for his coat. The captain would share a "wet" with the new sergeant in his mess.

He looked at the locked drawer but saw the rose in her hand.

There was a tap at the door. He was ready.

It was *not* a dream.

13 COMING TO TERMS

THE RUGGED STRETCH of parkland which ran down to the River Thames to mark the winding curve of Chiswick Reach was deserted. There were usually young riders exercising their skills here, as it was considered safe, at least during the daylight. It was July, and yet the wind off the river seemed cool, and strong enough to ruffle the bushes; the sky was almost hidden by cloud.

The smart landau in its dark blue livery stood alone, the matching greys resting now, shaking their harness after a lively trot across the park.

Catherine, Lady Somervell, tugged the strap and lowered one of the windows, tasting the air, the nearness of the river even though it was not visible from this place.

This place. She felt a shiver run through her. Why? Was it guilt, excitement? She stared across the park but only saw her own reflection in the glass. It was speckled with rain too. She shivered again.

There were two leafless trees standing apart from all the others. They had died long ago, but something or someone had decreed they should remain. It was said that they marked the last rendezvous for many duellists over the years. Pistol or blade; for officers from the nearby garrison, falling out over women or cards, or in a momentary fit of ill humour, it often ended here.

Her fingers tightened around the strap. Her husband had been killed in a duel. *Someone else.* She had never regarded him as a husband.

She heard the carriage creak as the coachman shifted his position on the box. Ready for anything. One of Sillitoe's men, most of whom looked more like prizefighters than servants.

He had not asked where she was going, or why. He would know. It was his way, and she had become used to it. Like this finely sprung carriage, unmarked, unlike his others, with the arms of Baron Sillitoe of Chiswick, the one he sometimes used for private business meetings. She shook herself, as if to drive it away. She had stopped questioning him.

She looked at her reflection again. The beautiful Catherine, who had won the hearts of the nation, and had been their hero's lover. Who had spurned the hostility and envy of society . . . She touched a lock of the dark hair at her brow. Until that man had fallen in battle and her world had ended.

She turned her thoughts aside, as a swordsman might parry a blade, and focused on Sillitoe.

Powerful, respected and feared. The man who had used his influence to keep her from Richard, and had never denied it. And yet he had been the rock which had saved her. From what? She still did not know.

She could sometimes even consider the horror of the night when she had returned unescorted to her little Chelsea house on the Walk. She would have been raped but for Sillitoe bursting into the room, where she had never slept again without remembering.

Now she lived in Sillitoe's house, which lay just around this sweeping bend of the Thames, and had accompanied him to Spain, on the excuse that she might help with his business affairs, as she spoke good Spanish. Or was the truth more simple, like the word *whore* carved on the door of the Chelsea house: because she needed him, now more than ever?

She often thought of her last visit to Cornwall, her talks with Richard's sister Nancy.

At first she had been tempted to return to Falmouth, and to live in the old house he had made into a home for her. She was, after all, used to spite and cruel gossip; it would have taken time, but they would have accepted her.

She knew even that was a lie. Nancy had said, *envy and guilt walk hand in hand.* She would know better than anyone.

And Adam, and his letters, which she had left unanswered. What else could she have done? She suspected that Adam knew as well as she what disaster would have resulted, intentional or otherwise.

The house by the river was almost spartan when compared with the mansions of other men of influence. And it would soon be empty, with only the servants to care for it, and memories she could only imagine. Like the portrait, alone on that wide landing, of Sillitoe's father, who had founded an empire upon slavery. There had been pride in Sillitoe's voice when he had spoken of him.

He might be thinking very differently now; rarely a day had passed when the issue of slavery did not appear in the news-sheets. And now Algiers again. She controlled her breathing. Richard would have lived but for those ships at Algiers. Napoleon had landed in France after his escape from Elba; it had been inevitable. She thought suddenly of the man who was meeting her today. Now . . . Vice-Admiral Sir Graham Bethune, a rising star in the Admiralty but still young, and alive. He should have relieved Richard in the Mediterranean. She had heard her lover say it so often; time and distance, wind and tide. A few days sooner, and he would have been replaced. *Safe.*

She heard the coachman shift again, the click of metal as he loosened the weapon he always carried. Something like a club, but it could change at the twist of a wrist to a foot-long stiletto.

"Comin', m' lady!"

She dabbed her eyes and looked again. A solitary horseman, approaching at a loose canter. Unhurried. Watchful.

She realised that it was the first time she had seen Bethune out of uniform. It was easy to recall her private visits to his office at the Admiralty. *Up the back stairs,* he had always called it.

She watched him wheel round towards the carriage. Another one who had done little to hide his feelings for her. The youngest vice-admiral since Nelson, with a brilliant career ahead, and a wife and two children to support his endeavours. He was taking a risk simply by meeting her today. She had never forgotten the savage cartoons, herself, naked and shedding tears while looking out at the assembled fleet. The caption *Who will be next?* had roused Sillitoe's fury more than anything she had seen; he was usually too clever to show emotion.

William called down, "This 'im, m' lady?" No chances, or he would answer for it.

Bethune swung down from his horse and doffed his hat.

She said, "Come in," and moved along the seat. Richard had always spoken warmly of him; Bethune had been a mere midshipman in the *Sparrow*, his first command, and he had never lost that youthful look.

Bethune was studying her.

He said, "We can always meet here, when you need to see me. It is secure enough."

She said, "It was good of you to come." It was not so easy after all. They were like strangers. But it was safer this way. "I have something for Adam." She groped in her shawl, knowing that he was watching her, as she had seen him do in the past. He had never forgotten that it had been he who had allowed her to return alone to Chelsea, when the nightmare had been waiting for her.

He had blamed himself, and his wife for conspiring with Belinda on that same night.

She said, "It is Richard's Nile medal. I think Adam should have it." She knew Bethune was about to protest. "Richard gave it to me at Malta. That last time." She faltered, and tried again. "I think he knew then that he was going to die. Adam must have it. It will help him."

His hands closed around hers to cradle the little package.

"I will attend to it. *Unrivalled* will be at sea, but I can make arrangements." The grip remained firmly on her hands. "You are looking wonderful, Catherine. I think about you constantly." He attempted to smile, the midshipman again. "I did think that you might have married."

He hesitated. "Forgive me. I had no right."

She released her hands and smiled at him for the first time.

"I lost my way. And what of you, Graham?"

"Their lordships are very demanding at times." He seemed to come to a decision. "I have been hearing a great deal of Sillitoe's involvement with the slave trade. I am certain that he is in no way a party to the continuation of such illegal dealings, but his other connections may bring criticism. The Prince Regent, as you may know, has discontinued his seals of office. Some people are quick to forget past favours."

She nodded. She did not know about the Prince Regent. He had already revoked Sillitoe's appointment as Inspector General. Because of rumour. *Because of me.*

Bethune cocked his head to listen to a church clock somewhere.

"I have heard that Lord Sillitoe intends to visit the West Indies, some of his old interests?" He took her hands again, and this time he did not release them. "I would ask that you do not accompany him. I would feel safer if you remained in England." He looked at her openly. "In London. Where I might see you. Do not seek trouble for yourself, I beg you, Catherine."

She felt him touch her face, her hair, and she was suddenly ashamed. *Is this what I have become?*

The door opened and closed and Bethune was looking up at her again.

He said quietly, "Remember. I am always ready. Always at your call . . . but you know that?"

She watched him swing easily into the saddle. *My own age? Younger?* She wanted to laugh. Or cry.

"Back to the house, please, William."

The river came into view, a few coloured sails on the grey water. But all she saw was the door.

Whore.

Unis Allday walked slowly across the inn yard and felt the sunshine hot across her neck and bare arms. She enjoyed it, even after the heat of the kitchen and the baked bread, fresh from the oven. It was afternoon, in some ways the best time of the day, she thought.

She looked at the front of the inn, freshly painted and welcoming, a place to be proud of. She waved to a passing rider, one of the estate keepers, and received a greeting in return; they all knew her now, but nobody took liberties with her. If they did it would only be once, small though she was.

Even the inn sign had been repainted, The Old Hyperion under full sail. To strangers passing through Fallowfield, on the fringe of the Helford River, it might be just another name for a local inn, but not to Unis, or the man she had married here. *Hyperion* was a real ship, and had taken one husband from her in battle and given her another, John Allday.

She could smell the paint. The two additional rooms for guests were almost finished; the new road nearby would bring coaches, and more trade. They had done well, despite, or perhaps because of the struggle at the beginning.

At noon it had been busy, with men in from working on the road, and they were young men, proof that the war was truly over. Men who could walk free without fear of a press-gang, or the misery of returning home crippled and unwanted.

She thought of her brother, the other John, who had lost a leg fighting in the line with the Old Thirty-First. Now, at least, he would talk about it, instead of looking upon his injury as some kind of personal failure. Without him she would never have managed to build the inn into a successful, even prosperous business.

She heard the clatter of glasses and guessed it was Tom Ozzard, *our latest recruit,* John had called him. Another link, a veteran from that other world she could only imagine. Sir Richard Bolitho's servant, who had been with him until the day he had been killed. Out of nowhere, Ozzard had appeared here in Fallowfield, more like a fugitive than a survivor. A man haunted and hunted by something, and she knew that but for John's sake she would never have considered offering him a roof, and work which he understood.

Despite his dour and sometimes hostile manner he had proved his worth, with wine, and with some of the more demanding customers, auctioneers and traders in particular. An educated man, he had made the inn's bookkeeping and accounts seem simple, but he never shared a confidence, and she sensed that even her John knew little about him beyond that world they had shared at sea.

She saw a shadow pass the parlour door. It was Nessa. Tall, dark-haired, and rarely smiling, but she would turn the head of any real man. Her brother John, for instance. But it was hard to know if there was anything between them. Turned out by her parents because she had conceived and lost a child by a soldier from the Truro garrison, Nessa had become part of the family here, and had rejected the past. And she was so good with little Kate, necessary at a busy inn when you needed six pairs of eyes at once.

The Old Hyperion was doing well, and would do even better. She paused, one hand on the wall, the bricks almost as hot as new bread. So why was she worried?

She thought of the big, shaggy, some might say ungainly man who had burst into her life. Rough, but respected as a true seaman and Sir Richard's friend, John Allday had won her heart. He had come ashore now; he had done far more than his duty, but he was still not over it. When he made his trips to Falmouth she knew he would be watching the ships, coming or going; it was always the same. Trying to hold on. To remain a part of it.

She considered his last visit to Falmouth, when he had met Captain Adam Bolitho; she had been painfully aware of his uncertainty, his misgivings as he had tried to decide whether he should go back to the old house he had once called his home, when he was not at sea with Sir Richard.

She had heard Bryan Ferguson say that Sir Richard and her

John were like master and loyal dog, each afraid of losing the other. Perhaps that was so. She clenched her fists. She would allow no harm to come to him now.

She had asked John how he had found Captain Adam. He had thought about it, his chin in the big, awkward hands which could be so loving and so gentle in their private world.

He had said, "Like his uncle, a good and caring captain to all accounts, but stands alone. Shouldn't be like that." As if he felt somehow responsible.

She entered the parlour, so familiar now, the shining copper and pewter, the lines of tankards, and the mingled smells of food, flowers, and people. In the place of honour was the beautiful model of the old *Hyperion*, exact in every detail and scale, and made by those same big, scarred hands. But it had been moved, something forbidden to everybody except . . . She walked into the next room, the one with the fine view of a long line of evenly matched trees; when the light was right you could see the river, like molten silver beyond them.

John Allday was sitting at the table, his face deep in thought as he studied the canvas roll of tools, blades and strips of bone arranged in front of him.

Like many sailors, he could take on most jobs. He could make furniture, like the beautiful cot he had fashioned for little Kate, and the chest he had built for the lieutenant named George Avery who had become so much a part of Unis's life. Because Allday was illiterate, Avery had written his letters to her, and had read her letters to him. It would have been a rare and wonderful relationship in any walk of life, let alone aboard a man-of-war. Now the quiet, almost shy Avery was gone, one more name on the roll of honour. *For King and Country.*

"What is it, John?"

She put her arm around his massive shoulders. Sir Richard had called him *my oak*, but she could feel his slow, careful breathing even now. The terrible wound in the chest left by a Spanish sword, at a place no one could remember, and it was getting worse. But he had always insisted he could manage, when Sir Richard had needed him.

Now I need you, dearest John.

"When I gets time on my hands." He did not look up at her. "I gets to thinking, another model, mebbee?"

She hugged him. "You're *always* busy! Make some of the youngsters sit up an' take notice, I can tell you!"

He sighed. "You knows me, love, I'm not one for passing time with the old Jacks, swinging the lamp with every tankard of ale! Your brother's got the right idea, puts 'em in their place!" He looked round. "Where's Kate?"

"Resting. Nessa'll keep an eye on her."

She remembered his dismay when the child had turned away from him, when they had met for the first time on his return from sea. To her he must have seemed like a stranger, an interloper. But he had won her over in his own patient fashion. He could even pick her up and play with her now without fear of damaging her in some way. And Unis loved him for it.

Allday said suddenly, "I meant to ask about young Elizabeth, Sir Richard's daughter—she'll be growing up now, right enough. I wonder what the King of Cornwall thinks about having her in his great house."

She hugged him again, and said nothing. Sir Lewis Roxby had died back when Lady Catherine was still living at the Bolitho house.

She said, "You're going to make a model of the *Frobisher*," and bit her lip to steady herself. "We'll have to find a real special place for that!"

Then Allday did look at her, his eyes very clear, the frown gone.

"I shall give it to Cap'n Adam. From both of us."

Afterwards, alone in their room, she wondered. *Who did he really mean?*

Nancy, Lady Roxby, saw the rambling old building swing into view as the carriage swayed over the rutted track.

It was an open vehicle, and she could feel the dust gritting between her teeth, but she liked it this way, always had since she was a small girl, the younger daughter of Captain James Bolitho. She often thought about her father, the man; she sometimes felt that the one she knew existed only in the portrait at the Bolitho house, while his character and upbringing were like entries in a diary or history book.

"Go straight in, Francis. I doubt this will take long."

The shadow of the old glebe house rose above her, as always grim and unwelcoming. Ideal perhaps for an artist and a recluse, but few others.

She felt a twinge of excitement and rebuked herself. Roxby would have called her too curious for her own good. She smiled sadly. But he would have loved her for it.

The dark windows were blind to the outside world, the ruined chapel adding to the air of mystery. Gossip, more likely; this place was well known for its tales of witchcraft and evil spirits.

The coachman said doubtfully, "I don't think we are expected, m' lady."

He had not been with her very long. Otherwise, he would have known about her impulses. She heard Roxby again. *Damn impudence, more like!*

The sky was bright and clear, without even a wisp of cloud over the hills or the sea beyond.

Adam would be out there now somewhere, doing what he had always wanted and dreamed about. She thought of his face, so near, when she had last spoken to him, and then had pressed his cheek against her own. *Doing what he wanted and believed in.* But this time had been different. As if he was leaving something behind.

She said impatiently, "Get down and knock on the door, Francis!"

She saw the horse shaking its ears, irritated by the buzzing insects. She could remember a time when she would have ridden here herself, and across country if the mood took her. It was wrong to look back too often . . . perhaps because since Roxby had died there had been so little joy, and nothing to anticipate.

So many things had changed. Like young Elizabeth, who had been so surprised at the way local children lived and played . . . how could it be, that she had been so sheltered from an endless war which had threatened every mile of this coastline? She thought of the girl's mother, Belinda, and tried once again to come to terms with it.

She heard voices, Francis, tall and ramrod-straight like the soldier he had been until a year ago, and the servant she had met on her previous visit, when she had called to arrange for the portrait.

She climbed down, and grimaced a little. Her breathing was fast. *Just to remind me.* On her next birthday she would be fifty-seven years old. People told her to settle down and enjoy these years. She was secure, and had two fine children, and now two grandchildren. *She should be more than satisfied . . .*

She grimaced again. She was not.

Francis called, "He says that his master is not here, m' lady. He will gladly take a message." It was as if the servant was invisible. Perhaps they were like that in the cavalry.

She said, "It is about my nephew's portrait." Even that made her sound ancient. "In Captain Bolitho's absence I thought I should enquire . . ."

"May I be of any help, my lady?"

Nancy turned in the direction of the voice.

"Thank you, my dear. Have we met before?"

The girl looked towards the house, as if regretting her first impulse. But she said, "I am Lowenna. I am staying here."

Nancy took a deep breath and stepped into cool shadows. In her heart, she had hoped for this meeting with one who until now had been little more than a name, an occasional visitor to these parts, and then only in the company of Sir Gregory Montagu.

She followed her along the deserted passageway, conscious of her poise, her apparent confidence. She remembered her vaguely as a child; it was coming back to her like her father's history, like fragments from the pages of a diary. She had been born in Bodmin, where the family name had been Garland. A successful arrangement, they had said at the time, between a promising scholar soon to be appointed to a prestigious college in Winchester, and the daughter of a Bodmin corn chandler . . . Nancy saw the girl pause, as if to ensure that she was still following . . . She saw the date in her mind. Around 1790, when news had reached her of Richard's fever in the Great South Sea; he had been in command of the frigate *Tempest*. Allday had been with him even then.

"We may talk in here, if you wish." Very composed, and, in the filtered sunlight, quietly beautiful. A woman then, aged about twenty-six or twenty-seven.

Nancy glanced around the room. Untidy, but she was aware of the order of things in this, a painter's domain. A place wherein he could work, leave for a week or a month if he chose, and know that it would be exactly how he wanted it when he returned.

She often spent her spare time painting flowers, or scenes on the shore, and she had been moved by Elizabeth's readiness to copy her. It had been their first real point of contact.

She observed the girl. Dressed in a pale blue robe without any sort of decoration, or even a belt. Loose and airy. She had already noted the long hair, and the easy way she walked, but now that she was facing her she was more aware of her eyes. So dark that they concealed her thoughts, like a barrier between them.

Lowenna said, "The portrait is over here. Sir Gregory is pleased with it, I think."

Nancy waited as she uncovered the canvas; she even did that with a graceful, unhurried movement. She knew she sat for Montagu: perhaps that was it. Poise . . .

She studied the unfinished portrait; unbelievable that one man could possess such a great talent. It was Adam to the life, the way he held his head when listening, or answering a question. The dark eyes, like the eyes of the girl she knew was watching her, instead of the painting. There was an uncompleted yellow rose in Adam's coat and she almost mentioned it, but some deeper sense seemed to warn her that this tenuous contact would be broken instantly. And Adam's small, elusive smile; Montagu had caught it precisely. No wonder he could turn any woman's head, and break his own heart.

She said, "It is exactly right. How I think of him when he's away. Which is too often these days."

She turned, and saw the astonishment which for only a second had broken through the girl's composure.

Lowenna said quietly, "I had not realised . . ."

"That we were so close?" Nancy looked at the portrait again, the flood of memories pushing aside all reserve. "He came to me when his mother died. He had walked all the way from Penzance. He was only a boy." She nodded slowly, without knowing she had done so. "Came to *me*."

"Thank you for telling me." So simply said, like a very young girl again.

"Will you be staying here long, Lowenna?"

She shook her head, the sunlight touching her hair like fine gold. "I don't know. I may be going back to London. Sir Gregory has several paintings to finish." She glanced at the portrait again, almost shyly, as if she were testing something. "But he will complete this first."

Nancy walked to a window, seeing the harp and the stool beside it. Then she saw the other unfinished painting, the naked girl chained to a rock, the sea monster about to break surface beside her.

She looked at her again. Defensive, or defiant? The dark eyes gave nothing away.

She said softly, "You are very beautiful."

"It is not what it may appear, my lady."

"I am far older than you." She shrugged. "Unfortunately. I have been in love twice in my life. I know how it feels." She made to hold out her hand, but instinct prevented her. "I also know how it looks. I care deeply for my nephew, perhaps, dare I say it, more than a son. He is brave, loyal and compassionate, and he has suffered." She saw the words reaching her. "As I believe you have."

"Who said that of me?"

"Nobody. I am still a woman, still young at heart."

She tried not to listen to the sound of carriage wheels. Montagu was back, but it would make no difference who it was. She made up her mind. "You see, I believe my nephew has lost his heart to you. It is why I came here today." She walked towards the door. "Now that I have met you, I am glad I came." She turned, one hand on the door. "If you feel the need, Lowenna, come to me."

She did not move. But the hostility was gone.

She said, "As Adam came?" It was the first time she had used his name.

Then Nancy did reach out and take her wrist. "As a friend, if you like." She felt that in another moment the girl would have pulled away.

She said calmly, "A friend, then, my lady."

Along the same bleak passageway, and the bright square of sunshine through the opened doors.

It was not Montagu, but a man she recognised from a wine merchant's in Falmouth. He touched his hat and beamed at her.

"'Tes a fine day, m' lady. Summer at last, mebbee?"

Nancy looked back at the pale blue figure by the stairway. "Yes, Mr Cuppage, it is a fine day." She raised one hand to the girl and added, "*Now* it is."

She walked out into the dusty air again. Afraid to stop and consider, even to look back.

Francis and a stable boy were by the horse; the dour-faced servant had disappeared. She might have imagined all of it.

She thought of Adam and his ship, under orders again after so brief a respite. It was his life, and she was a sailor's daughter and the sister of England's naval hero. She took Francis' arm and pulled herself up into the carriage before glancing back at the house. *But now, I am Adam's aunt.*

She saw a brief movement by a window. Pale blue. Where she had seen the harp, and the other painting.

She said aloud, "There *is* nobody else!"

As the carriage moved away, she imagined she heard Roxby laugh.

Rear-Admiral Thomas Herrick got up from the chair and walked to a nearby window. He could not remember how many times he had done so, or how long he had been here.

He stared down at the familiar scene, the unending parade of carriages, mostly open to the watery sunshine, a few bright parasols and the wide-brimmed hats of ladies being driven from one form of amusement to another. A troop of dragoons trotting past, a young helmeted cornet turning in his saddle as a straight-backed man stepped from the crowd to raise his hat to the colours at the head of the troop. He had only one arm.

Herrick turned away, angry with himself, unable to ignore or forget the raw pain in the stump of his own arm, even at the slightest movement, and all the more so in his heavy dress coat.

He sat again and stared at the opposite wall, and two paintings of sea fights: colours flying, swirling gunsmoke, the enemy's canvas riddled with shot-holes. But they never showed the blood, the dead men, and the pieces of men.

He studied the polished marble, the neat array of gilded chairs. It must take the equivalent of a watch of seamen to maintain this great vault of a building. He grunted and eased the shoulder of his coat, beneath the heavy bullion epaulette whose presence could still surprise him.

This was the Admiralty, where their lordships and an army of staff officers controlled the strands of the web connecting them to every squadron, every ship, and every captain on every ocean where their flag flew, almost unchallenged.

And after this? He thought of the lodgings he was using close to Vauxhall. Not fashionable, especially for a flag officer, but comfortable enough. And cheap. He had never been careless with his hard-earned money. He had come up the hard way, and was well aware of the navy's habit of reversing a man's fortunes along with his destiny.

He had been at the Admiralty the whole forenoon, going over the charts and reports of the anti-slavery patrols with the admiral concerned, and he knew men well enough to understand that the admiral, pleasant though he was, had not the least idea what Freetown and the appalling conditions of slavery entailed. Perhaps it was better, safer that way.

There would be more discussions tomorrow; a Member of Parliament on the interested committee would also be there. Herrick had explained in his reports, and face to face, that they needed ten times the number of agile patrol vessels, and a diligent leadership in direct command, before any real results would be manifest. Money was always the objection; there was none to spare for an overall increase. And yet Herrick had been hearing nothing else since he had arrived in London but the rumour of a massive show of force against the Algerine pirates and the Dey who had persisted in defying all attempts to unseat him. This time it would be no less than a fleet, and under the command of Pellew himself. Herrick could not be bothered with the frills and fancies of grand titles; "Pellew" was good enough for him.

There did not seem to be much in the way of secrecy; even *The Times* had hinted at a "determined intervention" to free the Christian slaves who languished in the Dey's prisons.

And now this had happened. A messenger had caught him just as he had been about to leave the building.

He had been requested to present himself to Vice-Admiral Sir Graham Bethune, the newly appointed deputy, and no stranger to the lords of admiralty.

He had no thoughts on Bethune as a senior officer. *I was Richard's first lieutenant a year after Bethune was one of his midshipmen. Now he outranks me.* He had grown used to such distinctions. He did not have to like them.

He found that he was at the window again. Perhaps Adam Bolitho had told a superior officer, maybe Keen, what he had divulged about Sillitoe and his part in the slave trade. No. Adam might be hot-headed, even indiscreet, but he would not violate something as strong as personal trust. He watched a smart carriage passing among some market vehicles, saw the woman who sat alone, her face shaded by a broad-brimmed hat. It could have been Richard's mistress. *That woman.* Why had he told Adam Bolitho? Concern, or was it guilt?

It had been Adam who had brought the news to him, that his own very dear Dulcie had died. Just as Herrick had once carried the tragic news of Bolitho's young wife's death . . .

He stared with something like hatred at the garishly painted battles. The roots and memories were stronger than many believed.

He heard unhurried footsteps approaching, and braced himself. Perhaps it was a mistake, or Bethune had taken another appointment.

"Sir Graham Bethune can see you now, sir."

Herrick stood up, and winced as the heavy dress coat dragged at his stump. So damned typical of this place. *Can* see you now. As if it was a favour!

He knew he was being unreasonable, and blamed his pain for it. He hated the way people stared, or clucked sympathetically when they met him. He could recall a surgeon suggesting that he should wear ostrich quills on his coat to steer people away from jostling or reopening the wound. He could even hear himself.

Afraid of war, are they? Or of what it does to those who have to fight it?

If Dulcie had been alive . . . He saw the doors swing inward, and Bethune waiting to greet him. Standing, his arm outstretched, his left arm, to match his own.

"Good to see you, Thomas!" His handshake was firm, his palm still that of a sailor. "Seat yourself. There'll be some wine in a moment, but we are served by snails in this cathedral!"

Herrick sat down, taking time to adjust himself in the chair, like someone searching for a trap. Then he looked directly at Bethune. He had always prided himself in being honest and open with others, and grudgingly he recognised those qualities in Bethune, something which the vice-admiral's lace and the grand office could not hide.

Bethune said, "I saw your reports. I was particularly interested in your views on Freetown and the Windward Coast—I have said as much to the First Lord. You should get the credit you deserve. I suspect you may be requested to return to that or some other aspect of the slave trade, but I don't suppose you'll mind about that." It was not a question.

Herrick almost smiled. *Requested;* a term they used when you had attained flag rank. It still meant that you had no choice in the matter.

Bethune strode to a window and opened it, admitting the ceaseless din of iron-shod wheels and the clatter of many horses: London on the move, never at rest.

Herrick watched him. He too was restless, full of energy. Still a young man, like the one who had commanded that fine frigate depicted in this room's only painting.

Bethune went on, "I especially liked your report on Captain Tyacke, another officer who might well have gone unnoticed, passed over, but for someone caring enough to act."

Herrick clenched his remaining fist. As if Tyacke were also in this room, listening to the street, watching the dragoons, like the man in the crowd. He said without hesitation, "Sir Richard did as much for me, Sir Graham."

Bethune nodded, satisfied perhaps. "You served with him at the Nile?"

Herrick rubbed the arm of his chair. This was not what he had expected.

"Yes. In *Lysander.* I was Sir Richard's flag captain then."

Bethune turned from the window. Herrick would say no more, but it was enough.

"Tyacke was at the Nile also, where he was so cruelly wounded."

A servant entered and began to place glasses on a tiny square of cloth. More like a woman than a grown man, Herrick thought.

For a moment he thought he had misheard as Bethune dismissed the servant and repeated, "Lady Somervell. I saw her here, in London." He glanced over at him. "This is Rhenish—I hope it will suit? It should be cool, although after its journey up those stairs one can only hope!" And laughed, completely relaxed. Or was he?

Herrick said, "It is some time since I saw her. It was in Falmouth, when I was intending to take up an appointment with the revenue service."

Bethune critically examined a glass. He knew about that, and thought he knew why Keen had intervened. Not all grudges faded with the years.

He said, "A brave and lovely woman. I admire her greatly." He thought of the Nile medal she had entrusted to him. Another link. But it had always been there. He suspected that she knew how he felt.

He tried to shut it from his mind and said, "I think that Baron Sillitoe may become more involved with his business affairs in the West Indies, even Cuba."

Herrick stiffened. Cuba, still the world's clearing house for slaves.

Bethune said, "We must put all past disagreement aside. The fleet is committed to the Algiers venture, as it is elsewhere where the trade flourishes. You know this, and I know it. I would take it as a great favour if you would pass on to me what you may hear about said involvement, so that the innocent can be protected." He raised his glass very slowly until their eyes met.

Herrick swallowed; if the hock was warm or ice-cold, he did not notice it.

"I understand, Sir Graham." It was utter madness, and if anything went wrong Bethune would deny any association.

He watched Bethune's tanned hand refilling the glasses.

When Dulcie had died of typhus, Lady Somervell . . . he hesitated even over her name . . . Catherine had stood by her. The only one, to the end. She could so easily have been infected by the fever herself. But she had stayed.

"It shall be done."

Their glasses touched.

Committed, then. And Thomas Herrick was suddenly alive again. Restored.

Tomorrow he might regret it. He smiled quite openly.

But that was tomorrow.

14 SUDDEN DEATH

JAMES BELLAIRS, *Unrivalled*'s young third lieutenant, touched his hat and said, "I relieve you, sir."

Eight bells had just rung out from the forecastle. The first watch was about to begin.

Lieutenant Varlo saw his own men hurrying away to their various messes and remarked, "If you are certain you can manage 'til the hour of midnight?"

Bellairs watched him walk to the companion-way and tried not to dislike him. A competent officer, but never without the last-minute jibe, the sarcastic quip at someone else's expense.

One of Bellairs' watch had been adrift when the hands had mustered aft; he had fallen and injured his wrist. Varlo had remarked, "Shall we rouse out the master-at-arms to find him, eh?"

He allowed his anger to settle. It was not in his nature, and anyway . . . He spread his arms and stared along the length of the ship. Already in deep shadow, with an incredible orange glow to starboard as the sun dipped towards the horizon. To larboard it was lost in a purple haze. You could sense the nearness of land. He put Varlo from his mind and smiled. Not so near: Lisbon lay about sixty miles abeam according to the last calculation. He listened to the creak and hum of taut rigging as *Unrivalled* leaned more steeply on the larboard tack. Every watch brought him fresh confidence, like the sounds which had once made him uneasy, but usually unwilling to call for advice from a lieutenant. Now he was a lieutenant himself, and those years as a "young gentleman" seemed a lifetime ago.

He glanced at the cabin skylight. There was a glow there, brighter than usual. The captain, going over his orders again. Was he ever unsure, he wondered, with nobody to advise *him?*

He walked to the compass, the two helmsmen watching him as he passed. Soon it would be too dark to recognise faces, but it no longer mattered. He felt that he knew every man in the ship. Even the bad ones. He grinned. Especially the bad ones . . .

He thought of Plymouth, now five days astern. A smooth if lively passage so far. Skirting the Bay and its foul moods, they had been out of sight of Cape Finisterre except from the masthead, when they had changed tack yet again to steer south-west by south and follow the coast of Portugal. Standing well out to sea, perhaps to avoid rumour or suspicion. He had heard the older hands joking about it. That everybody in the whole world would know more than *Unrivalled*'s people.

He peered at the compass card. South-south-west. Two more days, maybe less, and they would lie beneath the Rock's great shadow.

His thoughts returned to Plymouth. His parents and sister had come to see him, to present him with the new sword they had purchased to mark his commission. He looked again at the skylight. Before that, he had worn a curved hanger which belonged to Captain Bolitho.

Galbraith had remarked, "I can't say I've heard of any other captain doing that!"

He allowed his mind to return to the girl named Jane, who

had also been there. A friend of his sister's. A ready smile and dancing violet eyes; they had got on well together, encouraged, he realised, by his sister. She was of a good family, so what prospects could he offer as a lowly luff?

But she lived at Dartmouth, which was not that far from Plymouth. When *Unrivalled* returned after completing this mission, he might be able to see her again.

"Cap'n's comin' up, sir."

"Thank you, Tucker." He had learned well the risk of trying to be popular, or showing favouritism to this man or that. All the same, he could not imagine anyone warning Varlo if the captain was on the move.

He saw one of the helmsmen turn his head to make sure the windvane was in position. It got dark very suddenly hereabouts.

Bellairs waited near the wheel while the captain walked to the compass, and the log which was protected by a canvas hood; he had probably already been in the chartroom to make his own estimate of their progress. He made it seem so effortless; even when he stared up into the black tangle of rigging and the trimmed angle of each yard, it was as if he already knew. When they had been in action it had been impossible to register every act or injury. Only afterwards, when your heart and breathing steadied, could you realise what you had done. And those who had not come through it.

Bellairs could recall the captain's part in it, His apparent disregard for both danger and the nearness of sudden death. Or, far worse, a lingering despair in the agony of the surgeon's knife.

He straightened up as Bolitho said, "Holding her course and progress well, Mr. Bellairs." He tapped the pale planking with his shoe. "But she's feeling it, with all that extra weight of stores and shot." He turned away to watch a leaping fish, bright gold in the sunset. "We'll be needing all of it, I daresay."

He could have been talking to the ship.

Adam could feel Bellairs watching him. It was strange: when he had been a lieutenant he had never considered his captains young in thought and heart. Except his uncle. They had sometimes been mistaken for brothers.

He would know nothing until he was in Gibraltar. The prospects of battle might all have blown away by then. It happened often enough. But until then he thought of his carefully worded orders. Nothing which any captain could misinterpret if an opportunity offered itself. Lord Exmouth had been a great frigate captain. He would know every trick in the book.

Like the vessel they had sighted two days back after they had weathered Cape Finisterre. He had sent Sullivan aloft, and had then joined him with a telescope, as if something had driven him.

A large ship, a barque as far as they could tell; there had been a stiff wind and a lot of spray which made proper recognition almost impossible. But they had seen her again, and she had immediately changed tack, her sails like pink shells in the dawn light. To avoid *Unrivalled*'s closer scrutiny? Cristie had suggested that she might be standing closer inshore and heading for Vigo. It made sense. But Adam could not shift it from his mind. There were hundreds of ships in these waters, probably the busiest seaway in the world. And some of them would be barques. In any case his orders were clear. Blunt.

He said, "I hear you had the good fortune to meet a young lady during our stay in Plymouth."

He was aware of Bellairs' confusion. Had it been full daylight, he might have been blushing.

"This is a small ship, remember!"

Bellairs said, "A friend of my sister's, sir." He faltered. "She cannot yet be seventeen."

"I see." Adam walked to the rail and stared down at the boat tier. Bellairs was just nineteen. *Whereas I . . .* He stopped it there.

They were at sea. It was all that counted.

He said, "Time will pass quickly. You will know if your feelings are strong enough to endure the life we follow."

He took two paces away, angry that he should or could offer advice.

He said, "I note from the log that there are two men for punishment tomorrow?" Like cutting a cord. Safe in their ordered world.

"Yes, sir. One for drunkenness." It was now too dark to see his expression, but Adam knew he was frowning. "Craigie. The other one is Lucas, maintopman. He threatened a warrant officer." No hesitation this time. "Mr Midshipman Sandell."

"I shall speak with the first lieutenant directly. I am not pleased about this." He sighed. And it would be another two years before Sandell could even be considered for promotion to lieutenant. What Luke Jago would call "the rotten apple." He had heard his uncle say that it only needed one.

He said suddenly, "We shall alter course two points, Mr Bellairs. I fear the wind is backing a little."

He half-listened to the rush of feet, the shrill of calls, as more men ran to braces and halliards.

It might give an extra knot. At least it would keep his mind from her face. Her body framed against the soiled canvas, the imaginary rock, her eyes so dark, defiant, challenging him.

So different from the girl in the church, her pleasure over the rose which would be in that portrait. He touched his empty belt. And the sword.

"Steer sou'-west! Helm a-lee there!"

The squeal of blocks, men hauling on snaking lines and halliards before they could fling a sailor off his feet. Even the new hands were working like veterans.

Adam crossed to the empty nettings and waited for the deck to sway upright again. Still, faintly, he could see the beautiful figurehead's naked shoulders, showing only for a moment through the gloom while *Unrivalled*'s stem ploughed into a deeper trough in a welter of bursting spray.

Like the girl on the rock. Helpless and in need.

He heard Bellairs say something and then laugh, somehow carefree despite the chorus of sea and thrashing canvas.

"Steady she goes, sir! Sou'-west, full an' bye!"

Adam raised one hand to Bellairs and walked to the companion-way. The first watch could settle down, without its lord and master overseeing every move.

He went down the ladder, feeling the ship closing around him. The marine sentry, his figure angled effortlessly against the deck, stiffened as he passed, and Napier had the screen door open, as if he had been listening for his step on the ladder.

Everything as it should be, and a weighted-down pile of letters and orders in Yovell's round hand awaiting his signature.

He stared at the sloping stern windows, one side in darkness, spray dappling the thick glass like spectres, the other tinged with dull copper, the last of the sun on the western horizon.

The whole ocean, and yet he was bound by his orders, tied to the fleet's apron strings.

Napier asked, "May I bring your meal, sir?"

Adam stared at him and was touched by his concern. He knew what it must have done to him to be so well received in Falmouth, as if he was one of the family.

"Not too much, David. I'll have some cognac while I sign that little mountain."

He saw the boy smile and hurry away to the pantry. Why was it so easy to help others when you were helpless to rally your own spirits?

Tomorrow things might seem different. The final approach to Gibraltar. The formalities. The new orders. If any.

Bellairs would be thinking of the girl he had met in Plymouth;

Napier might still be remembering the excitement and laughter over his first ride on the new pony.

The hands had piped down now, and the ship was unusually silent. Overhead, the watchkeepers took note of the course and behaviour of the wind, and in the wardroom there might still be a few lively enough for a game of cards, or the unfinished letter to a wife or lover somewhere.

He yawned and sipped at the goblet Napier had put by his side before returning just as silently to the pantry, feet pale against the checkered deck covering.

And tomorrow he would speak with Galbraith about the punishment book. But he looked at the desk and pictured the rose pressed in the small log. It was little enough. He watched Napier arranging the table for him, a plate rattling suddenly in time with the rudder as the keel sliced into another long trough.

He moved to another chair and regarded the neatly laid table. Being captain kept you apart from the ship's routine, watchkeeping and everyday work on hull and rigging; it also left you without an ordered programme of eating and sleeping. The carefully prepared meal consisted of slices of fat pork, fried pale brown with bread crumbs. That must be the last of the loaves, he thought; iron-hard biscuit from now on until the next time. And there was a bottle of red wine.

He looked at Napier and smiled. "You do a good deal for me, David, with precious little thanks."

The boy poured some wine, frowning slightly as he usually did. He said simply, "It's what I want, sir."

He walked back to the pantry, and Adam noticed that he was limping again. Not much, but he would mention it to the surgeon.

Later when Napier came to clear the table he found the captain in the one deep chair, legs out-thrust, and fast asleep.

He carried the tray to the pantry again, pausing occasionally to allow for the deck's erratic movements. Then he closed the shutter on one of the lanterns and stood beside the chair again, uncertain but characteristically determined.

Using two fingers he loosened the captain's neckcloth, holding his breath, waiting for the motion to settle.

The captain opened his eyes wide and stared at him, seizing his wrist, holding it, but saying nothing.

Napier waited. He knew that the captain was still asleep. It was important that he should remain so.

He released his hand and backed away, satisfied.

It was what he wanted.

When Adam did awaken it took a few moments to recover his awareness, the instinct of any sailor, the feel and movement of his ship, no matter what hour of day or night it might be.

Too much cognac, or that red wine which rasped on the tongue. It was neither. He had hardly slept since leaving Plymouth. And now . . .

He stared at the partly shuttered lantern, and the empty table. It was still dark, but the sounds overhead were different. He sat upright, feeling his way. It must be eight bells. The morning watch was taking over.

He had been dreaming. He touched his neckcloth. In the dream she had been there, with him.

He saw the figure darkly outlined against the white paintwork. He pushed his fingers through his unruly hair and said, "You should have roused me, man!"

Luke Jago stood up and looked at him. "I would've. I just thought I ought to come."

He was instantly wide awake. Like those other times, so many of them. Like a fox's scent of danger. Even his voice was clear, sharp.

"What is it? Trouble?"

Jago turned his head and glanced at the shuttered skylight,

as if he could see the disruption in the order and discipline.

He said flatly, "Mr Sandell's gone missin', sir."

Adam was on his feet. "Are you sure?" His mind was reaching out like a beam of light, a warning. Galbraith had had the middle watch. He would not leave it for somebody else to act.

Jago replied, "They've searched the ship, sir."

Napier was here now, a jug of water held ready. Adam wiped his face and neck with a wet cloth, seeing it for himself. Sandell was in Galbraith's watch. The night was reasonably calm but for a steady wind; an unemployed person could not come on deck without being seen by one of the watchkeepers. An accident? Somebody would have seen that too.

He blinked as Jago unshuttered the lantern. It would be first light very soon, the ship coming awake to a new day.

Jago lifted a hand as someone shouted something, the voice carried away by the wind.

He said, "They've not found him, sir."

Adam looked at him. Nobody liked Sandell; some hated him. He should never have been selected. He could guess what Jago thought about it.

He turned and faced the door, hearing Galbraith's familiar footsteps. The responsibility, as always, lay here, in this cabin.

He heard the sentry stamp his boots outside the screen door.

Accept it, then. It was murder.

Lieutenant Galbraith strode aft, his shoes sticking on the deck seams as the sun bore down on the anchored ship. It had been a long and slow approach to the anchorage, as if the Rock's majestic presence defied the wind to intrude. He squinted his eyes against the reflected glare at the other ships anchored nearby, and the guard-boat which had waited with tossed oars to mark their journey's end, rolling evenly above its own image.

He looked at the fortifications and batteries, which seemed

like part of the Rock itself, a flag flapping listlessly above one of them. There was a lot to do. All boats would be lowered no matter how short their stay here, to seal the sun-baked hulls. The captain would expect windsails to be rigged, to draw what air there was into the cramped quarters between decks. Galbraith had known captains who would never have contemplated it, would have insisted that the ungainly canvas spoiled their ship's appearance, no matter what discomfort they averted. But not this captain. The gig was already being hoisted out over the starboard gangway, Jago's voice urging or threatening as required.

He saw Lieutenant Varlo speaking with Hastie, the master-at-arms, arranging another search, maybe. The captain had told the second lieutenant to carry out a final investigation, although it seemed unlikely that anything would be gained by it. But Galbraith could feel a difference in the ship and amongst the various sections of men he had come to know so well. Resentment, suspicion; it went deeper than these.

To many of them it would seem a betrayal of something personal and intimate, that bond in any fighting ship which made each man look out for his friends. Sailors owned little enough, and a thief, if caught by his fellows, would suffer a far harsher fate than that meted out by the Articles of War. And a man who would kill another in this ship was like something unclean. Midshipman Sandell would not be missed, but the threat would remain.

He saw the captain by the taffrail, a telescope trained towards the main anchorage, but unmoving, as if he was unwilling to let it go.

Galbraith touched his hat and waited. "Ship secured, sir. The gig is being lowered now."

He followed Bolitho's telescope. A little apart from the other vessels, and larger than most of them: they had seen her on the last two cables before the anchor had plummeted down and the cable had taken the strain.

A receiving-ship, they called such vessels, used mainly as temporary accommodation for officers and personnel on passage to other appointments. Mastless, and with most of her upper deck covered by a protective awning, her gun ports empty and opened to attract any offshore breeze, she was another hulk. The last time they had seen her, she had worn an admiral's flag at the mainmast truck. *Was that only last year?* Even now, her "gingerbread," the ornate scrollwork about her stern and counter, was still brightly gilded in the sunlight, and her name, *Frobisher*, was not to be forgotten. Least of all by the man at his side.

Adam said, "Is that all they could find for her, Leigh?" He closed the glass with a snap and looked directly at him.

"I saw my uncle's old coxswain when I went to Falmouth." He looked at the ship again, but Galbraith knew he was seeing something else. "I am only thankful that John Allday is not here today to see *this!*"

He seemed to pull himself out of it with a great effort and said, "I will be going ashore directly. In the meantime, perhaps Mr Tregillis will loosen his purse strings again and attempt to obtain some fresh bread. The garrison will be the best chance."

"I'll deal with that, sir."

He looked down, surprised, as Bolitho's hand gripped his arm.

"What do *you* think happened to Midshipman Sandell?"

"Lucas, the maintopman accused of threatening him, denies all knowledge, sir. And in any case he was in the care of the ship's corporal, in irons during that watch." He added bitterly, "*My* watch!"

Adam released his grip and stared at the towering Rock. There was mist or low cloud around the summit; Cristie had said it might promise a wind for the return passage.

Varlo seemed to be enjoying his investigation, had even made a sketch showing where every man would or should have been stationed in what he had calculated was the last half hour of

Sandell's life. At the second eighteen-pounder on the starboard side he had discovered that two balls were missing from the shot garland. Enough to carry a body swiftly down before the keel had had time to pass over it. And up forward, so close to the lively bow wave, it would hardly make a sound.

Sandell had had the makings of a tyrant, given the opportunity. But it could have been anybody.

You never spoke of it, but it was always there. When you realised that if the worst happened and you were sailing alone, only the afterguard and the thin line of marines stood between a captain and mutiny.

He saw Jago at the top of the ladder, his dark features expressionless. Waiting.

"I want both counts of punishment to be stood down. One man was drunk, and you know from experience that flogging has never yet cured a drunkard. As for Lucas, he is a *good hand.* Remember how he saved two raw landmen from falling to the deck when we first commissioned? A man of spirit and courage, and I'll not see him broken without proper evidence."

"Sandell's people are quite important, I believe, sir?"

Adam was looking at the *Frobisher* again. "They shall have the truth, Leigh. When I know it."

He walked to the rail and joined his coxswain.

"Man the side! Attention on the upper deck!"

Rist, master's mate, stood with the others while the calls trilled and the captain went quickly down the side into his gig.

He said, "You reckon Mr Sandell's gone to the sharks?"

Cristie overheard and said calmly, "If I was a shark I'd throw the little bastard right back at us!"

Rist forced a smile, but turned away as the calls shrilled once more and work recommenced.

He thought about it again; he had done little else since it had happened. It would soon be forgotten, and as everybody knew but would not say, Midshipman Sandell with his arrogance and secretive cruelty was no loss to anyone. *Think of it, man.* The fleet was growing again, you could see that for yourself at Plymouth, and here beneath the Rock there were more craft than on their last visit. The real cutting down was over. For now, anyway. Rist was not young, but young enough for promotion if it was offered or fell his way. To sailing master like old Cristie, or maybe to a command of his own, no matter how small, just given the time and the chance.

He watched the first lieutenant speaking to Partridge, the boatswain. He liked and respected Galbraith, trusted him also.

He faced it for the hundredth time. How long would that last if he revealed that he had witnessed the murder?

He had to go down to the chart room. It was no use just going over it again. He felt the fine new spyglass the youth Ede had made for him. *Put yourself first.* But it would not go away.

Luke Jago perched his buttocks against a massive stone bollard and picked his teeth with a piece of whalebone. The stone was still warm, and yet looking across the dark, heaving water there were already lights showing on some of the ships, like fireflies at his home in Dover. What he could still remember of it.

The gig's crew was close by, where he could keep a weather eye open for some last-minute chancer, although he had to admit they had become a fairly reliable boat's crew. He heard someone kicking stones into the water. Midshipman Deighton, doing his share on this duty. A "young gentleman," and one day he would be a lieutenant, and maybe another jumped-up slave driver. But he had to admit that he liked him, shared something which even his keen mind could not define or accept. Always ready to listen and learn, never threw his weight about even with the most junior hands, but it went deeper than that. Like the one most important thing which had brought them together, the fact that Jago had been there when Deighton's father had died. Shot down by one of his own men, although nobody ever spoke of it. Not even the captain.

He thought of the missing midshipman. San*dell*. He smiled grimly. San*dell*, as he had always insisted. Nobody spoke much about that, either. Deighton was affected by it, although he had never liked the other midshipman. It was like a presence moving between decks.

Captain Bolitho had been ashore for most of the day, but had sent word by messenger that the gig would not be needed. *Until now.*

He watched the passing throng of people; it was always the same at the Rock. It was funny when you thought about it. A few years back and you could imagine the Dons, just over the water at Algeiras, waiting to spy on ships arriving and leaving here, ready to send fast horsemen with the news, *where from?* or *where bound?* The enemy. Now there were ships of a dozen flags at anchor here. He could recall all too easily when there was only one flag. The rest were the foe.

But they were not making much of a secret of their presence here; he had heard the first lieutenant say as much to young Bellairs. Why *Unrivalled?* Any fast schooner or courier brig could have done it. They did it every day somewhere or other.

He hid a smile in the dying sunlight.

Two sailors from another vessel had looked at the gig, and had asked what was their ship?

When he had told them, one had exclaimed, "That's Captain Bolitho's ship, matey!"

Jago had been forced to give in to a feeling of pride, which before would have been laughable.

Neither of those two Jacks had ever laid eyes on the captain. But the name was enough.

Deighton stood up and brushed his white trousers. "The captain's coming."

Jago pushed himself away from the bollard and spat the whalebone into the water. *Must be getting old.* Deighton had seen him first.

He could sense the impatience, anger even, as the captain stepped down into the nodding boat.

Jago gauged the mood. Took a chance.

"We sailin' again, sir?"

He saw the upturned face, the dark eyes framed by the hair, the familiar cocked hat. He had gone too far this time.

But Adam said quietly, "We are so, my friend. In Falmouth I heard of an errand boy who rose to be a rich and powerful man. Now you can see a captain who has become an errand boy!"

The boat's crew shifted on their thwarts, sharing it, some without understanding. Midshipman Deighton rested one hand on the tiller to lean forward and listen. So very different, yet these two men had filled his life when he had believed himself to be alone.

He remembered the day he had met Captain Bolitho for the first time. He had been sympathetic, but not out of mere duty, as his father would have reminded him. Like a friend. Someone who had understood what he was going through.

"Cast off! Bear off forrard!" His voice confident and strong.

As the gig pulled away into the lengthening shadows, Midshipman Richard Deighton would have changed roles with no one.

Jago smiled and settled back to watch the regular rise and fall of the blades.

Once, he saw the captain turn to look at the big hulk he had seen on their arrival. The last time had been when Admiral Lord Rhodes had ordered *Unrivalled* to stand fast, to discontinue the chase of the renegade frigate, and this captain had ignored the signal. And together they had won the day.

But in his heart Jago knew he was seeing the moored hulk and her empty gun ports as she had once been, as his uncle's flagship.

He saw him remove his hat and hold it against his breast, and was surprised that it touched him so deeply.

And yet, beyond even that, he felt something else. Like a warning.

It was the scent of danger.

Two days out of Gibraltar, *Unrivalled* was heading north again after standing well clear of Cape St Vincent to find more sea room. As was expected, Cristie's prophecy about the wind had proved true. Within an hour of leaving the Strait, the Rock had vanished into thick mist, probably rain deeper inland, and now, close-hauled on the starboard tack and leaning steeply into the wind despite her reefed topsails, the frigate was constantly swept by a sea which thundered over her weather side, making any movement on deck dangerous.

At first light the masthead had reported a sail directly to the north, but with such poor visibility any recognition was pure guesswork.

While they reeled over, fighting into a wind which at times seemed to be from directly abeam, most of the hands, especially the older ones, were glad they were well clear of the land.

Adam climbed to the quarterdeck as the forenoon watch relieved other soaked and exhausted seamen, who, under these conditions, were unlikely to be offered anything to warm their insides before they were called once more to trim or reef the salt-hardened canvas. But rum could work wonders; he had even heard two of the relieved topmen sharing a joke as they groped their way below, no doubt wondering what all the fuss and urgency had been about.

Adam wondered also. He had had a meeting with the Captain-in-Charge at Gibraltar; the acting flag officer was otherwise engaged, being entertained aboard one of the visiting Dutch ships. How long would it take to accept this change of allegiance, enemies becoming friends overnight?

The captain had told him that the information he had given to be carried in *Unrivalled* would be useful and important to Lord Exmouth. He had not said that it was vital.

Nothing, it seemed, had changed. Several small vessels had been attacked by Algerine pirates, their crews taken as prisoners to the Dey's stronghold. There had been other reports of innocent fishermen being slaughtered by Turkish soldiers at Bona, a port Adam had good cause to remember.

The documents and despatches were now locked in the strong-box, *to be guarded at all times,* the Captain-in-Charge had insisted.

He braced himself as his head and shoulders emerged from the companion, his hair blowing unheeded as he waited for the deck to rear up again.

Bellairs greeted him, eyes reddened by the onslaught of wind and spray.

"Steady she goes, sir! Nor' by west!"

Adam gripped the rail, feeling the ship plunge and rear again, like a thoroughbred fighting a halter. Despite his weariness, his regular visits to this windswept place of command, he could still feel the old excitement. The challenge: man, ship, and ocean.

He stared along the upper deck, aware of the sharply braced yards, the spray pouring from the hard-bellied canvas like icy pellets, conscious that everything was in its proper place, stays and running rigging taking the strain, boats on their tier firmly secured. With this sea, it must have been a fight just to accomplish that . . .

He watched the water boil against the guns on the lee side, saw crouched figures snatching at handholds until the miniature tidal wave had passed over them before running to the next task, another repair to cordage and canvas.

"*Deck there! Sail on the starboard bow!*" There must have been a momentary lull as the lookout yelled again, "*Two* sail, sir!"

Bellairs wiped his streaming face with his sleeve. "Our two companions of yesterday, sir?"

"Perhaps." Adam peered up at the swaying topmasts, trying to picture *Unrivalled* as another lookout might see her. Whatever they were they were not running away, or trying to avoid an encounter. Common enough when ships' masters knew there was a man-of-war about, on their lawful occasions or not. They had not forgotten the press-gangs, either.

He thought of the Dutch ships he had seen at Gibraltar. Part of Exmouth's plan? Or was it mere coincidence?

He saw a man clambering up the main shrouds, fingers and toes expertly hooked around the ratlines as the hull reeled over again, so that he appeared to be hanging bodily above the leaping wave crests. He saw the seaman turn and stare down at him. It was Lucas, whom Sandell had accused of threatening behaviour. It was still hard to believe that an officer had gone missing. They might never discover what had happened. He tried to shut it out. *Somebody knew.*

He glanced at the masthead again. "Mr Cousens, take your glass and go aloft, will you? I'd value a second pair of eyes up there."

Cousens grinned. Signals midshipman, as Bellairs had been such a short while ago, and with luck the next one for the board for lieutenant. He should do well; he worked at his studies, but had a reputation for practical jokes. Also, he had a good head for heights.

Woodthorpe, the master's mate of the watch, asked carefully, "D' you think them ships want to speak with us, sir?"

Adam watched the midshipman climbing steadily up the

shrouds, the signals telescope hanging across his shoulders like a small cannon.

"We shall likely lose them soon." He looked at the compass, imagining the spread of shark-blue ocean which separated the vessels. The bearing was the same, as far as he could estimate in this unruly sea. A converging tack, then. With the benefit of a wind under their coat-tails they should pass well ahead, heading west, deep into the Atlantic.

"Deck there! Leading ship is a frigate, sir!"

Some of the seamen on deck had stopped work to listen, anything to break the aching monotony of hauling on ropes and hammering wedges into position. Adam moved a little apart from the others. Without looking, he knew Cristie had come on deck. In a moment Galbraith would appear. They never had to be told.

He swallowed and tasted the treacle he had spread on a biscuit, with some of Napier's strong coffee. He had questioned him about his leg, and Napier had said that he had picked up a splinter in his foot; otherwise he was quite well. In some ways the boy reminded him of himself at that age. He was not a very good liar, either. He would speak to the surgeon.

"Deck there! She's a Yankee!"

Someone gave an ironic cheer, and a boatswain's mate remarked, "Don't them buggers 'ave somethin' useful to do?" Another man laughed.

Adam looked at the masthead again, the spray running over his face like rain. *Come on. Come on.* With that big telescope Cousens would be able to see the ship well enough to identify it. But what about the other? What was an American ship doing out here? Perhaps, after all, the United States government was taking the slave trade seriously, although until now they had strongly resisted any attempt by patrols to stop and search their vessels in the known vicinity.

Adam took a telescope from the rack and climbed up into the

weather shrouds. He was soaked through in any case; he hated wearing a heavy tarpaulin coat. If you slipped it could carry you down as quickly as any round shot . . .

He waited, the tarred shrouds biting into his skin while the hull went over once again. *Unrivalled* must have lifted suddenly on a freak crest; he saw the other ship quite strongly, her buff sails and most of her shining side before she dipped into the sea again. But not before he had seen the bright patch of colour standing out from her peak like polished metal, the Stars and Stripes.

He clambered down again and saw Galbraith waiting for him.

He said, "Yankee frigate." He looked at him, his eyes steady despite the biting spray. "The other one's a barque."

"*The* barque?"

"Could be. In which case . . ."

"*Deck there! The next vessel's a prize—she's flyin' the same flag!*"

Adam bit his lip. "*In which case,* the Americans have beaten us to it. This time."

Galbraith said, "They're still closing with us, sir."

Adam turned away and walked down to the leeward side. Perhaps Rear-Admiral Herrick had made a report to their lordships about *Osiris,* the mystery slaver. It would further involve Sillitoe. He frowned. And therefore Catherine. He pictured Herrick again, aboard this ship. Intense, stubborn, but sincere. Finding it impossible to break a code he had almost been born to uphold. *Sir Richard's oldest friend.*

He climbed into the shrouds again, hearing two bells chime from the forecastle as he settled himself in a suitable position. An hour had passed. It felt like mere minutes since he had come on deck.

He tried again. It was clearer this time, the other frigate much closer, two miles at the most. He shifted the glass with great care, gritting his teeth against the raw pain in his arm and thigh with each steep plunge. The Stars and Stripes were very bright and clear now. And men too, lining the gangway and clinging to the rigging to stare at this ship. He moved the glass again. To gloat, probably. Then he found the barque, graceful for her size, closer but angled away from the frigate's quarter. And he saw the flag. It was flying above another which had been crudely tied into a knot, the mark of submission. The prize.

He saw some of the sailors waving from the other frigate, well aware that telescopes were watching them.

Cristie said, "Proud as peacocks now, ain't they?"

Bellairs said, "The wind's easing, sir." It was a question rather than a report.

Adam nodded, impatient to end it. "Call all hands. Shake out those reefs, and we shall take her closer to the wind." He glanced at Cristie. "Show them how it's done, eh?"

High on his perch in the crosstrees, Midshipman Cousens heard the faint squeal of calls, and guessed what was happening far beneath his dangling legs. Clinging to a stay, the lookout watched him patiently, eager to be alone again. Cousens trained his glass. It felt like a bar of ballast in his wet hands.

He studied the frigate and then wiped his eye, thinking he had missed something. Somehow the picture had changed, which was impossible.

The waving, cheering sailors, soundless and tiny in the lens, were gone, and . . . he could scarcely believe it . . . the Stars and Stripes had vanished also.

Even as he watched, the line of ports opened, as one or so it seemed, and he stared with disbelief at the guns which shone in the hard light like black teeth.

He groped for the lookout and punched his arm.

"Alarm! Alarm!"

All else was blotted out by the growling roar of a broadside, and one last scream as he fell.

15 THE OLDEST TRICK

"BEAT TO QUARTERS and clear for action!"

For an instant longer there was chaos as the men pouring on deck to obey the last order broke into groups, the constant drills taking charge, even as a few stared with disbelief at the other ships.

Adam cupped his hands. "Alter course two points! Steer nor'-west by north!"

Men were running past to take station at the braces while gun crews ducked around them, looking for familiar faces, driven to a faster pace by the staccato rattle from the drums of two marines by the mainmast truck.

Adam gripped the rail with both hands, watching the other frigates, the open gun ports, the sudden menace of their black muzzles.

It was too late. Already too late. *I should have known, guessed.*

"Steady she goes! Nor'-west by north, sir!"

All else was drowned by the rolling thunder of a broadside. Perhaps the other captain had sensed that *Unrivalled* had been about to spread more sail, and maybe thought it was his only chance.

It was like a wild wind, shots screaming through the rigging and punching holes in topsails and jibs. And the tell-tale quiver of iron smashing into the hull.

He looked again. One 18-pounder had been flung inboard from its port and a man was pinned under it, his arms reaching out, as if he were drowning. His lower limbs did not move. Nor would they.

Two other seamen lay by the foremast, one cut almost in half by a ball, the other trying to drag himself away. To hide.

Galbraith shouted, "If he'd waited, he'd have dismasted us!"

Adam saw the shattered telescope, broken across one of the guns, and Cousens's body, dislodged from the main-yard as the hands hauled at the braces to fall like a rag doll to the deck.

He felt the grief changing to fury, white-hot, and beyond reason. *They died because of me. Not because of the stupid, over-cautious orders, but because of me.*

The guns were running out again along the other frigate's side, and he tried to clear his mind. Not quick, but fast enough. There were trained men working those guns: renegades, rebels, whatever he chose to call them was irrelevant. Still on a converging tack, the second vessel still wearing. The frigate mounted 38 guns, so perhaps the barque carried armament of her own. Her master had also expected *Unrivalled* to change tack, come fully aback perhaps, and leave her stern exposed for just long enough.

"Ready, sir!"

He ignored the faces around him and sought out Varlo at the first division of guns. He was standing motionless, his hanger drawn and across one shoulder as if this were a formal inspection, and one of his boots had left a bloody footprint, from the man pinned under the eighteen-pounder.

"As you bear! Fire!"

The broadside was well timed, crashing aft along the side, the orange tongues spurting through the dense pall of smoke funnelling inboard through the ports and over the gangway.

The other frigate had the wind-gage but, held over by the same wind, her muzzles high-angled, *Unrivalled* had the range.

Adam knew the enemy had fired again; cordage, severed blocks and charred strips of canvas fell and scattered across the gun crews who, working like demons with handspikes and rammers, were already responding to the hoarse shouts of command. *Unrivalled* was alone, and ordered to be so until her mission was completed. If anything vital carried away now, the other vessels would lie off and take their time, until there was no one left alive to prevent a boarding. A slaughter.

He seized Midshipman Deighton's arm and pushed him against the rail, and trained a telescope across his shoulder. The youth was staring at him; he could even feel his breath, his body shaken to another ragged salvo. But his eyes were steady, trying to tell him that he was not afraid.

Adam acknowledged him without speaking and concentrated his gaze on the other frigate. There was a black flag at her peak now, and he recalled with insane clarity the words of the dying renegade captain in that same cabin beneath his feet. *In war, we're all mercenaries.*

He saw the shot-holes in the sails, raw timbers protruding from a bulwark, a few empty gun ports. He lowered the glass. But it was not enough. *Not enough.*

He flinched as he felt hands fumbling around his waist, the sudden drag of a sword against his hip. It was Jago, face half shaved, caught by the sudden call to arms.

More shots slammed into the lower hull, each one a body blow. Jago reached out and gripped his arm, unsmiling, and said harshly, "No matter, sir. I'll finish shavin' when we're done with this scum!"

Adam stared at him, and realised, perhaps for the first time, how close he had been to breaking, failing the ship, and the men like Jago who never questioned why they were here, or who would die next.

"We'll hold this course!" He saw Galbraith cup his hand over his ear to listen as the roar of cannonfire drowned out all else. The gun captains, blinded by smoke, were barely able to see their enemy, and yet with practised fingers they gripped their trigger-lines even as each carriage lurched up against the side. *Fire! Sponge out! Load! Run out! Fire!* If the pattern was broken, they were finished.

A boatswain's mate dropped to the deck without a sound. Unmarked, his face shocked, as if he couldn't accept the haste of death.

The range was down to less than a mile, with both ships firing, the churning fog of gunsmoke hiding everything but the upper yards and punctured sails of the adversaries.

Galbraith yelled, "He's badly mauled, sir! One shot to our two, if that!" He was actually grinning, and waving his hat to the quarterdeck gun crews. Adam walked to the centre of the deck, his legs suddenly able to carry him again.

"Then he'll try to board us, Leigh!" He found he had the sword in his hand. Not his own: Jago must have snatched it from somewhere. There must be no more mistakes. *Could not.* "All guns double-shotted and with grape. Warn the smashers up forrard to be ready." Over his shoulder he called, "Bring her up a point, Mr Cristie—we don't want to keep him waiting!"

He watched the topmasts of the other ship rising through the smoke, saw small, bright flashes from the tops or yards where marksmen had taken up their most effective positions. Distant, without apparent danger, until you felt the heavy balls thudding into the deck, or gouging up splinters as if raised by some invisible chisel. And that other sound. Lead smashing into flesh and bone, a man's pitiful cries as he was dragged away to the orlop, and the surgeon. A ball ploughed into the boat tier, and severed the bow of the big cutter like an axe. More men fell as the splinters cut amongst them like arrows.

Adam thought suddenly of Napier. *That last time.* When he swung round he saw the youth on one knee, tying a bandage around a marine's forearm, his fingers red with blood, and with the same serious expression he wore even when preparing a meal for his captain.

"Keep *down*, David!" Their eyes met, and he thought he heard him reply. It sounded, insanely, like ". . . a pony ride!"

"Ready, sir!" Every gun captain who was able was peering aft, fist raised. Galbraith had drawn his hanger, and the marines at the packed hammock nettings had already fixed bayonets.

The carronades, too, would be ready. If they failed now . . .

He shouted, "Stand fast, and take them as they come, lads!" He saw faces, eyes staring. Wild, fearful, desperate. And they were his men.

He waved the unfamiliar sword. "Remember, lads! *Second to None!*"

With a shuddering lurch, the enemy's jib-boom and bowsprit drove over the forecastle like a giant tusk. He could hear the crack of muskets, and voices merged above the din of grinding hulls and snapping cordage like a hymn of hate. A severed halliard snaked through the crouching seamen and marines, and had somehow become entangled with Midshipman Cousens's body, so that it swayed upright again, as if to answer the call he had followed without question for most of his young life.

The sword sliced down. *"Fire!"*

Towards the bows, the gun muzzles must have been overlapping those of the enemy now looming high alongside. At point-blank range, double-shotted and with added grape for good measure, the explosion sounded like a ship being blasted apart. Where seamen had been standing and shaking their weapons, waiting for the moment of impact, there was now a smoking strip of water. Men and pieces of men, the dead and the dying ground together as the hulls were brought to another embrace by the wind.

But a few had taken the risk and had somehow gained a foothold, some by the smoking carronades which had transformed the enemy's foredeck into a bloody shambles.

"Forward, Marines!"

That was Captain Luxmore. Adam could not see him beyond

the smoke, but imagined he would be immaculately turned out, as always.

He could hear a new sound, like a horn, rather than a trumpet or bugle. Galbraith was shouting at him. "They're casting off, sir!" His voice was harsh with disbelief. "On the run!"

Adam swung round. "Grapple her!" Galbraith was staring at him, as if he could not understand. *"Grapple her!"*

But it was too late; the hulls were lurching apart, like two prizefighters who had given and taken too much.

Adam gazed up at the sky, clear again now above the smoke, in that other, impossible world.

Where was the barque? Why could Galbraith not understand?

He felt the solitary explosion, and was only partly aware of the deck splintering behind him. Half the double wheel had been shot away; one of the helmsmen still clung to the spokes, but his legs and entrails painted a grisly pattern on the planking.

And above it all he heard the lookout's cry. Far, far away, beyond all this pain.

"Deck there! Sail on th' larboard quarter!"

He felt Jago holding his shoulders, and realised that he had dropped on his knees. And then came the pain. He heard himself cry out; it was like a branding iron. He tried to grope at his side, but someone was preventing it. For some reason he thought of John Allday. When they had last met. Had spoken, and had held hands . . . as it must have been . . .

Galbraith was here now, eyes anxious, moving to others around them as if to seek assurance, or grim acceptance.

He heard himself speaking, anguished, incoherent.

"They-broke-off-the-action-because-of-this-newcomer."

He almost bit through his lip as the agony lanced him. "Otherwise . . ." He could not go on; there was no need.

The smoke was clearing; he heard the guns run out yet again.

Someone was calling pitifully, another was insisting, "I'm 'ere, Ted! 'Ang on now!"

He turned his head and saw Napier bending down to wipe his forehead with a cloth.

Cristie's voice. "Surgeon's comin'!"

He tried to rise, but felt the blood running across his side and down his thigh.

"Mr Galbraith." He waited for his face to move into focus. "Get the ship to Plymouth. Those despatches must reach Lord Exmouth."

Galbraith said, "God damn the despatches."

"How many did we lose?" He gripped his sleeve. "Tell me."

"Eight at a count, sir."

"Too many." He shook his head. "The oldest trick, and I did not see it . . ." A shadow shut out the misty glare. Small, strong hands for so burly a figure. The Irish voice, calm, taking no nonsense, even from the captain.

"Ah, be still, sir." A pause, and some sharp pain, insistent. Pitiless. "A close thing. I'll deal with it now." The shadow moved away, and he heard O'Beirne murmur, "Marine Fisher was killed. Dropped his musket as he fell, and it fired on impact. It found the wrong target!"

He felt hands lifting him, others reaching out as if to reassure him, or themselves.

Galbraith waited until the little procession had disappeared below, then he looked at the scars and the pitted sails, the drying blood, and the deck where men had died. And more would follow them before they saw Plymouth Hoe again.

He shaded his eyes to look at the other ships, but they had become unreal in the mist and the drifting smoke. Already he could hear hammers and saws, men calling to one another as they worked high above the embattled deck.

How was it that the captain had seemed to know what was happening, at the moment of truth, and later, when the other frigate had tried to free herself from their deadly embrace? And what if the barque's captain had realised that *Unrivalled*'s steering had been disabled by that single shot?

He took a mug of something from one of the wardroom messmen, and almost choked on it. It was neat rum.

And when he had seen the captain stagger and then fall to his knees, he had heard himself speaking aloud. *Anyone but him. Please, God, not him!*

It was like a voice. *Because you could not have done it. Nor will you.*

He stared at the flag locker, overturned in that brief but savage encounter.

"Attend to it, Mr Cousens!"

Then he turned away, sickened, remembering, and murmured, "Forgive me."

There was nobody to hear him.

Daniel Yovell critically regarded the nib of a new pen before testing it against his thumbnail. Beyond the white-painted screen he could hear the constant sounds and movements of men working to repair damage, reeving new cordage, or replacing sails which had been shot through in the engagement.

It seemed that the work had never stopped, and it was sometimes difficult to believe that the brief action had been more than four days ago.

It was as if the labour was a need, the only way sailors could put their anger and sadness behind them. Yovell had watched men die, and had been there when they had made their last journey, down into permanent darkness.

He looked across the littered table at the sheaf of notes the captain had used to compile his report. In spite of the wound he seemed unable to rest, or make any allowances for his pain and loss of blood.

Even O'Beirne seemed baffled by the will and determination which was driving him.

He was with the captain now, in the sleeping quarters. They made a good pair, Yovell thought, neither willing to give in to the other.

He saw Napier by the stern windows, watching some gulls swooping across *Unrivalled*'s lively wake, their strident screams lost in this cabin. It was like a haven, separate from the rest of the ship, yet closely linked by the comings and goings of officers and messengers from the working parties, no matter how lowly. The captain had to be informed.

Yovell thought of his own part in it. Assisting the surgeon, seeing men he had come to know suffer and sometimes die, stretched out on that bloodied table. He had held the hand of one seaman and had recited a prayer for him, inserting his own words when he had forgotten some of it, and all the while the dying sailor had been very still, watching him. Finally O'Beirne had pulled the man's hand away and signalled for his assistants.

"Gone, I'm afraid." Almost callous. How else could he do his work?

He thought, too, of the burials, the uncanny silence falling over the ship as if even the dead were listening.

Anonymous canvas bundles, weighted with round shot. But as each name was read out the face would come to mind, with maybe a word or a deed remembered.

Captain Bolitho had insisted on doing that as well, the familiar, much-thumbed prayer book in one hand, this boy, Napier, holding his hat, and Jago standing at his elbow, ready to support him if the pain became too much.

O'Beirne came into the cabin and dragged on his coat; Yovell had already seen the dark stains of blood on his shirt. He did not seem to need sleep, either.

O'Beirne saw Napier pouring a glass of brandy.

"Well trained, boy!" But the usual humour evaded him. He looked at Yovell and waved one hand despairingly. "Can't *you* do anything about it? The man will kill himself if he keeps to this pace." He swallowed the brandy gratefully and held out the goblet to be refilled. "When we reach Plymouth I shall submit my papers for a transfer, see if I don't!" Then he did grin, very wearily.

They both knew he had no intention of quitting *Unrivalled*.

Yovell asked quietly, "How is he?"

O'Beirne tilted the goblet in a shaft of sunlight. "Lucky, I would say without hesitation. The musket ball cut across the old wound he received when he lost his other command, *Anemone*. We'll not know the total damage for a while. I've stitched him up as well as I may under these circumstances. Another inch . . ." he shook his head, ". . . and he'd have gone outboard with those other poor fellows."

He closed his worn leather bag with a snap. "I'm away now, before he makes me forget my sacred oath!"

He paused by the screen door. "Napier, come and see me later. I want to have a look at that leg of yours." The door closed behind him.

Yovell sighed. The captain had even found time to tell O'Beirne about the boy's injury.

Adam Bolitho heard the door, and O'Beirne's unmistakable voice as he spoke with the sentry.

With care, he sat on a chest and leaned forward to study himself in the hanging mirror. Calmly and intently, as he might examine some failing subordinate.

He was naked to the waist, his sunburned skin dark against the most recent layer of bandages. Like a tight waistcoat, and a constant reminder, throbbing now after O'Beirne's examination. The bowl was beside the hanging cot, some bloodstained water shivering in time with the dull boom of the rudder-head.

He listened, seeing the ship as she must appear to any other vessel, responding to a freshening wind. It had veered overnight, south-easterly. He found that he was holding his side, reliving it. The closeness of disaster: death had seemed almost secondary.

Tomorrow would see them off Ushant: the Western Approaches, and the English Channel.

But he could find no satisfaction in it. He could only think about the unknown barque; there was no certainty that she was *Osiris*. But she had made the signal causing the frigate to cast off when they had been about to grapple and board *Unrivalled.* So that the barque's master could bring his own armament to bear. But for the unexpected sighting of another sail, *it could have ended there.* The unknown vessel had made off almost immediately, as had their two attackers.

The barque had made the signal. So she must have the authority and the intelligence to plan and undertake so dangerous a venture. His mind repeated it. It could have ended there.

He glanced around the sleeping quarters. Quieter now; a stand-easy must have been piped to allow his men to rest from their countless tasks.

He thought of Jago by his side, dark features grim and challenging as they had buried the dead.

During the action and in the days which had followed they had lost a total of fourteen men. Some others lingered on the verge, but O'Beirne was hopeful. Fourteen, then. Too many.

In his mind's eye he could still see them. Midshipman Cousens racing up the shrouds, the big telescope swaying over his shoulder. *So full of life.* A boatswain's mate named Selby. Adam had not known much about him; perhaps in some way he had avoided it. Selby had been the alias used by his own father when he had been escaping justice. *When he saved my life, and I did not know him.* The Royal Marine, Fisher, an old sweat who had never gained promotion in the Corps. But a popular man, who had always been proud to boast of his service in the old third-rate *Agamemnon,* Horatio Nelson's last command as a captain. It had marked him out, lent him a certain celebrity. He had died without knowing that he had nearly killed his own captain.

He found he was holding his side again. Fourteen men. He stood up slowly and grimaced as the pain seared across his ribs. *And Midshipman Sandell.*

The hammers had started up once more. Stand-easy was over.

He saw Napier by the door, and that he had a clean shirt over his arm.

Adam smiled. He could not remember the last time he had done so.

"We'll go on deck, David. Are you ready?"

Napier shook out the clean shirt and nodded gravely. It was what he had been waiting to hear.

"Aye, *ready,* sir!"

Yovell looked up as they entered the great cabin. "Mr Midshipman Deighton was here, sir. I told him it was not convenient . . ." He saw the clean breeches and shirt and Napier's face.

Adam said, "I sent for him. I am appointing him signals midshipman. He is more experienced than the others, keen too." He raised his hand. "Never fear, my friend, I shall see him directly. On deck."

Yovell pushed the spectacles on to his forehead and gazed at his hands. They felt as if they were shaking. With God's help he could usually conceal emotion. It was not like him at all.

He heard the door close, and the stamp of the sentry's boots.

It was what they all needed.

The captain was back.

The admiral's servant moved the chair a few inches as if to indicate that it had already been selected for the visitor. Adam had noticed that there was little conversation between Lord Exmouth and his personal servant; perhaps they had been together for so long that spoken instruction had become unnecessary.

He lowered himself into the chair, afraid that the pain would return at this moment when he needed to be fully alert. Galbraith had warned him about it, had almost pleaded with him, and Jago had been unable to conceal his indignation.

"What do they expect, sir? You have been wounded—you shouldn't be here at all, by rights!"

Adam thought of Herrick, overcoming his disablement, visiting *Unrivalled* at Freetown, and the stubborn determination which had made him refuse the offer of a bosun's chair to hoist him aboard.

He had had misgivings of his own as the gig had approached the flagship's side. Like a cliff; he was still not sure how he had reached the entry port without losing his hold and falling headlong, as Herrick would have done but for Jago's swift action.

Jago had touched his hat, standing in the gig while Adam had reached out to pull himself on to the "stairway," and he had heard him murmur softly, "Nice an' easy does it, sir."

And now he was here, in the admiral's great cabin. The din of his reception had been the worst part, not the calls, or the slap and click of muskets, but the faces on the fringe of the side party and the waiting officers. Curiosity or excitement, he was not certain. Like the silence which had fallen over Plymouth's busy harbour and jetties as *Unrivalled* was moved slowly to her allotted anchorage. Her company had worked without complaint, for him, for the ship, and for one another, but they could not conceal the scars of battle, and only the most pressing tasks could be accomplished while the ship was still under way.

It was the first anyone had known of the action, and he had

sensed the shocked stillness of those same vessels which had seen them depart less than three weeks ago. Some store ships had stopped work when the frigate's shadow had glided slowly abeam, the hoists and derricks motionless, as if it were a mark of respect.

The request for his appearance on board the flagship *Queen Charlotte* had been brought by the guard-boat and not by any signal, and the officer of the guard had signed for and carried the secret despatches to this very cabin.

Lord Exmouth sat back in his chair, outwardly relaxed, but his keen eyes missed nothing.

"I read your report, Bolitho. Very thorough, especially under the circumstances." His hand moved very slightly and a tray with two fine glasses appeared on his table. Another small movement, and the servant began to pour wine. "You might like this. I keep it for myself, usually."

He continued, "I also read other things which you did *not* put in your report, and I appreciate how you felt, *feel*, about the sly and unprovoked attack made under false colours." He shook his head. "An old trick. But you were under orders. *My* orders. Which is why I selected you in the first place. Any other vessel, brig or fast schooner, would have stood no chance at all."

There was a discreet tap on the door and a lieutenant moved soundlessly to the table and placed a note by the admiral's glass. He left the cabin just as quietly, giving Adam only a brief glance in passing.

Lord Exmouth read the note and screwed it into a tight ball. "It is as I surmised, Bolitho. The Dey has gathered more ships to his flag, like the frigate which attacked *Unrivalled*. French, Dutch, who can say? But I don't have to explain that to you, do I?" He made another small gesture and the glasses were refilled.

Adam tried to stretch his body in the chair, testing it, feeling the immediate drag of the bandages. He did not remember even drinking the wine. It was almost cool in the great cabin, but he felt as if his body was burning.

The admiral was observing him calmly. "You did not mention that you were wounded. I am not a mind-reader, Bolitho, nor should I have to remind you." He did not wait for any reply. "Time is running out. I intend to sail from here at the end of the month. To Gibraltar, where we shall be joined by a Dutch squadron under Baron van de Capellan, an officer who is known to me, and whom I greatly respect." His eyes crinkled in a smile. "In your report you mention that you did in fact see some Dutch ships at the Rock. Very astute of you—perhaps you had already guessed what their purpose might be?"

"I had good cause to remember one Dutch frigate, my lord."

"Indeed, indeed. But as Our Nel was given to say, *war makes strange bedfellows*. And peace creates even more!"

He glanced at the skylight as the trill of calls drifted down into this remote cabin. The admiral was a great man, but perhaps still a frigate captain at heart. The sound of running rigging in the middle of the night watches . . . someone calling a command or a warning . . . Like young Cousens, who had seen the danger before anyone. And had paid for it.

"I have a good squadron already, Bolitho. To say that I need a certain captain is too frivolous a term for my taste. You have the experience and the skill for this venture. I want you in the van when I begin the attack on the Dey's defenses and his ships. If your ship is not in fit repair by the time I make that move, then I will find you another!"

Adam caught his breath, astonished and dismayed.

"She *will* be ready, my lord! With some local help, I can . . ."

The admiral held up one hand. "I will arrange that. Shall you be fit enough to follow the flag?"

His whole world was suddenly compressed into this moment, with this famous man, and the threat of losing *Unrivalled*.

"I will be ready, my lord. You have my word."

The admiral frowned and pressed his fingertips together. "Your word may not be enough. I knew your uncle, and I can see something of him in you. You'd not rest and leave the routine to others."

Adam stared around the cabin, the truth stark and very real. He would lose *Unrivalled* . . .

The admiral stood up and walked aft to the tall windows. The big three-decker had plenty of headroom, even for him. Perhaps he was still with his own frigate, somewhere . . .

He turned swiftly.

"Your first lieutenant, Galbraith. I met him. He seemed competent enough." It sounded like a question. "I read somewhere that you recommended him for promotion, even though you were short of trained people at the time? So you must have confidence in the fellow's ability."

"Yes, sir." Why was it so strange, that he had hesitated? "He is a fine officer."

"That settles it, Bolitho. You will take a week or so, and spend the time ashore. Cornwall is my home too, y' know." He smiled, but his eyes never wavered from Adam's face. "I am not giving you an order, Bolitho. I want you in the van. If you do not think you can do it, then tell me now. I would not hold it against you, not after what you've done."

"I can, my lord. So will *Unrivalled*."

Discreet voices. It was time.

Adam stood up and gasped involuntarily with pain.

Lord Exmouth held out his hand and took Adam's between both of his own. As Allday had done.

"I will make certain that your ship has all the aid she needs. I may even be able to hurry up the bounty money owed to your people. It will not raise the dead, but it will lift a few spirits, I daresay!"

The flag lieutenant had returned; the door was open and ready.

Then the admiral released his grip and said almost curtly, "You will go to your boat by bosun's chair. This time. Pride is one thing, Bolitho, but conceit is an enemy!"

The servant was already leaving with the tray and the two glasses; the next visitor was to receive other than the admiral's own wine. Lord Exmouth smiled, almost sadly.

"He is a good fellow. Lost his hearing back in '93, after we captured the *Cleopatre* when I commanded *Nymphe.*" He glanced around the spacious cabin, and his eyes were momentarily wistful. "Now, she *was* a fine little ship."

Adam went on deck, past two other captains waiting to see the admiral. Unbelievably, the great man would have been the same age as himself when he had commissioned *Unrivalled.*

He turned and raised his hat to the flag, and to the assembled side party.

Then, hardly trusting himself to hesitate, he walked directly to the group of seamen waiting with the bosun's chair.

One, a boatswain's mate, made a quick adjustment and raised his fist to those handling the tackle.

Only for an instant, their eyes met. Then he whispered, "You showed 'em, Cap'n! Now us'll do it together!" He cupped his hands and yelled, "'Andsomely, lads! 'Oist away, there!"

The marines presented their muskets but he barely noticed. The flagship's people were cheering him as he rose above the gangway and then swung easily above the waiting gig.

Jago steadied the tackle until he had freed himself and reached the sternsheets.

Midshipman Martyns was at the tiller, and looked as if he was about to say something, his face full of excitement and pleasure as the cheers echoed over and around them, as if the whole ship was joining in. But Jago silenced him with a scowl.

Adam felt the gig move away from shadow into sunlight, and thought of the unknown seaman who had spoken to him. *Together.*

He looked at Jago and shrugged. Like hearing someone else. "So be it, then," he said.

The girl sat facing the tall mirror, her hand moving steadily up and down, the brush running through the full length of her dark hair. *Brush . . . brush . . . brush*, unhurriedly, in time with her breathing. She wore a long, loose gown; this was a private moment, and there would be no visitors.

Around and beneath her, the old glebe house was very still. Empty. Montagu had ridden into Falmouth to speak with a carpenter there: some work he wanted carried out while they were away.

Away. London again, that endless journey in their own coach. It was Sir Gregory's wish.

She studied herself in the glass, meeting her own gaze like a stranger. Outside the house it would be hot, very hot, the shrubs and flowers drooping in the sun's glare. She would have to arrange for the roses, at least, to be cared for.

The brush stopped, and she thought of the deserted studio directly beneath her feet. The portrait was finished, but Sir Gregory would still not be satisfied until he had given it more time "to settle in." She had looked at it on several occasions. Interest or guilt; she could not describe her feelings. Would not. The brush began to move again, this time the other side, her long hair draped over her shoulder and down to her thigh. Beneath the gown she was naked. Something she shared with no one.

She thought of the portrait again. Anybody who knew Captain Bolitho, *Captain Adam* as she had heard people call him, would recognise it as fine work. Lady Roxby would be pleased with it. But something was missing. She tossed her hair impatiently. How could she know?

The rose was there in the portrait. Sir Gregory had seemed satisfied with that, if a little surprised.

She tried to think of London and the house, which even the Prince Regent had visited several times.

She plucked at the gown; even the thick walls of the glebe house could not hold the heat at bay. Her feet were bare, and she rubbed one on the tiled floor as she recalled the stone house where she had last seen Adam Bolitho, and that tense little group, and the courier with the recall to duty.

She had heard the cook talking about a man-of-war which had entered Plymouth a day or so ago. Damaged, as if in battle, although there had been no news of any such event. She put down the brush and shook her hair out. This place was so isolated. She rubbed her thigh with her hand. *For my sake.*

She looked at the window, the creeper tapping against the dusty glass although there was no breeze.

She stood up and stepped back from the mirror, her eyes never leaving her reflection. She might be asked to sit for Sir Gregory in London, or for one of his students. Why did she do it? He had never insisted. She stared at herself and touched her body, the hand in the mirror like that of a stranger. *Because it saved me.*

She let the hand fall to her side and turned away from the stranger in the glass. She had heard a horse; Sir Gregory was back, earlier than expected. The house would be alive again. She wondered why he insisted on riding when he could afford any carriage he wanted. *The old cavalier.* He would never change. *What will become of . . .*

She swung round, startled. Someone was banging on the door. She hurried to the window and looked down. No one was supposed to be coming today . . .

She saw the horse, tapping one hoof and idly chewing some overgrown grass, then she saw the stable boy, looking straight up at her, his eyes wide with alarm.

"What is it, Joseph?"

"You'd better come, Miss Lowenna! There's bin an accident!"

She almost fell back from the window. *The horse.* The one he had ridden here. But that was impossible . . . She dragged a shawl around her shoulders, only half aware of some bottles being knocked from the table. It was suddenly clear, like one of Montagu's quick, rough sketches. There was nobody else. Only the cook, and she was probably asleep at the back of the kitchen.

She flung open the doors and exclaimed, "Where is he?"

The boy gestured towards the gates.

"'E be bleedin' bad, miss!"

She ran from the house, heedless of the loose stones cutting her bare feet.

He was sitting on a large piece of slate, part of the original wall when the Church had ruled here.

One leg was bent under him and he was leaning forward, bowing his head, eyes tightly closed, his hair plastered across his forehead. She saw his hat lying in the lane. It was as if she had been there, seen it happen. Then she saw the blood, so bright in the cruel sunshine, on the leg of his breeches. It was spreading even as she watched.

Go now. Leave it. You do not belong here. Go now. It was like some insane chorus. As if all the spirits people had spoken of had come to taunt her. To remind her.

But she said, "Help me, Joseph." She was walking towards him, saw her shadow reaching beyond her, as if the girl from the mirror had taken her place. Then she knelt and put her arms around his shoulders, feeling the sudden, uncontrollable shivering, knowing it was her own.

Joseph was a good, reliable boy. But he was only thirteen.

She heard herself say, "Run to the inn, Joseph, and fetch some men. We must get him into the house." Her mind was reeling. Suppose there were no men at the inn? They might be back in the fields by now. She could not even remember what time it was.

Somehow she steadied herself, and waited for the understanding to show itself on the boy's freckled face.

"Rouse Cook. I want hot water and some clean sheets." She tried to smile, if only to restore his confidence. "Go on, now. I'll stay here until help comes."

She watched him scamper along the pathway. She was alone.

She tried to open his coat, but it was fastened too tightly. There was blood on his shirt also, and it was fresh.

She felt the tremor run through her again. It must have been his ship which had been damaged, the rumour which had eventually reached here all the way from Plymouth. It did not seem possible . . .

She realised that he was staring at her, moving his head slightly as if to discover where he was, what was happening.

He said suddenly, "Blood—it's on your clothing!" He struggled briefly, but she held him.

She wanted to speak, but her mouth seemed dry and stiff. She made another attempt.

"You're safe here." She held him more tightly as she felt his body clench against the pain. "What happened?"

She looked along the lane, but there was no one. Only his hat, lying where it had fallen. Like a spectator.

He said hoarsely, "There was a fight." His head rolled against her shoulder and he groaned. "We drove them off." It seemed to trigger something in his mind. *"Too late. I should have known."*

He was still staring at her with wide eyes, perhaps only just understanding what had happened. She could feel it; he was momentarily without pain. He said, "Lowenna. It *is* you. I was coming . . ." He pressed his face into her shoulder again and gasped, "Oh, dear God!"

She took his hand, gripping it tightly. "Help is coming! Soon now!"

She twisted round to stare down the lane again, and felt his hand on her breast. She looked at it, seeing the blood on his fingers, and on her gown where he had touched her. The fear, the scream was rising in her throat. But she did nothing, and watched the hand on her breast, feeling the heat of his skin through the thin material, like fever.

And then, all at once, everyone was here, even the landlord from the inn.

"We'll take Cap'n Adam, miss," and young Joseph was saying, "There was blood on the road, Miss Lowenna, on the horse too. Must've thrown him."

She stood up as two of the men eased Adam into a chair.

"We kin carry un to the inn, missy!"

She looked down at her gown, the bloodstains, and the smudges of blood around her breast. There was blood on her feet also. She felt nothing. Like taking a pose for a painting. Empty the mind. Wipe away the memory.

She scarcely recognised her voice. Perhaps it was the girl in the mirror.

"Carry him carefully—I will show you the room. I must stop the bleeding. Send someone for a doctor. The garrison will send one if you tell them who it's for."

She held the door open wide and the men lurched against her.

She saw his hand reaching for her, although he could not know what was happening. She seized it, holding it against her, ignoring the people all around her, not even aware of them.

"You are safe now, Adam." And she thought she felt his hand respond. She had called him by name.

16 "WALK WITH ME"

ADAM BOLITHO lay quite still, for how long he could not tell, counting seconds, waiting, finding himself.

He moved slightly, waiting for the pain to bite into him. It was late, sunset. He tried again, and realised that there was a curtain drawn across a window; the sun was still shining, he could see it bringing colour to the bed.

He closed his eyes tightly again, and attempted to fit the pieces together. He was in a bed, covered up to his chin by a sheet. His hand explored his body, his side, and the bandages. Different ones, and there was no blood.

As if through a haze he saw his coat hanging from a chair, the buttons glinting dully in the filtered glow.

His hand moved again, touching his skin, damp, but without the terrible pain. And he was naked.

He groped above the sheet to push the hair from his eyes, but someone had already done that for him. It was like seeing a picture at the end of a dark corridor, remembering. The horse trotting steadily into the lane, the vague outline of the old house through a rank of trees. He had pulled one foot from its stirrup to lessen the strain, the raw reminder of the wound in his side.

A shadow; it might have been a fox, or even a stoat, but it had taken the horse by surprise. *At any other time.* But it was not any other time, and he had pitched headlong from the saddle. How long? How long? He moved his legs, afraid of losing the fragments of memory. Faces and voices, more pain while he was carried somewhere. He felt the bed beneath him. Then other voices, firm, deliberate fingers. He must have fainted again.

But he had not been alone. He was certain of that. Perhaps

O'Beirne had been right about his stubbornness, the admiral, too. *Pride is one thing. Conceit is an enemy.* He let his head fall back again. He could remember! He listened to the sounds. Some birds, rooks most likely. Voices, not in the yard but somewhere in the house. Perhaps they had already sent word to the ship? He tried to move on to one elbow, the returning memory like a threat.

Only then did he see her figure beside the window. In shadow, but she was watching him, he could sense it. Just as he could recall her being here, with him, in that lost space of time before someone else, a professional, had come to attend him.

"Lowenna?" His voice seemed like an echo in this strange room. He did not see her move, but felt her sit carefully on the bed and take his hand in hers, as he thought he could remember before . . .

She said, "Easy, now, Captain. Your wound is dressed. I am sorry you were caused such pain." He felt the fingers moving in his, as if she were suddenly aware of something. "I have sent word to your aunt." She must have sensed his surprise. "She told me I could call upon her. As a friend."

More voices, louder now. One was Montagu's. *Not yet.* Adam said, "You were with me. I can just recall it. You stayed with me." He tightened his grip as her hand attempted to pull away. "No, Lowenna, don't go. You took care of me." He made another effort and raised his body but she laid the hand on his bare shoulder and pressed him down.

"Please, *don't.*"

Adam stared at the ceiling. The voices reminded him of the men who had carried him here. When she had stroked his face with the cloth, when he had protested at the blood on her gown.

He gazed at her. *Seeing it.* Like a word or a sound bringing back a dream. She had stood beside the bed and had dropped the stained gown to the floor. Then she had laid down beside him, dabbing his face with a damp cloth, stiffening when he had reached out for her, and had touched her.

She was looking down at him now, her hair hiding part of her face, lying against his shoulder like warm silk.

She said, "You kept saying that you wanted to save me. I worried so much—every effort seemed too much for you." She looked away, the hair now concealing her eyes. "You wanted to save me. Perhaps you saw me as the captive in the painting. Andromeda?" Her hand touched his mouth. "Don't say anything. I will think of it like that."

He said quietly, "I was coming to see *you*, Lowenna. Because I wanted to, needed to. But for my horse throwing me, I might have been unable to tell you things. Riding here was madness anyway. I have been at sea too long, I fear . . ." He held her hand to his lips. "And I must go back to it soon."

She said, "Your steward is here."

"Bryan Ferguson?" Remembering what he had told Lieutenant Bellairs. "But then Falmouth is a *small* place."

She did not take her hand away but watched as he kissed it. She could recall the eyes of the men who had come from the inn, and her gown in disarray. It would make a good yarn over a glass or two of ale. She had seen and heard it all before, like the creeping terror which she had fought, year after year . . .

She removed her hand. "I never forgot your kiss, my tears, when you left." And today, here, in this room, she had lain beside him, nude, like one of the poses she performed for Sir Gregory. Which had taught her to fight and defy the shame and disgust, and the faces that turned to stare and condemn her.

He had been lost in pain, but aware of her. His hand had found her, and she had done nothing to prevent it.

She still could not believe it. She had wanted to end it then and there, but her mind had cried out for it to continue.

She must face it. Not merely give in like some innocent child.

She said, "I must go to London." She felt his eyes on her. "Tomorrow."

Adam said, "I behaved badly. Abused you, when pain and sickness are no excuse." He kissed her hand again. "But I must see you. It was intended, fate if you like. But I have to be with you."

She saw the smile, the edge of sadness which was lacking in the portrait. She hesitated; this was their last moment alone. "Perhaps . . ."

The door opened and Montagu, with Ferguson peering anxiously over his shoulder, strode into the room.

Adam released her hand. *Perhaps.* It was enough.

John Allday seized his friend's arm and all but pushed him through the doorway into the parlour.

"I'll fetch you a wet meself, Bryan. You sit here—an' I'll want to hear everything about the battle." He paused in his stride. "An' you says young Cap'n Adam is all right?"

Bryan Ferguson glanced around the room, at the model of the *Hyperion* on the table, and Allday's kit of tools beside a rough plan of another fine piece of work.

Unis hurried through to the Long Room but paused to greet him. "Good to see you again. We're busy today—the new road, y' know."

Allday shouted from the cellar, "Only just heard about *Unrivalled* an' the battle—wouldn't have known anything but for one of the revenue men passin' through! My God, Bryan, what are we here? Six miles from Falmouth? You'd think we was on the other side o' the real world!"

Unis touched his shoulder and carried on with her work, but not before Ferguson had seen the hurt on her pretty features.

He took the mug from Allday and waited for him to settle in another chair.

"I see you've started on *Frobisher*, then?"

Allday waved a hand. "Tell me about the battle. Did *Unrivalled* dish the buggers up? Who were they anyway? Why, in our day . . ."

Ferguson sipped the rum, recalling all the excitement, but not the sort his old friend wanted to hear. The urgent message from the glebe house, and going over with Young Matthew to collect Captain Adam. Everybody wanted to know about it. Even Lady Roxby had driven over to see her nephew. A surgeon from the garrison had examined and treated him and had offered a few blunt warnings of his own.

"If you were one of my dragoons, sir, I'd have you flogged in front of the troop for your behaviour. What the *hell* did you expect to happen?"

And he had met the girl, the one who had brought Captain Adam from the town that day when he had got his orders to report back to Plymouth.

He had recognised the change in her, even on so slight an acquaintance. There were rumours about her, how she posed for an artist, no matter that he was one of England's greatest painters to all accounts. His wife Grace had relatives still living in Bodmin, where the girl Lowenna had been born. Lowenna's family had not approved of the match. Hard-working farming people, and the biggest corn chandlers in that part of the county, they had considered their daughter to be out of her depth marrying a scholar, a man who had never known the demands of bending his back and working with his hands. They had moved away after the birth. Vanished, "foreigners" again.

There had been some scandal, although Grace had said little about it. He had not pressed her; he knew what he owed her for nursing and restoring him after the Saintes. He glanced at the model again. Before *Hyperion*'s time, that was . . .

On this occasion the girl had been warmer, but outwardly

correct despite all the upheaval. Withdrawn, many would have said. But Ferguson had recognised something which was still as clear as yesterday. When Sir Richard had brought Lady Catherine to Falmouth for the first time . . . If only . . .

Allday leaned forward. "He was wounded, y' say? Is he taking it well?"

"The ship's repairing at Plymouth." He saw the old light in his friend's eyes. Living it. "The fleet's standing to, if you ask me."

"We should have finished the job last time, matey! Them buggers don't understand a soft hand, that's it an' all about it!"

Ferguson looked at the tools on the table. Captain Adam had told him about *Frobisher*, and that he had seen her at Gibraltar, maybe for something to say as they had driven back together in the new dog-cart, as it was called. More comfortable on that rutted track, it had bigger wheels than his little trap, but Poppy had pulled it like a champion. He thought Adam must have felt every stone and hole on that journey, but his mind had seemed elsewhere. He had been wounded, but in some way, Ferguson thought, he looked better than when he had been here before, only weeks ago.

Afterwards Young Matthew had said with unusual vehemence, "So that was the girl? I heard about her from a loudmouth I used to know."

Ferguson had waited; Young Matthew was not by nature a gossip.

"In Winchester, I was told. Beaten an' raped, an' left for dead, the story had it. Tried to end her own life, poor lass."

He had said no more. Nor would he.

Perhaps Grace also knew.

He felt Allday's big hand tap his knee. There was no avoiding it.

"Well, they sighted these two vessels, and right away Captain Adam guessed what they were up to."

Unis paused at the door, and after a few seconds smiled at what she heard and saw.

Her John was back at sea again. He had never really left it.

The wine cooler stood in one corner of the cellar, its polished woodwork and silver mounts gleaming in the flickering light of the lanterns.

Adam Bolitho ran his hand over the inscription and crest, identical to that carved on the fireplace in the room above. *For My Country's Freedom.* He thought again of the forlorn hulk at Gibraltar; it was hard to imagine this wine cooler on board, with men working and following their daily routines, like the world he had left in *Unrivalled.*

Catherine had given this fine piece of furniture to his uncle; its predecessor lay on the seabed in the old *Hyperion.* It was a marvel that it had reached here unscathed, changing ships, being signed for again and again, until eventually it had arrived in Falmouth. And the chair she had given him.

He heard Ferguson's breathing behind him; he had scarcely left his side since the accident.

"I think we should move it upstairs, Bryan." He looked at the chair, covered with a sheet. "I might have that taken to the ship."

Ferguson nodded, unwilling to speak, and strangely moved.

"And the wine cooler, Captain?"

"It were best kept in the house. To come home to."

He turned away, suddenly lost within himself. Still the interloper, always feeling that the house waited for someone else.

"I shall attend to that." Ferguson followed him up the stone steps.

It should have been so different, he thought. This was another homecoming which would soon be interrupted by some urgent message. He had heard more about the sea fight in which *Unrivalled* had been damaged, and men had died. He closed the iron-studded door. It could have been Adam. And next time . . .

He shook some dust from a heavy curtain and looked at the flowers in the walled garden. *To come home to,* he had said. But this was no home. Not anymore.

He thought again of what Young Matthew had told him. Maybe someone should consider the girl's feelings, and this spectre which still obviously haunted her. He sighed. Anyway, she had gone to London, so that was the end of it. But her eyes had said something else. He smiled awkwardly. How Grace would laugh if she knew. But he had not forgotten how it felt.

Or how it looked. He glanced down at his empty sleeve. The past was the past.

Adam was only partly aware of Ferguson's concern as he walked through to the study, where John Allday had seen Captain James Bolitho hand the old sword to his younger son.

He felt the leather case in his pocket, the Nile medal which Catherine had sent to him by special messenger. Somebody must have arranged it. There was only a brief note, echoing the one she had left for him in this house with the sword. *He would have wanted you to have it.*

He looked up at the portrait of Captain James, with the arm painted out. By right the sword should have been Hugh Bolitho's. The traitor.

My father.

His eyes went involuntarily to the empty fireplace. It was even the same rug, where he had loved and been loved by Zenoria. And now Catherine had broken the link which had brought them together.

Ferguson knew the signs. The ship was his world, and soon he would be away again. *This house will be empty.*

"A meal perhaps, Captain?"

Adam had opened the little case and was gazing at the gold medal. *The Nile.* So many memories. So many faces, gone forever.

"I think not, Bryan."

Ferguson said nothing. He would seek Grace's advice. She might know . . .

He was unable to believe what he saw.

She was standing just outside the opened French windows, by the roses, one finger to her lips, smiling but unsure, as if at any second she might turn and vanish. She was dressed in pale grey, and wore a wide-brimmed straw hat fastened beneath her chin with a blue ribbon. Her hair was tied back, and Ferguson saw that she carried a yellow rose, like the one rumoured to be in the portrait.

Adam said, "I think I shall take a walk, Bryan." He closed the little case and turned towards the sunlight.

She said, "Then walk with me."

Adam crossed the room, and paused as she held out the rose. "This is for you." Her poise seemed suddenly a lie. "Please . . . I should not be here." He took the rose from her hand; her breathing was unsteady, as if she were fighting something, needing to speak, unable to find the words.

Adam slipped his hand gently beneath her arm.

"I will show you the house, Lowenna." He pressed her arm to reassure her, feeling its tension. And then, "You came. It is all I care about. You are here beside me, and I shall not awake and find only a dream."

"I could not go, to London, or anywhere else, without coming to discover how you are." She averted her face slightly. "No, do not look at me so, I am not sure if I can . . ."

She was trembling. Afraid. Of him or herself?

He repeated, "And you *came*."

"Joseph brought me. I told him to wait." She looked at him directly, her eyes suddenly determined, pleading. "I had no right . . ."

"You, of all people, have every right."

She smiled, for the first time. "Just walk with me, Adam. Show me your home. The way you offered, that day . . ."

They moved from room to room, scarcely speaking, each intensely aware of the other. And not knowing how to proceed.

She said abruptly, "I saw the portrait. I told Sir Gregory it is not *right*." She seemed shocked by her own outspoken comment. "Who, *what* am I, to say such things?"

He smiled. "Tell me. I'll not bite."

It was like a cloud passing away. She said, "Like that, Adam. Exactly that. The smile, as I remembered. And *will* remember it!"

He put his hand on her shoulder, touching her skin, feeling her body's resistance. Like a reminder. As if it had happened before.

He said, "I would never hurt you, Lowenna. I would kill any man who harmed you."

She touched his face. "A man of war." Gently, she took his arm. "Walk me to that garden. The roses . . . What are you thinking, Adam?"

He walked with her to the steps, feeling the sun on his face, on her arm. The girl who had visited him in a dream had returned.

He said, "I think that you belong here, Lowenna."

She did not answer, and he said, "That was badly put. Given time, I would learn to express myself . . . as I feel . . . and *how* I feel. You do belong here."

They walked on, pausing while he stooped to pat Young Matthew's dog, Bosun. Old and almost blind now, the dog allowed nobody to pass unchallenged.

Adam winced as he straightened again.

"That will teach me a lesson!"

Ferguson was standing by the door of his office, and lifted a hand as they passed.

From another doorway Grace Ferguson also watched, and felt a tear in one corner of her eye.

They made a perfect picture. Like something from the past, and yet something so new and radiant that it was beautiful to see after all the sorrow this house had known. And all the happiness, too . . .

She thought she heard the girl laugh, at something he had said, perhaps. A closeness, a new discovery.

She went back into the house and closed the door, in spite of the heat.

Would she tell him? Could she share something which had all but destroyed her, without destroying this hope of a fresh beginning?

She hurried into the cool shadows, annoyed at herself that she was weeping.

Aware only of the girl holding his arm, Adam strolled through the stable yard and towards the gates. Several people working in the yard turned to look at them; a few, who had served here longer, waved.

She said, "I want you to tell me about your life. Your ship, the men you lead." She said it so seriously that he wanted to throw caution aside and embrace her. Like the girl in the dream.

"Then you can tell me all about *you*, Lowenna."

She turned away, pretending to watch some ducks flying across the surface of the pond. She could not answer. And she was afraid.

Bryan Ferguson stood just outside the library door, his hand moving up and down the buttons of his coat, a habit he no longer noticed. It was rare for him to be so agitated.

"I heard a horse, Captain. I thought it was mebbee a courier."

Sir Gregory Montagu removed his hat and gave a curt bow.

"It is not uncommon for people to call upon *me* without prior arrangement. The times we live in, perhaps?"

Adam stood up from the table, the letter unfinished. Barely begun. *My dear Catherine.*

It was hard to compare this straight, elegant figure with the paint-daubed one in the grubby smock. He had ridden here along that same dusty track, but looked as if he could have been arriving at Court.

"Very well, Bryan. Thank you." He glanced at the open door, the windows beyond. For a moment more he had imagined that she had come, too. Was it only yesterday, their walk in that same garden, while he had told her about *Unrivalled,* and some of the people who had made her the ship she had become? For those precious moments, so close, and yet quite apart.

Montagu gestured towards one of the paintings. "That must be some of Ladbroke's work. Ships all out of proportion. Wouldn't know a block from a beakhead!"

Adam was suddenly alert, on the defensive. Montagu had not come here to pass the time of day about a painter who had died years ago.

"I thought you might be in London, Sir Gregory."

"Did you? Indeed." He plucked at the short cavalier's beard, his eyes everywhere. It was the first time Adam had seen him uncertain, perhaps unsure how to continue.

"You saw Lowenna, here in this house?"

Adam tensed. It would be easy to lose his temper. Maybe Montagu wanted just that.

"She was concerned about my injury. She would not stay for long." He could see that his words were having no effect. "I made certain that she was properly escorted."

Montagu nodded abruptly. "So I heard. As it should be. One can never be too careful these days."

He walked to a bookcase, his riding boots squeaking on the waxed floorboards.

"Lowenna is very dear to me, otherwise I should not be here. She is my ward, but that cannot last forever. Nothing does. She is a lovely woman, but in some ways . . ."

Adam said quietly, "Then you must know, Sir Gregory, that I care for her greatly." He raised his hand. "Hear me. I was unprepared for it, but now I can think of little else, only her future happiness."

Montagu sat down heavily and gave him the same unwavering stare as some subject for his canvas.

He said, "I knew her father for some years. I had occasion to work with him at Winchester. A scholar, and a fair man. But not of our world, yours or mine. He cared and trusted too much. His wife died in Winchester—a fever of some sorts. It was a foul winter that year—many went the same way. Lowenna tried to take her mother's place, and I did my best to help when I could. I felt I owed it to her father. As I said, a fair man, but weak. Unable to find his way after her death."

"I felt there was something."

Montagu seemed not to have heard him. "They had a house outside Winchester, near the woods, pleasant enough, I suppose, but remote." He leaned forward, his eyes very steady, sharing something which he must carry like a sacred trust. "Some men came, asking for food, shelter maybe. Anyone else would have sent them packing. But as I said, he was not of our world."

Adam felt himself gripping his leg, chilled, held in suspension, as if watching the gun ports of an enemy opening.

"They wanted money. Afterwards, we heard they were deserters from the army, common enough in those times. He had none, in any case, but they would not believe him."

He was on his feet again. "I am only telling you this because

I trust you. If I thought or discovered to the contrary, I would use everything at my disposal to destroy you."

He had not raised his voice, and yet it was as if he had shouted it aloud.

"It was some time before it was discovered. A visitor from the college where he was employed, I believe. For four days that girl was held captive, at their mercy. I can see from your face that you can form your own assessment, and I shall leave it there. It broke her in mind and body, and she would have died, I know that now. She is a brave, intelligent person, and I have seen what she has given to force that horror behind her."

Adam said, "With your help. Yours alone."

"Perhaps I need her as much as I think she needed me."

"Thank you for telling me, Sir Gregory."

Montagu regarded him impassively. "Has it changed things?"

"How could it?"

"She may never be able to tell you herself. Who can be that certain of anyone?"

Adam said, after a silence, "Did they catch them?"

"Eventually. They were hanged as felons, not as soldiers. Even at the scaffold they tried to soil her name. Some of it found a receptive ear. *No smoke without fire*, isn't that what the Bard said?" He moved one foot sharply. "I would have burned those scum alive for what they did!"

Adam heard someone leading a horse from the yard. Montagu had timed his visit to the minute.

"The subject of this conversation is safe with me, Sir Gregory."

Something in his tone made Montagu cross the room and take his hand, their first contact since his arrival.

"No secret is ever safe, Captain Bolitho. Be ready. I think maybe you are the one who can save her. From those four days, and from herself."

Adam followed him into the sunshine. There was cloud coming in now, blue-grey, from the sea. A change in the weather . . . He watched his visitor climb up into the saddle. Or an omen?

For a moment longer Montagu sat motionless, then he said, "Your portrait will be ready very soon. I was told of a few alterations I should make." It seemed to thrust some of the earlier anxiety aside. "And I would not wish to annoy your aunt. That rascal Roxby knew a thing or two when he married her, eh?"

Adam watched the horse until it was through the gates.

He knew Ferguson was loitering nearby; it was something they shared, without truly understanding how or why.

He turned and looked at him, surprised by his own calmness. "I shall need Young Matthew early tomorrow, Bryan."

Ferguson nodded. No questions were needed here. He had seen it all too often. And yet this was different in some way.

"I have some letters to write." He was looking now towards the walled garden, at the roses.

To come home to.

He was ready.

17 THE ONLY KEY

AT THE CLOSE of July, Lord Exmouth's fleet weighed and put to sea. It was an impressive armada, even to the eyes of those who had grown up in war, and Plymouth drew crowds from miles around to watch its departure. Because of indifferent winds it took a whole day for the ships to clear the Sound and take formation upon *Queen Charlotte*, the flagship. They left behind a powerful sense of anti-climax. For weeks anyone who could scull a dory or lay back on a pair of oars had pulled spectators around the anchored ships. Entertainers, and even a performing bear, had joined with pickpockets and tricksters to make the most of the unusual crowds.

Now, apart from local tradesmen and the usual idlers, Plymouth appeared strangely deserted. In the main anchorage only lifeless and laid-up vessels in ordinary and the hulks closer inshore remained. Except for one anchored frigate, lying apart from all the others, yards crossed, upperworks and rigging alive with seamen as they had been since her return with a hull scarred and blackened from that brief but pitiless encounter. True to his word, the port admiral had sent every spare shipwright and rigger to assist with *Unrivalled*'s hasty overhaul, and now she seemed reborn. Only the experienced eyes of watermen and the old Jacks on the Hoe could see beyond the fresh tar and paint, and the neat patches on much of her canvas.

The carriage stood at the roadside below the wall of a local battery, the paired horses resting after the journey, the hills and the hot sunshine.

The coachman leaned outwards slightly and said, "Close enough, I think, Miss Lowenna."

The girl nodded but said nothing. Like all those who worked for Sir Gregory, the coachman was polite, but firm. He had his orders for this expedition, as he would if he had been transporting a valuable painting from one address to another.

He was concerned about the loitering crowds, she thought. Some were looking over now. A smart carriage, a liveried coachman . . . they were all men. She plucked at her gown; it was hot, and the leather was damp against her body. One of the men raised his hand in a mock salute, and she heard the coachman mutter something under his breath.

You saw them in every seaport. Men who had once served and fought in ships like the frigate now shimmering above her own reflection. They had suffered, lost an arm or a leg; two had patches covering empty eye sockets. And yet they always came to watch. To cling to something which had so injured or disabled them.

It was something no painter could recreate. She thought of the portrait again. The smile, about which Sir Gregory had at first been so adamant. Or was he merely testing her? Sounding out her strength?

Two more men had joined the group by the wall, but stood slightly apart, their clothing marking them out as shipyard workers.

One said, "She's up an' ready to go, Ben. Tomorrow first thing, if this wind 'olds."

The other one seemed less certain. "Under orders, then? I thought she was too badly knocked about when she first came in!"

His companion grinned. "My father's out there now with the freshwater lighter—she's sailin' right enough. I was talkin' with one of the ropemaker's men. Tells me 'er captain's a real driver! A firebrand to all accounts!"

Some of the others had moved closer to listen. As if they were jealous, she thought.

An older man, walking heavily on a wooden leg, said, "'Er cap'n is Adam Bolitho, matey."

"You were *afore* 'is time, eh?"

He ignored the laughter. "I served under 'is uncle, Sir Richard, in th' old *Tempest,* when 'e took fever in the Great South Sea. There was none better."

The girl gripped the lowered window. Nancy Roxby had mentioned that ship when she had come to see the portrait.

She looked towards the old sailor, the sudden determination making her head swim. She had seen the old-fashioned telescope under his arm.

"I'm getting down!" She held up her hand. "No. I shall be *all right*." She could not even remember his name. "I have to see . . ."

The coachman fastened the reins, and glanced around uneasily. He liked his work in spite of Montagu's changes of mood, and his demands for a carriage at any time he chose; there were few enough jobs, and too many men being discharged from the fleet and the army to be careless.

He saw the girl extending her hand to the burly, one-legged figure.

"May I have it?" They were staring at her, close enough to touch, to smell the strong tobacco, the tar. "Please?" The hand was steady, but felt as if it were shaking uncontrollably. She was even calm. The way Sir Gregory had taught her, insisted, for her own sanity.

The man suddenly smiled. "But certainly, young lady. 'Tis a bit old an' dented—" He shook his head as if to exclude the others, especially the one who called, "Like you, eh, Ned?"

She raised the glass carefully, heard the coachman's boots slam down on the cobbles as the one-legged man put his arm around her, taking the weight of the telescope, as a marine will test the measure of his musket.

"There, miss." The hard hand tightened over her fingers. "*There.*"

She shook some hair from her eyes, feeling a trickle of sweat run down her spine, like an intruder. A memory.

Then she saw *Unrivalled*, and almost stopped breathing as the ship, slightly angled on the current now, swam into the lens, the raked masts and black rigging shining like glass in the sunlight, the loosely brailed-up sails, a long, tapering pendant occasionally whipping out from one masthead.

Tiny figures moving, apparently aimlessly, about the decks, but each having a purpose. Others motionless, officers perhaps. She felt the tension returning. Adam. He would be there. The stable boy had told him when the carriage had left, when she had asked Sir Gregory if she could be driven to Plymouth.

It was important, although even she did not know how important it was. Like opening a sealed room, with the only key.

"Not without *me*, you won't!" But his sharpness had been to cover something else. Something only they had shared. Until now.

She steadied the glass on the proud figurehead, the hands thrust behind her streaming hair. The uplifted breasts, like herself in the studio that day when he had walked in.

She lowered the telescope and saw the ship fall away, become only a fine model again.

"Someone you know aboard *Unrivalled*, miss?"

They were all looking at her, but there was no malice. No lust. No hands reaching out to hold and force her down, down . . .

She said quietly, "Yes." *How can I say that? He will leave here, tomorrow, someone said, and in any case . . .* "I would like to get a message to him. Is it possible?" She looked towards the coachman. "I can pay."

The coachman relaxed muscle by muscle. A patrol of soldiers was coming along the road. He was no longer alone.

He said, "I'll drive us down to the waterfront, Miss Lowenna. I can barter with the wherrymen there."

The one-legged man said firmly, "I can do it. I've got me own boat." There was a kind of defiance in his voice. Pride, too.

Then he looked at her, eyes taking in everything, reliving memories, perhaps.

"It'll be the cap'n, then?"

"Yes," she said.

"I can take you too, if you wishes it?"

She shook her head. "I will write a note, here and now."

She opened the little case she had brought with her. As if she had known.

It was impossible. It was madness.

And all at once it was done.

The man took it with great care and said, "*My* Cap'n Bolitho in *Tempest,* 'e had a fine lady like you. Lovely, she was."

She laid her hand on his ragged sleeve. "Was?"

"We buried 'er at sea. Same fever."

He gripped her hand and folded her fingers firmly over the coins she held ready for him.

"Not this time, missy. "'E's a lucky man, I'll give 'im that. None luckier, eh, lads?"

She climbed into the carriage, eyes blind to everything, even the anchored frigate.

If they knew, they would pity her. She bit her lip until the pain steadied her. Everyone did, who knew.

She recalled crying out in the night. Not caring.

It's love I want. Not pity, can't you see that?

Like the sealed room. The only key.

Vice-Admiral Sir Graham Bethune waited for his servant to close the doors and said, "It was good of you to come, Thomas. I am aware that you are very busy at this time."

He watched his visitor sit carefully, holding his shoulder, and frowning as if in anticipation of pain. He looked tired, more so than on the previous visit.

Rear-Admiral Thomas Herrick looked around the room, with its glittering chandeliers and a splendid portrait of Earl St Vincent as First Lord of the Admiralty.

Bethune knew Herrick disliked any contact with this seat of Admiralty; hated it, was a better description. He felt out of place here.

"I received your last report." Bethune paused, like a wildfowler testing his ground. "I found it very informative. Helpful, especially to me."

Herrick looked up at him, his blue eyes very steady. "Commodore Turnbull needs more ships, Sir Graham. And he needs them *now.* I doubt if we shall ever stop the slave trade completely, but without proper patrols we will be outmanoeuvred at every stage. A waste of time, and money too, if that is their lordships' only yardstick."

Bethune walked to a window and looked down at the carriages and the riders heading towards the park, seeing that other stretch of parkland, the leafless trees that marked the old duelling site.

He had spoken to Catherine just a few days ago. There had been more people about, and she had seemed surprised that he had come to meet her wearing his uniform. He touched the gold lace on his sleeve. It had been a reckless thing to do, but he had already read Herrick's report and had acted swiftly. He had not even stopped to consider what it must have cost Herrick to break his silence.

He tried to put it from his mind. Herrick was not doing it for him, but for Catherine and Catherine's lover, Richard Bolitho.

He said, "I hope you will take a glass with me, Thomas? We shall not be disturbed."

Herrick shrugged. It could have meant anything.

But Bethune was ready. He knew Herrick well enough by now. *I think I do.* Stubborn, single-minded, loyal. The navy was his whole life, and, like an hour-glass, it was running out.

He opened a cupboard and poured two glasses of cognac. From the dusty shop in St James's where Catherine had bought wine for Richard . . .

He saw her face again, her eyes flashing when he had mentioned Baron Sillitoe of Chiswick.

"We are *not* lovers. But I owe him so much. He stood by me when others did not. I would have died but for him."

Herrick took the glass and studied it gravely. "Early for me, Sir Graham." Always the title, like a last barrier, just as he never used "Lord" in connection with Sillitoe, either in his report or in this room.

"It seems certain that Lord Sillitoe is deeply involved with business affairs in the West Indies." Bethune hesitated. "And in Africa?"

Herrick said, "No doubt about it. The offices in the City of London have confirmed it. Sillitoe may have been unaware of the extent to which it was tied to the slave trade, but ignorance is no excuse in the eyes of the law." He added with sudden bitterness, "Anyone who has faced a court martial will say as much!"

Bethune turned back to the window. He must have been mad; Catherine had been right. So near the Thames, where anyone might have seen them. A promising flag officer, well placed for further promotion, with a wife and children, and still young enough to rise to the new demands of the navy in peacetime. He thought of the fleet which had sailed from Plymouth, to an inevitable confrontation with the Dey of Algiers. Hardly peace, and there was growing friction between the new allies over the slave trade.

He had even touched her, held her hand, prevented her from pulling it away.

"I don't want you to go, Catherine. You could remain here, in London. I can make certain of your privacy."

He had seen her eyes.

"As your mistress, Graham? Another scandal? I have too much respect for you to ruin your whole life."

Herrick asked abruptly, "Is there news of Catherine?"

Bethune faced him. "I spoke with her. A few times." He saw the disbelief, then the caution. "She intends to go with Lord Sillitoe to the West Indies." He thought suddenly of the Nile medal, her relief when he had told her that it had been delivered safely to the Bolitho house in Falmouth.

He heard the clock chime, more of a tremble than a sound, and refilled the glasses while he considered what he had done.

He would be blamed for warning her. His future would be in ruins. Perhaps a sea appointment might have saved him . . . He put down the bottle.

He saw her walk towards her carriage. She had paused once, and had asked quite calmly, "Are you in love with me, Graham?" He could not recall his answer, only her final dismissal. "Then you are a *fool*."

Herrick said, "Can nothing be done?"

"Their lordships are too concerned with Algiers at the moment. Afterwards . . ." He shrugged. "Perhaps Lord Sillitoe will absolve himself."

Herrick stood up carefully. "I must take my leave, Sir Graham. I am told that I will be required to return to Freetown shortly. That damnable place! And afterwards, I shall be put on the beach." As if he could see it, face it, like a man with one foot on the scaffold.

Bethune said, "Will you go back to Kent?"

Herrick studied him. "I am a stranger there now."

He watched the door, knowing that a servant was waiting, ready to spirit him out.

"I ask you, Sir Graham. Do what you can for Catherine. Sir Richard gave me my life. She gave me back my trust."

Something seemed to hold him by the door. "Adam Bolitho. Is he at sea yet?"

"I am informed that *Unrivalled* left Plymouth yesterday."

Herrick said, "How I envy him."

The door closed, and Bethune picked up the bottle again, which was unlike him.

He raised the glass, and said aloud, "Yes, Catherine, I am a fool!"

He thought of her hand in his, her resistance. And something more.

The servant was back. "I thought to remind you, Sir Graham.

We have an appointment with the First Lord at noon."

"I see." He glanced at the empty glasses. "Then we had better not keep him waiting."

He was reminded sharply of the room he had seen in Malta, the last place she had joined Richard Bolitho.

He had used the same words then. *How I envy him.*

It was not over.

Lieutenant Leigh Galbraith followed his captain into the stern cabin and waited by the door, half-expecting him to remember something and hurry to another part of the ship. It had been like that since his return, a boundless energy which was infectious, something you shared without knowing why.

Even O'Beirne had been at a loss for words, which was most unusual. He had redressed the wound and had snorted, "Riding a horse—I ask you, man. Does he have a death wish, this captain we follow?"

Yovell was here, coat draped on a chair, his table and some of the surrounding deck covered with folders and lists, and still more letters, Galbraith noticed.

He realised that the captain had halted by the stern windows, hands spread out on the lower sill as if embracing the anchorage.

"It's good to be without an admiral's flag to rule our days, eh? The fleet will be well on its way now." Galbraith saw one hand pat the freshly painted wood. "Never fear, we'll soon catch them up." He turned. "And you recommended Lawson for promotion to bosun's mate to replace . . ."

"Selby, sir. Lawson was cox'n of the jolly-boat, and a good all-round seaman. But if you think . . ."

Adam smiled. "I had thought that Sanders might be the right choice, but no, I agree with you. Lawson it is. I shall speak with him directly."

"And the new midshipman, sir. Shall I deal with him?"

"No. I shall see him. It's important, I think."

Galbraith watched him touch the wound again.

Napier came from the sleeping cabin, some clean shirts folded over one arm. He wore no shoes, and Adam knew the reason for it. O'Beirne had told him. There was a splinter in the boy's thigh, teak like the other, but deeper, and dangerous. All sailors hated teak. *Triton* had been a Dutch ship, and most of them were built of timber brought from far-off Dutch possessions.

Napier had said, "It will be all right, sir. I won't have a limp if . . ." *If* was always the threat.

Adam said, "I'm pleased with the ship, Leigh. And with what you've achieved while *Unrivalled* has been here." He shook his head. "And I know what you're going to say about all the help steered our way by the admiral. I was a first lieutenant myself, and I have not forgotten who truly gets things done." He smiled at him. "It will look well when I write your report."

"Report, sir?"

Adam had turned to look at a passing yawl and did not see the sudden apprehension.

"When the time comes for promotion!" He swung round, half-blinded by the glare from the anchorage. "Be ready, man! It will come, or I'll know the reason why. And now let us go over that list again. Gun crews and their captains. Topmen and boat crews." He remembered the shattered wheel, the mangled corpses clinging to the splintered spokes, and touched the fresh paint-work once more. As if the rest were only a memory.

Never again.

"Tell me about the new midshipman. Is there anything that might put him at his ease when we meet?"

He thought of the surprise, even the pleasure, he had seen in faces he thought he already knew.

He was back in command. And it mattered. A close thing,

O'Beirne had said. Would they be watching him when next they were called to quarters? *Never question it. Do it.* Was it ever that simple?

Galbraith said, "His name is John Bremner, late of the frigate *Juno.* He is fifteen."

"I remember *Juno.* A French prize, fifth-rate. When I last heard, she was about to be broken up. He should be experienced, anyway. What we need now."

He watched the wind ruffle the water of the anchorage; Cristie said it would hold. Even he had been pleased, he thought. *"We owe that bugger one, sir!"* He had almost smiled.

He felt the strain running out of him. Even the wound was not painful, at the moment.

And they were leaving again. Tomorrow.

He saw a small boat pulling away from the side, the oarsman pausing to shade his eyes and peer up at the gilded gingerbread around the quarter.

They would make full use of the time on passage to join the fleet; gun drill would be paramount. He could almost hear the admiral's words. *Unrivalled* had been there. The others had not. *I want you in the van.*

There was a tap at the door: the new midshipman. His most important time. *So it must be mine, too.*

But it was Lieutenant Bellairs, his face scored by the sun even now.

"I'm sorry to trouble you, sir. But I thought it might be important."

Adam looked at him and knew he had Galbraith's full attention as well. Bellairs, only recently a midshipman himself, had changed since young Cousens had been killed. They had been close, and Bellairs had helped to train the other midshipman in flags and signals before his own promotion to lieutenant. As if he had hardened, matured almost overnight, not the Bellairs who had blushed when telling him about the girl named Jane who lived in Dartmouth.

He opened the small, hastily-folded cover.

For a moment the cabin was gone. The faces, the individual concerns and responsibilities were at another's door.

A clear, unfamiliar hand, but he knew it instantly.

I was here. I saw you. God be with you.

He stared at the wind-ruffled water, just in time to see the boat vanishing around two hulks.

It was not possible. Like the dream, when he had almost lost his mind in pain and despair. When she had always been with him . . .

He faced them again.

"Thank you for that, Mr Bellairs."

He sat down, in the chair which he had brought from Falmouth.

"Send in Mr Bremner, will you?"

He was leaving someone. And that, too, mattered.

"Steady she goes, sir! Sou'-west by south!"

Adam braced his legs on the wet planking as *Unrivalled* ploughed her stem into the curling breakers of the Channel, levelling the glass with care, measuring the distance, the bearing of the last jutting spar of land. Penlee Point, the sea lively there too, spray drifting like pink shadows in the morning light.

He lowered the glass. Cristie was right; they would weather the headland with half a mile to spare. You could take no chances with a lee shore. He walked up the tilting deck, feeling the ship quiver as she lifted and then bit into deeper water. What she did best. And wide across the bows lay open water.

All hands had been piped before dawn, the last mail and

despatches were lowered to the guard-boat, and after a hasty meal
the capstan was manned, the shantyman doing his best above the
rising south-easterly wind.

During the ship's stay at Plymouth, Galbraith had managed
to find seven recruits to fill the dead men's shoes. Surprisingly,
they were all prime seamen, so that would make up the difference far more than mere numbers. Perhaps it was because
Unrivalled was the last ship to leave port, with only the listing
hulks to remind men of hard times ahead? With all boats stowed,
and the anchor hove short, she had left as the day was just dawn-
ing, giving colour to the land.

He strode aft, men dodging out of his way, rigging groaning
and taking the strain, experienced eyes watching new and old
cordage for weakness, or a job too hastily completed in harbour.

He thought of the new midshipman, only fifteen but already
well trained in his previous ship. A dark, serious-looking youngster, a little too serious perhaps, probably comparing Adam with
his previous captain. There were no passengers in a frigate, and
the real personality would soon be forced to emerge. It would help
to take the minds of the other midshipmen from Cousens and
the missing Sandell.

He came out of himself and called, "Mr Galbraith, get the
courses on her, once we are clear of the Point." He stared up at
the sloping masts, the angled yards where topmen were already
spread out like monkeys, indifferent to the height or the sea boil-
ing along the weather side. *One hand for the King.* It was the first
lesson for any true seaman. The other one you kept for yourself.

He turned away as Galbraith yelled his orders to the
boatswain's party waiting by the foremast. *Leaving port.* Would
he never get used to it? The excitement, the small pictures you
never left behind. Fishermen standing in their frail craft to wave,
their cheers soundless in the din of canvas and feet running to

halliards and braces. A small packet ship under French colours, dipping her flag as they had passed her. The old enemy; the sea, perhaps, was the only true thing they held in common.

He had levelled his glass on the land, the Sound already swallowed up astern, and imagined her as she must have been, writing the note, some sudden whim or determination making her give it to some waterman for delivery. Maybe she was already regretting it, fearing it might be misinterpreted or worse. He had put his own letter to her in the guard-boat. It would be delivered to Bryan Ferguson; if she had not already gone away, he would find her.

He heard one of the helmsmen curse quietly, saw him gesture at something on the big double wheel, the replacement for one shot to pieces.

He touched his side again. There might have been no letter. He thought, too, of the marine who had died, dropping his musket. A man well liked, and remembered because he had once served under the young Captain Nelson in the *Agamemnon,* "*Old Aggie,*" as she was affectionately known.

Was there someone left, perhaps in Plymouth, who would grieve for him? Or would it be yet another lost name, like the *Paradox*'s boatswain, who had come from St Keverne overlooking the Manacles, which they had discussed while he lay dying. So many. Too many.

He had contained a sudden and, he knew, unreasonable anger when he had read the letter from a retired rear-admiral who had served with Sandell's father, and had sponsored the boy for his appointment as midshipman. No sadness, no pity. If anything, only a resentful disapproval that a would-be officer had been lost at sea, without proper investigation, a fault, surely, of his captain. Would he have cared so much for procedure if a lowly landman had been missing overboard?

He saw Midshipman Deighton standing by the flag locker with his chosen hands, frowning slightly as he studied his signals card, then he smiled at something said by a master's mate. And he saw Lieutenant Bellairs turn from his station with the after-guard, to watch with, he thought, a certain sadness, as if seeing someone else. Then he was with his men again. He would get over it. There was no other way.

He seized the hammock nettings as the ship crashed into a long, unbroken roller. And what would be the outcome of this venture? It was the admiral's total responsibility; his was the deci-sion whether to call the Dey's bluff, or commit all his ships and men to the onslaught of battle. No ship could match gun for gun with a carefully sited shore battery. And there might be heated shot, and fire, every sailor's only real fear. According to the writ-ten orders, the Dey had mounted a thousand cannon or more, perhaps in those same old crumbling batteries he had seen for himself when he had cut out an enemy ship from the anchorage, and afterwards when Admiral Lord Rhodes had made his attack with bomb vessels and his own heavier ships in support. But too far out to find and destroy those hidden guns.

Exmouth was a frigate man. *Had been.* How would he per-ceive, and accept, a challenge which might end in disaster?

He saw Galbraith studying him, trying not to show it. He, too, was changed in some way. Troubled by his captain? Unsure of him, after what had happened?

Adam faced into the wind, coming harder now across the quarter, tasting it. Like the tears that day, fallen on his hand.

Whatever happened they must be ready, for treachery and for traps.

A voice seemed to insist, *You must be ready. You.*

He called, "Get the courses on her, Mr Galbraith! Another hand on the helm, too!"

He saw him lift his speaking-trumpet, men poised and ready to respond to his orders, their bodies stripped and shining with spray. Like those warriors to whom she had alluded, in the myths and traditions of ancient times of which he knew so little. She had described him as a man of war. Perhaps she had not truly understood how apt that had been. There had never been opportunity or leisure to become anything else, for the boy who had walked from Penzance to Falmouth. The frigate captain.

He heard the thunder of released canvas as it filled and hardened to the wind. *Unrivalled* was standing hard over, every eighteen-pounder on the weather side throwing its weight on the breechings.

They might walk together again. And she would share it with him.

He stared into the wind until the spray almost blinded him.

She must know. It came like a fist from nowhere. Why she had written that brief note, which now seemed to hold such urgency.

God be with you. It was like hearing her voice.

"More hands on the weather forebrace, Mr Fielding! *Move yourselves!*"

Adam stared at the land again, almost lost now in the wind and spray. A green haze, without real form or substance. It would soon be gone once they changed tack.

He waited for the ship to steady, the sails shining like metal breastplates, then he strode to the quarterdeck rail and gripped it with both hands.

Fear was an enemy, but it could be held at bay. When others looked to you, there was never any choice. The faces sometimes came back to remind him. He had seen it in Bellairs just now, Galbraith also. Seeking something, other than trust.

It was a long time ago, another voice. *I don't want to die. Please, God, not now.*

But the voice was his own.

18 "PREPARE FOR BATTLE!"

LUKE JAGO stood with his legs braced against the ship's easy motion, his hat tilted to shield his eyes from the unwavering glare. To some he might appear composed, even indifferent. Those who did not know him.

It was always the same, he thought, from the moment the order was piped through the ship. *All hands! All hands, lay aft to witness punishment!* It was a part of life in the navy: good or bad, you accepted it.

Often you never really knew how it had begun, or if it could have been prevented. Order, discipline, routine; he should be used to it by now.

Perhaps it was boredom. It was almost a month since *Unrivalled* had left Plymouth. They had caught up with the fleet at Gibraltar, anchored while many of the lame ducks were still making their final approach.

But after that the ship had spent almost all of her time at sea, keeping contact with other frigates, the admiral's scouts, only half aware of the planning and the scheming which must have been taking place.

He glanced over the heads of the assembled company at the horizon, like molten metal from a furnace, and, beyond it, what looked like a far-off, unmoving cloud. Africa.

He heard Hastie, the master-at-arms, call, "Prisoner seized up, sir!"

Jago moved forward, a few feet behind the captain's left shoulder, his body angled only slightly against the quarterdeck rail.

He looked briefly at the prisoner. Stripped to the waist and seized up to a rigged grating, head twisted round to stare up at the figures on the quarterdeck. A small group of midshipmen on one side, the officer of the watch, Bellairs, on the other, a mass of off-watch and unemployed sailors filling the usually busy deck, "the market-place," they termed it.

The watchkeepers were going about their normal affairs, on the gangways, splicing and attending to the running rigging, some working far above the deck, while topsails and jibs flapped or filled to a wind which was little more than a hot breeze.

Jago had heard the master cursing it. Maybe some fast sailing, when every man was required to work the ship, was what they needed.

The prisoner, for instance, an ordinary seaman named Bellamy, not one of the usual troublemakers or hard men. Probably just his bad luck.

He half-listened to the captain's voice reading the relevant section of the Articles of War. Jago knew it by heart. He felt his shoulders stiffen, remembering the moment, the sickening blow of the lash across his naked back. He had been unfairly flogged; an officer had stood up for him and had proved his complete innocence. But he would carry the scars of the cat to his deathbed.

"All other crimes not capital, committed by any person or persons in the fleet . . ."

Jago looked again. Two boatswain's mates were waiting by the grating; one, Creagh, carried the red baize bag, and he saw that the other was Lawson, who had until his promotion been coxswain of the jolly-boat, and a good all-round seaman. His first flogging, and a prisoner he had probably known as a messmate.

The captain said, "Two dozen, boatswain's mate. Do your duty."

No heat, no contempt. But Jago knew differently.

As the arm swung back, over and down, and the cat o' nine tails cracked across the bare skin he saw the captain's hand tighten around his scabbard. The master-at-arms called, "One!"

Jago saw the first droplets of blood, heard the victim gasp, the air punched out of him. He had once witnessed a flogging around the fleet, on a charge of mutiny. The boat, carrying the prisoner spread-eagled on a capstan bar, had called at every ship, and each captain was ordered to award his allotted share of the punishment.

Three hundred lashes. The man had died shortly afterwards.

"Two!"

The ship leaned into a slight swell and Jago swayed forward to look at the officers.

Had it been one of the old hands, a seasoned warrant officer like Partridge, it might have ended there and then, a quick punch, or rap with a rope starter, all that was needed.

He watched Lieutenant Varlo's expression. Impassive, and yet with each crack of the lash he saw him purse his lips. He was enjoying it.

"Eighteen!"

Jago saw O'Beirne the surgeon bending to study the prisoner's back. He made himself do the same. He must not forget.

The man's back was like something inhuman. Torn, flayed flesh, blackened as if burned by fire.

O'Beirne stood aside. The punishment continued.

Lawson was using the lash now, probably holding back, even though the prisoner was beyond pain. Jago could recall a captain who had suspected leniency in one boatswain's mate, and had threatened him before the entire ship's company. *Lay it on harder, man! Or by God you'll change places with him!*

He glanced at the captain's sunburned hand. The knuckles were almost white around the sword at his side.

"Twenty-four!"

"Cut him down." The captain turned aft and saw Jago's expression. He said, "Give me an enemy I can fight, not *this!*"

Jago stood aside. He doubted if the captain had even seen him, or knew he had spoken aloud.

Galbraith asked, "Dismiss the hands, sir?"

Adam looked at him. He had recalled Lawson's pleasure and pride when he had told him of his promotion. Now he would understand the other side of the bargain. The line he had crossed, which set him apart from the rest.

And Martyns, their youngest midshipman, who had come through the fighting like a brave, if inexperienced, lion. But just now, as the flogging had been carried out, that same resilient boy had been in tears.

He realised that Galbraith was still waiting.

"Yes. And I would like you to have a word with Mr Varlo at your earliest convenience."

Galbraith turned his back to exclude the others. "I hardly think that it should come from me, sir."

Adam removed his hat and touched his damp forehead. *Why should it matter?*

"Because you are experienced, and you understand the importance of standing together. If I see him myself it may well end in a court martial, his or mine, I am still undecided!" He saw O'Beirne waiting by the companion-way. *"Do it!"*

It was like a shutter falling. Perhaps it had never really lifted.

He seemed to hear her voice again. *I want you to tell me about your life.* Had it really happened? *Your ship, the men you lead.* What would she think if she could see him now?

O'Beirne bided his time, recognising his distress, which he guessed no one else would even imagine.

"Bellamy will be up and about soon, sir. I've seen far worse."

Adam looked at him. Almost time to change tack again. An unending rectangle of sea. An invisible fleet, and a handful of small vessels holding the strings. The eyes of the fleet, Nelson had called them.

He said, "What about the lad, Napier? Can you do something for him?"

O'Beirne assessed him gravely. *For you, you mean.*

"Yes, sir. While this weather holds. There's a risk, of course ..."

"No risks, please."

He walked to the nettings as seamen and marines broke ranks and drifted away. Some hands were already scrubbing the grating and the deck, while down on the orlop the seaman called Bellamy would be drowning his agony and degradation in more rum than he could handle.

A fateful equation. Too much to drink, a loose tongue, and the wrong officer. Varlo would claim, rightly, that he was only doing his duty. An admission, not a defence.

He looked up, past the main-yard, where Cousens's body had broken its fall to this deck, and saw the lookout, a tiny shape against the empty sky.

"Sail on th' weather bow, sir!"

The link in the chain. It had to be. Everybody else would stay clear.

For a moment more he stared at the cloud-like outline of the distant coast. Maybe it was already over. He blinked to clear his vision and looked down at the main deck, the last traces of blood being washed into the scuppers.

It was not over. Fate, destiny, how could anyone know?

He thrust it aside. "Our best lookouts aloft, Mr Galbraith. We will alter course directly, and let her run down on us."

"I'll be ready, sir."

Bellairs had been watching them, and tried to relax as the ship slowly returned to routine, normality.

He liked to think that, had he been dealing with the seaman Bellamy, he could have managed to avoid a flogging, just as he knew that in a ship's tight world of discipline and purpose an officer's word had to be respected. Obeyed. He thought of the girl named Jane who lived in Dartmouth, imagined her face lighting up when he walked up to her one day as a captain. With a frigate of his own . . .

Cristie called wearily, "When you can *spare* a moment, Mr Bellairs, I would like to have the log witnessed and signed."

Bellairs shook himself out of it.

"At once, Mr Cristie!"

Beneath their feet, Adam walked right aft and slumped in the high-backed chair he had brought from Falmouth.

What thoughts must he have had, sitting here like this? Hopes too, before fate had marked him down. He touched the wound. He must ask O'Beirne to examine it again.

He listened to the sudden thud of feet, the muffled bark of commands, and knew he should go on deck once more.

And what of trust? He recalled Galbraith's face. The barrier again.

Yovell appeared, without letters or documents for once.

"Shall we fight, sir?"

As one man might ask another about the weather, in some country lane.

"I believe so, Daniel." He did not see the surprise at the casual use of his name.

Yovell said uncertainly, "I attended to the letter, sir. The legal one." His eyes rested briefly on the chair. Perhaps remembering.

Adam listened to the thud of the tiller-head and imagined the wheel going over, Cristie watching compass and helm, Rist or another master's mate waiting to lay the ship on her new course.

He heard the *click-click-click* of Napier's shoes. Preparing to go to the sickbay.

He said quietly, "If anything should happen, to me, for instance, that boy should be cared for. He reminds *me* of *me*." He smiled faintly. "As I believe I once was."

Yovell said, "The surgeon is a good man, sir."

"I am relying on it." He stood up, his hand running over the back of the chair. He could see them all in his mind. As he would describe them to her.

The men you lead.

The door opened and Jago stepped into the cabin.

"The sail is changin' tack, sir. A frigate. One of ours."

He recognised the strain and was angered by it. Any captain could decide if you lived or died. But this one cared. "Sullivan is at the main, sir."

Yovell adjusted his spectacles. He sensed the unlikely bond between them, although he did not fully understand it, yet. A man who scorned authority, and had been quick to say so. But one who had earned respect by giving his hand to Adam Bolitho. Yovell was not a seafarer, but he had noticed that when Jago entered the sentry had not even challenged him.

Adam said, "I'll come up presently." Their eyes met. "Call me."

He looked around the cabin again, trying to find the words to describe it to her in his mind. But the other voice intruded.

I want you in the van.

It had already been decided.

Midshipman Deighton wedged his book beneath one arm and levelled the telescope again. "She's *Halcyon,* twenty-eight, Captain Robert Christie, sir!" He peered quickly at the others, and seemed startled by the authority in his own voice.

Adam folded his arms and watched the other frigate, almost bows-on now, her sails in disarray as she changed tack to converge on *Unrivalled.*

Even now he could feel the shiver of memory, of instant recognition. As if he had known.

Was it only a year or so since they had last met? When Admiral Lord Rhodes had ordered *Halcyon* to chase and attack the big frigate *Triton,* the day so many faces had been wiped away.

Outranged and outgunned, *Halcyon* had stood no chance, and Rhodes must have known it. But he had been so eager to prevent *Unrivalled* from giving chase that he had ordered her to remain on station. Adam had ignored the signal, and they had won the day. When Martinez, the Dey's agent and advisor, had died, shot down by Corporal Bloxham as he had been about to fire. The day young Napier had taken the great splinter in his leg.

And yet despite the pain and the hate, the rejoicing and the sadness, one picture always stood out in his mind. He glanced at Galbraith's strong profile; he would recall it, too. They had swept past the mauled *Halcyon* and he had seen her destruction, the thin threads of scarlet running from her scuppers, as if the ship were bleeding to death. Young Deighton had been there also. And he had heard Galbraith's voice, harsh with emotion. *"They're cheering! Cheering us!"*

Somehow *Halcyon* had survived, and her captain with her; James Tyacke had spoken of him when they had met in Freetown. He felt his lips crack into a smile. That seemed so long ago. Tyacke had been a lieutenant in the *Majestic* at the Battle of the Nile, and Christie had been a young midshipman. He thought of the medal now in his strongbox. *The Nile.* It had affected so many in this naval family. The Happy Few . . . Where Tyacke had had half his face blasted away. Just before it had happened, he had saved that young midshipman from breaking. When Christie had become a man. *A better man,* he had later said to Sir Richard. He wiped his mouth with his hand. Less than two years ago, in this same Mediterranean Sea.

"Heave-to, if you please." He saw Galbraith's eyes. He had remembered.

Deighton called, *"Have despatches on board, sir!"*

He could almost feel the tension of those around and closest to him dissipate. The waiting and uncertainty were in the past. Jack always knew . . .

Cristie muttered, "Not wasting any time, is he?"

Unrivalled came round easily, her sails all aback, that same Corporal Bloxham, now a sergeant, shouting at some marines to form up at the entry port. The deck was still rising and falling heavily while the ship hove-to, so that they swayed in an untidy dance until they found their feet again.

Some of the seamen were grinning broadly. Sailor and "bullock" would never really mix.

Adam watched the frigate's gig pulling strongly across the dark blue water, a cocked hat in the sternsheets. Christie was coming in person.

Galbraith was observing *Halcyon* through a telescope. For some reason, it made him feel like an intruder. Even without the glass he had seen the scarred and blistered paintwork, her figurehead still unrepaired and partly shot away. He lowered the glass. Battered and hard-worked, with obviously little time spent in harbour, but a ship any man would give his right arm to call his own.

The calls trilled and Adam saw Christie climbing from his boat. Tall, a keen, intelligent face; *probably posted a year or so after me.* The sort of man who would catch any woman's eye. The frigate captain.

But when he raised his hat to the guard and quarterdeck Adam saw the legacy of that terrible day.

Above either ear his hair was not merely greying, it was white, as if it had been dyed. The touch of war.

The meeting in *Unrivalled* was brief, Adam sensing both the urgency and the relief of this rendezvous.

One of the wardroom messmen served refreshments, and he was surprised that Christie chose rum.

He said, "My supplies are all in chaos. His lordship has kept us busy indeed. I am glad the muddled thinking is over and done with."

Adam waited while Yovell unfastened the envelope, and looked up sharply at his visitor as Christie said, "Lord Exmouth sent word to the Dey. Surrender all the Christian slaves, and disband the fleet of renegades—pirates, I'd call them—or defeat is inevitable." He smiled for the first time, and Adam could see him as Tyacke's midshipman at the Nile. "Needless to say, it was ignored. The emissary was damned lucky to leave alive!"

Adam glanced at the messman, face very intent, ears taking full note of everything that was being said.

He thought of Napier. The sea was calm enough, for the moment. O'Beirne might take the opportunity to extract that one, dangerous splinter.

"Lord Exmouth is joined by a Dutch squadron, six good ships to all accounts. But between ourselves, I'd prefer to act without anyone else becoming involved."

Adam recalled Jago making much the same remark. "Let the *meneers* stay away an' smoke their own pipes." The war was over. The mistrust was not.

He stood up and walked to the stern windows, feeling the jerk and tremble of the big rudder. Ready to go. To obey.

He heard himself say, "The day after tomorrow, then." August twenty-seventh. Exactly a month since Bellairs had given him her note. *Here.*

Christie had his hat in his hand, and his glass stood empty. "I must leave. Lord Exmouth is all in haste. He insisted you were to be found without delay."

Adam followed him to the door. *The last in the line. And the first to lead.*

"You have a fine ship, Captain Bolitho." But there was no envy.

Adam said, "After this, perhaps you may return to England."

Christie faced him; the messman and the rigid marine sentry meant nothing. They could have been quite alone.

"England has nothing to offer me. They would take my ship

from me. Without her . . ." He broke off, and said almost abruptly, "I could ask for no better ship or captain in the van." He shook Adam's hand, lingering over it. "If you meet Captain Tyacke again . . ." He could not continue.

But when the marine guard and side party stood in swaying ranks to show respect, one ship to another, they saw only the two captains.

Galbraith waited for the gig to bear off from the side and watched some of his own seamen's eyes, critical or impressed as their station dictated. It was something no landsman would ever understand, he thought.

He looked up at the men aloft, and standing loosely by braces and halliards. Waiting for the next order. Their captain would tell them, but everybody from the cook's slush-monkey to the elegant captain of Royal Marines would already know. And soon, sooner rather than later, these guns would be in action again. In earnest and without mercy.

He glanced towards Lieutenant Varlo, who was up by the foremast with Rist, the master's mate.

The wardroom had been empty, which was rare in any ship. Even the messmen had been elsewhere; he had made certain of that.

There had been just the two of them. Varlo had been confident, almost amused as he had told him what he thought of his behaviour in general, and in particular over the flogging.

Galbraith had lost his temper. Something he had sworn to avoid. Something he had wanted to do.

Varlo had said, offhandedly, "The captain could have told me himself, if he had thought it important. In all my experience, I've never heard such abuse. As first lieutenant you are entitled to dictate matters of duty if or when it is justified. This is not. I'll take no insolence from any lout, drunk or sober—I'll see the backbones of anyone who tries it!"

Galbraith had listened to his own voice. A different sound, another person.

"*In all your experience. I was forgetting. Forgive me.*" He had seen the slight smile forming. Strangely, it had helped. "Flag lieutenant to a flag officer, albeit a junior one. But he thought highly of you, his aide, so much so that anybody might have expected further promotion." The smile had gone at that point. "Instead, you were appointed to *Unrivalled*, to fill a dead man's shoes, as it happens. I know some who would have killed for the post, but to a flag lieutenant surely something more promising should have been offered!"

Varlo had snapped back, "I don't know what you mean!"

It had gone far enough. Now, he knew for certain. Soon they would fight.

He had said, "The admiral wanted to end it there. Your liaison."

Varlo had stared at him, stunned. He had seen him just now, watching him from the foremast trunk. Shock, fury, and something far deeper.

How silent the wardroom had seemed. Even the sounds of rigging and timbers were stilled.

Then Varlo had said softly, "Had we been ashore, anywhere but in this ship, I would have called you out, and you would have danced to a different tune!"

Galbraith had walked to the door. "Do your duty, and remember that you rely on our people, just as they, poor devils, have to depend on you." He had turned, half expecting a blow or another threat, and had said, "Next time, *Mister* Varlo, ensure that the admiral is safely married, eh?" The pretence was ended. "And call me out when and where you wish. You'll find me ready enough!" He could still hear the door slamming behind him, and remembered the shock and the shame of his own words. But no regrets.

"Get the ship under way, if you please." The captain was

looking at him, his hat still grasped in one hand. "I will speak to the people tomorrow. It may be the last chance."

Galbraith understood, and turned to call a boatswain's mate. But something made him hesitate.

"You can rely on me, sir."

The other frigate was already spreading more canvas and going about, the gig hoisted and stowed.

Adam thought of her captain, Robert Christie, who had served under James Tyacke at the Nile. *We are of the same mould, the same generation.* A face you could trust when the signal for close action was flying.

He felt the chill again. The warning.

They would never meet again.

Joseph Sullivan, the ship's best lookout, settled himself comfortably on his perch in the crosstrees and glanced down at the deck far below. It was hard to believe that none of them down there could see what he could see. Not yet. They had been roused early, but nothing out of the normal run of things, almost unhurried, he thought. But purposeful, in earnest. A good breakfast, too; he could still taste the thick slices of pork, washed down with a pint or more of rough red wine. And, of course, some rum. A proper issue, with officers and warrant ranks looking the other way when the older hands pulled out their hoarded supplies. After all, you never knew if it was the last tot in this world.

He looked across the bow and studied the array of ships. They appeared still and unmoving in the morning sunlight, but they were coming right enough, a fleet the like of which they might never see again. Liners keeping perfect formation in the low breeze, all sails set and drawing well, considering. Not yet stripped for action. Frigates too, staying up to windward, ready to run down like terriers if the admiral so ordered. Dutchmen in their own squadron. He drew his knife and carved himself a wedge of chewing tobacco. He had been at sea almost all his life, or all that he could remember. He knew what was essential. Like the changing scarlet pattern of marines, mere puppets from up here, being arranged on the quarterdeck, some to be stationed at hatchways and what the old hands called bolt-holes, where a terrified man might run at the height of battle. A marine would prevent it. There was nowhere to run anyway, but only experience taught you that.

Sullivan was at a loss. The fine model of his old ship *Spartiate*, which had stood in the line at Trafalgar, was finished. It was hard to recall exactly when he had begun it. In his last ship they had pulled his leg about it. But he and the model were still here. The others were not.

He peered down again. More figures about now. On edge, wanting to get on with it. Get it over. He saw steam rising from the sea alongside, and loosened a last piece of pork from his teeth. The galley fire had been doused. *Almost time now.*

He twisted round and looked at the shore, no longer a shadow, an unending barrier of sand and stone. He could see the headland, a sudden stab of light, the sun reflecting from a window or telescope. He measured it with his eye. Three miles. It would be noon before they were close enough. He thought of the captain, yesterday, when they had cleared lower deck to hear him speak from the quarterdeck.

It was strange at such times, he thought. *Unrivalled* carried some 250 souls of every age and rank, and in a crowded hull you would expect to know every man-jack of them. And yet, packed together on deck or clinging to shrouds and ratlines to listen, you still found yourself beside someone you had never met before.

Every man-of-war, no matter how crowded, was divided by rank, status, and station. Soon the pattern would change again. Gun crews and powder monkeys, sail-handling parties, and men to repair damage. He watched the land, as if it had altered in some way. Others to drag away the wounded, or to pitch the dead overboard.

The captain had told them about the Christian slaves, and the murder and persecution of helpless people taken at sea or on land in the Dey's name.

He had heard Isaac Dias, the foul-mouthed gun captain, mutter, "They can only spare a few poxy schooners to put screws on the slave trade down south, eh, lads? But it's a whole bloody fleet for the Christians!" It brought a few grins; it did not do to fall out with *Unrivalled*'s best gun captain. Sullivan smiled to himself. He was useless for anything else.

He wondered what the captain thought about it. Really thought. His ship, his men, and his neck if things went badly wrong. He had asked his coxswain about him, but Jago was as tight as a clam. "He'll do me," was his only reply. Funny, for a man who had always loathed officers.

Sullivan looked at the fleet again. It was not possible, but they were closer now. He could see the Cross of St George at the masthead of the big three-decker at the head of the line, *Queen Charlotte*. The admiral's ship; a hundred guns or more, they said. The enemy had prepared and well-sited artillery. In all his years at sea he had heard the arguments about ships set against shore-mounted guns. He grinned. Who would be an admiral today?

He looked down between his bare feet at the great main-yard angled below him, overlapping either beam. Young Midshipman Cousens had fallen across it when he had been thrown from up here. *If I had been with him* . . . He shut it from his mind. He was not here. Another face had moved on.

He saw that the marines were climbing into the fighting-tops, marksmen, and a few to handle the deadly swivel guns, which could kill or maim more of your own mates than the enemy if badly laid and trained. *Daisy-cutters.* Invented by somebody who never had to use one, he thought.

He realised that one of the marines was gesturing at him with his musket. Sullivan waved. Somebody was coming . . . Did he never sleep? Sullivan had seen the skylight shining throughout the night, and had heard of him visiting the magazine, where Old Stranace the gunner ruled the roost, and even the sickbay, where his servant shared the space with the man who had been flogged. His lip curled. Because of Mister bloody Varlo. Like Sandell, he would not be missed.

He looked suddenly at his big, rough hands; scarred and pitted with tar, but they could still fashion a perfect ship's likeness. *Would I be missed?*

He watched the captain climb the last few feet, hatless, his brown face shining with sweat. He was still able to smile.

"A fine day for it, Sullivan!"

Surprisingly, he thought of an earlier captain he had served. In a boat's crew, he had accidentally brushed against the officer as they had come alongside the ship. The captain had damned his eyes for it, and had threatened to have him charged with assault. But at least you knew where you were with a bloody-minded tyrant.

Sullivan was close enough to reach out and touch him. A man like himself, without the authority and the Articles of War. He sighed. It was no use. Jago was probably right.

He saw the captain touch his side and take some deep breaths, his eyes first on the shore, then up to the masthead pendant, as if to take the measure of the wind.

Adam was aware of the lookout's scrutiny. One of *Unrivalled*'s best seamen, but more than that, like one of a ship's strongest timbers. *The men you lead.*

He studied the array of ships, and wondered how the brooding land mass would appear to the admiral. Like sailing into a giant trap. He checked the wind again. Almost easterly, as Cristie had assured him it would be this day. "Off this patch of the coast it's more likely easterly than westerly. Very definite, it is." He'd said it without a trace of a smile. Perhaps it was something he had had drummed into him many years ago, in this same sea.

He thought suddenly of the studio at the old house with the ruined chapel. Deserted now. Empty. She would know all about these waters, when the Pharaohs had ruled, and before that. Another world.

He looked at Sullivan.

"Noon?"

Sullivan nodded. "As near as hell's kitchen, sir."

They both laughed, and some of the marines in the maintop leaned out to try and hear.

He looked down at the ship again. Undisturbed, unhurried, as he had intended. It would be hard enough for them to stand to their guns and take the first onslaught without all the usual clamour and call to arms. But soon now. Very soon.

He pictured Midshipman Deighton, with his telescope trained on the flagship. Just one signal, and *Unrivalled* with *Halcyon* close astern would lead the attack.

Galbraith had said, when they had discussed the possibilities, "Simple enough, if you don't think too much about it!"

Surprisingly relaxed, even cheerful. He would need all of that today. If only he had been able to sleep, but it had evaded him. Except once, when he had fallen into an exhausted doze, neither one thing nor the other.

Then he had seen her, watched her fighting, her screams silent but no less terrible. The shapeless, beast-like forms holding her down, exploring her nakedness, tormenting and entering her.

He had awakened, fighting off the blanket, his body running with sweat, calling her name.

He had almost expected Napier to burst in from the pantry, but as his mind quietened he had remembered that he was still in the sickbay.

He had dragged on his shirt and gone through the ship, speaking with watchkeepers or men who were merely squatting on deck, like himself unable to sleep, without knowing what he had said or heard in reply.

But the dream had remained, stark and terrible. As it must have been.

He had found Napier asleep, the confined space heavy with rum.

O'Beirne had been there with one of his assistants, checking his instruments, which had glittered and shivered on the table as if they were alive.

He had said, "He took it well, sir. It was a deep incision—I found the thing after a struggle." He had almost smiled. "Brave lad. His only worry seems to be that he wants to be with you when the action begins."

Adam had put his hand on the boy's bare shoulder, and had seen the frown ease away from his unconscious face. As if he had known.

"You shall have your pony ride, my lad. Be sure of that."

He had left, the others staring after him.

He came out of his thoughts and realised that the foretop had also been occupied by a squad of marines. He looked at the land. A thousand guns, or more. Again he tested his feelings, but there was no fear, no uncertainty. It was more like a dull acceptance.

He felt inside his breeches pocket. The little note was there. All he had.

He thrust his leg out from the crosstrees and waited for the pain. There was none. That, too, was numb.

He said, "Remember, Sullivan?"

He grinned, the youthful eyes very bright in an old seaman's face.

"Aye, sir. *For th' King!*" Then, as if surprised at what he was doing, he reached out and shook hands.

Adam took his time, pausing occasionally to stare through the rigging at the panorama of ships and sails. And men, hundreds of them . . . into the inevitable.

I want you in the van.

He swung out and around the shrouds and dropped the last few feet to the deck. Cristie gave him a quick, crinkled smile.

Captain Luxmore, "the true soldier," as Galbraith had called him, looked as if he were about to mount a parade or a guard of honour. The new wheel was fully manned; Midshipman Deighton, assisted by young Martyns, a mere child, was with his small party of men by the flag locker. Bellairs, Rist, and Varlo, who was up forward again by the first division of eighteen-pounders. Unsmiling, even subdued. He wondered what Galbraith had said to him.

High above the main deck the chain-slings had already been shackled to the yards, to prevent heavy spars falling on to men working at sails or guns. Nets would be spread as well, and most of the boats cast adrift before they closed still further with the land. Always a bad moment for the sailors in any ship, but necessary; flying splinters cut down more men than any solid shot.

Two small fifers were standing by the weather side, moistening their instruments with their tongues, their eyes on their captain.

But only their drums would be used this day.

Jago walked towards him, eyes very calm, but watchful, no doubt taking in the breeches smeared with tar after his descent, and the open shirt, the neckcloth tied loosely around his bare throat. He was hatless, and wearing the familiar, sea-going coat with its faded and tarnished lace. Jago nodded in silent approval, as if he was putting his seal on it. No foolish chances today. *But still the Captain.*

He held up his arms and Jago clipped the old sword into place.

Deighton's voice shattered the momentary stillness.

"From Flag, sir! *Prepare for battle!*"

"Acknowledge!"

Jago said, "We've heard that a few times, eh, sir?"

Adam grinned and impetuously seized his arm. It had been a close thing. Jago must have seen just how close.

He said, "And a few more yet, old friend!"

He swung away, without seeing Jago's relief. "Come on, you drummers! Beat to quarters, and clear for action!"

He felt the waiting figures hesitate, and then come alive as if something far stronger controlled them.

Adam looked up at the long masthead pendant, streaming out now, pointing the way.

Men stampeding to their stations, screens being torn down, the hull alive with noise and purpose. A ship of war.

It was now.

19 CAPTAIN'S LEGACY

ADAM BOLITHO glanced at the compass and strode to the packed hammock nettings to train his telescope. In those few paces he saw the helmsmen watching the peak of the driver, flapping now as a warning, while *Unrivalled* held as close to the wind as was possible in the gentle pressure off the land.

So slow. So slow. He steadied the glass and watched the jagged spur of land reaching out towards the ships. It was as he remembered it: the rough landscape, where it was sometimes hard to distinguish between the country itself and the crumbling fortifications, and weathered towers built of sand-coloured stone, which looked older than time itself.

He swung the glass across the quarter. *Halcyon* was holding on station, a second ensign hoisted now, clean and very bright above the tanned sails and scarred hull. Their other companion, the 14-gun brig *Magpie,* was further astern, tiny against the great array of sails where the fleet was on its final approach.

Adam returned to the quarterdeck rail, and saw several of the seamen look up at him from the nearest eighteen-pounders. So many times, and yet you were never certain. He ran his eyes along the length of the ship. The decks had been sanded to prevent men slipping in the height of battle, and to soak up the blood of the first to fall. That was always the hardest to accept. Not that men would die, but that they were faces and voices you knew, of which you had become a part. He saw the slow-matches, each in a bucket of sand beside every gun. It was still not unknown for the modern flintlock to fail because of a gun captain's haste, or over eagerness to beat the others to a first broadside.

The nets were spread overhead, and the boat tier was empty, so that the deck seemed more spacious than it should. The gig and jolly-boat were towing astern; the rest were well away by now, drifting to a canvas sea anchor. Waiting for the victor to recover them, no matter which flag was still flying.

The land was curving away again, like the neck of a poacher's bag. He trained the glass ahead, moving to avoid shrouds and stays, or faces, intent as they leaped into the lens. He could see the main anchorage, exactly as it was described in the orders, and as his uncle's flag lieutenant, Avery, had reported after that first visit.

Adam lowered the glass and stared into the distance. There were ships at anchor, some no doubt waiting to attack and harry the slow-moving vessels of Lord Exmouth's fleet once his intentions were recognised. He had heard four bells chime, but precisely when, he could not remember. It was a wonder that the seaman had kept his head and was able to mark the hour.

Sullivan had been right. They had closed the land at noon. That was two hours ago.

He looked at the gun crew directly below him. Stripped and ready, their bodies shining with sweat, neckerchiefs tied around their ears, cutlasses freshly sharpened at the grindstone and within reach. Another glance aloft. The big yards were braced so tightly that they appeared almost fore-and-aft; she was as close-hauled as she would come. He heard the wheel creak sharply, and one of the helmsmen mutter something as if to silence it.

He saw Galbraith by the starboard ladder, speaking with Rist, master's mate, and Williams, the gunner's mate who had been with him on the chebeck raid. He dabbed his lips with his sleeve. *A lifetime ago.*

Bellairs called, "Flagship is altering course, sir!"

Adam moved the glass. It was impossible to imagine the strength and effort now responding to Exmouth's signal. Ponderous, slow, and some badly out of station, but the ships were moving as one, their shapes lengthening as they tacked like floating leviathans towards the shore.

It was still too far, but he could imagine the lines of guns running out, the muscle and sweat of hundreds of men like these around him, preparing to match their skills against the enemy. If Lord Exmouth had been expecting some last-minute submission he would be disappointed. The Dey was relying on his massive armament. Adam thought of that brief meeting. *Trick for trick.* Exmouth was still a frigate captain at heart.

There was a dull bang, the sound dragged out by echoes from the land, then they saw the ball splash down before ripping across the water like an enraged dolphin.

Cristie had his watch in one hand, but his voice was almost indifferent.

"Make a note in the log, Mr Bremner. At half past two o'clock, the enemy opened fire."

Adam turned away. Nothing seemed to unsettle the old sailing master. He had even remembered the name of the midshipman who had only recently joined the ship. Like a rock. The man who had been born in the next street to Collingwood.

Perhaps the watchers on the shore had expected the fleet to sail directly into the anchorage, loose off a few shots at long range, and then go about without risking the mauling of close action. If so, they were wrong. A flag dipped above the *Queen Charlotte* and the air was split apart by the crash of gunfire. Unlike any broadside, it went on without cease, guns firing and reloading with barely a pause, the bay and the land already covered by drifting smoke.

What the gun crews must have trained for, all the way from Plymouth, and from Gibraltar to this mark on the chart.

Adam gripped the rail and felt the vibration of the bombardment jerking at the wood, as if some of the shots had smashed down alongside.

He thought of his own service in a ship of the line, and knew that *Halcyon*'s captain would be remembering it also. The incredible din, which scraped the inner walls of a man's mind, so that only drill and discipline saved him from madness. Down on those gun decks, the overhead timbers brushing your hair, the confined space thick with smoke and the stench of burning powder, and only an open port beyond each crew, a hazy outline or shadow which had to be the enemy.

Sponge out! Load! Run out! Ready! Nothing else existed.

Adam called, "Two points, Mr Cristie! Steer sou' by west!" It was impossible, but he could feel his mouth fixed in a grin. "That'll give her more freedom!"

He swung round to watch a twisting column of sparks rising far beyond the nearest ships. Perhaps one had blown up, or a random shot had found its mark in one of the citadel's magazines. Nobody could survive that.

He beckoned to Jago. "We shall be up to the anchorage directly. Keep with Mr Galbraith." He lifted the glass again and held his breath until he had found the vessel in question. A schooner, moored apart from all the others. He moved the glass slightly and saw the frigate, anchored fore-and-aft, a floating battery, another man-of-war lying just beyond her. Guarding the anchorage, the ships which were the Dey's lifeblood. "You know what to do, yes?"

He realised that Jago had remained silent. He looked at him, his ears cringing to yet another tremendous explosion, and saw the expression he had come to recognise since that day when they had settled on a handshake.

Jago said flatly, "My place is 'ere. With you." He saw Lieutenant Varlo hurry past with a party of seamen. "Let 'im go!"

Adam contained his sudden anger. "I did not hear that, Luke." He waved his hand towards the anchored ships. "That schooner is our weapon. The wind is right. Boat action, over quickly. Trust me."

Jago touched the double-bladed weapon at his belt. "Burn the bastards out, before they can cut an' run."

Adam nodded. "Or get amongst the fleet. Some of our ships will be in a bad way by now."

Jago frowned, his eyes elsewhere. Recalling another battle perhaps.

He said shortly, "Gig an' jolly-boat. Might leave you short-'anded." He glanced at somebody below the rail. "Some still wet behind the ears. If you gets boarded . . ." He looked at him and shrugged. "You command, *sir*." Adam felt his limbs shaking. Not fear. It was worse. The madness. *Just being here.* It made no sense, and never would.

Jago was staring around, already seeking faces, names. "I'm ready."

He swung himself down the ladder, his eyes still lifted to the quarterdeck, to the helmsmen barely moving as the sails filled again to the wind. Even that was full of acrid smoke. And when you looked astern it seemed the whole fleet had been swallowed up in it, broken here and there by flashes of gunfire, and the lasting patterns of burning timbers. Like a scene from hell.

This deck was quiet by comparison: Cristie beside his small rigged table, his eyes moving restlessly from masthead pendant to compass, from individual sails to his master's mates and assistants, Midshipman Deighton at the flag locker, Bellairs waiting to make more sail, and the marines in position behind the hammock nettings, their only protection when the time came.

Jago said, "Watch yer back, sir." Then he was gone.

More flashes darted through the smoke. From the anchorage this time. Adam winced as iron thudded into the lower hull. Not dangerous. He tried not to move, or to wipe his face. Even the slightest change in behaviour might be seen as doubt, or loss of confidence.

The frigate which was anchored fore-and-aft fired again, but the shots were haphazard, the gun crews perhaps confused by the spreading barrier of smoke. Adam crossed to the side and looked for the brig. She was holding on station. It was only too easy to close on one another, if only for a false sense of security.

He heard Cristie say, "That's the same ship, sir! No Yankee colours this time, God rot him!"

Adam felt someone beside him. It was Napier, his eyes defiant as if he expected the worst.

But Adam said only, "Stay with me, David. Get down if I tell you." He saw the youth nod, and then bite his lip as he took the weight on his injured leg.

"The surgeon said . . ."

Adam gripped his shoulder. "I can imagine what he said— much as he did to me, I have no doubt!"

Some seamen at the quarterdeck nine-pounders watched and nudged one another. The captain passing the time of day with his servant, as if they were still at Plymouth. It could not be that bad.

Galbraith was here. He looked very alert, no more time left for mistakes.

"Ready, sir. I'm taking Rist as my second-in-command—he's a good hand. Williams has made up the charges. I already know what he can do!"

Adam did not look away as a ragged broadside crashed and echoed across the anchorage.

Bellairs exclaimed, "*Halcyon*'s hit, sir!"

Adam shut it from his mind and concentrated on Galbraith. A good officer who was used to taking risks. Who was about to lay his life on the line yet again. Who wanted his own command, and was watching *Halcyon*'s fore-topmast stagger and then pitch down into the water alongside. As if he was seeing his own ship under fire.

"I shall come about as soon as you slip the boats. If everything goes against us, then make your own way to the fleet. As you see fit, Leigh. I already know what *you* can do, too!"

Galbraith touched his hat and ran lightly down the ladder, shouting orders as he went. He paused only once, to stare across at *Halcyon* as she was raked by another full broadside. Then he, too, was gone.

Adam saw Partridge turn and wave his arm; the boats had cast off, and they were already pulling like madmen towards the anchorage.

He measured the distance as if he were studying a giant chart.

Varlo would remain up forward to direct the guns when *Unrivalled* came about. That inner voice persisted. *If the wind holds.*

He could also be called to command if the worst happened and the quarterdeck became a bloody shambles. He looked around, at Bellairs with the afterguard, Captain Luxmore with Sergeant Bloxham and his marines. He had already sent his lieutenant, Cochrane, to cover and protect the carronade crews on the forecastle. He saw Midshipman Deighton staring at him over his signal locker, and his unexpected smile when Adam tossed him a casual wave. Casual? It was like raising the dead.

"Stand by on the quarterdeck!"

Cristie was waiting, slightly hunched as if anticipating a stray shot. Beside him the boy Ede, who had been spared the rope for an attempted murder, made an unlikely companion on the threshold of battle. Cristie had proclaimed that none of his navigational equipment had ever been in such good hands. It was praise indeed.

He counted seconds, all else but the narrowing triangle of smoke-hazed water thrust aside.

Another quick glance aloft: the masthead pendant was lifting and falling as before. But steady. The wind held.

His hand had found the folded note he had crammed into his breeches pocket.

Lowenna. In the old Cornish tongue it meant "joy."

He swallowed, but his mouth was dry. *So it will be.*

"Ready ho! Put the helm down!"

He had to shout, above the noise of wind and canvas, and the continuous thunder of the distant battle. And because of his heart, which surely those around him must hear.

"Helm a-lee, sir!"

They were beginning to turn, to swing the jib-boom across the anchored shipping as if they and not *Unrivalled* were moving.

"Off tacks and sheets!"

Adam stared above the heads of running men, while the ship continued to answer the wheel until she was pointing directly into the wind.

"Run out the larboard battery." He drew his sword, and found time to imagine *Unrivalled* as she exposed her opposite side to the anchored frigate. They would have been expecting an immediate challenge, and they would have been ready.

"*Run out!*"

He gripped the boy's shoulder and knew he must be hurting him badly.

He saw the guns lurch against the side, muzzles lifting to the thrust of wind and wheel, as if to sniff out their old enemy.

The sword was above his head. All else was forgotten. Even the tearing crash of iron slamming into the hull meant nothing.

Not a voice he recognised.

"As you bear, lads! *Fire!*"

Lieutenant Leigh Galbraith half rose from his place in the gig's sternsheets as another ragged broadside crashed across the water. He saw the flashes reflected in the stroke oarsman's eyes, but forced himself not to turn. It seemed so much deadlier, more personal, in spite of the unbroken thunder of heavier weapons which, as far as he could tell, had not stopped since the opening shots.

He had seen *Unrivalled*'s topgallants, taut and filling again as she came fully round on to the opposite tack, had heard the squeal of blocks, and imagined the shouted commands and stamping feet while men threw the full weight of their bodies and souls on braces and halliards.

Then the broadsides, *Unrivalled*'s, and the sharper bark of the brig *Magpie*'s nine-pounders as she sailed deliberately amongst the anchored shipping.

Here in the gig it was all so different, like being a spectator, or a victim, without the usual stealth and cunning of a boat attack.

He felt the heavy pistol at his side, the hanger already loosened in its scabbard. Puny against the thunder of battle, ships of the line matched against the Dey's batteries. The smoke over the town was thicker than ever, the fires rising through it, the gun crews probably half blinded and too dazed even to be afraid.

He said, "Ease the stroke, cox'n. We'll lose the jolly-boat if we're not careful!" He thought he heard Jago grunt, and saw the quick exchange between him and the stroke oar. The jolly-boat was abeam, heavier and slower because of Williams' explosives and some extra hands to allow for opposition, and sudden death.

He twisted round as another broadside cracked through the smoke. The anchored frigate was still firing, but the rate was slower; *Unrivalled*'s sudden attack had worked. There were more shots on a different bearing, probably *Halcyon*. Wounded or not, she was well able to hit back.

Galbraith peered ahead as two anchored barges loomed through the haze. He found he was gripping the hanger as if to steady himself. The schooner lay directly beyond them.

He saw the bowman on his feet with the swivel gun on the stemhead. There would only be time for one shot. After that . . . Jago muttered, "There she is!"

The schooner's counter seemed to loom through the smoke. Galbraith measured the distance. One grapnel would suffice. Each man was hand-picked. They all knew what to do. How to die without complaint if their officer made a mistake. He knew Jago was looking at him. Probably thought him mad anyway, if he could actually grin in the face of death.

Someone hissed, "*Boat, sir! Larboard bow!*"

It should not have been there. A major battle was in progress. Nobody sane or sober would venture out from a safe mooring.

There were wild shouts, and a sudden crack of musket fire. Galbraith heard and felt the balls smacking into the hull, saw the stroke oarsman throw up his hands and fall across his thwart, the oar trailing outboard like an extra rudder.

He shouted, "Fire, man! Rake the bastards!"

So close to the water, the bang of the swivel gun was deafening, the packed canister smashing into the other boat at almost point-blank range. The oars were in total confusion, the boat slewing round in a welter of spray, the air torn apart by the screams of men scythed down by the blast.

The bowman stumbled aft to help push the stroke oarsman over the gunwale and take his place. It all took time. Galbraith glanced at the corpse as it floated astern, turning slightly on one shoulder as if to watch them press on without him.

More shots now, from overhead.

Galbraith gasped as a blow flung him hard against the tiller bar. As if a white-hot bar of iron had been dragged across his back; he could even smell the cloth of his coat burning, then Jago's hard hands as he tore it away and slapped a wad of rags across the wound. But no pain. Just breathlessness, as though he had been kicked.

Jago said sharply, "*Easy,* Mr Galbraith. We'll get you fixed up, good as new!" He turned as the jolly-boat passed abeam, oars rising and falling without cease, as if they had only now cast off from the ship's side. "Frank Rist can manage." He felt Galbraith turn to listen, to understand, and added, "He always wanted a bloody command of 'is own, anyway!"

Then the pain did come, and Galbraith found himself lying by the first stretcher, his head propped on somebody's hat. He was alive. But all he could think of was that he had failed.

Jago held out a hand. "*Oars!*" He gauged the overhanging stern. Young Deighton would have enjoyed this, he thought vaguely. But his mind was still like ice. "*Ready in the bows!*" He heard the hiss of steel being drawn, and knew a couple of them were armed with boarding-axes. He trusted that the grapnel had been thrown, and lurched to his feet as the gig came under the counter with a violent jerk. A swivel gun exploded, it seemed only a few feet away, and for an instant he imagined that the schooner's crew had been ready and waiting for them. Instead he heard a wild whoop and knew it was Williams, the mad Welshman. *"At 'em, lads!"* Then he was clawing his way up and over the stern with all the others.

He paused only to peer down at the gig, where Galbraith lay where he had been dragged into a safer position. He even grinned. *Bloody officers!*

Frank Rist, master's mate, had heard the burst of firing and the swivel gun's murderous response. As ordered, he had brought the jolly-boat alongside. He knew he would have done it in any case. *Even if a friend is cut down in battle, don't offer your hand. Or it's your turn next.*

He rubbed his stinging eyes; the smoke was everywhere. Miles and miles of it. He swore silently as his boots skidded on blood and fragments of flesh. There had only been one man to challenge them, and he had taken the full blast of canister, all on his own. Some other whimpering shapes had been seized without even a struggle. The anchor watch were alone on board, eight men in all. One had tried to escape, but a boarding-axe had stopped him in his tracks. A splash alongside told the rest.

He found that he could relax, albeit holding his nerves on a leash. He heard the battle roaring in the background, men being killed and maimed, ships disabled or sunk. It was all meaningless in the distance and the smoke.

And *Unrivalled*'s guns had stopped firing. With her two consorts, she would be waiting. He stared around the unfamiliar deck, scarcely able to believe it. *Because of us.*

He heard Williams calling to one of his mates, pictured his nimble fingers twisting and fixing fuses, like that other time with the chebecks. Galbraith had been there then.

He thought Williams was humming to himself, unconcerned about everything beyond his immediate reach. Rist felt himself smile. The madness of a fight. Williams would probably lay a bet on the outcome of this raid, down to the last minute. Although he was a powerful man, he made his strength seem effortless; Rist had seen him pick up a handspike and use it to train an eighteen-pounder gun to explain something to a green landman at Plymouth. He had used no more effort than somebody moving a chair up to a table. But a gentle man in many ways, despite his trade of gunner's mate. Like the time he had carried the young black girl in his arms, on board that damned slaver when her master had recognised him, or thought he had, from the past. The girl had been abused so badly that it was unlikely she would recover. It was common enough. But she had not said a word or protested once when Williams had carried her to her own people, when by rights she should have seen him as just another white devil.

Williams could have been promoted long ago, but for his love of gambling. With him it was like lust, and, discipline or not, nothing would change him. Dice, or simply laying odds on the most common daily occurrence: how many knots sailed in a single watch, or how much rum would be consumed in one mess in the course of a week. He had a loyal group of fellow gamblers, his clutch, as he called them, and as he was able to read and write he was the one who kept a tally of the wins and, more likely, the losses. Rist had heard some of them say they had already laid down their slave- and prize-bounty in Williams' care, and they had not even received it yet!

Williams was his own man. If he liked you, it was enough. If you pushed him too far, then beware.

It had all been so quick. If Mister bloody Sandell had not been nosing around between decks when he should have been standing watch, it would not have happened. Maybe the midshipman had heard something and was out to prove himself. But he was there that morning, when Williams had been returning to his mess after yet another secret session with the clutch.

Sandell had probably attempted to seize the list of bets, or even some of the money, as evidence. It was all so fast, you would never know for sure. One moment there had been the two of them, Williams towering over the irate, gesticulating midshipman, then there was only Williams. Sandell had fallen back against one of the carronades, his head striking the iron "smasher." Dead or unconscious, the sea had received him. And bloody good riddance.

He swung round guiltily as Williams shouted, "Done, Frank! Cut the cable, and we'll be going!"

Rist hurried forward and called, "Cut it, lads!" He stared ahead at the overlapping shapes of anchored vessels. They would soon do the same when they saw a fireship drifting down on them.

A seaman shouted, *"Look out!"* It was almost a scream.

One of the anchor watch must have hidden below, undiscovered, when the boarding party had swarmed up from the boats. He just seemed to rise out of the deck, from a small hatch which nobody had cared to investigate.

Rist aimed his pistol; he did not even recall having drawn it. The two shots sounded as one. He ran to help Williams, who had fallen to his knees; the other man had no time even to cry out as a cutlass smashed into his skull.

"Where is it, Owen?" Other hands were helping, but Rist and Williams were completely alone.

Williams said thickly, "It's a bad one, Frank. This time, I think . . ." His head lolled, and he groaned, as if to bite back the agony. Rist could feel the blood on his hand, running over his wrist. *A bad one.* He had seen enough of them.

"We'll get you to the boat."

Williams tried to protest but the pain held it back. Then he said in an almost normal tone, "You too busy to see the wind, man? It's shifted. Not much. But a bit. *Enough,* see?"

Rist stared around. "I don't give a damn!"

With sudden strength Williams pulled himself up to the schooner's wheel. Gasping with pain, he slowly wrapped and fastened the old-style crossbelt he always wore around and through the spokes, so that it took his weight.

"Get to the boats, Frank. Time to move, see? Nothing more you can do. The ship'll need you now!"

Somebody asked, "What d' you say, Mr Rist?"

For a moment longer he stared up at the masts, and the loosely flapping jib. A command of his own. What he had always wanted. He shrugged, as if to the world. What Galbraith wanted too, although he would never admit it.

He looked down as a hand gripped his.

Rist lowered his head until their faces almost touched. Feeling the agony, the sudden determination.

"What is it, Owen?"

Williams gripped his hand harder. "You saw me, Frank, that morning. I knew you did." He fought a bout of coughing. There was blood on his shirt. Rist heard the distant guns. *It could not last.* He had others to think of.

"Yes, I saw it."

"And you never said?" He tried to smile, but it only made it worse. "Save yourself, see? Time to go, cut the cable. *Now!*" He reached out suddenly and Rist heard the sharp click of his flintlock. The realisation seemed to freeze him, but he could see it stark and clear in his mind. Williams had fired the fuse.

"*Cut the cable, Billy!* Into the boats, the rest of you!"

The deck was deserted, the only sound the regular thud of a heavy axe. He heard Williams mutter, "A life for a life, see, Frank? So I was taught!"

"*Cut!*" The seaman was already running aft to the waiting boats.

Rist stood motionless, seeing the wheel respond to the hands, the jib hardening enough to swing the hull very slightly.

Adrift, and at any second the fuses would blow.

Then he ran aft, his leg over the rail even as the first muffled explosion spurted sparks through the forehatch.

Voices were yelling at him to jump; he thought he had heard Galbraith too, but all he could think of was the figure strapped to the schooner's wheel. And how strong his Welsh accent had sounded, in the face of death itself.

Someone thrust a bottle into his hands. It was rum, like fire in his throat. He raised the bottle again and murmured, "All bets down, my friend!"

Then the world exploded.

"Hold your fire!" Adam had to shout twice to gain Varlo's attention. The guns had fired three broadsides, the havoc on the other frigate's deck easy to see despite the smoke and confusion. Perhaps their forecastle party had been cut down in the first double-shotted onslaught, when *Unrivalled* had come about to show her true intention. The ship was swinging now, moored only by her forward cable, the stream anchor aft having been cut to escape the second broadside. Purpose or panic, it mattered little now, but the blazing schooner Galbraith and his two boats had boarded had been enough for the crowded shipping which had been relying on the warships' moored broadsides.

The fireship had become entangled with another schooner and both were now drifting like one huge torch.

Even as he watched, Adam saw another, smaller vessel catch fire, the flames leaping up the sun-dried rigging and turning the sails into scattered ashes. He heard warning shouts from the maintop and saw two oared galleys sweeping past the other ships, turning as one towards *Unrivalled* and increasing speed to the urgent beat of a drum.

Such fanatical daring should have achieved a better settlement. But the brig *Magpie* was ready, and raked the leading galley with canister and grape, in an instant changing it to a shattered wreck. The second paid no heed and met with more grape from *Unrivalled's* larboard carronades.

The long sweeps splintered like boxwood as the galley lurched and shuddered alongside. In the next instant figures were swarming up and over the gangway, only to be confronted by the boarding nets, probably something they had never before encountered.

Men snatched up cutlasses and axes, while others dragged the deadly boarding-pikes from the racks and impaled the screaming, crazed attackers before they had even cut through the nets.

And yet there were a few who managed to hack their way past the defences. One, a bearded giant, marked out from the others by a scarlet robe, reached the quarterdeck ladder, his eyes fixed on the man he recognised as captain.

Adam had his sword balanced in his hand, loosely, some of the others might have thought. As if he no longer cared . . .

He saw the great blade swing down, heard someone, Napier perhaps, yell out a warning. Like being someone else, able to measure the weight and force of the blow. He felt it lance through his arm, heard the scream of steel as the two blades crossed, the heavier blade sliding down to lock against the hilt of his sword. He could even smell his attacker, feel the overwhelming hate which excluded everything else.

He stepped aside, gasping as pain seared his wounded side, but keeping his balance as the giant lunged forward.

It was the madness. The moment when risk and caution meant nothing. If anything, he felt light-headed, and knew only that he wanted to kill this man.

A shadow sliced across the smoky sunshine and he saw the giant reel aside, eyes still blazing as he pitched down the ladder.

The hard man, Campbell, wielding a cutlass with both hands like a claymore, had almost severed his head from his body.

Campbell turned now, showing his mutilated back, the evidence of a dozen or more floggings, with something like a gladiator's triumph.

Adam raised the old sword to him.

"Thank you!"

Campbell, streaked with blood, his own or that of his victims, gave a mock bow.

"Your *servant*, Cap'n!"

And then, all at once, impossible though it was, it was over. Like a sudden deafness left when the last broadsides have exploded.

Adam grasped the quarterdeck rail and stared along his command. The dead lay where they had dropped, as if they had fallen asleep. Others reached out as grim-faced seamen and marines hurried around and over them: the wretched wounded. A captain's legacy, so that he should not forget.

Midshipman Deighton shouted, "From *Flag*, sir! *Discontinue the action!*"

Adam tried to sheathe his sword, but it was sticky with blood. The signal made no sense. Someone had removed the sword and was wiping it clean with a piece of rag.

He looked at Napier and wanted to smile, but his lips would not move. "You did well, David. Your mother . . ." He made another attempt. "*I* am proud of you!"

Small but stark pictures stood out. Like those first moments, the waiting. The aftermath was even worse.

Bellairs, sitting on a water barricoe, his face in his hands, the fine sword his parents had given him to mark his commission as lieutenant discarded at his feet, its blade also stained with blood. And now Yovell, coming from below for the first time, from the orlop where he had been helping the surgeon with the wounded and the dying. Staring around, a length of soiled bandage trailing from one pocket. A man wrestling with his beliefs.

And the boats returning alongside, Rist hurrying to the quarterdeck, peering at the planking, pock-marked with musket balls from the enemy's sharpshooters, and at the dark bloodstains where men had stood together and had died. Lastly he had looked at Cristie, the old sailing-master, and remarked almost casually, "You got through it, then?"

And Cristie, looking and feeling his age, who had never quit this deck throughout the attack, had smiled, perhaps because he knew what Rist had expected, and replied, "Got through *what,* Mr Rist?"

Adam walked to the hammock nettings, his hand feeling the torn canvas where musket balls had cut through the tightly-packed bedding. Some had been meant for him.

The bombardment was over. Through the pall of drifting smoke he could see the freshly set sails: Lord Exmouth's fleet on the move again. Withdrawing. The casualties would be terrible, but not a ship had been lost. On the shore there were fires raging, and the guns were silent. Many must have been buried with their crews when the old fortifications had crumbled under Exmouth's barrage.

He recalled his own relief when he had seen Galbraith being helped aboard, in pain, but quietly determined, like a man who had discovered something in himself which he had not suspected.

And the moment when Galbraith, his wounded shoulders covered by a seaman's jacket, had paused by Varlo, at the place where he had controlled every gun and every man of the full broadside.

Galbraith had said, "You did well."

Varlo had half-smiled, and retorted, "Go to hell!"

And now they were leaving this place. Many vessels had been destroyed or left abandoned. The enemy barque had not been one of them. They would meet again. He gripped the nettings until the pain in his side reawakened. And tomorrow Lord Exmouth would demand that all his previous terms be met. The Dey would have no choice.

He turned away from the smoke and the fires.

"Turn the hands to, Mr Bellairs! We will prepare to get under way."

He stared along the ship yet again. The first in, the last to leave. And they had done it.

He looked at the dead where some had been dragged from the places they had lain to clear the guns' recoil. One was a marine officer, his face covered with a bloodied cloth. Lieutenant Cochrane. *Unrivalled* was his first ship.

"Move yourselves!" He walked to the rail again. A captain must never show weakness. His authority was his armour. It was all he had.

Bellairs called, "Shall we put them over, sir?"

Adam stared down at him. So simply asked. Was that all it took?

He said, "No. We'll bury them when we clear the land." He saw Yovell watching him. "Perhaps you could read a suitable prayer, Mr Yovell?"

Afterwards, he thought it was like seeing Yovell's despair clear away. Another memory had been sparked. All he needed.

"For all of us, sir."

And tomorrow . . .

Galbraith straightened his back in spite of the bandage, and said quietly, "Here comes *Halcyon*."

Adam walked to the opposite side, feeling their eyes following him. The helmsman, Sergeant Bloxham, leaning on a musket on which the bayonet was still fixed. Midshipman Deighton, his telescope still trained on the distant ships, gnawing his lip to make a lie of his composure.

And Jago, watching the slow-moving frigate, feeling her pain.

Sharing it. Foremast shot away, sails riddled with holes, the hull gouged by gunfire at close quarters.

Magpie was following astern; she had been in the thick of it, but looked unmarked by comparison.

The second ensign *Halcyon* had hoisted when the flagship had made the signal *Prepare for battle* had been lowered to half-mast, for the man who had been Tyacke's midshipman at the Nile, and had loved his ship above all else. Both ship and captain had fought their last fight.

Adam climbed into the shrouds as if something had snapped, releasing him from frozen immobility, and shouted, "A cheer, lads! Give them all you have!"

He waved, and imagined he saw a telescope being trained from *Halcyon*'s splintered quarterdeck.

Then he climbed down and felt Jago's hand steady his arm. It must be the smoke. The fight had continued all afternoon. It would soon be dusk.

He stared around at the damage, his mind dulled by *Unrivalled*'s wild cheering, which *Halcyon*'s people would always remember, even when they were sent to other ships.

He said, "Pipe the hands to the braces, if you please." If only his eyes would stop smarting.

He looked at the anchorage again, already hidden in smoke and shadow.

Unrivalled was the last to leave. As ordered.

And tomorrow . . .

He heard Jago remark, "Our gig will need more than a couple of new planks when we gets home, sir."

"Yes." He did not trust himself to say more.

Home had a new meaning now.

Jago watched him, and was satisfied.

Like his ship, he thought. Second to None.

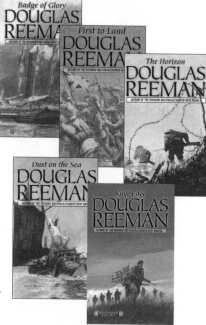